Brutus of Troy

Dedication

Respectfully dedicated to my tenth cousin twice removed, HRH Prince George of Cambridge, the future heir to Brutus's sea-girt realm.

Also by Anthony Adolph:

Tracing Your Family History

Tracing You Home's History

Need to Know? Tracing Your Family History

Tracing Your Irish Family History

Who Am I? The Family Tree Explorer

Tracing Your Scottish Family History

The King's Henchman: the Commoner and the Royal who saved the monarchy from Cromwell

Tracing Your Aristocratic Ancestors

In Search of Our Ancient Ancestors: from the Big Bang to Modern Britain, in Science and Myth

Illustrations

Unless otherwise credited, all drawings, diagrams and photographs are by the author.

Brutus of Troy

And the Quest for the Ancestry of the British

Anthony Adolph

Pen & Sword
FAMILY HISTORY

First published in Great Britain in 2015 by
Pen & Sword Family History
an imprint of
Pen & Sword Books Ltd
47 Church Street
Barnsley
South Yorkshire
S70 2AS

ISBN 978 1 47384 917 4

A CIP catalogue record for this book is available from the
British Library

Typeset in Ehrhardt by
Mac Style Ltd, Bridlington, East Yorkshire
Printed and bound in the UK by CPI Group (UK) Ltd,
Croydon, CRO 4YY

Pen & Sword Books Ltd incorporates the imprints of Pen & Sword
Archaeology, Atlas, Aviation, Battleground, Discovery, Family
History, History, Maritime, Military, Naval, Politics, Railways, Select,
Transport, True Crime, and Fiction, Frontline Books, Leo Cooper,
Praetorian Press, Seaforth Publishing and Wharncliffe.

For a complete list of Pen & Sword titles please contact
PEN & SWORD BOOKS LIMITED
47 Church Street, Barnsley, South Yorkshire, S70 2AS, England
E-mail: enquiries@pen-and-sword.co.uk
Website: www.pen-and-sword.co.uk

Contents

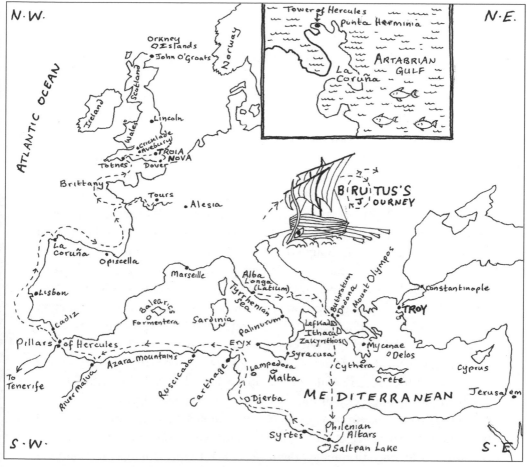

Brutus's world. The dotted line shows his route as given by Geoffrey of Monmouth (though precisely how Brutus reached Buthrotum is not stated). Inset is a map of La Coruña, showing the Tower of Hercules in relation to the old city and harbour.

Introduction

On the second Saturday of November each year, a great procession winds through the City of London, leading the new Lord Mayor on his journey to take his oath of loyalty to the sovereign of Great Britain. The tradition of the Lord Mayor's Show is as old as the office of Lord Mayor itself, dating back to 1189. In early times he travelled by barge to Westminster, and now he goes in his magnificently gilded coach to take his oath at the Royal Courts of Justice on the Strand. But though the route has changed, his journey has always been accompanied by great spectacle and pageantry. Crowds line the streets waving Union Jacks at a long succession of marching bands and floats. There are the Royal Marines jogging along in their combat gear, the Royal Yeomanry in their splendid uniforms, the Honourable Artillery Company marching along with buttons and belt buckles shining, and many other representatives of the British armed forces too. There are floats from the venerable City Livery Companies – the Fruiterers' float piled up like a market stall, the Fishmongers' led by an enormous green fish and the Paviors' accompanied by a huge, inflatable pig. There go the Freemasons in their colourful sashes, and representatives of the great City law firms, chartered accountants and banks, the powerhouses of the world's economy. In amongst them all are many representatives of London's modern and diverse population, on the floats of charities for the handicapped and disadvantaged, arts foundations, musical groups and choirs, and the Scouts and Guides and many, many, more – 'as much of life as the world will show', as Dr Johnson said of London, and as true now as it ever was in his day.

At the rear comes the new Lord Mayor himself, in his sumptuous red robes, waving cheerily to the crowds. But up near the front, what have we seen? Amidst the thunder of the drums, the skirl of bagpipes and cheering of the onlookers there loom two tall, wicker figures like monstrous Iron Age warriors, towering above the robed humans who escort them (see plate 1). As they gaze solemnly down from beneath their antique, crested helms they seem arcanely frightening, fiercely armed with spear, sword, shield and a quiver bristling with arrows. Their names, written on flags beside them, seem hoary too: Gog and Magog. The giants seem crudely out of place as they pass by the slick steel and glass frontages of the City's offices and coffee shops, yet they seem also to be, strangely, *in* place, as if all this, anciently, was theirs. As if they alone are the guardian spirits of the old stones of the City. They have been here always, they seem to say, and always will be.

How they came to be here, leading the many faces of modern Britain through Britain's capital in this way, is told in this book, though this book is not about them specifically. London's giants arose as an almost accidental byproduct of a far greater story; that of Britain's quest for its own identity. They appeared first as bit players in a story that our ancestors invented to explain where they came from – the story of Brutus of Troy. That Brutus is not the same as the Brutus who founded the Roman Republic, nor the Brutus who murdered Caesar. Originally, our British Brutus was called Britto, a name derived deliberately from the name of Britain itself, but the Roman one sounded grander, so it was adopted for the island's founding hero instead. More than half a millennium before there was a Lord Mayor in London, our Dark Age forefathers used Brutus of Troy to link their ancestral story back into the overarching narratives of world history as told in the Christian Bible and the Greek tales of the siege of Troy.

For more than a thousand years, anyone who thought about Britain's origins thought about Brutus and his sidekick Corineus and the giant Gogmagog from whom they wrested control of Britain in the first place. The crowds of medieval London who cheered on earlier Lord Major's Shows knew their names and deeds by heart. The royal genealogies stretched back to Brutus as the ultimate founder of the monarchy. London was even known sometimes by the name that Brutus was said to have given it when he laid the city's first foundations: Trinovantum, 'New Troy'. But then, when this grand myth faded in the face of modern, scientific rationalism, the identities became confused: Brutus was almost forgotten, Corineus became Gog, and Gogmagog ended up as plain old Magog. But the two statues, now known as Gog and Magog, were still wheeled out from Guildhall every year, as they are to this day, to lead the Lord Mayor's procession. Through them, in a strange, convoluted and very British sort of way, does the Matter of Britain, as the ancient myths of our island are termed, live on.

I must have seen Gog and Magog and wondered who they were when my parents took me to see a Lord Mayor's Show when I was four. But my fascination with Brutus's world – that deeply arcane world of the ancient Britons – was reignited by a televised production of Shakespeare's *Cymbeline* in the mid-1980s, which led me back to read *King Lear*. In both plays Shakespeare evokes a world hovering fantastically between myth and reality, a spine-tingling land

Brutus, from Guillaume Rouille's *Promptuarii Iconum Insigniorum* (1553).

of sickle on mistletoe and ivy on timeless stones, a Britain drenched in druidic secrets, so old that its mornings seem like the sunrises at the dawn of the world.

Then I became a genealogist, and sometimes encountered Cymbeline and Lear near the tops of dusty old royal pedigrees in the library of The Institute of Heraldic and Genealogical Studies in Canterbury, where I learned my profession, which had a whole, timber-framed room with creaking floorboards devoted to musty, leather-bound, gilt-edged books about blue-blooded ancestry. And when I traced my finger further back up those same arcane pedigrees, which showed Lear to be a forebear of Cymbeline, I would find Brutus there, impossibly far back, the ancestor of them both. And before him still were other wonders, for Brutus's great-grandfather was Aeneas, hero of Virgil's *Aeneid*, the Trojan prince who had survived the fall of Troy and sailed away to lay the foundations of Rome in the west. And Aeneas's mother was the love goddess Aphrodite, and his father Anchises, according to the pedigrees, was descended, via Noah, from Adam and Eve.

It was a genealogical wonderland and seemed impossible to understand. Was it true or at least partly so, or had it all been made up? Was there a kernel of reality in the story that Trojans had founded Britain? I wanted desperately to unearth some evidence that Brutus had been a real historical character, heavily disguised by myth, but eventually I came to realise that he was entirely fictitious, just like the character in Hughes Mearns's poem:

> *Yesterday upon the stair,*
> *I met a man who wasn't there.*
> *He wasn't there again today…*

But the more my research confirmed that Brutus had never existed, the more remarkable his endurance and hold on the psyche of our British ancestors seemed to be. He was, like Mearns's character, a *literary* one: when treated as a historical character, Brutus makes no sense, but when viewed as someone conjured out of nowhere and given life by words, then he becomes suddenly very comprehensible indeed. However non-existent Brutus had been, his stories were very real indeed and they had enjoyed an extraordinarily long life in our ancestors' minds. And this, together with the reasons why our ancestors invented them at all, is truly fascinating.

I realised that, if we want to understand the mindsets of our ancestors in the age of Arthur, struggling to come to terms with the collapse of the Roman world; of the Dark Age Britons, valiantly forging their Welsh kingdoms in the face of brutal Anglo-Saxon expansion; of the people of the Middle Ages, peering back into the past through the dusty stained glass of the medieval psyche; of the Tudor and Stuart kings, bolstering their regal credentials by claiming direct descent from Trojan royalty; of the builders of the British Empire, drawing courage from epic tales of the heroes of old – and thus to gain a better appreciation of how modern Britain came to be, we must first understand Brutus. From the perspective of them all, Brutus lay at the beginning of Britain and all else flowed from that simple fact.

This story will take us from the glories of ancient Greece to the mouldering stones of Britain, and also to the goat pastures of Judea and the cloisters of early Christendom. For in all these places lie the many, interconnected roots of that most magnificent of ancestral tales – the myth of Brutus of Troy.

Part I

Conceiving Brutus

Chapter 1

In Alma's Tower

In a scene towards the beginning of his great Elizabethan epic *The Faerie Queene*, Edmund Spenser imagines Sir Guyon and the future King Arthur – then just a knight errant, ignorant of his true origins – being led up the alabaster steps of a magical castle by its doyenne, Alma. As they ascend the turret, they see the green hills of Albion spreading out below them. Gazing up, they see a high-arched roof, fretted with flowers and illuminated by two blazing beacons.

Alma shows the young men each of the turret's three rooms. The first buzzes with flies of prophecy and is the home of a saturnine young visionary. In the second sits a middle-aged man, deep in meditation, the walls covered with images of the arts and sciences. The third chamber 'seemed ruinous and old' and is full of ancient scrolls and books 'that were all worm-eaten, and full of canker holes.' Here sits Eumnestes, who has lived since the start of human history and remembers every detail of it all.

Arthur and Guyon start browsing through the dusty books, as Alma intends. Her name means 'nurturer' and her purpose is to aid the boys' knightly quests by educating and elevating their youthful minds. Guyon, who is an elf, becomes absorbed in a history of his own land of Faerie. And Arthur's own hand closes on the spine of a dusty tome entitled *Briton Moniments*. He realises at once that this must be the story of his own country, Albion. 'Burning both with fervent fire' to learn the origins of their respective countries, both the young men 'crav'd leave of Alma, and that aged sire, to read those books.'

Spenser proceeds to tell a story-within-a-story, as Arthur reads the fabulous history of Britain. Gripping the book in his strong young hands, his noble brow furrowed in concentration, Arthur reads how, long ago, fair Albion had been but 'savage wildernesse, unpeopl'd, unmanner'd, unprov'd, unprais'd'. Its only inhabitants were giants, 'like wild beasts lurking in loathsome den, and flying fast as roebuck through the fen, all naked without shame, or care of cold [who] by hunting and by spoiling lived then; of stature huge, and eke of courage bold.'

Now Arthur learns how Brutus, the great-grandson of Trojan Aeneas, had come to Britain. Brutus's wanderings had started through his 'fatal error' of killing his own father at Alba Longa, near Rome. Brutus then travelled to northern Greece, where he found many Trojans living in slavery. He freed them and led them on a long journey to Spain, where they joined forces with another colony of exiled Trojans, led by a formidable giant slayer, Corineus. Together, Brutus and Corineus led their people north, ravaging Gaul (modern France) and then landing in Britain, where they fought the giants Goëmagot, Coulin and Godmer. Spenser describes Godmer as a son of 'hideous Albion, whose father Hercules in Fraunce did quell'. Godmer flung 'three monstrous stones' at Brutus's companion Canutus, but Canutus slew him.

Once all the giants were dead, Brutus settled the island with Trojans. He 'raigned long in great felicitie.' From his son Locrinus descended a long line of kings, including Lear and Cymbeline, under whose successors Joseph of Arimathea brought the Holy Grail to Britain. The story continues down to Uther Pendragon. Arthur does not yet know that Uther is his father – so the book he is reading ends so abruptly, says Spenser, that there is not even a full stop on the page.

Arthur sits in silence for a while, thinking about Britain and then exclaims, 'How brutish is it not to understand, how much to her we owe.' Britain had nourished Arthur, yet of Britain's origins he had known so little, and understood even less.

Arthur's initial lack of understanding is understandable. Even Spenser, repeating the age-old litany of the 'Matter of Britain', had no idea how it had all originated. The true origins of the Trojans in Britain were as much of a closed book to Spenser as they had been to Arthur himself.

Whilst Spenser managed more or less to relate a coherent mythological history for Britain, the material he was using came from a variety of different sources, some complimentary, some contradictory, which reflected very well the complex, real history of Britain and the cultural influences to which the island had been subject – native British, Greek, Roman and then Christian. We might want to think of our island's mythology as the best of what each of these rich storehouses of myth had to offer. A better analogy, though, might be that Spenser's tales represent the flotsam left behind by a series of mighty waves of myth that washed over the imaginative landscape of Britain. But whilst a lot of old wood was left behind here by these waves, there are genuine treasures too, onto which we need only splash a little water to make them shine as brightly as they did when they were first imagined.

The tale of Troy, in which Brutus's myth is rooted, is best known now through its retelling in the 2004 film *Troy*. But to most people, that film is simply one swashbuckling historical drama amongst many. Many people have read the books from which the film's story is taken, Homer's *Iliad* and *Odyssey*, not to mention the story's continuation in Virgil's *Aeneid*, either for pleasure or as part of school or university curriculums. But again these might seem like three old stories amongst many – nothing remarkable, nothing of which we need take much notice in our modern world. So it is astonishing to realise that, in Roman times, the Trojan myth was not just one story, one 'classic' among many. Far from it: the myth of Troy was *the* narrative that informed the Romans about their past, and their place in the greater scheme of things. And for the Ancient Greeks, too, Homer (see plate 8) and his tales of Troy lay at the beginning of literature and the heart of their psyche.

The story of Troy concerns the conflict between the Mycenaean Greeks and the Trojans, who lived due east of them across the Aegean Sea, on the western coast of Asia Minor. Paris, son of Priam, King of Troy, abducts Helen, the beautiful wife of Menelaus, King of Sparta. Menelaus and his elder brother Agamemnon, King of Mycenae, summon all the lords of Greece including Odysseus (see plate 7) and Achilles, who assemble a mighty fleet at Aulis, and sail across the wine-dark sea to lay siege to Troy.

The siege lasts ten years. Homer's *Iliad* covers part of the tenth year only, focusing on the quarrel between Achilles and Agamemnon over a slave girl, but in the course of the telling we hear the entire background of the siege and its heroes, and the origins of the Greeks and Trojans, and we discover much about the Greek gods who had engineered the conflict in the first place and who interfere in every detail of the war. We have to wait until the *Odyssey* to hear how the siege ends: the Greeks are ready to give up and go home, but crafty Odysseus suggests that they should pretend to retreat, withdrawing from the beaches and hiding behind the island of Tenedos. They leave behind a wooden horse, which the Trojans misguidedly take into their city. At night, Odysseus and his men, who are hidden inside the horse, creep out and open Troy's gates. The Greek ships return and the Trojans are either butchered, or are taken back to Greece as slaves, or flee to safety (see plate 5).

If such a war ever took place at all, it is generally dated to 1194–1184 BC, just before the dramatic collapse of Mycenaean civilisation. By the time Homer sang of it, about the 800s or 700s BC, the Greek world had recovered itself and started its rise towards Classical civilisation. For the Greeks of Homer's time, the war had come to symbolise the last, destructive, hubristic flourish of Mycenae's greatness, the reckless act by which Agamemnon's empire lost its wealth, its manpower and its moral fortitude.

The fate of the Trojans played on the Greek imagination. Wherever Greeks encountered worthy adversaries of unknown origin, they wondered if these were descendants of the dispersed survivors of Troy. Of those Trojans who survived and fled, the best known was Aeneas (see plate 6). Conceived through a passionate encounter between the love goddess Aphrodite and Anchises, a cousin of Priam's, Aeneas was a mortal hero who, as Poseidon prophecies in book twenty of the *Iliad*, was 'destined to survive'.

As Greece's colonies in southern Italy edged ever closer to the little Iron Age city of Rome, the Greek champion, Pyrrhus of Epiros, scoffed that the upstart Romans were descendants of the Trojans, waiting to be wiped out by a new Trojan war. When the Romans achieved the impossible and hounded mighty Pyrrhus out of Italy in 275 BC, they adopted the Trojan myth as a badge of honour. They started imagining that Aeneas had indeed led the survivors of Troy to Italy. Because Troy was called Ilium by Homer, the Roman Iulii family fantasised that their ancestor Iulus had Trojan origins, and developed a family story that he had been identical with Aeneas's son Ascanius. Thus, Julius Caesar (100–44 BC) grew up believing that his ancestry went back to Iulus/Ascanius, and thus to Aeneas and Aphrodite.

It is small wonder that Caesar had the nerve to accomplish all that he did, including his audacious attempted invasions of Britain in 55 and 54 BC. Later, his great-nephew Augustus (63 BC–AD 14) commissioned Virgil (70–19 BC) to enshrine the myth in verse, in the *Aeneid* (see plate 9). Ironing out all the contradictions and problems that existed in the many versions of the Greek and Roman stories, Virgil wove a smooth, poetic tale that brought Aeneas safe from Troy on an odyssey through the Mediterranean to Italy, in obedience to the will of Zeus and Fate. He forms an alliance with King Latinus of Latium, the region just south of where Rome was later to rise, but is opposed by Turnus of the neighbouring Rutulians. War ensues, which ends, as the *Aeneid* ends, with Aeneas's killing of Turnus, after which he marries Latinus's daughter Lavinia. During Aeneas's journey, Virgil describes his visit to Hades, where the shade of his deceased father Anchises shows him a parade of their descendants yet to be born, including Romulus, who will found Rome, Julius Caesar and Augustus. It was a story that was destined to survive, and which would exercise a profound effect upon the British imagination.

Chapter 2

Brutus's Isle

The myth that Britain was first settled by Brutus and his Trojans in about 1100 BC is just that – a myth. In fact, Britain has been inhabited by humans, on and off as the Ice Ages allowed, for almost a million years: the earliest remains left by *Homo erectus*, a distant ancestor of we *Homo sapiens*, were found at Happisburgh, Norfolk and are about 950,000 years old. But continuous occupation by our ancestors started only when the ice receded for the last time, about 9,500 BC. Then, from about 4,300 BC onwards, that first tiny population of Mesolithic hunter-gatherers was overlaid by new waves of Neolithic farmers from the Rhine and Brittany. Their agrarian way of life was inherited, ultimately, from the Near and Middle East, where farming had started about 5,000 years earlier. The incoming farmers' genes may have included a few from families who, many generations earlier, had farmed around Troy – but if that is so, it is completely coincidental to our story.

Later, metalworking spread with itinerant smiths – first the art of working copper and tin, then the more complex science of mixing the two together to make bronze, and finally the technology of smelting and working iron. Always, Britain lagged far behind the Mediterranean: bronze first appeared about 2,000 BC followed by iron as late as 400 BC. Similarly, the art of writing, which spread from the Middle East and established itself in Greece during the 600s BC, did not reach northern Europe until the Romans came. The lack of any written records created in Britain prior to the Roman period is one of the reasons why our ancient history and mythology is so powerfully and impenetrably mysterious.

In about 320 BC, however, Pytheas, a merchant explorer from the Greek colony of Marseille, became Britain's first-known, named tourist. Surviving quotes from his book *On the Ocean*, written back in Marseille, provide a tantalising glimpse of the Britain he saw from the heaving prow of his black ship. Much that he wrote, or might have written, has been lost, but we know at least the names of the patchwork of tribes he encountered. In the far north of what is now Scotland were the Cornavii. Working south through the Highlands towards the Central Belt were the Carini, Smertae, Carnonatae, Decantae, Taexali, Creones and Cerones, Caledonii, Vacomagi, Venicones, Epidii (the 'people of the horse'),

Damnonii and Selgovae. Together, these were the people who probably called themselves the Piti, and whom the Romans later called *Picti*, 'painted ones', as a pun, because they painted their bodies with blue woad.

Their Mother Goddess was Bride, or Brigid. They had kings, whose power lay in their swords, but whose authority and sanctity was vested in their membership, via their mothers or wives (or both), of each tribe's dynasty of hereditary queens, the true rulers of the land. These female–line dynasties claimed they were descended from Bride herself, and through their rites, each queen was an embodiment of the goddess.

To the south, in Dumfries and Galloway, were the Novantae, and to their east, around and to the south of the great volcanic rock of Edinburgh, were the Votadini. Dominating the entire north of what would become England were the Brigantes. The Parisi and Coritani were in Yorkshire and Lincolnshire, the Deceangli in Cheshire, the Cornovi in the upper Severn Valley, the Ordovices in North Wales, the Demetiae and Silures in South Wales and the Iceni were in East Anglia – they whose last queen, Boadicea, who died opposing the Romans, ensured that history would never forget the era when Britain's hills were ruled by a goddess's descendants.

The land to the south was dominated by kings whose right to rule depended on their membership of enormous, extended families of warriors related through the male line. They, if not the poor tillers of the lands they ruled, were probably of Gaulish origin. In Essex and Hertfordshire were the Trinovantes, the Cantii were in Kent and Sussex, and in the tin-producing west lived the Dumnonii. Between, all along the upper Thames Valley and down to the Channel, including the sites of Stonehenge and the White Horse of Uffington, was a single tribe who later split into the Durotriges and Dobunni.

Between Pytheas's time and the day when Caesar's ships crunched ashore on the stony beach at Pevensey in 55 BC, the picture altered due to fresh invasions by the Belgae, a fiece race of warriors resulting from the interbreeding of Gauls with the Germanic tribes to the east. They appeared in southern Ireland as the Fir Bolg and in southern Britain as the Regnii, who took over Sussex, the Catuvellauni in Hertfordshire and the Atrebates in Hampshire and the upper Thames Valley.

These were the peoples of Britain when the Romans came. They lived partly by hunting and fishing and partly by farming, mainly herding goats, sheep and cattle, but also growing wheat, oats and barley to make bread and beer. For most, home was an isolated village of little round huts of wattle and daub or stone, thatched with reeds, straw or turf, perched up on a hill. The warrior élite lived in more substantial hill forts, in larger roundhouses with high thatched roofs: food brought in from the hinterlands supported a more complex society including horsebreeders, metal and leather workers and traders who brought in luxury goods from the south. But there were no cities. Any aspects of life that might vaguely resemble the way things had been in Bronze Age Troy were due to occasional imports. The archaeology of ancient Britain rules out the idea of a great wave of Trojan immigrants, as described in Brutus's myth, as firmly as can be.

Brutus's name is a Roman one, reflecting the awe with which Roman culture was remembered in the centuries following its collapse. But early versions of his story call him Britto, a more obvious eponym for Britain. An eponym is the name of a person who is said to have given their name to a city or county. But often things are really the other way around, for many place names were used to create personal names for entirely fictional founding heroes. Thus, from the name of Britain, came Britto, or Brutus.

Pytheas called the island he encountered 'the island of the Albiones', from *alba*, 'white', probably from the dramatic chalk cliffs and downs of the south coast, which greeted any mariner voyaging up from the south. It was not until the last century BC that both Strabo and Diodorus Siculus referred to the island, which they knew about through the reports of traders, as 'Pretannia'. The name might be from *pretanii*, 'painted ones', because the Britons painted their bodies with blue woad, but it could mean 'the island of the *prytaneis*', a Greek word for lawgivers or magistrates, and referring to Britain's law-giving druids. If so, it would fit well with the Dark Age belief (recorded in an ancient bardic triad in the medieval *Red Book of Hergest*) that Britain had once been named 'the precinct of Myrddin', after that archetypal druid, Merlin.

Long before Brutus of Troy, and perhaps inspired by Greek precedents, the ancient Britons had imagined their own eponymous founders. Another triad in the *Red Book of Hergest* refers to Britain being 'conquered by Prydain son of Aedd Mawr', who gave the island its name. 'Aedd Mawr' may mean 'great fire': he may have been a sort of thunder-and-lightening god, like the Greek Zeus. Pedigrees recorded in the Dark Ages show this god-born Prydain as the ancestor of the semi-mythological British king Bran the Blessed. Prydan's otherwise forgotten story may have been a mythologised memory of genuine invasions of southern Britain by Gauls during the Iron Age. But, if so, Prydan was only one invader amongst many: once Brutus's myth was finally formed, its tale of a heroic leader of invading colonists contained a great resonance because there had been so many genuine waves of incomers to Britain, from the end of the Ice Age onwards.

Any eponym derived from 'Britain' had immense sacred and royal resonance as well, for the name of the ancient British goddess Bride was probably also derived from the name of Britain. She was surely seen as the great spirit of the island long before the Romans came and civilised her as Britannia, an Athena-like Olympian goddess and the island's official patroness. Even after the Romans left, Bride remained a potent deity amongst the indigenous Picts in Scotland. Until the AD 800s, their royal dynasty of queens continued to be seen as incarnations of the goddess, and some of their king-consorts prefixed their own names with the honorific title Bruide, or were called Bredei or Bred. So in those parts, 'Bruide' and 'sacred king' may have been virtually synonymous until at least the AD 800s, by which time Brutus's legend was well established in Wales. The role of sacred king of Britain, therefore, was ready and waiting for the mythical Trojan Brutus to step into.

Throughout Britain's prehistory, there was contact, however sporadic and remote, between Britain and the Mediterranean world. The 'Amesbury Archer', who was buried below a round barrow near Stonehenge about 2,300 BC, had with him gold and copper artefacts, some of which had clearly been fashioned in southern France and Spain, and his tooth enamel contained chemical signatures that place his origins in the Alps. Some of the best sources of tin anywhere in Europe were the opencast mines of Devon and Cornwall. Trade routes that brought British tin to the Mediterranean existed in Mycenaean times, and resumed from about the time of Homer (the 800s BC) onwards. The tin travelled south-east via a lengthy chain of Gaulish middle men and Greek traders. We know that the Greek merchant Pytheas visited Britain; and he may not have been the only one.

Via such connections as these, myths may have been exchanged. The Greeks' stories about the Hyperboreans, who lived in the north and danced around a stone circle dedicated to the sun god Apollo, may well reflect some genuine knowledge of Britain, and specifically of Stonehenge, which was built to respect midsummer and midwinter sunrises and sunsets. We know about the Hyperborean myth because the Greeks wrote their stories down. But until Roman times, Britain had no writing, and without writing, myths are infinitely mutable. Maybe Britons living in the first millennium BC heard stories of Troy, perhaps from Pytheas himself, and wove them into their own tales. But without writing, and with no real appreciation of what a city was, such tales are likely to have degenerated quickly into unrecognisable adventure stories. At any rate, no discernible traces of such stories remain today: there is no indication, to be clear, that Prydain had anything Trojan about him whatsoever.

But at the end of the Iron Age, the Trojan myth did wash for certain over northern Europe, and this time it did leave traces, in Gaul at least. The tale of Troy must have been known in southern Gaul once the Greeks had established their colony at Marseille about 600 BC, and it spread north for sure, through the Roman conquest of Gaul in 58–50 BC. When the Aeduii tribe in central Gaul made an alliance with Rome back in 61 BC, the Senate referred to them diplomatically, according to Caesar's *Conquest of Gaul*, as *fratres consanguineique*, 'brothers and kinsmen'. This may have fostered a belief in Trojan origins like those claimed by the Romans because, shortly afterwards, Timagenes wrote that 'Some again maintain that after the destruction of Troy, a few Trojans fleeing from the Greeks ... occupied these districts [Gaul], which at that time had no inhabitants at all.' Any Gauls tempted into such a belief might have had it enforced by the settlement of an eastward-roaming branch of their people in Anatolia, in the region that became known as Galatia, in the 200s BC. The Gauls back home now had kin living in close proximity to Troy, and the Galatians may have started claiming Trojan ancestry for all the Gauls, so as to make it appear that they had not so much conquered Galatia, as simply returned back home.

Some Gauls may, therefore, have thought of themselves as Trojans, but there was an alternative. In 279 BC, when an eastern branch of the Gauls marauded their way as far as Greece, they sacked the sacred oracle at Delphi. Cowering behind the walls of Athens, Timaeus struggled to find an appropriate mythological explanation for this all-too-real nightmare race. He knew the Sicilian story of the hideous Cyclops Polyphemus, who fell hopelessly in love with a sea nymph who happened to be called Galatea. So Timaeus hypothesised that the brute monster had had his way with the poor nymph and fathered the eponymous ancestor of the Gauls. Later, the Roman historian Appian recorded an expansion of this story, that Galatea and Polyphemus had produced three offspring: Galas, Celtus and Illyrius.

The Greeks' insulting view of the Gauls' origins, which nonetheless placed their origins firmly within the framework of Classical mythology, must have filtered back to Gaul itself. But they, or more likely the Greek colonists of Marseille on their behalf, came up with a better idea. The new version concerned a Gaulish princess who was so tall and strong that no man was good enough for her, until one day Hercules passed by, on his way back from his tenth labour, the stealing of Geryon's cattle in Spain (see plate 23). From their passionate union, according to Diodorus Siculus, was born 'Galates', the eponymous ancestor of the Gauls.

Julius Caesar conquered Gaul by discovering which tribes were at war with each other, and forming alliances with some in return for their help in fighting the rest. These tribal alliances of Caesar's were expressed sometimes in terms of the ancient, mythological struggle between Troy and Greece. Thus, in 52 BC, a great rebel army of Gauls, led by Vercingetorix of the Arvernii, who were neighbours and enemies of the Aeduii, was besieged by Caesar at the great Mandubii hill fort of Alesia (now Alise-Sainte-Riene), in central Gaul. Outside the walls, Caesar was busy honouring his urbane Trojan ancestor, Aeneas. So within Alesia's stockaded banks and ditches, we hear from Diodorus Siculus that Caesar's Gaulish foes were sacrificing to Greek Hercules, as the reputed founder of Alesia and (by implication) the ancestor of the rebel tribes.

But we should not be surprised when, after Vercingetorix's rebellion had been crushed, his own tribe seems to have realigned itself mythologically, rejecting Hercules in favour of Aeneas. For about AD 50, the Roman poet Lucan quipped about the 'the Arvernian race, that boasts our kinship by descent from Troy'.

In 55 BC, Julius Caesar stood gazing across the English Channel towards the white cliffs of Britain. In the Greek world view, the landmass of Europe, Asia and Africa was girdled by a mighty river called Ocean, which flowed, uninterrupted but for a few scattered islands of varying sizes, to the edge of the world. Only Alexander the Great had tried to conquer as far as Ocean's shores – east, in his case, and he had failed. By reaching the western shores of Ocean, Caesar felt he had at least equalled Alexander's achievements. By crossing the Channel, Caesar might outshine Alexander completely. In his body, he believed fervently, flowed the blood of Aeneas and Aphrodite. To conquer Britain was the will of the Olympian gods who protected him as one of their own.

But the gods had other ideas. Caesar's first attempted invasion was repulsed: he returned with more troops the next year, and battled through Kent and up into Hertfordshire, where he agreed a truce with Cassivellaunus, overlord of south-eastern Britain. But then he left for good.

Under Cassivellaunus and his successor Cunobelinus (Cymbeline), more traders than ever before came and went between Britain's south coast and Roman Gaul, eagerly exploiting the opening markets of southern Britain. Honouring the terms of the peace treaty, the south-eastern British tribes sent tributes to Rome, first to Caesar and then to his successor Augustus. They also sent *obsides*, young princes destined to rule their people, who were both nominal hostages and also willing pupils who came back to their island fully Romanised, their heads bursting with tales of Greece and Troy. Hercules appears on a handful of British coins from this period, suggesting, perhaps, that some of

Dido and Aeneas, drawn
from the mosaic floor of
Low Ham Roman villa,
Somerset.

the southern British tribes had imported a belief in Herculaean origins from Gaul. Some of them were recent immigrants from Gaul anyway, so the extension of such a belief to Britain is certainly possible.

The question of whether the *obsides* also developed a Trojan myth for Britain – perhaps even containing the seeds of Brutus's story – was discussed by John Creighton in 2000. He described it as 'exactly the sort of unification of the mythological support for the Augustan regime and the descent of the British kings which we would expect'. Creighton concluded that it was possible – but he admitted that he could find no hard evidence for any such Trojan myth in Britain at that time.

After old Cunobelinus died, the Roman-British truce broke and in AD 43 Claudius led a successful invasion. Within a few decades, all of Britain except for the far north had become the Roman province of Britannia. From then on, the *Aeneid* was read and sung throughout Britain and we can see the results in archaeological finds, from Lullingstone Villa in Kent's Darenth Valley, where a mosaic of Europa and the bull is accompanied by a quote from book one of the *Aeneid*, to the floor of Low Ham Roman villa, Somerset, on which Aeneas's love affair with Dido is depicted in fourth-century mosaic tiles.

But a knowledge of Aeneas in Britain does not automatically equate to a belief that he, or his Trojan descendants, were the ancestral founders of the British population. Such a national myth did not arise then, for the good reason that Roman Britain was a Roman province, not a nation, so it had no need of its own foundation myth. The myth of Troy, embodied in the arrival of Aeneas's descendant Brutus, was destined to arise – but not until several centuries later, when new nations formed in the aftermath of Rome's collapse. And before that happened, a new force was set to burst upon the mythological landscape of the western world – Christianity.

Chapter 3

The Age of Arthur

Although Brutus was a Trojan and a great-grandson of the Classical hero Aeneas, he was conceived by Christian monks as part of a chain stretching back beyond Aeneas to Adam and Eve (see plate 3). Christianity itself emerged in the first century AD in Palestine, which was then a province of the Roman Empire. Despite early, savage persecution, it spread across the empire. The Romanised Britons embraced the new faith early on, first in small numbers and then in ever greater ones, not least, perhaps, because they hoped it might induce the Roman authorities to show them some compassion.

Only a few generations before, their Iron Age ancestors had worshipped their own gods in their own woods and on the banks of their own rivers. The Romans embraced these local deities happily enough: the nymphs of the river Darenth can still be seen painted on plaster in an alcove in the excavated Roman villa at Lullingstone, Kent. For their part the Britons, presented with the overwhelming, written majesty of Classical lore, drew the Mediterranean myths up enthusiastically to embrace their island. Though written down in many books, Classical mythology lacked a single, orthodox version so was infinitely adaptable. It was no problem for the Britons to believe, should they have desired to, that it was Zeus's thunderous voice they heard when storms rumbled across the Pennines, or that Perseus had roamed the Berkshire Downs in his quest for the Gorgon, or that Hercules had visited Britain in the course of his labours. Romans and Britons alike were interested in equating the island's gods with Classical ones, too. Sometimes, a British and Roman deity might actually be the same entity, both derived from the same, Neolithic, archetype. Other times, less reliable identifications were made, due to perceived, but actually coincidental similarities, such as the equation of Hercules with Ogmios, a Gaulish deity famed, oddly enough, for his eloquence.

And then, within only a handful of generations, came Christianity. The multi-textured mosaic of beliefs that had resulted from Britain's full exposure to Classical mythology, all crowned with Virgil, was not swept away completely. Wisps of it curl through our island's myths like strands of mist from behind the veil of Christianity. It is this covering of Britain's older indigenous and Classical beliefs by Christianity that makes British mythology so obscure, so arcane and so fascinating.

Christianity brought a welcome message of love and compassion, but it was not without problems. As the newly converted Romano-British Christians read their Bibles by the light of oil lamps in their elegant villas, they could readily imagine Yahweh moving over the face of the waters of the Thames Estuary. But it was inescapably clear that all of the Bible's action was set in distant Palestine and its environs. Unlike the infinitely mutable Greek myths, Christianity was encapsulated in a single, authoritative book – and from that book the name of Britain was completely absent.

So myth-making stepped in again. Just as their ancestors had tried to connect themselves to the matrix of Classical mythology through tales of Classical heroes coming to western Europe, so now, in similar fashion, the early Gaulish and British Christians longed to bring the heroes of the Bible to their shores. By the AD 300s, according to Eusebius, British bishops were claiming that 'the Apostles passed beyond the ocean to the isles called the Britannic Isles.' Imagination focused most sharply on Joseph of Arimathea (see plate 4), a biblical follower of Jesus who was transformed by myth into the uncle of the Virgin Mary. Joseph was said to have come to Britain after the Crucifixion and spread Christianity from his base at Glastonbury. (In the Middle Ages, a further layer of myth was added, with the story that Joseph had also come to Britain earlier, landing at Falmouth and walking up Smithwick Hill, leading by the hand his young great-nephew, Jesus himself. And such wilful transplanting of biblical stories to Britain has never really stopped: even in the twentieth century, members of the Bloomsbury Set painted the nativity in Berwick parish church, Sussex, taking place below the sweeping curve of Firle Beacon, and Stanley Spencer painted the adult Jesus's life unfolding, Crucifixion and all, amidst the leafy lanes of Cookham, Berkshire.)

Enforced by Joseph of Arimathea's myth, Christianity spread throughout Roman Britain. Christianity received official toleration from Constantine in 313, and became the official religion of the Roman Empire under Theodosius in 380. But then the magnificent, gilded edifice of the empire creaked, groaned, and came crashing down in ruins.

On a bitterly cold day at the end of December 406, the Rhine, that broad, strong-flowing barrier that protected the Roman world from the barbarous forests of Germany, froze solid. Cold and hungry, the Germanic people called the Franks, who had been crowded along the east bank, seized an opportunity denied them for generations and started to pour across the ice to start pillaging the food, wine and gold of Roman Gaul. Four years later, the emperor's relations with Alaric and his army of mercenary Visigoths turned sour, and the barbarians he had employed to protect the empire besieged the capital itself. On 24 August 410, they burst through Rome's gates and sacked the city.

Back in 330, having toyed with the idea of establishing a new eastern capital for the Roman Empire at Troy, Constantine had opted instead for Byzas, which became Constantinople. Later known as Byzantium (and now Istanbul), the new capital, with its separate, eastern Roman emperor, withstood the carnage that followed, for a thousand years. But that was small comfort for the peoples of the Romanised west, who saw their rulers in Rome degenerate rapidly after 410 into the puppets of barbarian warlords, while their formerly orderly provinces disintegrated like icicles in the sun.

As Rome's marble columns crashed down, pagan Romans rounded on their Christian neighbours, accusing them of having precipitated the disaster by abandoning the empire's stalwart, Virgilian values. Against such criticism, St Augustine of Hippo thundered back through the pages of his *De Civitate Dei,* 'the city of God'. For too long men had placed their trust in the strong walls of earthly cities, he proclaimed. Lofty Troy had fallen and risen again as Rome: but now Rome too had perished on the pyre of earthly evil. Those who placed their trust in walls and gates were doomed to taste the bitterness of death. Let them turn instead to the City of God, roared Augustine. Let them place their trust in the greater city that lay within each person's soul, and which was a microcosm of the eternal city of Heaven: the inviolable dwelling place that was the City of God.

Until this point, Virgil and Aeneas had been the bedrock on which the Romans' self-image was based. The poet Claudian (c. AD 370–404) had even presented Aeneas's (albeit pagan) piety as a fine example for Christian emperors to follow, praising the Emperor Theodosius for using Christianity to restore the Golden Age of which Virgil had sung. But Zeus's promise made in the *Aeneid,* 'I have granted them [the Roman descendants of the Trojans] empire without end', now had a distinctly hollow ring to it. 'But what was I to do,' asks an imagined, snivelling Virgil in one of Augustine's sermons, 'when I was selling my words to the Romans, except flatteringly to promise them something that was false?'

Then Augustine's pupil Orosius took up the new theme: follow Jesus, he urged, and reject Aeneas, for 'the strifes he aroused, the wars he stirred up over a period of three years [and] the many peoples he involved in hatred and afflicted with destruction'. There was no comfort to be drawn any more from

Virgil's stirring tale of the founding of earthly cities, when every day walls were torn down and churches were burnt by unstoppable waves of barbarians.

Britannia fared no better than most Roman provinces. When the legions withdrew in AD 410, the Romano–British were exposed first to raids and then to outright invasion by Anglo-Saxons from the Danish and German coast, Picts from Scotland, and the Irish. Those Roman soldiers and officials who remained behind tried to maintain authority, especially around Hadrian's Wall in the north, and along the heavily fortified Saxon Shore of Kent in the south. The most successful created power bases that survived to form the cores of the later British kingdoms – Rheged, Strathclyde, the Gododdin, Ebrauc, Elmet and so on – which clung to the vestiges of Roman civilization as the tide of barbarism surged around them. They used the Roman military title *dux*, 'leader', for which the British translation was *guletic*, or *wledig*.

Tradition, as opposed to firmly established history, remembers the succession of wledigs who tried to stave off disaster: Coel Hen ('Old King Cole'); Cunedda Wledig; Amlawd Wledig; Ceretic Guletic; Vortigern; Vortimer Fendigaid; Ambrosius Aurelianus; Uther Pendragon and Arthur. The first four were in the north and the latter four – though it is the subject of much debate – were probably in the south. Vortigern was the foolish king who invited the Jutish brothers Hengist and Horsa into Kent, and then found he could not get rid of them. Vortimer was the heroic son of Vortigern, who drove the Jutes out, temporarily, but was poisoned by Vortigern's Jutish wife. Once brave Vortimer was dead, resistance to the Germanic invaders shifted west. The decimated Romano-Britons flocked, 'as eagerly as a hive of bees when a storm is threatening ... burdening the air with unnumbered prayers', as Gildas reported, around the standard of an unassuming survivor of the Romano-British aristocracy, Ambrosius Aurelianus. Ambrosius organised a vigorous resistance, and for a while he held the invaders back.

It was under Ambrosius that there emerged a new leader, Arthur. Later myth makes him the son of Ambrosius's alleged brother, Uther Pendragon. More likely, he was simply an able Romano-British soldier. Arthur fought a series

King Arthur, reimagined as a medieval knight by W.H. Margetson.

of battles against the Saxons, culminating in AD 518 with the battle of Mount Badon, which is probably Badbury Rings, Dorset, 'in which,' report the *Annales Cambriae*, 'Arthur carried the Cross of our Lord Jesus Christ on his shoulders for three days and nights, and the Britons were victorious.'

It was a mighty triumph that checked the advancing tide of Saxons for a generation. But in AD 537 a disaster struck, which myth remembers as a family squabble and the *Annales Cambriae* record as 'the strife of Camlann', Camlann perhaps being South Cadbury hill fort in Somerset (see plate 2), which was in turn later mythologised as Camelot. 'Arthur and Mordred perished, and there was plague in Britain and Ireland,' recall the annals, and the Saxons swept west. With these brief references in the annals, Arthur appears and vanishes from recorded history. Everything else about him belongs to the realms of supposition and myth.

But the little we do know about Arthur fits exactly with his times. Unlike the prince later evoked in Edmund Spenser's *Faerie Queene*, who discovered that he was descended from Trojan Brutus, the real Arthur had not drawn his inspiration from any imagined Trojan antecedents. Like any good disciple of Augustine, he had cast aside his *Aeneid* and placed his trust in the cross of Christ alone.

Writing a few years after Arthur's death, as the Anglo-Saxons rampaged west across Britain, Gildas, the first British historian whose work has survived, wallowed in the rhetoric of *The City of God* to bemoan the sinfulness of the Romano-British. This alone, he believed, had brought the Germanic hordes crashing down upon them. Gildas was not remotely interested in myths about Britain's origins: his concern rested purely with the fate of the souls of the people living in Britain in his own time, either in the eternal joy of Heaven or, more likely, in the vengeful fires of Hell.

Yet, slowly, the storm abated. The Angles, Saxons and Jutes settled down in the great swathe of Britain that they had overrun, and called it Angle-land, or England. The Romano-Britons stemmed the tide short of the western sea and fortified the borders of their remaining lands – Strathclyde and Cornwall, and the land that became known as Cymru, 'the land of the compatriots', which the English called Wales, 'the land of the foreigners', the land in which the myth of Brutus was destined to emerge.

Chapter 4

'The Coastal Peoples'

While the dust of the Anglo-Saxon invasion of England slowly settled, Brutus waited in the wings. The two main elements of his myth, the Classical story of Aeneas's journey from Troy to Italy and the Christian belief that all humans were descended from Noah, were in place. The time had not come yet to fuse them together, but when it did, it happened for the good reason that the Christian Bible provided a compellingly clear account of who we humans are, and where we come from.

The Bible's origin myth for humanity, which takes up the first part of the Book of Genesis, must have come as a refreshing change for the people of the Roman and post-Roman world, who had to wrestle with numerous tribal origin myths that didn't agree with each other, and also with the complex and contradictory written mythology of the Classical world. Now, with Christianity, there was just one clear, orthodox story taking everything back to Adam and Eve.

But what was the genesis of Genesis? The old view is that it recorded traditions handed down faithfully by many generations of Semitic tribesmen, but many modern scholars express a different opinion. In 597 BC Jerusalem, like Troy before it, was besieged and sacked by foreign enemies. The king and many of his people were carried away by Nebuchadnezzar to Babylon, where they began a long period of exile. In his *Prologue to History*, John Van Seters argues that Genesis was composed during this period of exile by newly literate Hebrew scribes. It was a literary synthesis of oral, tribal Jewish tradition and the powerfully arcane written origin myths of Mesopotamia, which they encountered in Babylon, with a structure borrowed direct from Hesiod's *Theogony*. Probably written in the 700s BC, Hesiod had taken all the contradictory stories he had heard about the Greek gods and welded them into a single genealogical narrative poem, starting with the beginning of the world, out of which emerged Earth (Gaia), who gave birth to Heaven (Uranos), and from the union of Heaven and Earth came the Titans, who were parents of the Gods and all the rest. Hesiod was the first known, named genealogist, and his work was truly groundbreaking, because to our knowledge nobody had ever created such a genealogical narrative before. Now, taking its inspiration from

Hesiod, Genesis followed a similar, relentlessly genealogical structure, starting at the beginning with God creating Adam and Eve and then working steadily down to Noah and beyond. The momentum of this narrative created waves that rippled out far beyond the pages of the Bible and led, ultimately, to the invention of Brutus as one of Noah's numerous descendants.

The story starts, of course, with God. The Jews' belief in a single deity was unusual, and had been born, perhaps, through simple practicality: the fewer statues of gods a nomadic people had to carry about with them, the better. But earlier in their history, it seems likely that Yahweh had been part of a pantheon of gods, the victor in the Jews' own version of the cosmic succession struggle that was common to the culture of the entire Near East and eastern Mediterranean. Yahweh, runs the argument, was the Hebrew equivalent of the Hittites' supreme god, Tarhunta, the Phoenicians' Baal and the Greeks' Zeus, all of whom had risen to power by overthrowing their fathers. Biblical scholars such as Raphael Patai and Dr Francesca Stavrakopoulou argue that, like them, Yahweh even had a consort, Asherah – the equivalent of Zeus's wife Hera.

The story of Yahweh creating the world seems like a version of a much older origin myth found right across the region too. The Babylonians, for instance, attributed the creation of the world to their own city god, Marduk, who, they said, had made the Earth, plants, animals and humans. In numerous versions of the Mesopotamian origin myth, the gods made man out of clay, just as the biblical Adam's name seems to derive from the Hebrew *adamah*, 'earth'. Perhaps the idea of Eve as the primordial troublemaker mirrors Helen's destructive role in the myth of Troy and also Hesiod's misogynistic view of Pandora as the origin of all evils, as expressed in his *Works and Days*. The story of the serpent persuading Eve to eat from the Tree of Knowledge seems to have borrowed both the serpent and the tree from an ancient Mesopotamian myth of Inanna and Dumuzi, in which Dumuzi is transformed into a snake and takes refuge in an apple tree.

Genesis then provides a genealogical line of nine long-lived patriarchs coming down from Adam's son Seth to Noah. This, as Van Seters argues, seems like a Jewish adaptation of the Sumerian King Lists, which start with Alulim and come down through nine long-lived monarchs to Ziusudra or Uta-napishtim. The Mesopotamian epic *Gilgamesh* explains that Uta-napishtim survived a great flood sent by the gods to keep human numbers in check. Genesis keeps this flood story, changing Uta-napishtim to Noah and introducing a moral slant, not present elsewhere – that humanity's near-extinction was the result of its own sinfulness.

The Mesopotamians used the story of the Great Flood as the great dividing line between the dim and distant, primordial past and their own times. The Greeks of Homer's time used the Trojan War for the same purpose – to draw a line in the sands of time between 'then' and 'now', and this was one reason why the story of Troy loomed so large in the Classical mindset. The war's divinely ordained purpose, as with the flood, was destructive. The *Catalogue of Women* (probably written in Athens about 530 BC and falsely attributed to Hesiod, whose style it follows) states that the gods had been interbreeding with mortal women to produce the race of heroes. But the gods were so ashamed of these acts of passion that Zeus caused the Trojan War to wipe the heroes out altogether. The war therefore marked the end of the Golden Age and the start of our present, iron-bound era of war, misery, drudgery and disease. Genesis (6: 1–4) contains a strikingly similar story. Shortly before the Flood, we hear that 'When man began to multiply on the face of the land and daughters were born to them, the sons of God [*bene ha'elohim*] saw that the daughters of man were fair. And they took as their wives any they chose.' The children born of these unions 'were the Gibborim who were of old, the men of renown.' It is a confused, troubling passage and perhaps even its writers were not entirely sure what it meant, but the 'Gibborim' seem to equate to the Greek heroes. And God brought their era to an end, sending a great flood, just as Zeus had engineered the Trojan War for the same purpose.

So, whilst the idea of Brutus's story emerging not only out of Classical tradition but also out of the Bible may seem strange, because the two seem to be so different, we can see now that both belief systems had grown out of the same, older, broader eastern Mediterranean beliefs. They were both branches off the same ancient stem: both were attempts by different peoples, in the absence of science, to explain the human condition and the origins of humanity itself.

The Classical Greek view of the Trojan War was that it wiped out most of the heroes and ensured that no more would be born after the surviving ones, like Aeneas, had died. The Greeks did not assert that the war had had a major impact on the regular, human population. Later, it's true, some Greek writers tried to incorporate a flood story into Greek mythology as well, and at an earlier point than the Trojan War. Deucalion and Pyrrha, they said, survived a terrible flood by building a ship. When the waters receded, the ship was beached on top of Mount Parnassus, and they revived the human race by sowing stones in the soil, which was the body of Gaia, Mother Earth. But these stories never really caught on as an integral part of the Classical world view.

For Genesis, however, the repopulation of the world was a pressing concern. It is described in detail in the section known as the 'Biblical [or Hebrew] Table of Nations'. Noah survived the Great Flood and his first, beloved son was Shem, ancestor of Eber, the eponymous progenitor of the Hebrews: his genealogical line is described down to and beyond Jacob, from whose sons the Jewish tribes claimed descent. The genealogies continue down to include many of their leaders, prophets and kings, particularly King David and his son King Solomon. It was to this stem that Matthew and Luke later attached the genealogy of Jesus himself in the New Testament.

Noah's second son was Ham, ancestor of the Jews' neighbours, including the Egyptians, Babylonians, Canaanites (Phoenicians) and Hittites – the ancient Near-Eastern empire out of whose ruins had emerged the independent kingdom of Troy. The Jews had little love for their neighbours, so they told the story of Noah (Genesis, 9: 21–5) becoming drunk and lying naked in his tent, where Ham saw him and told his brothers, for which Noah cursed him. The original Hebrew tradition on which this idea is based probably stopped with these two sons, pious Shem and cursed Ham, but in Genesis, a third son appears, Japheth. He was presumably borrowed directly from Hesiod's *Theogony*, in which the Titan Iapetos was father of Prometheus, whose son Deucalion was father of the Greeks' eponymous ancestor, Hellenos. Thus, in Genesis, the Greeks ended up as the descendants of Eli'shah (i.e, Hellenos), son of Javan, son of Noah's third son Japheth (i.e. Iapetos). And Japheth was also ancestor of 'the coastal peoples' – everyone else in the world for whom the writers of Genesis wished to account.

Originally, of course, the Old Testament, including Genesis, was the holy book of the Jews alone. Many Jews, both those in Palestine and the many who were increasingly dispersed across the Roman Empire, knew, precisely or vaguely, their family connections back to the Old Testament's genealogical stem. That situation remains to this day. For example, the priestly clan of the Cohenim, which is dispersed throughout Jewry, claims male-line descent from Aaron, the brother of Moses, whose ancestry back to Noah is recorded in Genesis.

But as the Old Testament started to be used as the holy book for other religions as well, other peoples started claiming descent from Noah too. When Islam arose in the Middle East, for instance, the second Caliph, Omar I (d. AD 644) commissioned eminent genealogists including Dagfal and Ibn Sharya to codify the mesh of Arabian tribal genealogies into clan registers. These then connected back to the Biblical Table of Nations, to Noah's most prominent son, Shem.

Flavius Josephus was an aristocratic Jewish soldier-turned-historian who settled in Rome after the fall of Jerusalem in AD 70. In the first book of his

Jewish Antiquities, Josephus listed the modern peoples of the Greco-Roman world and explained from which of the grandsons of Noah he thought they were descended. The wild peoples of Asia, for instance, whom the Greeks called Scythians, came from Japheth's son Magog. From Magog's brother Gomer, asserted Josephus, came the Gauls, and from Gomer's brother Javan came the Greeks. Oddly, the Trojans and the Romans who claimed descent from them were not mentioned, but perhaps, because the Trojan pedigree went back to Dardanos son of Zeus, who was Greek, they were thought to have come from Javan too.

Josephus's work was probably of little interest to the Romans until some of them started converting to Christianity. Once they had, however, it became a matter of more than mild curiosity to know how they fitted into the Biblical Table of Nations, so Josephus's work was expanded and improved upon by an early Christian scholar, Hippolytus (c. AD 170–236). He made Japheth's son Magog the ancestor of the Celts and Gauls. No eulogist of Imperial Rome – the pagan emperor was later to have him torn apart by horses – Hippolytus placed the Trojans (and thus their Roman descendants) scornfully under the 'cursed' progeny of Noah's son Ham.

That must have been galling for the Romans, but newly converted Britons, leafing through Josephus, would have been sorely disappointed not to find an ancestor identified for them at all. They may have concluded, as we must, that Josephus considered the British to have been a mere offshoot of the Gauls. Hippolytus was scarcely more satisfactory. Having assigned the most important European peoples to particular grandsons of Japheth, he gave up with the lesser ones and just listed them as general descendants of Japheth himself, without specifying which of his grandsons was their specific ancestor. Jumbled into this unsatisfactory list were *Brittones qui et in insulis habitant* – the island-dwelling Britons, mentioned, but still to some extent orphans, lacking a specific genealogical connection to what has been termed the 'Genealogy of Salvation'. That was the bleak mythological situation for the British in the time of Arthur.

Other nations fared better in this game of biblical ancestry. Between the 500s and 700s, monkish chroniclers in the newly built Christian monasteries of Armenia and Georgia boldly reimagined their countries' old, Greek-inspired eponymous founders, Hayk, father of Armenak (Armenia), and K'art'los, father of Mts'xet'os (Georgia), declaring them to have been sons of Thogarmah, son of Gomer, son of Japheth, son of Noah. As the kings of Armenia and Georgia already claimed descent from Hayk and K'art'los, they could now bolster their status with impeccable pedigrees coming down from Noah himself – an idea they did not think implausible, because Mount Ararat, where Noah's Ark is said to have settled when the flood waters receded, was within the borders of the old Armenian realm.

Just over twenty years after Arthur died, Isidore of Seville (c. AD 560–636) was born into an old Romano-Spanish family struggling to come to terms with the recent Visigothic invasion of Spain. Isidore reworked Josephus and Hippolytus in a new attempt to list races under their correct progenitors in the Biblical Table of Nations. His *Etymologiae* (or '*Origines*') reverted to Josephus by making Japheth's son Gomer the ancestor of the Galatians and Gauls, with his own Iberian ancestors under Japheth's son Tubal, and his Gothic overlords under Magog. Following this came a list of former barbarian tribes, Franks, Saxons and Germans, whom Isidore seems not to have been able to place specifically under any of the seven sons of Japheth, and then we read that 'certain people suspect that the Britons are named Brittones from Latin because they are stupid, *bruti*. It is a nation placed as if outside the world, in the ocean, with the sea pouring between. About them Virgil says: "the Britons, sundered from the whole world".'

It was clear that, as far as the Britons were concerned, relying on the Church Fathers for their genealogical origins was never going to provide them with all the answers they wanted. And yet the stage was now set. The system of assigning origins to races based on eponymous ancestors, whose names were derived from the names of the races themselves, was now extremely familiar. The continued omission of a founding ancestor for Britain created a demand for just that – an eponymous ancestor through whom the British could discover their connection back to the Biblical Table of Nations, so that they could trace their history right back to Adam and Eve and the start of the world. Isidore had even suggested a name, albeit in a derogatory tone – *Bruti*. It was almost time for Brutus of Troy to emerge from the wings. But why, when Troy had been condemned so roundly by St Augustine, might the British ever wish to imagine their ancestor as a Trojan?

Chapter 5

Troy Reborn

While Arthur was battling against the Saxons in England, Theoderic the Great (d. AD 526) was growing old on his throne in Ravenna and dreaming of Troy. His people were the Ostrogoths, the eastern branch of a barbarian horde that had swarmed across great swathes of the Roman Empire. A Christian from birth, Theoderic had been sent as a hostage to Constantinople, where he sloughed off the last traces of his barbarian past and entered adulthood as a fully fledged Roman. The Emperor Zeno made him a patrician and a consul, and encouraged him to invade Italy to overthrow the troublesome Germanic warlord Odoacer, who had made himself master there. Theoderic used a combination of Roman and barbarian techniques to achieve his goal. He invited Odoacer to a banquet to celebrate a truce, and then murdered him while he was chewing his mutton. While Rome celebrated, the golden mosaics in the palaces and basilicas of Theoderic's new capital, Ravenna, glittered bright with the reflected glories of Italy's past.

The Goths' genuine, orally transmitted tribal history was recorded and embellished by Cassiodorus shortly after Theoderic's death. As the Goths were from Scythia, and Josephus had said the Scythians were descended from Japheth's son Gomer, Cassiodorus decided that Gomer must indeed have been the ancestor of the Goths. His work was improved upon in AD 551 by Jordanes (who commented indignantly on the earlier writings of Josephus, 'why he has omitted the beginnings of the race of the Goths ... I do not know'). Jordanes included a fascinating new element in the story by asserting that the Goths had once been ruled by Telefus, 'a son of Hercules by Auge, and the husband of a sister of Priam [King of Troy], [and Telefus was] ... of towering stature and terrible strength. He matched his father's valour by virtues of his own and also recalled the traits of Hercules by his likeness in appearance.' Telefus fought a war against the Greeks and later his son Eurypylus, who was Priam's nephew, took part in the Trojan War on the Trojan side.

Thanks to Jordanes, the Goths now had an origin myth rooted in the Biblical Table of Nations. But, as the heirs to the glories of Imperial Rome, they were clearly willing to lay aside St Augustine and Hippolytus's negative connotations of Troy and to enjoy again the nation-building tales of Virgil's *Aeneid*. For they had dared bridge the gap between Noah's time and their own with a new chapter drawn from the myth of Troy.

All over the western world, barbarian tribes took stock of the new lands they had conquered and the traumatised remnants of the Imperial aristocracy, hiding inside the robes of priests and bishops, began the slow process of converting and civilising their new, long-haired masters.

Quite independently of the Goths' historians, someone else was trying to work out how the races who peopled the former Roman Empire were related to each other. Walter Goffart thought this unknown person was a pagan living in Constantinople about 520. The result of this man's ponderings was a new table of nations that became so popular in Christian France that we know it now as the Frankish Table of Nations. The compiler had started with a passage in Tacitus's *Germania*, written about AD 98, which described how the German tribes sung stories of their descent from 'an Earth-born god called Tuisto. His son Mannus is supposed to be the fountainhead of their race and himself to have begotten three sons

Francus (Francio), eponym of the Franks, re-imagined for the frontispiece to Jacques de Charron's *Histoire Universelle de Toutes Nations* (1621).

who gave their names to three groups of tribes – the Ingaevones, nearest the sea, the Herminones, in the interior; and the Istaevones, who comprise the rest.' Basing his ideas in Tacitus, the unknown writer of the Frankish Table listed under each of these three brothers the peoples who, by the AD 520s, were living in Europe. Under the third son, Istio (i.e. a name derived from the eponym of the Istaevones), he listed four races in western, Continental Europe: Romanos [Romans]; Brictones [Bretons]; Francos [Franks]; Alamanos [Germans]. In some versions, the three brothers gained a new father, Alaneus: his name might be derived from a semi-independent Roman commander who tried to retain control of Gaul after the western Empire collapsed.

It was a curious piece of work. One version is endorsed 'monks' pastimes'. But it stuck a chord with the Franks because it appeared to make them brothers of the Romans, and the Romans, of course, had claimed Trojan ancestry. Thus, one version of the Frankish Table makes the three founding brothers sons of

Mulius rex, 'King Mulius', a name possibly derived from Iulus, the byname of Aeneas's son Ascanius.

It may have been this – along with the Goths' newly manufactured myths that gave them a glorious part in the Trojan War – that encouraged the Franks to begin searching for their mythological roots in earnest. By now thoroughly Christianised and Romanised, the Franks knew from Isidore of Seville that they belonged in the Biblical Table of Nations under Japheth's son Gomer. But their place in the Trojan story, comparable to that invented by Jordanes for the Goths, remained unknown until about AD 642, when a Burgundian monk called Fredegar produced the *Gesta regum Francorum*, a chronicle of Frankish history.

His imagination inspired by the *Aeneid*, Fredegar invented a story that, after Troy was captured by the cunning of Odysseus, some of the escaping Trojans were led away by a brother of Aeneas called Friga ('Phrygians' was an Homeric byname for the Trojans). They split into two groups: one migrated to Macedonia, to become the forebears of Alexander the Great, whilst Friga led the other party into Asia, where they were called Frigians. These Frigians split again: one party, led by Turchot, became the Turks, who eventually reconquered Anatolia, and the other party, led by Francio or Francus, went west. They settled near the Rhine and started building a new Troy there – a detail inspired by Colonia Traiana (modern Xanten), whose name meant 'Trajan's colony' but which sounded temptingly like 'Troy'. But soon they abandoned this project and invaded Gaul instead.

The Turkish element of the story, incidentally, was later embraced by the Turks themselves, who liked seeing themselves not as barbarians who had invaded Asia Minor, but (as Sultan Mahomet II delighted in telling the Greeks on a visit to Troy, after he had captured Constantinople in 1453), as Trojans who had come back home.

Back in Dark Age Europe, Fredegar's work was of immense satisfaction to the Franks, but it did not explain everything. In the AD 720s, the anonymous *Liber Historiae Francorum* tried to plug some of the gaps by reworking Fredegar's story. This told how a party of Trojans was led to Pannonia (Hungary) by Priam (who, contrary to Homer, had survived the fall of Troy) and his cousin Antenor. Priam was father of Markomir, father of Faramund, father of Clodio, the father of Merovech, founder of the Merovingian dynasty who still ruled the Franks in the AD 720s.

It was a good attempt at an invented history, but the pedigree was far too short. Later chroniclers improved on it, extending it by numerous repetitions of existing names and adding other names drawn from Trojan and Frankish history until eventually the French kings had a plausibly long pedigree, running back from Merovech to the Homeric kings of Troy. Later, Jean Lemaire de Belges, in his *Illustrations de Gaule et singularitez de Troye* (1510–14), even went so far as to claim that Troy had been founded by Gauls in the first place.

These claims of Trojan roots were deeply embedded in the Franks' consciousness by the late AD 700s, when their ruler Charlemagne was expanding his empire, based around his northern capital at Aachen. Charlemagne's coronation as Holy Roman Emperor in Rome in AD 800 was a triumph not only of actual, military and political power but also of the West's desire to revive the long-lost *pax Romana*, the Roman peace established under the Caesars. In accomplishing this *translatio imperii* from Rome

This woodcut from Jean Bouchet's *Les Anciens et modernes Genealogies* (1531) shows Francus, Aeneas and Antenor leading different parties of Trojans away from burning Troy. Aeneas and Antenor were known to the Greeks as survivors: Francus was an invention of the AD 600s.

to Aachen, the Franks made extensive use of Virgilian language and imagery. Charlemagne's court scholar Alcuin was said to have loved Virgil more than the psalms, and whilst he was Christian enough to hail his master as the new King David, not the new Aeneas, he drew heavily on Virgilian imagery, quoting Trojan Anchises' admonition to his son in book six of the *Aeneid* to 'raise up the defeated and now put down the proud, so that peace and holy piety may everywhere reign'.

These continental experiments had made Trojan ancestry respectable and desireable again. The time was ripe for the Trojan myth to spread across the sea to the British Isles and for Brutus to appear at last.

Chapter 6

The Birth of Brutus

W ere it not for the work of the British monk we know as Nennius or Nemnivus, we would have absolutely no idea how the myth of Brutus of Troy had arisen.

'I bore about with me an inward wound,' explains Nennius in the introduction to his *Historia Brittonum*, 'and I was indignant, that the name of my own people, formerly famous and distinguished, should sink into oblivion, and like smoke be dissipated. ... Many teachers and scribes,' he continued, 'have attempted to write this, but somehow or other have abandoned it from its difficulty, either on account of frequent deaths, or the often recurring calamities of war. I pray that every reader who shall read this book may pardon me, for having attempted, like a chattering jay ... to write these things, after they had failed.'

This extraordinary man, who probably worked about AD 809–829, collected material on Britain's history, 'partly from the writings and monuments of the ancient inhabitants of Britain', partly from the annals of the Romans, and the chronicles of the Church Fathers, and also by correspondence with the monasteries of Ireland and Gaelic Scotland, whose people had settled there from Ireland some 300 years earlier, and whose monks were deeply concerned with the history of their Irish forefathers.

Most historians before and long after his time attempted to synthesise contradictory stories into clear, but in fact very misleading, narratives that often bore little relation to the earlier sources. Nennius, however, followed the example set, but rarely followed, by Dionysius of Halicarnassus, a near contemporary of Virgil's, who had painstakingly collected varying stories about Aeneas and Roman history and set each one out clearly, stating his sources. Nennius thus presented the different accounts he had collected concerning the origins of the British side by side, to enable each 'diligent reader to winnow my chaff, and lay up the wheat in the storehouses of your memory' – as we continue to do now.

Nennius successfully collected and recorded a number of different pedigrees concerning characters called Britto or Brutus, and amongst these is the one that stuck and became the 'orthodox' version of Britain's origin myth for more than a thousand years. In this, Brutus was a heroic son of Silvius, son of Ascanius, son of Aeneas, and he settled Britain with descendants of the survivors of the siege of Troy.

Several copies of Nennius's collection exist, but unfortunately each contains slightly different versions of the early Brutus pedigrees, and we cannot be sure which might be the originals. Thus, we have not only the different accounts that Nennius had found, but also different versions of what those accounts had been: and it is from these that we shall try to piece together the story of how the 'orthodox' version of Brutus of Troy's myth had arisen.

It would be have been convenient if Brutus's story had one, clear point of origin, but the inescapable conclusion from studying Nennius is that there were two, both of which ended up providing him with Trojan ancestors. There must have been considerable interplay between these, and between them both and the developing Trojan myths on the Continent, echoes of which resound in the records. The outcome is clear: our job now it is to penetrate those origins.

The first likely origin for Brutus and his Trojan ancestry is the story of the very real Decimus Junius Brutus Gallaicus (180–113 BC), consul of Rome in 138 BC. Two generations before Caesar set out to conquer Gaul, Brutus Gallaicus led the Roman conquest of western Iberia (Portugal and Spain), capturing and fortifying Lisbon and penetrating as far north as the river Minho. His story was related by Strabo and the Church Fathers such as Eusebius, so it was readily accessible to Dark Age scholars.

Gallaicus's cognomen, Brutus, sounded rather like the name of Britain, especially when Isidore of Seville had written so scathingly that the Britons were so called 'because they are stupid, *bruti*'. It was probably for this reason that Brutus Gallaicus became associated with the Britons. So Nennius records a British story that 'Brutus was consul when he conquered Spain, and reduced that country to a Roman province,' adding incorrectly that 'he afterwards subdued the island of Britain.'

Ascanius, son of Aeneas and, as it was eventually decided, grandfather of Brutus, from Guillaume Rouille's *Promptuarii Iconum Insigniorum* (1553).

Brutus Gallaicus was descended from Lucius Junius Brutus, consul in 509 BC, who had founded the Roman Republic. Lucius's maternal grandfather was Lucius Tarquinius Priscus, the fifth king of Rome in succession (according to Roman tradition) to Romulus, the legendary founder of Rome, who was held to have been a descendant of Aeneas. This was known from Roman histories accessible to Dark

Age historians but, more importantly, it was enshrined in Virgil. In book six of the *Aeneid*, Aeneas descends into Hades, where he meets the shade of his father, Anchises. Standing on a mound, they see the 'parade of heroes', the ghosts of all their descendants yet to be born, down to Augustus himself, and amongst these is 'Brutus' (meaning Lucius Junius Brutus). Therefore, the Brutus who was (falsely) believed to have conquered and named Britain was also believed (correctly, in terms of Roman myths) to have had the potent, Trojan blood of Aeneas.

It is perhaps for this reason alone that the story of Brutus Gallaicus's alleged conquest of Britain was preceded by a brief history of the family of Aeneas, down to Romulus and Remus. This version, which appears in J.A. Giles's edition of Nennius, does not state explicitly that Brutus Gallaicus was descended from Aeneas's family, but instead it says that the Britons whom he conquered were 'the descendants of the Romans, from Silvius Posthumous', who was a son of Aeneas and Lavinia. This Silvius was so called 'because he was born in a wood. Hence the Roman kings were called Silvan, and the Britons from Brutus, and rose from the family of Brutus.' The story, recorded faithfully by Nennius, does not make any logical sense, but it is a perfect example of Dark Age monkish reasoning. It starts with two loosely connected 'facts' and then, in the course of a few sentences, synthesizes out of them a new fact that had not existed before: the British were not only named after the Roman Brutus who had conquered them, but were also sprung from the same stock as the Romans, from Silvius Posthumous, son of Aeneas.

This account, as copied by Nennius, also traces Aeneas's ancestry. It follows broadly the established, Classical version (the earliest version of which comes from Aeneas's own mouth in book twenty of Homer's *Iliad*), but with a couple of mistakes (for instance, it makes Aeneas's father Anchises a brother, not a cousin, of Priam). It correctly states that they were descended from Dardanos, who was in Greek mythology son of Jupiter (Zeus), son of Saturn (Kronos), but this version makes Dardanos the son of Saturn, 'King of the Greeks'.

John Morris's edition of Nennius quotes two different versions of this pedigree. These dispense with the idea of Brutus Gallaicus and turn Brutus (or 'Britto') into an earlier hero, the one with whom we shall become familiar throughout the rest of this book. In the first version, 'Britto' is the son of Silvius, who was in turn a son of Aeneas by 'a wife' and it includes a descent of Aeneas's wife Lavinia from Saturn. The other version is prefaced variously, 'This is the genealogy of that Brutus the Hateful, who has never been traced to us, when the Irish, who do not know their origins, wished to be under him', and also,

'This is how our noble elder Cuanu gathered the genealogy of the British from the chronicles of the Romans'. St Cuanu was a monk at Kilconna in Galway, Ireland, who died in AD 640. His pedigree makes Brutus son of Silvius, son of Ascanius, son of Aeneas. Deciding on who Brutus's immediate ancestors were was made difficult for the Dark Age monks because the Roman accounts of Aeneas's genealogy each differed subtly from each other (none, of course, mentoned Brutus, for he had not been invented in Roman times). St Cuanu's genealogy disagreed with Dionysius of Halicarnassus, Virgil, Cassius Dio and Diodorus Siculus, who all made Silvius the son of Aeneas, but it followed Livy, who made Silvius son of Ascanius, son of Aeneas. This seems to mark the beginning of the 'orthodox' version of Brutus's ancestry, which made him Aeneas's great-grandson.

St Cuanu then provides a version of Aeneas's ancestry that is accurate within the Homeric myth, going back to Dardanos, who, Cuanu states correctly, was son of Jupiter (and who, we know, was son of Saturn). In all these versions, it was taken as read that Jupiter and Saturn were not great gods, but mere mortals, hence Saturn being described in Giles's version as 'King of the Greeks'. All humans, of course, were descended from Noah, and Saturn was no different. But the route chosen was a terrible one. For Saturn, ancestor of Aeneas, Brutus and thus of the British, was descended from 'the people of Ham, the accursed son who saw his father Noah [drunk] and mocked him'.

This story was clearly influenced by Hippolytus (d. AD 236), as it places the Trojans under Noah's accursed son Ham, and by Isidore of Seville (d. AD 636), because of the earlier association of the name of Britain with *bruti* and thus with the Roman consul Brutus. It must date to before AD 640, the year in which St Cuanu died. It may be fair to place it, therefore, in the early part of the 600s.

It comes as a shock to realise that this Trojan pedigree of Britain's founder, Brutus, had not been invented by the Britons to glorify themselves. It seems instead to have been contrived as an insult by their neighbours, the Gaels of Ireland and Scotland, in whose ears the anti-Trojan sentiments of *The City of God* were still echoing, loud and clear. It explains why Brutus was described as 'the Hateful'. The phrase about Brutus never having 'been traced to us, when the Irish, who do not know their origins, wished to be under him' is misleading, for the Irish had never claimed descent from him, but the statement underlines the horror felt by some British clergymen at the thought of the Britons being descended from Ham. The Britons might have found their exact place amongst the progeny of Noah at last. But if the Trojans were indeed descended from

Noah's cursed son Ham, then Brutus seemed to be in danger of plunging his British descendants straight down into Hell.

Whilst the Irish were thinking up ways to belittle their British neighbours, they and their Gaelic cousins in Scotland were also becoming fascinated by the Frankish Table of Nations. They developed a new version of this, which was copied out, later, at the start of various versions of that great treasury of Irish mythology, the *Lebor Gabála Érenn*, which was compiled by Christian monks about AD 1000. The Irish version of the Frankish Table was subtly different to its predecessors. Of the four brothers in western Europe, Romanus and Francus remained unchanged, but 'Alamanos' (Germans) was altered to 'Albanus' – in other word, the Scots, who were Gaels from Ireland – and 'Brictones' (Bretons) became 'Britus' – Britons. Unlike any version of the Frankish Table known on the Continent, the Irish version provides a line of ancestors for the brothers' father, Alaneus. Rendered 'Elenus', he becomes son of Dohe, son of Bodb, son of Ibath, son of Gomer, son of Japheth, son of Noah. Ibath is an Irish version of 'Ripath', the Bible's name for a son of Gomer. From what source Dohe and Bodb were concocted, I have never discovered. This new, Irish pedigree made the Frankish Table into something it had never been thought of originally: a continuation of the Biblical Table of Nations, and a stepping stone in the Genealogy of Salvation, down from Noah's respectable son Japheth to the Irish and, accidentally, to the British. It might possibly have been this that Nennius had in mind when he wrote that 'The Irish, who do not know their origins, wished to be under [Brutus]', even though it actually places the Irish next to Brutus, and not under him.

Gomer, son of Noah, re-imagined as ancestor of the Gauls, in the frontispiece of Jacques de Charron's *Histoire Universelle de Toutes Nations* (1621).

As with the Franks, this genealogy made the 'Albanus' (the Scots and, by inference, their Irish forebears) into 'brothers' of the Romans and capable, potentially, of sharing their Trojan ancestry. St Cuanu would have been horrified, but some Irish monk, inspired by the Goths and the Franks, seems to have used this to develop a

Trojan myth for the Irish and the Scots. It does not survive in a coherent form, but an intensely garbled descendant of it appears in the *Life of St Cadroe*. This story as we have it now was written in the late AD 900s, but its raw simplicity suggests that it dates back a good few hundred years. It claims that the Gaels of Ireland were originally Greeks from 'the town of Chorischon in Choria'. They sailed to Thrace, where they met 'the people of Pergamus' and also some 'Lacedemonians' (Spartans) who included Nelum or Niulum, son of Aeneas. From Thrace their ships were blown through the Cyclades to Crete and then west through the Pillars of Hercules (the Straits of Gibraltar), eventually making landfall at Cruachan Feli in Ireland.

The story is clearly based on the *Aeneid*, for Aeneas's journey took him to Thrace, the Cyclades and Crete too. Niulum, son of Aeneas, is Iulus, Virgil's name for Aeneas's son Ascanius. Though the story has turned Aeneas into a Spartan, he is still associated with the Pergamese, and Pergamum was Homer's byname for the acropolis of Troy. So the original idea on which this story is based was presumably that the Gaels met Aeneas in Thrace, where (in the *Aeneid*) he had paused on his way to Italy. They travelled with him to Italy, and then proceeded to Ireland with his son Iulus/Niulum.

It is likely that a story related to this one lies at the root of the *Lebor Gabála* itself. This too concerns the wanderings of the Gaels from their origins in the Near East (where they were descended from Noah) to Ireland, where they wrested the island from the monstrous races who were already there. Though often held up as an accurate record of very ancient, oral Irish tradition, the *Lebor Gabála* is much more likely to be a monkish compilation with its principal roots in Classical and biblical tradition. Its story of the wanderings of the Gaels is probably derived in part, at least, from tales of Aeneas, as John D. McLaughlin first realised. In the *Lebor Gabála*, Troy and Aeneas are forgotten, but Aeneas lives on as Feinius Farsaid, leader of the wandering Gaels, the father of Neolus or Nel, where the name 'Feinius' is derived from Aeneas and Neolus is derived, via Niulum, from Iulus, the byname for Aeneas's son Ascanius.

So Ireland briefly gained a Trojan myth, which then became so garbled that the explicitly Trojan elements disapperared from view. But Britain gained a Trojan myth that stuck, and remained explicity Trojan. This brings us to the second likely origin for Brutus and his Trojan ancestry. Amongst the material collected by Nennius through his correspondence with monasteries in Scotland and Ireland was a version of the Irish pedigree derived from the Frankish Table, linking 'Albanus', the eponym of the Scots – and, incidentally, his 'brother' Britus – back to Noah via Japheth. Nennius's version has a much longer pedigree going back from their grandfather 'Alanus' to Japheth, but it includes the names Thoi, Boibus and Jobath, which are clearly derived from Dohe, son of Bodb, son of Ibath in the Irish version. It seems likely that some unknown monk had realised that the pedigree was far too short, and lengthened it accordingly.

This pedigree did the job of linking both the Irish and their British neighbours back to Noah's son Japheth. This was of course very good news for the British, who had been fascinated by their descent from Brutus and the family of Aeneas, but were disturbed by the awful suggestion that the Trojans were descended in turn from the accursed race of Ham. This new pedigree not only confirmed that Brutus (or 'Britto', as he is also rendered here) was related to the Romans, but it also deduced him, safely, not from Ham, but from his much more respectable brother, Japheth.

In Nennius's time, there was a severe conflict in Britain between the native British church, whose roots went back to Roman times, and the English church of the Anglo–Saxons, who had been converted by missionaries from Rome in the AD 600s. The English wanted the British church to reform its ancient practices and conform to the rulings of the Pope. It seems that envoys from Papal Rome had been using the derogatory 'Ham' pedigree of Brutus to undermine the British church, because in the contents section of his manuscript, as quoted by Morris, Nennius wrote that his book demonstrated how the 'insult of the Romans, that they unjustly twist against us, can be rebutted'.

This 'rebuttal' must be a pedigree that usually appears after the others; as if Nennius thought it was the culmination of them all. This keeps Brutus as the son of Istio (here rendered 'Hiscion'), who was son of Alaneus, and it retains Alaneus's descent from Japheth. But it makes important changes to the generations that connect them. Gone are the Gaelic names Thoi, Boibus and the rest. Instead, as if 'Alaneus' was an echo of 'Aeneas' and thus a name appropriate for a descendant of the Trojan dynasty, it makes Alaneus son of Rhea Silvia, daughter of Numa Pompilius (both being well-known characters from early Roman history), who it says was son of Ascanius, son of Aeneas, son of Troius, son of Dardanos, who (as a 'Greek') was son of Elishah, son of Japheth's son Javan. This pedigree is badly flawed in its recitation of Roman and Trojan history, but as an attempted synthesis of two completely different genealogies, it is not a bad first attempt.

It may have been influenced by St Cuanu's Trojan pedigree of Brutus, but it lacks any negative mention of Ham and clearly does not regard the Trojans as a malignant influence. And that is where Nennius leaves us, with an accurate

Trojan pedigree for Brutus going back to cursed Ham, and an inaccurate one going back to worthy Japheth. Later, or perhaps even within Nennius's lifetime, Welsh genealogists tidied this up and synthesised a new, clear one, going back through the accurate Trojan generations to Japheth, as we shall see in the next chapter.

From the early 600s to the early AD 800s, out of the names of a Roman consul, a reference to the Bretons in the Frankish Table of Nations and the name of Britain itself, had been conjured an eponymous founding hero, Britto or Brutus. He was then re-imaged as a Trojan *oikistes*, or founding hero, a great-grandson of Aeneas, with an impeccable line of descent back to Noah, not via the accursed son Ham, but through the well-regarded son Japheth. Following the Goths' and the Franks' brilliant examples, the Britons had drawn the confidence they needed to affirm their own ancestral links, via Brutus, to the fabled city of Troy and to forge through this a positive place in the Genealogy of Salvation. And that was just what was needed to kindle Trojan fire in the hearts of the Britons of the late Dark Ages.

Chapter 7

'The Monarchy of Britain'

After their first contact with the Roman world, the Iron Age Britons had probably fantasised about Classical heroes such as Hercules visiting their island. Later, under Christianity, they had connected themselves to the story of Jesus by imagining Joseph of Arimathea coming to Glastonbury. Now, by the AD 800s, they had invented Trojan Brutus sailing up from the Mediterranean to settle the island with the earliest ancestors of the British. We know this because, besides the bare pedigrees of Brutus described in the last chapter, Nennius recorded his story, briefly, too. It is clear from this that the version of Brutus's pedigree that had most inspired the British imagination was the one that led back most directly to Aeneas. It reads as if the imagination of the Welsh storytellers had been at work on the bare genealogies, encouraging the made-up names to open, like buds on a sapling's stem, to reveal their leaves and blossoms.

After the Trojan War, relates Nennius, Aeneas comes to Italy, vanquishes Turnus and founds Lavinium. Later, his son Ascanius founds Alba Longa. Different versions of Nennius's text make either Aeneas or Ascanius the father of Silvius: the second option became the orthodox one. When Silvius's wife becomes pregnant, Ascanius summons a magician to determine the child's gender and fate. Again, the versions vary: either, the child 'would become the most valiant among the Italians, and the most beloved of all men' or he 'should slay his father and mother, and be hated by all mankind,' and the latter must be the original version because then we read that Ascanius has the magician put to death.

Yet the magician's prophecies come true nonetheless, for Brutus's mother dies in childbirth and later, while playing with his friends, Brutus accidentally shoots his father with an arrow. Brutus is expelled from Italy and 'came to the islands of the Tyrrhenian Sea'. The Tyrrhenian Sea lies immediately to the west of Italy and contains the large islands of Sardinia and Corsica and many smaller ones, such as Capri and Prochida: there is no way of knowing which were intended here. Brutus then reaches Greece, but is driven out, in some versions, because his great-grandfather Aeneas had slain Turnus (who was an

Italian of Greek descent). Then he goes to Gaul, where he founds Tours, which he names after Turnus, who had been slain by Aeneas. 'At length he came to this island [which was] named from him Britannia, dwelt there, and filled it with his own descendants.'

It was a heroic tale that lacked, but at the same time invited, the further embellishments that would later be added. But it was appropriate for its time and place.

Nennius was a pupil of St Elvodug, Bishop of Bangor (d. AD 809) in the north-western Welsh kingdom of Gwynedd. Gwynedd was one of the Welsh realms that had emerged out of the collapse of the Roman Empire, 400 years earlier. Its kings claimed descent from Cunedda, one of the wledigs or Romano-British leaders of the resistance to the Anglo-Saxons. Latterly, under Merfyn Frych (d. AD 844), to whom Nennius refers as being on the throne while he was writing, Gwynedd was becoming a formidable state in its own right.

Merfyn's court aspired to the Romanesque cultivation of its Carolingian counterparts in France and Germany. Somewhere, in a corner, St Augustine's *The City of God* lay mouldering and unread. It was the *Aeneid* now that was retold around the smoking fires in King Merfyn's banqueting hall, and he and his people dared hope that their strongholds might one day blossom into lasting and protective earthly cities. As Theoderic and the Franks had done before, they could even dream of themselves as the heirs to the glories of Rome, and of Troy itself.

Gazing out from the twin rocks of his ancestral *llys* or stronghold of Deganwy, on the north coast of what is now Caernarvonshire, with the towering mountains of Snowdonia to the south and the magical isle of Anglesey to the north-west, Merfyn saw an expanding empire. Dynastic marriages were drawing the north-eastern Welsh kingdom of Powys under his control. With his son Rhodri Mawr's marriage to the heiress of Ceredigion, the entire northern half of Wales would fall under his dynasty's sway. The divided realms of southern Wales lay within his grasp. Beyond that, King Merfyn allowed himself to dream that one day the gleaming lances of his *comitatus* might sweep over the marches and into Loegria (England), smashing through the Anglo-Saxon kingdoms and driving those barbarians back into the eastern waves, whence they had come.

This was the dream of Merfyn Frych, which would never come true: to restore Britain to the unity it had enjoyed in the time of its Trojan founder, Brutus. His dream was sung in the halls of Gwynedd, and later across all Wales. It was recorded in about AD 930 in a now lost book, *Armes Prydain Vawr*, 'the great prophecy of Britain', a song to be sung by king's *comitatus*, as they donned their shining helms and prepared for battle.

It seems likely that all the Welsh descendants of the Romano-British, including Merfyn Frych himself, thought of themselves generally as descendants of Brutus, the great-grandson of Aeneas. But Merfyn's actual pedigree was more modest. Through the male line he claimed descent, through the rulers of the Isle of Man, from St Ceneu (who is not the same as the Irish St Cuanu), son of Coel Hen, the first of the wledigs. Through Merfyn's mother, Essylt of Gwynedd (through whom he had inherited his throne), he also claimed descent from the second wledig, Cunedda (who was said to have married Gwawl, daughter of Coel Hen).

These claims are probably not true, but if the dynasts of Dark Age Wales bolstered their authority and self-confidence by laying false claim to descents from the heroes of the Romano-British resistance to the Anglo-Saxons, we can hardly blame them.

The same can be said for the purported ancestry of Coel and Cunedda, as recorded in the genealogies of Merfyn Frych's family. Both of them had male-line ancestries stretching back to Beli Mawr, the father of Cassivellaunus, the great Catuvellauni warlord who had resisted the invasions of Caesar. Some of the later generations might be genuine – Cunedda's grandfather was 'Tagit', which may be the plausible Roman name Tacitus, whilst the Roman names Urban and Grat[ianus] appear in the recent ancestry of Coel. But the chances of the earlier sections of their pedigrees, which connect them to Beli Mawr, being genuine are extremely low. They are more likely a form of genealogical propaganda, contrived while the immediate descendants of Coel and Cunedda were attempting to secure their shifting borders, in order to arrogate to their families the prestige of the greatest of the Iron Age Britons.

Around Merfyn's time, the Welsh princes made a new addition to this genealogy, inspired by the developing myth of Joseph of Arimathea. From the collection of Welsh pedigrees now known as Harleian manuscript 3859, we learn that Beli Mawr was married to Anna, 'cousin of the Virgin Mary'. The conceit was possible because Anna was supposedly a daughter of Joseph of Arimathea, he who was already believed to have visited Britain. This one piece of genealogical fabrication led to more stories – that Joseph's wife was the daughter of Longinus, the Roman soldier who had pierced the crucified Christ's side with a lance, and that Longinus was an illegitimate son of Julius Caesar himself. But as Joseph of Arimathea shared the Virgin Mary's descent from King David, the Welsh kings could now claim not only a cousinship with Jesus, but also a direct descent from David, who provided the most prestigious of all routes back to the family of Noah.

Yet even this was not enough. It went without saying that Beli Mawr must have had the Trojan blood of Brutus. Maybe at first the bards simply said he was

Brutus's son. It was in similar fashion that the early Romans had claimed that Aeneas was father of Romulus, the founder of Rome in 753 BC. But in the 200s BC, and with a greater historical sense than their predecessors, Rome's scholars realised that many generations must have come between Aeneas and Romulus, and they set about inventing who those generations were. Likewise, it dawned on the Welsh after Nennius and Merfyn's time that a great many generations must have elapsed between Brutus and Beli Mawr. There ensued a scholarly scramble for material to fill the gap, either from made-up pedigrees or, possibly (as I argued in *Tracing Your Aristocratic Ancestors*), from genuinely old Iron Age tribal pedigrees recorded in Roman times – ancient genealogies that, had they not been re-used as 'space fillers', would have mouldered away and been lost entirely.

We hear, tantalizingly, of a now lost poem called *The Monarchy of Britain*, which probably contained a prototype pedigree linking Merfyn's ancestor Beli Mawr back to Brutus. Gerald of Wales wrote in the 1190s (but clearly referring to a situation that had pertained for a long time) that 'the Welsh bards, singers and jongleurs kept accurate copies of the genealogies of these princes [of north and south Wales] in their old manuscripts, which are, of course, written in Welsh. They would recite them from memory, going back from Rhodri Mawr to the time of the Blessed Virgin Mary, and then further still to [Brutus's father] Silvius, Ascanius and Aeneas. They then continue the line back to Adam himself.'

Several such genealogies survive amongst the old Welsh pedigrees collected by Peter Bartrum. Some traced the rulers of Brittany (who were ancestors of Merfyn Frych through his mother's great-grandmother Afadda) and Gwent (who were also female-line ancestors of Merfyn's) back to the semi-mythical Iron Age hero Bran the Blessed, whose own pedigree they capped with an alleged descent from Brutus. But the main genealogies show several different experiments with Beli Mawr's ancestry, one in fact using some of the same ancestors as Bran (the two tribal kings could conceivably have been related), but greatly lengthened by a pedigree that includes Leir, the king on whom Shakespeare's *King Lear* is based.

The ancestry of Brutus himself follows the version that Nennius attributed to St Cuanu, the early part of which, running back from Aeneas, was itself based in Homer's *Iliad*. It runs back to Dardanos, son of Jupiter (Zeus), son of Saturn (Kronos), son of Caelus (Uranos) – but here, as in Nennius, these Classical gods are alleged again to have been mere kings of Greece. An unknown scholar then added two further generations: Cretus/Creti (Crete) and Ciprius/Cipri

(Cyprus) – names derived from two ancient centres of Mediterranean culture. Ciprius was made into a son of Cetim, who appears in the Biblical Table of Nations as Kittim (which was, actually, an eponym for Cyprus too). And Cetim was son of Javan, son of Japheth, son of Noah.

The finest flowering of this pedigree-making appears in the *Hanes Gruffydd ap Cynan* – 'the history of Griffith ap Cynan', the genealogy of a descendant of Merfyn Frych, recorded in the 1100s and reproduced by Bartrum. It is reproduced below, with modernised spellings and some additional notes from other sources, in brackets. I have also continued it down with a genuine and proven genealogy from Griffith to the present day. It runs down in a continuous line, each person named being the parent of the next one in the list. It starts, as the original Welsh text started, with God:

God
Adam and Eve
Seth
Enos
Cainan
Mahalel
Jared
Enoch
Methuselah
Lamech
Noah
Japheth
Javan (everything down to here is
    from Genesis)
Ciprius (Cyprus)
Cretus (Crete)
Celius (Uranos)
Kronos (Saturn)
Zeus (Jupiter)
Dardanos (whose mother was Electra,
    daughter of the Titan Atlas)
Erichthonius
Tros (founder of Troy)
Assaracus (whose brother Ilus was
    father of Laomedon, father of
    Priam, father of Aeneas's wife
    Creusa)
Capys
Anchises (lover of Aphrodite)

Aeneas
Ascanius (Iulus) (everything back to
    Celius is from orthodox Classical
    mythology)
Silvius
BRUTUS (first king of Britain)
Locrinus
Maddan
Mempricus
Ebraucus
Brutus Ysgwyt Ir ('Greenshield')
Liel
Rud Hudibras
Bladud (founder of Bath)
Leir ('King Lear')
Regan, married to Henwinus
Cunedagius
Rivallo
Gurgustius
Sisillus
Antonius (Annun: he was probably
    originally a tribal god, but has here
    been spliced onto the bottom of the
    pedigree of Leir's dynasty)
Aedd Mawr
Prydain
Dyvynarth
Krydon
Kerwyt

Eneit

Manogan, probably wife of Diguellus
of the Catuvellauni

Beli Mawr (married Anna, cousin
of the Virgin Mary. Anna was
daughter of Joseph of Arimathea
and his wife, the daughter of
Longinus, natural son of Julius
Caesar)

Aflech, brother of Cassivellaunus

Avallach

Eudolen

Eudos

Enid

Eudygant

Eudeyrn

Rideyrn

Riuedel

Grad

Urban

Deyeweint

Tecvan Gloff

Coel Hen ('Old King Cole', first
wledig of Britain)

St Ceneu

Gorwst Ledlumm, king of the
north-western British kingdom of
Rheged

Meirchyaun Gul

Elidir Lledanwyn (married Gwair
of Breicheinog, descended from
Macsen Wledig and his wife St
Helena, a descendant of Bran the
Blessed)

Llewarch Hen

Dwc

Gweir

Tagit

Alcwn

Sandef, King of the Isle of Man

Elidir

Gwraid (married Essylt of Gwynedd,
descended through her Breton
ancestors from Elaine, the half-
sister of Arthur)

Merfyn Frych (married Nesta of
Powys, descended from Vortigern)

Rhodri Mawr (d. 878, married
Angharad of Ceredigion,

descended from St Cadwallader
and Cunedda Wledig)

Anarawd

Idwal Foel

Meuryc

Idwal

Yago

Cynan

Gruffydd ap Cynan (with whom
Hanes Gruffydd ap Cynan ends)

Owain

Iorwerth

Llewelyn the Great (d. 1240)

Helen, wife of Robert de Quincy

Hawise, wife of Baldwin Wake

Sir John Wake

Margaret, wife of Edmund Earl of
Kent

Joan, wife of Thomas Holland Earl of
Kent

Thomas, Earl of Kent

Margaret, wife of John Beaufort Earl
of Somerset

John, Duke of Somerset

Margaret, wife of Edmund Tudor

Henry VII (d. 1509)

Margaret, wife of James IV of Scots

James V of Scots

Mary Queen of Scots, wife of Henry
Stuart Lord Darnley

James VI and I

Elizabeth, wife of Frederick King of
Bohemia

Sophia, wife of Ernest Augustus
Elector of Hanover

George I

George II

Frederick, Prince of Wales

George III

Edward, Duke of Kent

Victoria, wife of Albert of Saxe-
Coburg-Gotha

Edward VII

George V

George VI

Elizabeth II

Charles, Prince of Wales

William, Duke of Cambridge

Prince George of Cambridge

Prince George is not really descended from Brutus, but he is descended from many, many generations of ancestors who believed they were. Griffith's ancestry is a superbly imaginative combination of the biblical genealogies and Trojan, Greek and British myths, all welded together to provide the most prestigious origins imaginable for the Welsh kings, to be used as a psychological weapon against the many enemies who beset them.

This is also the pedigree to which King Arthur belongs. According to the *Bonedd yr Arwyr*, Kerwyt, who appears in this genealogy, was father of Morunan, who was father of Arth, father of Keit, father of Secuyn, father of Gerein hir, father of Garar, father of Llyr Lletieith, father of Bran (the Blessed), father of Karadawc, father of 'Eudaf' (Eudaf Hen), father of 'Kynan' (Conan Meriadoc, Duke of Brittany), father of Kadienn, father of Morvawr, father of Tudwal, father of Kynnvor, father of 'Kustenn' (Constantine II), father of Uther (Pendragon), father of Arthur.

The success with which the Franks and the Britons had forged bridges back to Trojan ancestors emboldened their warlike neighbours, the Saxons, to seek their own Trojan origins. Based on a perceived similarity between the names 'Saxon' and 'Alexan[dros]', the Saxons had already started imagining that their forebears had been Alexander the Great's Macedonian soldiers. When Fredegar made the Macedonians into Trojans, the Saxons seized on this. Widukind's *Saxon Chronicle*, written in the AD 900s, provided a detailed account of the migration of the Trojans to Macedonia, and hence to Saxony, thus placing the Saxons on a genealogical par with the Franks and Romans.

In the AD 900s, marauding Vikings invaded part of northern France, which became Normandy, 'the land of the north-men'. The Normans rapidly absorbed the culture of their erstwhile victims and soon dreamed of reviving the Roman Empire though Virgilian chivalry and city building. Their own Trojan myth appears first in Dudo of Saint-Quentin's *Norman Chronicle*, written about AD 966. Rollo, the real founder of the Norman dynasty, was a Viking from Norway, but Dudo claimed Danish roots for him and his followers. He asserted that 'Dane' was a corruption of 'Danaan', an Homeric byname for the Greeks. This then inspired Dudo to forge a link back (admittedly, somewhat illogically) to Antenor, one of the survivors of the Trojan War. Adapting the *Aeneid* for Norman ears, he gave the part of Turnus to Hasting, a marauding Viking, and the part of his adversary Aeneas was given to Rollo himself, who became a pious, virtuous Norseman, whose rebuilding of ruined Rouen echoed Aeneas's rebuilding of Troy in Italy.

Encouraged by their kinsmen in Normandy, the Vikings themselves joined in with the *Heimskringla* and the *Younger* [or *Prose*] *Edda*, written in Iceland by Snorri Sturlason (1179–1241). For several centuries, Viking longships had been sailing south down the Russian rivers and across the Black Sea to the Bosporus and thus to Constantinople (Byzantium), where Viking warriors had formed the Byzantine emperors' Varangian bodyguard. Norse myth had had plenty of time to absorb the stirring tales of Troy that they heard there, before the northlands were converted to Christianity, and gained the fresh input of Classical mythology, which was an essential part of the civilising process. Sitting around their peat fires, the newly converted Norsemen heard from Snorri's songs how their supposed god Odin had been, in truth, a great human king who was descended from Priam, King of Troy. The ancestry of Priam was lifted from the *Hanes Gruffydd ap Cynan* and appears almost word for word in the Icelandic pedigrees. Snorri wrote that, anticipating the coming of the Romans, Odin had led his people north, first to 'Saxland' and then to Scandinavia. Asgard, home of the gods, was Troy. The cataclysmic battle of Ragnarok, the focus of Norse mythology, was the siege of Troy, in which cunning Loki was Odysseus and Fenris Wolf, the baying demon destined to kill Odin, was the avenging Neoptolemus, son of Achilles. Vidar, the Norse hero destined to slay

Vidar, the Norse version of Aeneas, drawn by Lorenz Frølich for Karl Gjellerup's *Den ældre Eddas Gudesange* (1895).

the wolf and re-form the world from the ruins of the old, said Snorri, was none other than Aeneas.

Long after the Vikings, the Trojan myth continued to spread. By the 1300s, even Wenceslaus IV, King of Bohemia, whose ancestors had been regarded as barbarian incomers by civilised Franks and Saxons alike, found himself the proud possessor of a Trojan pedigree.

But these Trojan tales were never origin myths in their own right. Always, they were preceded either by a statement, or in some cases a pedigree, showing how these Trojan founders of the European nations were descended from characters in the family of Noah, as identified in the Biblical Table of Nations. Troy had regained its ancient glamour, but, as in Greek times, it served a far greater end than as a mirror for its own glory. To the Greeks, the siege of Troy had represented the end of the Golden Age, and the start of the present age of Iron. Now, in Christian Europe, the end of that Golden Age was pushed back to the time of Noah's Flood. And the Trojan dynasty had become the bridge by which the peoples of Europe could connect themselves back to the Flood's pious survivor, Noah.

Now all of Europe had Trojan ancestors, and the British knew their Trojan roots through Brutus. Nennius had told an embryonic version of Brutus's story, but its brevity invited additions. It was time for Brutus's story to blossom into a much fuller biography. And the man to write it was Geoffrey of Monmouth.

Chapter 8

Geoffrey of Monmouth

The origins of Geoffrey of Monmouth are no less obscure than the sources he used for his story of Brutus. He may actually have come from Monmouth, but he refers several times in his works to Caerleon-on-Usk, which is nearby, so some scholars think he was born there.

In the decades after the Norman Conquest of England in 1066, both Monmouth and Caerleon were frontier towns. To the east lay the green fields of England, ruled by William of Normandy. But the purple mountains looming to the west belonged to a patchwork of Welsh kingdoms, ruled for the most part by the querulous descendants of Merfyn Frych. Both towns, too, were old Roman bases. Their mazes of medieval streets lined with wattle and daub houses were loomed over by new, Norman fortresses, but everywhere were reminders of the Imperial past, from ruins of barracks and bathhouses to the still functional Roman walls.

William the Conqueror had granted Monmouthshire to Wihenoc, a Breton lord, whose people believed themselves to be descendants of the Romano-Britons who had fled the Anglo-Saxon invasion. Monmouthshire's population was a mixture of Welshmen, Anglo-Saxons, Bretons and Normans. Geoffrey called himself Geoffrey ap Arthur, where *ap* is Welsh for 'son of'. At the time, the name Arthur was commonest amongst the Bretons, so it has been speculated that Geoffrey's father was from Brittany, and his mother may have been a native Welshwoman. It would make sense, because a Breton father could tell Geoffrey stirring tales of his namesake King Arthur – maybe he was even claimed as an ancestor – whilst a Welsh mother could tell her son the strange tales of Coel and Cunedda, and of Trojan Brutus, who settled the island of Britain in olden times.

Geoffrey's chief ambition was surely to read the ancient books in the monastery libraries, which recorded the high deeds of the past. He became a monk, studying on the Continent and earning the title 'magister'. Returning home, Geoffrey became an Augustinian Canon at Oseney Priory, on the west bank of the Thames. Through the priory's narrow casements, he could gaze out across the river and the water meadows to the thatched roofs of the little town of Oxford.

Geoffrey gained the friendship of three great men: Walter Map, called 'Calenius', Archdeacon of Oxford; Alexander, Bishop of Lincoln; and Robert, Duke of Gloucester (c. 1090–1147), an illegitimate son of the Conqueror's grandson Henry I. Despite his birth outside wedlock, Robert was considered by many to be a potential heir to the throne, for Henry had no surviving, legitimate sons. Robert may have employed Geoffrey to visit his Cornish estates, including the rugged cliffside castle of Tintagel, where, he heard, Uther Pendragon fathered Arthur by appearing before Ygerne in the form of her husband Gorlois, thanks to the magic of Merlin.

For the Bishop of Lincoln, Geoffrey translated an old Welsh text, *The Prophecies of Merlin*. In it, he explains:

As Vortigern, King of the Britons, was sitting upon the Bank of the drained Pond two Dragons, one of which was white, the other red, came forth, and approaching one another, began a terrible Fight, and cast forth Fire with their Breath. But the white Dragon had the Advantage, and made the other fly to the End of the Lake. And he for Grief at his Flight, renewed the Assault upon his Pursuer, and forced him to retire. After this Battle of the Dragons, the King commanded Ambrose Merlin to tell him what it portended. Upon which he burst into Tears, delivered what his Prophetical Spirit suggested to him, as follows.

There ensues an intriguing, bewildering, impenetrably arcane set of prophecies about Britain, which included this: 'The Island shall [again] be called by the Name of Brutus: And the Name given it by Foreigners shall be abolished.'

Later, Geoffrey wrote *The History of the Kings of Britain*, which includes the story of Brutus and the Trojans, and finally a *Life of Merlin*. The latter is interesting because of the discrepancies that exist between it and his *History*. For example, in Geoffrey's *History*, Arthur is mortally wounded and is taken to Avalon, having handed the crown to Constantine of Cornwall: in the *Life*, however, once Arthur has been taken to Avalon, Mordred's two sons seize the realm, and Constantine has to rebel against them to gain the throne. Such discrepancies argue strongly for Geoffrey as a serious translator and reworker of old texts, rather the fanciful inventor of fiction, an accusation so often levelled against him.

The History of the Kings of Britain, the greatest work of Geoffrey's life, was part of a broader project initiated by the far-sighted Robert of Gloucester. 'He would regulate his day so wisely,' one contemporary wrote about Robert, 'that he did not neglect his knightly duties for letters, nor letters for knightly duties.' In the prologue to his *History*, Geoffrey himself praised 'your refined Wit and Judgement … we see an accomplish'd Scholar and philosopher, as well as a brave Soldier and expert Commander.'

Unlike his thick-skulled, conquering relatives, Robert saw his family's expanding realm as the fragile patchwork of hostile races it really was, held together only by Christianity and the mail-clad fist of the king. It was Robert who recognised the enormous potential for myth and history to heal and unify the island so as, ultimately, to create a unified realm of Great Britain.

Geoffrey of Monmouth, woodcut in the frontispiece of the 1603 edition of his *Prophecies of Merlin*.

The Normans' Trojan roots, as invented a century and a half earlier by Dudo, were well known. Not untypical of their dinnertime ballads was Robert Wace's *Roman de Rou*, written at the end of the 1100s:

> *When the walls of Troy in ashes were laid,*
> *And the Greeks exceedingly glad were made,*
> *Then fled from flames on the Trojan strand*
> *The race that settled old Denmark's land*
> *And in honour of the old Trojan reigns,*
> *The People called themselves the Danes.*

During the First Crusade (1096–1099), Robert's father's generation had marched through Asia Minor on their way to the Holy Land. The journey took many of them past the Troad: they were foreign invaders, but they dared think of themselves as the descendants of Trojans returning to their own ancestral homeland.

Robert set four scholars the tasks of writing books that together would provide a full history of the English, the Welsh and their Norman conquerors, all set against the backdrop of their common, Trojan past. Geoffrey received the task of writing the early British section. His work would emphasise how the island was conquered and civilised by Trojans, and flourished under Brutus's descendants. The race reached its epitome under Arthur, but thereafter went downhill.

The Welshmen, being very much degenerated from the Nobility of the Britains, never after recovered the Monarchy of the Island; on the contrary, what by Quarrels among themselves, what by Wars with the Saxons, their Country was a perpetual Scene of Misery and Slaughter. But as for the Kings that have succeeded among them in Wales, since that Time, I leave the History of them to Karadoc of Lancarvan my Contemporary; as I do also the Kings of the Saxons [and the Norman Conquest] to William of Malmesbury, and Henry of Huntingdon.

Thus Geoffrey ended his *History*. In those other histories, we hear how the land was conquered by the Saxons and then by the Normans. Robert's subtext was clear: the Britons and Saxons were both of Trojan origin, but the former had lost half their island to the Saxons, and the Saxons had been unable to conquer Wales. God had ordained that the Normans, the noblest of all the Trojan descendants, should conquer and rule them all, restoring the island to the sole rule of one king, as it had been under Brutus of Troy.

The timing of Geoffrey's writing, about AD 1135, seems an extraordinary coincidence. The siege of Troy was probably fought between 1194 and 1184 BC, and if we allow fifty years between then and the mythical birth of Brutus we reach about 1135 BC. It is as if world history had folded itself in half along the division of BC and AD, and imprinted those two events upon each other, allowing the reverberations of the fall of Troy to give rise to Geoffrey's fully formed story of Brutus.

Bent over his writing desk in Oseney Priory, quill in hand and surrounded by sheets of prepared vellum, piles of leather-bound books and half-unrolled scrolls, Geoffrey worked painstakingly on his *History*. As his goose-feather quill scratched over the vellum, it brought to life the glories of a British past that had lurked only dimly in his mind before then. Instead of writing an epic poem in the manner of Virgil, Geoffrey chose a more matter-of-fact style of prose history. His models were probably the pseudo histories of Dictys Cretensis and Dares Phrygius, two purported eyewitness accounts of the Trojan War, one apparently by a Greek, the other by a Trojan, both probably composed in the first century AD and both widely available in Geoffrey's time in Latin.

Dictys begins with a conceit – that the author, Lucius Septimius, had in fact merely translated Dictys's ancient Greek manuscript into Latin, adding self-deprecatingly, 'I felt I had no special talent but wanted only to occupy my leisure time.' And Dares starts with the author, Cornelius Nepos, explaining that, when Dares's manuscript was found in Athens, he translated it into

Latin 'following the straightforward and simple style of the Greek original.' So it is no surprise that Geoffrey employed a similar literary conceit, which has haunted his reputation ever afterwards, that he had not written the book himself, but merely possessed 'that Book writ in the British tongue, which Walter [the] Archdeacon of Oxford brought out of [Brittany], and which being a true History published in Honour of those Princes, I have thus taken Care to Translate'. Geoffrey describes this troublesome tome in his prologue as 'a very ancient Book in the British Tongue, which in a continued regular Story and elegant Stile, related the Actions of them all, from Brutus the first King of the Britains, down to Cadwallader the Son of Cadwallo. At his [Walter's] Request therefore, though I had not made fine Language my Study, by collecting florid Expressions from other Authors, yet contented with my own homely Stile, I undertook the Translation of that Book into Latin.'

Although his contemporary Geoffrey Gaimar, who later translated Geoffrey's *History* into Norman French, claimed to have seen Walter the Archdeacon's 'Good Book of Oxford', it was not heard of again. Many have doubted that it ever existed.

The problem of credibility lies entirely with Geoffrey himself. If, instead of claiming that he had translated an older book verbatim, he had said that he had made very creative use of Nennius, some old Welsh pedigree material linking the Iron Age kings back to Brutus, and perhaps an old tale about Corineus (as will be discussed later), few would have doubted him. For that is actually what he appears to have done. As a medieval cleric Geoffrey felt no compunction about embellishing or altering, making up names where none were given and improving stories with tales he had read or heard elsewhere. He embellished not to create a falsehood, but to bring out – he would have believed – the greater, poetic truth of the tale he was recounting.

Henry of Huntingdon, avidly copying sections of Geoffrey's work into a later edition of his own history, expressed surprise at how much new material Geoffrey had produced, but did not question its veracity. William of Newburgh (d. 1198) objected strongly to what Geoffrey had written about Arthur, but did not question his earlier material about Brutus. Most telling is the reaction of Gerald of Wales (d. c. 1223). He was half Welsh, and he hated Geoffrey because his *History* starts by saying God had punished the Welsh with foreign invasion because of their pride, and ends with them degenerating into a useless race, ripe for conquest. Gerald thought Geoffrey's *History* was so repugnant that, when laid on the lap of a man possessed by demons, the devils themselves would flee in disgust, and he even claimed this had actually happened. Gerald did not criticise what Geoffrey had written about Brutus or his immediate successors, however, because he knew and believed the same traditions himself.

Geoffrey's 'old book' was a literary conceit, based on sound Classical precedents, but despite this the possibility that such an ancient tome might really have existed has tantalised scholars over the centuries. There exist fifty-eight translations of his *History* in Welsh, called *Bruts* because they start with Brutus, and over the centuries some scholars have tried to argue that one of these must have been the 'old book' from which Geoffrey made his translation. Sir John Price (d. 1555), Lewis Morris (d. 1765), Sir Flinders Petrie (1853–1942), the distinguished archaeologist of ancient Egypt, and the American scholar Acton Griscom (in 1929) have all championed this cause. Petrie argued that Geoffrey's 'old book' was the *Brut y Bryttaniait* (Jesus College manuscript LXI, which Archbishop Ussher called the *Brut Tysilio*, despite the story it contained continuing to AD 688, a good forty years after St Tysilio had died). The apparent clincher is that *Brut y Bryttaniait* includes this postscript: 'I, Gwallter, Archdeacon of Rydychen [Oxford], turned this book from Welsh into Latin. And in my old age I have turned it the second time from Latin into Welsh.' But quite why anyone would wish to perform such a double translation is questionable, and Skene found that other versions of the *Brut* contained variants of this postscript, one saying that the original had been in Breton, and another that it had been in Latin.

The oldest datable *Brut* is the Dingestow Court manuscript, dating from 1200, and this was the one Acton Griscom hoped was Geoffrey's 'old book'. It is virtually identical to Geoffrey's *History*, and the few differences are hard to interpret. It omits the Lefkada section and the Prophecies of Merlin, but adds a story of Llud and Llevellys, which Griscom thought fitted 'very well', though its weirdly magical details are in fact rather out of keeping with the rest of the story. The Dingestow Court manuscript also includes Geoffrey's dedication to Robert of Gloucester, albeit in a different hand to rest of the text: Griscom argued here that someone had added it in the mistaken belief that the manuscript was a translation of Geoffrey, and added that, whereas Geoffrey breaks his narrative during Arthur's war with Mordred to address Robert of Gloucester, the Dingestow manuscript does not. For Griscom, the many differences between the different *Bruts* argued for them not being direct translations of Geoffrey, but they are so hard to date that such discrepancies could have arisen over several centuries of copying and alteration after Geoffrey's time. Petrie and Griscom's arguments are not ultimately very convincing, and it's relevant that both had a greater agenda – to argue that the story of the Trojan settlement of Britain was true, whereas we now appreciate that it was a purely literary invention. In fact, if we accept that the core of the Brutus story was worked up from the raw material recorded by Nennius, about 300 years earlier, then the argument over whether Geoffrey's *History* was mainly a translation of the *Bruts*, or vice versa, loses some of its steam anyway. Although they tell of ancient times, the style and political agenda of the *Bruts* and *History* are very much of their time, reflecting the Virgilian spirit of Dudo's Norman chronicle and fitting into Robert of Gloucester's master plan. If Geoffrey was not the author of the 'original' then someone else living not long before him must have been. Modern scholarly opinion generally follows Rachel Bromwich's view that the *Bruts* show the Welsh *cyfarwyddiaid*, or storytellers, working hard from the 1130s onwards to 'interpret and expand Geoffrey's story for a Welsh audience', for example by substituting authentic Welsh names for Geoffrey's more obviously Latinised ones. Thus, most scholars now believe that the *Bruts* are creative retellings of Geoffrey's *History*.

Although Virgil lived about 700 years after Homer, his poetic additions to the Trojan story are accepted unquestioningly by everyone wanting to know about Aeneas's later life. But what about the later, imaginative extensions of the Trojan myth as recorded by Nennius and embellished with such flair by Geoffrey of Monmouth? Where do we draw the line?

When the poet John Keats was talking to Leigh Hunt in 1819 about the Renaissance poet Dante, 'he observed that whenever so great a poet told us anything in addition or continuation of an ancient story, he had a right to be regarded as a Classical authority. For instance, said he, when he [Dante] tells us of that characteristic death of Ulysses [Odysseus] in one of the books of his *Inferno*, we ought to receive the information as authentic, and be glad that we have more news of Ulysses than we looked for.'

So although Dante died in 1321, argued Keats, the additions he made to the story of Odysseus's death and afterlife are valid because he was such a great poet. Keats would probably have regarded Geoffrey as a pseudo-historian, not a creative artist at all. Yet if we regard Geoffrey's medieval prose as a form of poetry, then maybe we can better appreciate his continuation of the story of Aeneas's dynasty – and accept him as a 'classical authority' as well for the extraordinary story of Brutus of Troy that is to follow.

Part II

The Life of Brutus

NOTE: This part of the book retells the story of Brutus, as related by Geoffrey of Monmouth. Where I have paraphrased what Geoffrey wrote, I have used the present tense. I have done this in order to make it clear that I am relating a made-up story and not real history. It is, however, a wonderful story with its own internal consistency and, in many places, I have added explanatory details to help draw out its hidden qualities and also to make it more explicable and colourful for modern readers. In these cases I have used the past tense, qualified by a phrase such as 'he would have' or 'we may imagine', to make clear (I hope) what comes direct from Geoffrey's mouth, and what emerges from within the story he told.

Chapter 9

A Fatal Arrow

The ruins of the Italian Iron Age settlement of Alba Longa lie beneath modern Castel Gandolfo, the summer residence of the Popes, but its dramatic setting is largely unchanged since ancient times (see plate 10). Virgil's *Aeneid* relates how Aeneas had come from Troy to Latium, the ancient kingdom just to the south of what was later to become Rome. After winning a war with the Latins and Rutulians, Aeneas married Lavinia, daughter of King Latinus of the Latins, and founded Lavinium near the sea. According to the myths related by Livy and Dionysius of Halicarnassus, Aeneas became king of the united Latins and Trojans once Latinus died, but after three years' peaceful rule the Rutulians rebelled and he was killed subduing them. His son Ascanius – he whom Julius Caesar's family insisted had also been called Iulus – became king of Latium. Remembering a prophecy that Aeneas's new city of Lavinium would be the mother of many cities, Ascanius founded his own capital 8 miles to the north-east, up on the ridge of the crater of the extinct volcano in whose cold caldera lay the Alban Lake. Stretched out along the crater's western rim, Ascanius's city was called Alba Longa.

If Ascanius had ever really existed and looked west from his palace ramparts, he would have seen the landscape sweeping dramatically down to the plain of Lavinium, with the Tyrrhenian Sea glittering in the distance. Then his gaze could sweep north-west, where the sun flashed off the serene waters of the Tiber, above whose sinuous curves rose the seven wooded hills across which the city of Rome would one day spread. Following the panoramic sweep around came the high peaks of the Apennines, washed gold in the setting sun. To the east lay the cold, clear waters of the Alban Lake and the steep, dark side of the Alban Mount. On the summit, Ascanius could just see the massive blocks of black, volcanic stone out of which he had built the temple of Jupiter Latiaris, Jupiter of the Latins: a new throne for Zeus in Italy, where snow-white bulls were sacrificed to the deified Latinus.

Beyond the south-eastern rim of the crater and over a ridge, concealed from Ascanius's sight, was another smaller crater, also containing a lake, Nemi. On Nemi's wooded shores, the locals maintained a sylvian or woodland cult of

Diana, the Latin equivalent of the Greek Artemis, goddess of childbirth and hunting, whom they sometimes called Triple Diana – maiden, mother and old crone (see plate 12). From her sanctuary, hidden in the woods, high above the lake's dark depths, it is sometimes possible to see Diana's moon chariot in the sky above, and reflected in the lake, and also glittering on the gloaming sea beyond – three moons, for the triple goddess. And this is why, within the context of the myth, it made sense for Ascanius to have named his son after the sylvan woods: Silvius.

Geoffrey's history opens with a few paragraphs in praise of Britain, a reminder that the Britons had been overwhelmed by the Saxons as a punishment by God for their arrogance and a very brief summary of Aeneas's story. Then we hear how his son Ascanius founds Alba Longa, which Geoffrey places inaccurately 'upon the Tiber', and has a son Silvius, with whom the tale begins in earnest. When Silvius is a young man in Alba Longa, he indulges in a 'private amour' for a girl. Geoffrey does not give her a name, but later John Hardyng's *Chronicle*, abhorring a vacuum, calls her Crensa, a name clearly adapted from the name of Aeneas's first wife (Silvius's grandmother), Creusa: in 1857 the Reverend R.W. Morgan, less comprehensibly, renamed her Edra. This girl, says Geoffrey, was a niece of Aeneas's second wife Lavinia. This contradicts Virgil, who said Lavinia had no surviving siblings, but if we accept Geoffrey's right to act as a classical authority, then the girl was, nonetheless, a granddaughter of Latinus. Conventionally, Latinus was the son of Faunus, but Dionysius of Halicarnassus repeats a story that, when Faunus married his wife, she was already pregnant by Hercules. Thus, any child of Silvius and Lavinia's niece would possess not just the blood of Troy, but also the blood of that great, Greek hero, Hercules.

Maybe it was a concern over the outcome of the intermingling of such anciently opposed blood that caused Ascanius to send for his 'Magicians' – quite possibly including the priest king of the sanctuary of Diana above Lake Nemi – to determine the future of the unborn child. These magicians pronounce that Silvius's wife 'was Big of a Boy, who would kill his Father and Mother, and after travelling over many Countries in Banishment, would at last arrive at the highest Pitch of Glory.' The much briefer version of the story related 300 years earlier by Nennius had been less positive. In Morris's edition of Nennius, a magician foretold that the boy 'would be the child of death, for he would kill his father and mother, and be hateful to all men.'

Finally, Silvius's wife goes into labour and gives birth. And at once, part of the prophecy is fulfilled, for she dies in childbirth. 'The Child is deliver'd to a Nurse and called Brutus.'

Brutus would have grown up below the shadow of the Alban Mount, learning to fight with the other boys, the mixed-race offspring of Trojans, Latins, Rutulians and Etruscans, the first generation of Aeneas's great project of ethnic mixing that would result in the Romans. On the Alban Lake, and on the sea near Lavinium, Brutus would have learnt to row and sail, essential skills for his later adventures (see plate 11). And in the woods, he learned to hunt.

It is on a hunting expedition when Brutus is fifteen that the second part of the prophecy is fulfilled. The woods near Alba Longa today are full of wild boar, but Geoffrey chose a herd of stags to be driven towards Brutus by the beaters. He takes aim and fires, but instead of hitting his target, the arrow strikes his own father 'below the breast' and kills him.

Brutus's slaying of his father is mentioned first by Nennius: 'While he was playing with some others he shot his father with an arrow, not intentionally but by accident.' This is not mentioned by any Roman writers, because both Brutus and Silvius's untimely death were invented long afterwards in Dark Age Britain. But whoever created the Dark Age story that accompanied Brutus's family tree was a genius, because he helped elevate Brutus to the status of a Classical hero, drawing a parallel between him and Perseus, who accidentally slew his grandfather Acrisius. The story also provided a handy excuse to explain why Brutus did not appear in Roman accounts of Aeneas's family: he had committed patricide, so he must have been deliberately expunged from the records.

The detail that Silvius was killed in the woods is Geoffrey's addition. It suggests a detailed knowledge of Roman history on Geoffrey's part, and also draws out a poetic truth from the name of Silvius, which means 'of the woods'. It was the epithet of the real, original kings of Alba Longa, whom Virgil said were crowned with chaplets of oak leaves. Before the Romans invented the idea that the kings of Alba Longa had been descended from Aeneas's family, their pedigree had started with Silvius. Presumably this was because the Alba Longan kings had once claimed descent from Silvanus, a wild, Italian woodland god, 'in rustic coronet', as Virgil described him in his tenth *Eclogue*, with 'flowers of fennel and long-stemmed lilies tossing upon his head', one of those primordial entities born of Gaia, Mother Earth, imagined to have lived long before the cosmic struggles of the Titans and the Olympian gods.

Silvanus is the essence of the forest, that untameable, unknowable world beyond the edge of the fields: the spirit of the trees, an echo of the last of the mammoths, perhaps, glimpsed in dread by our Mesolithic ancestors through the opening leaves of the northward-spreading oaks. He was often imagined with horns, like the stags that haunted his forest shrines, so he was also Pan, and the Celtic deity Cernunnos, whom the people of medieval Berkshire knew as Herne the Hunter, and whose memory lingers on in the Green Man, and even in the more other-worldly aspects of Robin Hood.

Long after Alba Longa had been absorbed by Rome, vestiges of its traditions lived on. A tree grew in Diana's sanctuary by Lake Nemi, and any runaway slave who could break off one of its boughs automatically became *Rex Nemorensis*, the priest king of the sacred grove. But there was a catch: to take the bough, he had first to kill the incumbent, so once he had become king, he had always to be on his guard against the next fugitive slave who, sooner or later, would murder him for the same reason. In *The Golden Bough*, Sir James Frazer found roots for this custom right back in the Mesopotamian myth of Dumuzi and Inanna, a myth as ancient as farming civilisation itself. Dumuzi the shepherd was the mortal consort of the great goddess Inanna, but to ensure the continued life of the land he had to die each year. Frazer suggested that kings in many ancient civilisations were married symbolically to manifestations of Inanna, and were ritually slain to ensure the success of the all-important harvest. Thus, the *Rex Nemorensis* may have been regarded as the consort of the goddess Diana and an echo of the way ancient, sacred kingship may have operated in Alba Longa. This sinister aspect of the Alba Longan kingship was conveniently forgotten once the Alba Longan kings had been re-imagined as descendants of Aeneas. But the memory remained, haunting their names. Maybe it was this as much as anything else that bent the arrow of Brutus, so that instead of slaying the stag, it plunged deep into the heart of his father, Silvius. By killing the 'king of the woods', Brutus had earned his right to kingship: not in Alba Longa, though, but far away in the oak groves of Britain – and perhaps, also (as Geoffrey's narrative allows us to speculate later on) as the sacred consort of the goddess Diana herself.

Brutus had killed his father, so his angry relations expelled him from Italy. Geoffrey ignores Nennius's mention of his visiting the islands in the Tyrrhenian Sea, but takes him straight to Greece. Of the world Brutus encountered beyond the borders of his grandfather's realm, Geoffrey later quotes something Nennius wrote about Brutus's time, that 'Eli the priest governed Judaea, and the ark of the covenant was taken by the Philistines.' Of the Classical world he tells us only that 'the sons of Hector ... reigned in Troy.' But closer to hand, we know from Classical sources, Troy's fall had heralded a general disintegration of the empires of old. In Mycenae, Agamemnon had been murdered by his wife Clytemnestra and her lover, and they in turn had been slain in revenge by Orestes, the son of Clytemnestra and Agamemnon. Now, even Orestes was dead, poisoned by a snake bite somewhere in Arcadia. Helpless to prevent Greece from being ravaged by earthquakes and invading hoards of Dorians from the north, Orestes' son Penthilus had sailed away to seek refuge in the eastern Aegean, founding the colonies where, some 300 years later, Homer would be born. The terrible price paid by the Greeks for their hubristic triumph at Troy was everywhere apparent. In the Cyclades, sacred Delos's precincts lay in disarray, its altars cracked, only the crested larks whistling in the wind where once Apollo's pipes had played so sweetly. The gates of Olympus had swung closed: even the gods looked in, for the most part, upon themselves. Had Brutus but known it, it was in his fate alone that the Olympians now took the slightest interest.

The only place reasonably close to Italy where Brutus knew he might find other Trojans was Buthrotum, on the Epirote coast, which is now Butrint in southern Albania, just opposite Corfu (see plate 13). Geoffrey says that Trojans had been taken there as slaves by Achilles' son Neoptolemus. He omits to mention what Aeneas discovered in book three of the *Aeneid*; that two of them, Helenus and Andromache, had been freed, and had founded a Trojan colony besides the clear blue waters of the Vrina Channel. But when Brutus arrives, says Geoffrey, he finds that all is not well: a new king called Pandrasus has arisen in Greece and now the Trojans there are living in (renewed) slavery under him. The scene is set for Brutus either to fail utterly, or to shine in glory.

Chapter 10

The Castle by the Acheron

Virgil's *Aeneid* is the story of a journey, modelled on Homer's *Odyssey*, followed by the story of a war, echoing Homer's *Iliad*. In telling his story of Brutus, Geoffrey adopted a similar model, but in reverse order. An epic journey to Britain lies ahead of Brutus. But first comes a war.

Brutus appears quietly amongst the enslaved Trojans and 'begins to distinguish himself by his Conduct and Bravery.' He quickly gains their affection, especially that of the young men. Wise in counsel and generous in spirit, he would always divide any spoil gained in 'war' between his men so, whilst Geoffrey does not say as much, he seems to have become the leader of a band of renegades. 'His fame therefore spreading over all Countries, the Trojans from all Parts began to flock to him, desiring to be under his Command [so as] to be freed from the Servitude of the Grecians.'

At this crucial time, Brutus makes an ally, 'a noble youth named Assaracus'. Assaracus (whose name Geoffrey borrowed from one of Aeneas's ancestors, as listed by Homer) is the son, by a Trojan concubine, of a local Greek warlord who, on his deathbed, had left him *tria castella*, three castles, including one by the river Acheron called Sparatinum. However, Assaracus has a half-brother whose mother was Greek, who considers Assaracus to be a bastard and wants King Pandrasus to help him seize the castles for himself. Assaracus therefore joins Brutus's cause.

Brutus 'being therefore chosen as their Commander, he assembles the Trojans from all Parts, and fortifies the Towns belonging to Assaracus. But he himself with Assaracus and the whole Body of Men and Women that adher'd to him,' numbering 7,000 men alone, 'retires to the Woods and Hills.'

Assaracus's background echoes the plot of Euripides' play *Andromache*, which explains how Neoptolemus had brought Andromache, the widow of Hector of Troy, to Epiros to become his slave and concubine. They had a son, whom later tradition called Molossos. When Neoptolemus died, his wife had wanted (but failed) to kill both Andromache and Molossos, whom she considered a bastard because he was half Trojan. So just as Molossos was hard done by for being half Trojan, so too is Assaracus.

The reference to *tria castella* suggests that Geoffrey knew something of Epiros. He could have heard much in Oxford from people who had passed through the Balkans on pilgrimage to Jerusalem – or maybe, as a youth, he had made such a pilgrimage himself.

Epiros is a land of towering limestone mountains divided by steep, wooded gorges, a land ideally suited to rebels, as Lord Byron discovered when he visited the region in 1809. Fifty miles south-east down the rugged coast from Buthrotum is the mouth of the river Acheron. Having risen deep in the Thesprotian mountains, the river emerges briefly into a fertile valley, about 10 miles inland. It then plunges suddenly through a narrow gorge, which local historian Dr Harry Gouvas nicknamed 'the Gates of Hades', a name that stuck, though he told me he now regrets how locally popular this invented name has become. The gorge seems to have severed a whole mountain in two and the

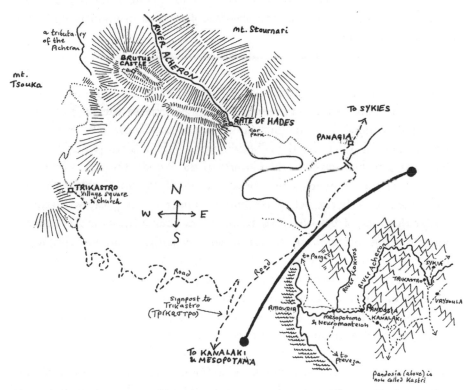

The village of Trikastro and the castle above it, backing onto the gorge of the Acheron. The smaller map in the bottom right-hand corner shows Trikastro's location within the wider area of northern Epiros.

Acheron roars through it to continue its passage through the mountains, after which it emerges to coil serenely across its coastal plain to the sea at Amoudia. Where the mountain is cleft in two by the Acheron, the cliffs rise up so high that you need to crane your head right back to see the sky, all the time being careful not to slip off the slimy rocks and into the torrential river roaring below (see plates 15 and 16). The western half of the split mountain stands with its long, sheer back to the roaring chasm, but its pale, rocky front slopes down less steeply into a valley. On this slope, it is still possible to find traces of two levels of walls built out of huge, well-hewn blocks, of the sort the Classical Greeks called Cyclopean, from the belief that only mighty Cyclopses could have undertaken such monumental work. In fact, the place was probably fortified by Pyrrhus of Epiros in the 200s BC.

The modern name of the village below this ruined castle is Trikastro. Unless that is an extraordinary coincidence, this must be the castle by the Acheron that Geoffrey called Sparatinum, 'the place of the spear' – one of the *tria castella* of Assaracus. Surely, this must be the place Geoffrey had in mind when he told the tale of what ensued.

From his mountain fastness, Brutus writes to Pandrasus:

> Brutus, General of the Remainder of the Trojans, to Pandrasus King of the Grecians, sendeth Greeting. As it was beneath the Dignity of a Nation descended from the illustrious Race of Dardanos, to be treated in your Kingdom otherwise than the Nobility of their Birth requir'd; they have betaken themselves to the Coverts of the Woods. For they preferr'd living after the Manner of wild Beasts, upon Flesh and Herbs, with the Enjoyment of Liberty, before continuing longer in the greatest Luxury, under the Yoke of your Slavery. If this gives your Majesty any Offence, impute it not to them, but pardon it; since it is the common Sentiment of every Captive, to be desirous of regaining his former Dignity. Let Pity therefore move you to bestow on them freely their lost Liberty, and permit them to inhabit the Thickets of the Woods, to which they have retir'd to avoid Slavery. But if you deny them this Favour, then by your Permission and Assistance let them depart into some foreign Country.

Affronted that runaway slaves should be so bold, Pandrasus summons his men and marches up into the mountains. He does not know the Trojans are ensconsed in Sparatinum, so as his men march past, Brutus and Assaracus are able to launch an ambush. For some inexplicable reason the Greeks are unarmed.

The Trojans briskly attack then [wrote Geoffrey] and endeavour to make a great Slaughter. The Grecians astonish'd, immediately give way on all Sides, and with the King at their Head, hasten to pass the river Akalon [i.e. the Acheron], which runs near the Place, but in passing are in great Danger by the Rapidness of the Stream. Brutus galls them in their Flight, and kills Part of them in the Stream, Part upon the Banks, and running to and fro, rejoyces to see them in both Places exposed to Ruin.

Geoffrey is spot on here, for the Acheron, though broad and calm elsewhere in its course, is indeed very rapid in the narrow gorge below Trikastro.

Now we meet Antigonus, Pandrasus's brother, who 'rallied his scattered troops', for he would prefer to die fighting than be drowned shamefully 'in a muddy pool'. They fight valiantly but are overwhelmed by the Trojans and Brutus takes him and his companion, Anacletus, prisoner.

Elated by his victory, Brutus garrisons the castle with 600 men and sets out with the rest to gather up the many bands of Trojans who are still lurking in the surrounding valleys. But in Brutus's absence Pandrasus reassembles his scattered troops and, now armed, returns to Sparatinum to try to rescue the prisoners. They cut off the castle's water supplies and, using wood from the nearby forests, they build battering rams and a *testudo*, or 'tortoise', with wooden walls and a bronze-plated roof, which shelters men trying to undermine the colossal masonry of Sparatinum's outer wall.

The valley must have reverberated with the dull thud of the rams, and the screams of Greeks being hit by spears and arrows or being scalded by the 'fire and scalding water' being hurled down at them. The defenders send a messenger to beg Brutus to help them, lest they become 'so weakened as to be obliged to quit the town'. But all Brutus can do when he returns through the woods is to watch, 'under great Perplexity', for he has far too few men with him to launch an effective attack.

Never was the distinction between Brutus and his god-born forebears more pronounced. Watching Pandrasus's army besieging Sparatinum, Brutus may have longed to lead his Trojans in an heroic charge, as Aeneas had done, once, at dawn, to rescue his beleaguered camp near the Tiber, but his men were far too few. So it was not Aeneas now, nor Hercules, but wily Odysseus whom he emulated.

They have with them two prisoners, Pandrasus's brother Antigonus and his comrade Anacletus, who have been captured in the initial battle. 'Noble Youth,' Brutus says to Anacletus, 'your own and Antigonus's Life is now at an

End, unless you will faithfully perform what I command you. This Night I design to invade the Camp of the Grecians, and fall upon them unawares.' His cunning plan is for Anacletus to lure the guards away on the pretence of helping Antigonus, who he will say has escaped from the Trojans and is lying in a valley nearby, encumbered by bronze fetters. With Brutus's sword held at his throat, and the promise that if he fails Antigonus will be butchered, Anacletus has little choice but to agree.

Night falls and the Trojans creep out from the sheltering trees, perhaps whispering prayers of gratitude to Triple Diana for veiling her crescent moon behind clouds. Anacletus does as Brutus has bidden him. 'I am not here to betray my own people,' he lies, and leads the credulous sentries down to the ambush. The Trojans inflict 'the most cruel slaughter' on them. Then, Brutus divides his men into three parties, all of whom creep with even greater stealth through the unguarded entrance to the camp and spread themselves out amongst the slumbering Greeks. Brutus makes his way towards the royal pavilion, in which Pandrasus lies asleep.

Brutus gives 'the promised signal' and immediately the Trojans 'forthwith draw their swords' and fall upon their victims. Though the Greeks outnumber their foes greatly, they are drugged by sleep and 'awak'd at the Groans of the dying and seeing their Assailants are dismay'd, as Sheep when seiz'd on a sudden … Some that could escape away half-dead, were in the Eagerness of Flight dash'd against Rocks, Trees or Shrubs, and increased the Misery of their Death,' whilst those who escape this fate are swept away by the fearsome Acheron. As to Brutus, he must have longed to plunge his bronze sword into Pandrasus's venal heart but – Odysseus-like again – he realises 'he could more easily attain his ends by preserving his life than by killing him.'

As the dawn comes the Trojans stride brazenly about the Greek camp, ending the lives of any Greek who has survived the massacre. Brutus, 'in Transports of Joy', leads his people back into the castle, where they divide the spoils of war.

The Greeks allowed rivers much more freedom than does our modern, gravity-constrained science. Every river in the world began in a great cavern below Mount Olympos, 'the pools enclosed in caverns, the sighing woods of weed', as Virgil wrote in his fourth *Georgic*. Guided in their courses by their own bearded gods wearing hats of grey-green reeds, they flowed through the pallid depths of the underworld until they came bubbling up through springs, to flow down their earthly courses and into the sea. Some then flowed under the sea or plunged back down into Hades, to rise up again elsewhere. Thus, one river could be imagined rising and flowing through one land to reach the sea and then reappearing – as the same watercourse – in a completely different place. It was through such beliefs that Greek travellers, settling in strange countries, could comfort themselves with the notion that the river flowing at their feet was the very same one by which they had grown up in their native land.

The Acheron had one of the most impressive imagined courses of all, for it was one of the seven great rivers of Hades. From the deep gorge below Trikastro, it rushes through the mountains and out onto the plain beyond. In the centre of the plain rises the rocky hill of the Nekromanteion, around which the river formed the Acherousian Lake, until it was drained away recently to create fields. At the lake, the river was believed to divide: part of it flowed out into the sea at Amoudia, but the other part tumbled down through the rocks, past the slavering jaws of Cerberus and back into Hades. From there it flowed underground to Italy, to feed Lake Avernus, near Naples, through whose tunnels Aeneas had gone down to visit his dead father Anchises in Hades in Virgil's *Aeneid*. And yet another branch of the Acheron was believed to emerge in southern Italy, where it flowed out into the Gulf of Tarantum, the bridge of the 'foot' of Italy.

This other, Tarantine, Acheron caused confusion in Classical times. The Greek geographer Strabo relates how, when Alexander I of Epiros was contemplating going to assist Greek colonists against the Brutti tribe in the toe of Italy, the voice in the oracle oak of Dodona whispered, 'Beware to go to the Acherousian water and Pandosia, where 'tis fated thou shalt die.' The king assumed this referred to Epiros, for a place called Pandosia lies on the Acheron, between Trikastro and the sea. He went off confidently to Italy – only to find there was a 'three-hilled Pandosia' and a river Acheron there too: and sure enough he met his doom in Italy.

Strabo's account may have provided Geoffrey with the original idea for Brutus's adventures in Epiros. The Brutti were a tribe in the toe of Italy, composed largely of runaway criminals and slaves. The Greeks called them by the insulting term *brutii* ('brutes'), but they quickly adopted the term as a badge of honour. The coincidence of 'Brutii' and 'Brutus' may have attracted Geoffrey to the story, and he may perhaps have imagined Brutus going south from Alba Longa to lead renegade slaves in a fight for freedom by the Italian river Acheron. Then, remembering the Acheron in Epiros, he realised it would make far greater poetic sense to transfer the action thence, so that the freed slaves could become descendants of Helenus and Andromache's Trojans from nearby Buthrotum.

The place name Pandosia may have influenced the name he gave the Greek king who had enslaved the Trojans, Pandrasus. Geoffrey does not explore Pandrasus's ancestry, but in mythology, Epiros was ruled after Neoptolemus's death by Molossos, his son by Andromache. Who else could Pandrasus have been but a descendant of Molossos? If so, then Brutus's victory at Trikastro can perhaps be seen as a poetic, Trojan revenge against the descendants of Neoptolemus, the sacker of Troy.

After his victory, Brutus leaves Sparatinum and 'retires with his forces to the woods in great joy for the victory.' Many of the Trojans want Pandrasus to give them part of his kingdom, but a wise Trojan called Mempricius points out that as long as they continue to live near Greeks, they will never be free of the ancient enmity between Greece and Troy. 'I propose therefore,' says Mempricius to the assembly, 'that you request of him [Pandrasus] his eldest Daughter Ignoge for a Wife for our General, and with her, Gold, Silver, Corn, and whatever else shall be necessary for our Voyage. If we obtain this, we may with his Leave remove to some other Country.'

Pandrasus is 'placed in a chair above the rest', and informed of the tortures prepared for him, unless he does what is commanded. He agrees: 'Since my ill Fate has delivered me and my Brother Antigonus into your Hands,' he says, 'I can do no other than grant your Petition ... though it is against my Inclination that I obey your Commands, yet it seems Matter of Comfort to me,' he added, attempting to put a positive spin on things, 'that I am to give my Daughter to so Noble a Youth, whose Descent from the illustrious Race of Priamus and Anchises is clear, both from that Greatness of Mind that appears in him, and the certain Accounts we have had of it. For who less than [Brutus] himself, could have released from their Chains the banished Trojans, when reduced under Slavery to so many and great Princes?'

Down they went by the course of the fast-flowing Acheron, towards the sea. They must have passed the Nekromanteion, where from Mycenaean times, if not before, pilgrims were lowered into a rocky cleft to commune with the shades of the dead rising up from through the Acherousian Lake from Hades. But Brutus did not go there: he would seek supernatural guidance for his journey soon, but not from the dead.

Geoffrey does not describe the wedding of Brutus and Ignoge, but a flavour of it can be borrowed from Sappho's poem *Andromache's Wedding*, about Andromache's first marriage to Hector of Troy, which describes how they brought 'jewels of twisted gold' and 'richly perfumed purple robes', and many embroidered clothes, innumerable silver cups and items carved from ivory. The men of Troy 'harnessed mules to the well-wheeled carriages, and the whole crowd of women and slender-ankled girls ascended … the men were harnessing their horses under the curved chariot, all young men in their prime … and the sweet-singing pipe was mixed with the lyre and the sound of cymbals, and the maidens sang clearly a pure song, and a wondrous echo reached to the sky.' The air was perfumed with myrrh, cassia and frankincense, and the older women 'raised a joyous shout; and all the men sang forth their lovely loud song, invoking Paean, the far-shooting god, the splendid harper.' And, wrote Sappho, they sang of Hector and Andromache 'who looked like gods'. In similar terms we may imagine the marriage of god-like Brutus and Ignoge.

For the Trojans' departure, King Pandrasus supplied 324 ships, all laden with the promised supplies and treasures. Though fashioned by Greek hands, the fleet was a literary reincarnation of the ships of Aeneas, the enchanted vessels that had borne the Trojans – and the myths of the Trojans – as far as Italy. Now, this new fleet would go further, carrying the myths of Troy to the shores of Britain.

We once spent a long summer evening at Amoudia, the sleepy village at the mouth of the river Acheron. As the sun hung heavily above the horizon, bathing the western sky in magisterial gold, it took no effort to imagine Brutus's black ships gliding away down the Acheron to meet the sea, dark against the shadowed hillside behind, half hidden by the gold-tinged reeds, oars sloshing impetuously through the peach-flushed river water.

Of their departure, Geoffrey tells us the precious details that:

Ignoge, standing upon the Stern of the Ship, swoons away several Times in Brutus's Arms, and with many Sighs and Tears laments the leaving of her Parents and Country, nor ever turns her Eyes from the Shore while it is in Sight. Brutus in the mean Time endeavours to assuage her Grief by kind Words and Embraces intermixed with Kisses, and

Brutus and Ignoge leave Amoudia.

ceases not from these Blandishments, till she grows weary of crying and falls asleep.

As we watched on that evening, imagining Brutus gazing eagerly west, the setting sun sank and described a glittering path of reddened gold, dancing out westwards across the gentle waves. It was a path, and a destiny, that grew ever brighter, ever bloodier, as the precious moments passed. Then the sun sank out of sight and the afterglow began; first intense gold, then deep crimson. It was easy to visualise – even actually to glimpse – the last of Brutus's ships clearing the promontory, the sails filling with the evening breeze, billowing out with their first precious taste of freedom.

Chapter 11

Diana's Prophecy

rutus's ships would have been typical of the Bronze Age, long and narrow, shallow-drafted and without keels, so they could easily be pulled up onto beaches. Their frames were of sturdy oak, covered with flexible pine planks, carvel style – laid flat rather than overlapping – held together with bronze nails, and painted black with pitch to protect them against rot and worms. They were hollow, just as Homer described the ships that sailed to Troy, covered with decking only in the bow and stern to provide both sheltered places for storage and rest, and platforms for the lookout and pilot. Some ships were painted above the waterline with blue indigo and most bows were painted with eyes (called *oculi*), derived ultimately from the all-seeing eye of the Egyptian sun god Ra. They had no fixed rudder: instead, they used a *peedalion*, a large paddle fixed on a peg near the right aft, or maybe one on each side. A single row of broad, spade-like oars bristled out on each side, attached to the gunwale by leather thongs. Usually, there were no more than ten on each side, but a well-crewed ship might carry more than twice as many men, who could work in shifts and leave some fresh and rested hands spare in case of emergency. With twenty oarsmen straining hard, such a ship might cover about 4½ miles in an hour, as Ernle Bradford calculated, and then about half that for subsequent hours, as the men tired. If the wind blew from anywhere behind them, they could raise the ship's slender pine mast, fastening it by stays fore and aft and hoisting the billowing white sail of linen or papyrus. Under such circumstances, a ship under sail might be able to cover 60 miles in a day.

Brutus could have sailed up the coast to Onchesmos (modern Sarandë in southern Albania, just north of Buthrotum) and crossed the Straits of Otranto, just as his great-grandfather Aeneas had done on his journey to Italy. But that would only have brought Brutus back to Italy, from which he had been exiled. So instead he follows the coastline south for 30 miles, past the Bay of Actium to Lefkada, which Geoffrey calls Leogetia. The prevailing wind, the Bora, is from the north there, but Geoffrey tells us the journey took two and a half days, so the Trojan oarsmen must have battled against an unusually strong southerly breeze that slowed their progress down to a crawl – but of course this was a journey invented in Oxford without recourse to modern maps, not an account of a real voyage.

In Classical times, the Corinthians cut through the rocky causeway that linked Lefkada to the mainland to create a shipping channel, turning Lefkada into a proper island. But that was long before Brutus's time, and the causeway still existed, a barrier to ships. Brutus had no choice, therefore, but to skirt around the island's northern and western shores.

Lefkada had been part of the realm of Odysseus and the peaks of his homeland, Ithaka, are visible, grey against the pale morning sky, from the southern part of the island. After Odysseus, his son, Telemachus, became king of Lefkada, but when the warships of the Dorians began to ravage the coast he had led his people away and settled, according to Servius, ironically, on the periphery of Ascanius's realm, at Clusium (modern Chiusi) in Italy. His abandoned archipelago realm fell into ruin, and this fits beautifully with Geoffrey's statement that the island 'had been formerly wasted by the Incursions of Pirates, and is then uninhabited.'

The Trojans probably landed in the bay of Frini, on Lefkada's north-western coast. Searching for fresh water and game, they find an abandoned city – probably the ruins of Nerikos, which can still be found amongst the olive groves along the north-eastern shore (see plate 17). And also, much closer to hand, they find a grove sacred to Diana, in which is:

> a Statue of that Goddess which gave Answers to those that came to consult her. … At last loading themselves with the Prey they had taken in hunting, they return to the Ships, and give their Companions an Account of this Country and City. Then they advise their Leader to go to the City, and after offering Sacrifices, to enquire of the Deity of the Place, what Country was allotted them for their Place of Settlement.

Kallimachus describes a great statue of Artemis, the Greek equivalent of Diana, that once stood in a temple dedicated to her, somewhere in Lefkada. The statue's golden crown was stolen by raiders from Epiros, who replaced it irreverently with a mortar that had been used for crushing garlic. The Lefkadans made a new crown, but it kept falling off and, on consulting the Delphic oracle, they learned that the goddess wished to wear the mortar instead – an odd arrangement depicted on some Lefkadan coins. Kallimachus does not say where the statue stood, but on the hill just west of Frini, overlooking the sea, stands a Christian monastery dedicated to Our Lady *Faneromeni*, 'of the revelations'. Is it, perhaps, built over a sanctuary where pilgrims once sought prophecies from Diana?

Brutus approaches the sacred place at sunset, accompanied by old Gero, an augur expert in the interpretation of omens, and twelve elders, hoping to find out from Diana where their true destination lies (see plate 18). 'With Garlands about their Temples, as the ancient Rites required, they make three Fires to three Deities, viz, Jupiter [Zeus], Mercury [Hermes] and Diana, and offer Sacrifices to each of them.' They probably included Mercury because he had conveyed messages from Zeus to Aeneas, encouraging and guiding him on his journey from Troy to Italy. Then, 'Brutus himself holds before the Altar of the Goddess a consecrated Vessel filled with Wine, and the Blood of a white Hart, with his Face looking up to the Image, breaks the Silence in these Words.'

Geoffrey then quotes Brutus's prayer. This and the goddess's response are in such a different style to the rest of Geoffrey's writing that the Tudor chronicler Holinshed attributed them (almost certainly incorrectly) to Gerald of Wales, whilst Milton later guessed they had been composed for Geoffrey by his contemporary, Joseph of Exeter, 'the only smooth poet of those times'. This is Alexander Pope's translation of Brutus's prayer:

> *Goddess of Woods, tremendous in the chase,*
> *To Mountain-wolves and all the Savage race,*
> *Wide o'er th' aerial Vault extends thy sway,*
> *And o'er th' infernal Regions void of day,*
> *On thy third Reign look down; disclose our Fate,*
> *In what new Nation shall we fix our Seat?*
> *When shall we next thy hallow'd Altars raise,*
> *And Quires of Virgins celebrate thy praise?*

Brutus repeats this prayer nine times, and then four more while circling the altar. He 'pours the Wine into the Fire, and then lays himself down upon the Harts-Skin, which he has spread before the Altar, where at last he falls asleep. About their third Hour of the Night, the usual Time for deep Sleep, the Goddess seems to present herself before him.'

What did he see? Geoffrey does not say. An aged crone, a proud woman in her prime of fertility, a slender-ankled maiden? Anybody who has seen the statue of Artemis that once stood in her great sanctuary at Ephesus can imagine how terrifying she would be in a vision, with lions roaring by her side. All over her headdress, and about her legs, lurk a multitude of nightmarish beasts, griffins and bat-winged goats, all with pendulous breasts, each with their mouths thrown open in the infernal screams of childbirth. About her slender neck flash the constellations of the zodiac, and across her breasts lie the scrotal sacks of sacrificed and emasculated bulls. Bees swarm everywhere, buzzing menacingly, whilst above her head rises her awesome crown, alive with tiers of beasts like gargoyles on a medieval cathedral and plump-bosomed sphinxes beat their dreadful wings. Over all, tower the ramparts of a great city. But what city is that, Brutus may have wondered: Troy? nascent Rome? – or another, in a far-off land, which he had yet to build?

And now the goddess speaks. This is how Milton translated her words:

> *Brutus, far to the west, in th' ocean wide,*
> *Beyond the realm of Gaul, a land there lies,*
> *Seagirt it lies, where giants dwelt of old,*
> *Now void, it fits thy people; thither bend*
> *Thy course, there shalt thou find a lasting seat,*
> *Where to thy sons another Troy shall rise;*
> *And kings be born of thee, whose dreaded might*
> *Shall awe the world, and conquer nations bold.*
> *Thus to the race of Brute, kings of this island,*
> *The whole Earth shall be*

subject ...

The vision is so powerful that Brutus awakes with a start. He calls over his companions, who 'very much rejoyced' at what he tells them.

Lefkada is composed entirely of limestone, grey on the mountainsides but brilliant white along its western cliffs, and from this it gained its name, from the Greek *leukos*, 'white'. It therefore shares the same Indo-European root as Loegria, the Welsh name for England, so called also because of England's white cliffs. It must have seemed entirely appropriate to Geoffrey for Brutus to receive news of one white island through a vision seen on another.

What also seems appropriate is that, if Brutus were to spend the night in the sanctuary of

The sleeping Brutus receives Diana's prophecy.

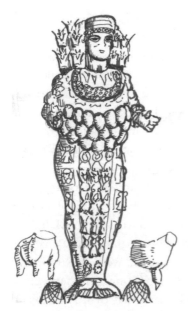

The statue of Artemis (Diana) in the archaeological museum in Selçuk (Ephesus), Turkey, from her great temple there, flanked by what is left of her two lions.

any deity, it should be that of Diana-Artemis. By slaying his father Silvius in Alba Longa's woods, Brutus had won himself the role of sacred king, and consort of the goddess. Now, by sleeping in her sanctuary, Brutus had effectively consummated that role. All this is implicit, not explicit, in Geoffrey's story – but it is there, nonetheless. And it is this sacred aura that then passes down, by implication, to Brutus's offspring – and thus to all the kings of Britain.

Yet again, they cannot sail west. The Bora must have risen at last. Brutus has no choice but to allow the wind to sweep his fleet south. 'After a Course of thirty Days [they] come to Africa. ... From thence they come to the Philenian Altars, and to a Place called Saline, and sail'd between Ruscicada and the Mountains of Azara.'

Brutus's route along the African coast is taken from Nennius. It is not from one of Nennius's Brutus stories, though, but from a completely different section of Nennius's collection of ancient writings, describing the route imagined for the Gaels on their journey from Egypt to Ireland. That story in turn has multiple origins, but the route itself must be derived from a Roman *periplus*, a written description of a sea route created to help mariners, and it is perfectly accurate. By travelling almost due south from Lefkada, Brutus's fleet reaches the *Aræ Philænorum*, 'the Altars of the Philaeni'. The Philaeni were two brothers who were buried alive to save their country. Their altars and bronze statues marked the western border of Egypt at the southernmost point of the Gulf of Syrtis Major (Khalīj Surt), about 150 miles south-south-west of modern Benghazi, Lybia. Nearby was 'the saltpan lake', now called Sabkah al Kabirah, Geoffrey's 'lake of Salinae'.

The Trojans' westward route would then have taken them along the shores of the Maghreb desert and past the place where, about 300 years later in 814 BC, the Phoenicians would build Carthage. Virgil's Aeneas spent a year there in love with its queen, Dido, despite his having lived long before the city's traditional founding date. Geoffrey does not mention Carthage and Sir Flinders Petrie once cited this as evidence for the voyage of Brutus being a true story. We know

now that it is not, and Geoffrey probably left out Carthage simply because Nennius had not mentioned it either.

Their next port of call, Ruscicada, means 'the promontory of fire'. Here the Phoenicians would later build the port now called Skikda, on the mountainous coast of Algeria. The 'Azara' mountains were part of the great Tell Atlas range that sprawls along that stretch of coast. Here, says Geoffrey, 'they undergo great Danger by Pirates, but notwithstanding vanquish them, and enrich themselves with their Spoils.' In Geoffrey's time, the Algerian coast was renowned for its Barbary corsairs, so this detail is probably anachronistic.

'From thence passing the river Malua they arrive at Mauretania, where at last for want of Provisions they are oblig'd to go ashore; and dividing themselves into several Bands they lay waste [to] that whole Country.' The 'Malua' is the river Moulouaya, which flows down from the High Atlas mountains and enters the Mediterranean at Ras el Maa, about 500 miles west of Ruscicada. Beyond it lay what would later become the Roman province of Mauretania Tingitana, modern Morocco. So it was here in Morocco that Brutus's Trojans foraged for food, anxious to replenish their ships' stores against the uncertain journey ahead. For now it was time for them to leave the encircling safety of the Mediterranean. Ahead of them lay the limestone rocks of Gibraltar and Cueta, the gateway to the shifting grey waves of the Atlantic.

Precious few heroes had ever sailed so far west and the straits were named after the only one who certainly had. Indeed, in some versions of his myth, that hero had even gauged the passage out and erected the guardian rocks with his own bare hands. With trepidation in their hearts, Brutus and the Trojan fleet approached the Straits of Gibraltar, which the ancients called the Pillars of Hercules.

Chapter 12

The Tower of Hercules

The Mediterranean loses two thirds more water to evaporation driven by the heat of the Sun than it gains from the rivers that feed it. As a result, there is a constant flow of cold water in through the Straits of Gibraltar from the Atlantic. To go the other way, the Trojans must have strained with all their might, beating against the current with their oars.

As they struggle along, they begin to hear sweet singing lilting over the heaving waves and see the heads of lovely maidens gazing up at them from the frothing tide. Geoffrey's decision to people this spot with sirens is surprising, for most writers accepted, then as now, that they lived south of Naples. Still, here they are, beckoning the Trojans to their doom (see plate 24).

'Drive your ship past the spot,' the sorceress Circe had warned Odysseus, prior to his own encounter with the same peril in book twelve of Homer's *Odyssey*, 'and to prevent any of your crew from hearing, soften some beeswax and plug their ears with it.' Maybe Brutus had been forewarned (by Diana?) in similar vein, and he must have taken similar precautions, for otherwise the helmsmen would have driven their ships straight onto the rocks whilst the crews leapt willingly into the water to cavort with the ethereal singers. And once the sirens had eaten the Trojans' flesh, their remains would have been discarded along with all the rest 'in a meadow piled high with the mouldering skeletons of men,' as Homer said, 'whose withered skin still hangs upon their bones.'

But the sirens were nothing compared to the physical dangers of the Atlantic. Brutus's keelless ships were built for Mediterranean travel, but in the violent swell of the ocean they could be pitched and tossed about at alarming angles. Only the good will of the ocean god Poseidon, whom the Romans called Neptune, they must have thought, could possibly save them all from drowning.

The Atlantic winds would have buffeted their worn sails as they battled north up the Spanish coast (Geoffrey calls this 'the Tyrrhenian Sea', but that is the name of the sea off the west coast of Italy. Holinshed thought Geoffrey had meant to write '*Mare Pyrenæum*', i.e, 'the Sea of the Pyrenees', but the confusion goes deeper due to Geoffrey's desire to associate Corineus, whom we shall encounter soon, with the giants of Italy: whatever the reason, it is a geographical slip). They would have approached rocky Cape Finisterre, the most westerly point of Spain (and Europe) and a treacherous place, then and now, for shipping. They would then have started to make their way north-west along the Galician coast until they rounded a rocky headland and found the Artabrian Gulf opening up before them. 'The Artabrians have many thickly peopled cities on that gulf,' wrote Strabo, inhabiting a land 'blest in fruits, in cattle, and in the abundance of its gold and silver and similar metals,' but they spent most of 'their time in brigandage and in continuous warfare with each other.' But that was over a thousand years after Brutus's time, so we must imagine the gulf much more sparsely populated, its great expanse of calm, blue water bounded on almost all sides by a low shoreline, thickly wooded with oaks, rising up to low, dark mountains covered with pines.

It was most likely here, 'upon the Shores', as Geoffrey wrote, that 'they found four several Nations descended from the banish'd Trojans, that had accompanied Antenor in Flight. The Name of their Commander was Corineus, a modest Man in Matters of Council, and excelling in Greatness of Courage and Boldness, who in an Encounter with any Person even of Gigantick Stature, would immediately overthrow him, as if he engag'd with a Child. When they understood from whom he was descended, they join'd Company with him and those under his Government.'

Antenor was a kinsman of Aeneas, to whom the foundation of various western cities, including Venetia and Padua in Italy, had been attributed. Antenor's son Ocela was in turn said by Strabo to have founded Opsicella further east along on Spain's northern, Cantabrian coast, not far from modern Bilbao. Geoffrey does not specify where Brutus met Corineus, indicating merely that it was somewhere between the Straits of Gibraltar and France. Maybe he was thinking of Bilbao, but the most likely place is in the Artabrian Gulf. For here, as Brutus's ships rowed in around the headland, they reached the deep, sheltered harbour of La Coruña.

The name 'Corineus' is borrowed from the *Aeneid*, where it belonged to a minor Trojan character who fought bravely on the side of Aeneas. Geoffrey's Corineus was clearly not this same man, for all of that generation were long dead. Rather, it seems likely that Geoffrey had used a Virgilian name to provide a Trojan veneer for a decidedly non-Trojan hero, perhaps an eponymous hero from La Coruña called something like 'Corunus'. This is possible because Geoffrey's Corineus had decidedly Herculean character traits, and there exists a Spanish myth that asserts that La Coruña had been founded by Hercules (see plate 23). That suggests in turn that Geoffrey may have known an older, now lost version of Corineus's story in which he was not a Trojan at all, but a son of Hercules called Corunus, an eponymous hero of La Coruña. That is an idea to which we shall return later, once Corineus has landed safely in Britain.

On the gorsy headland at the western opening of the Artabrian Gulf stands a lighthouse built towards the end of the first century AD by the Romans. It was a stout, square building, about 100 feet high with three floors and a ramp winding its way up the outside walls. This ramp fell down, but in 1788 the lighthouse was restored with a new façade around the outside of the Roman building, decorated with an ascending diagonal band to retain the memory of the ramp, and a lantern house was added on top.

The lighthouse stands there to this very day and is known as the Tower of Hercules because of a local myth that it had been built, back in the Bronze Age, by Hercules. This myth relates – as, doubtless, Corineus would have told Brutus as they feasted together – how Hercules came to Spain on his tenth labour, just as the Greek myths said, to steal the cattle owned by the giant Geryon, whom he fought and killed. The Greek myths imagined this fight taking place at Cadiz, on the south-western Spanish coast, but Galicia developed its own version of the story. It is probably as old as the AD 900s, when Al-Razi's *Muluk Al-Andalus* relates that 'this fight took place 3 miles from the city now called La Coruña'. The *De Rebus Hispaniae* by Rodrigo Ximinez de Rada (c. 1170–1248) says that Geryon ruled lands including Galicia, that Hercules killed him in Galicia and then populated the land with Galatians (from Anatolia). A much more detailed version appears in the *Primera Crónica General* of Alfonso X 'the Wise' (1221–1284), King of Castile, in whose realms Galicia lay. The charge that Alfonso invented the whole story is palpably incorrect, and improbable too, for how wise would he have seemed if he produced a Hercules story for Galicia out of thin air?

There is no way of proving for sure that it is a very old myth, but there is a good chance that it is older than Geoffrey. It might have arisen in the Dark Ages or it could even go back to Roman times, even though, admittedly, no Roman writings have survived that mention it. Alfonso's version includes details that he may have invented, but which he could just as well have heard locally – that Geryon had lived between the rivers Tagus and Duro, in Portugal, and that, once Hercules had killed him at La Coruña, he buried the giant's head on the headland and built the lighthouse over it. That idea may come from the large, rather skull-like boulders that are still there, immediately to the north of the lighthouse, whilst very nearby on the Punta Herminia, within clear sight of both, are rocks with natural indentations that look like giants' footprints (see plate 26), of the sort that have inspired giant stories elsewhere (in the Hazel Brook Gorge near Bristol, for example). It would only take one person, who knew about Hercules coming to Spain and fighting Geryon, to hear a local, Artabrian story about a giant being killed and buried below the lighthouse, and to suggest that this giant had been Geryon, slain by Hercules. A modern depiction of Hercules fighting Geryon is on the lighthouse's bronze door, and La Coruña's coat of arms shows the Tower of Hercules above the skull of the giant Geryon, making this place a potent meeting point between myth and reality.

The local place names are confusing and should be explained. The lighthouse's headland is at the northern end of a horn-shaped peninsula, attached to the mainland by a low isthmus. Near the southern end of the horn, commanding this isthmus, the Romans built a port city, which they called Brigantium, a name that probably reflected that of the earlier, Iron Age tribe who had lived there (and which was part of wider tribal grouping of the Artabrians). Thus the lighthouse became known as *Turris Brigantina* and Orosius, who was himself Galician, refers in about AD 416 to 'the city of Brigantia [which] lies in Galicia [where there is] a high tower, an observation point towards Britannia'. (Therefore, claims that Brigantium was the ancient name of the modern town of Betanzos, on the southern shore of the Artabrian Gulf, are without foundation, and there is precious little evidence of ancient settlement there in any case.) But whilst the port city was called Brigantium, the horn-shaped peninsula itself seems to have been called Crunna, a name presumably derived from the Indo-European root *cornu*, meaning 'horn'. It probably had this name long before the Romans built Brigantium and the lighthouse. During the Dark Ages the port city declined dramatically but it remained a settlement, referred to as Crunnia, as Floriano Cumbreño's work shows, and this name was used for sure in the 1100s, as is asserted in the work of López Alsina. Thus, when Alfonso the Wise's grandfather, King Alfonso IX of Leon, granted La Coruña a charter to become a city in 1208 and wrote 'I am building a new population near the Tower of the Lighthouse, in a place called Crunna' he was, certainly, adding to a settlement that was already there. And that matters, because it confirms the possibility that Geoffrey's Corineus was indeed based on a much older eponymous hero from the place called Crunnia or La Coruña.

Did Corineus ever take Brutus up the Tower of Hercules to show him the view? Besides British myth, the lighthouse also features in Irish mythology, for the *Lebor Gabála* imagined this region being settled, and the tower being built, by King Breoghan, whose name was an eponym derived from the Roman name for the place, Brigantium (see plate 25). 'Once,' according to O'Clery's redaction of the Irish story, 'when [Breoghan's son] Ithe, of a clear winter's evening was on top of Breoghan's Tower, contemplating and looking over the four quarters of the world, it seemed to him that he saw a shadow and a likeness of a land and lofty island far away from him. He went back to his brethren, and told them what he had seen; and said that he was mindful and desirous of going to see the land that had appeared to him. Breg son of Breoghan said it was no land he had seen but clouds of heaven,' but Ithe persists, and sails there – and discovers Ireland.

The story owes something to Orosius, who referred to the lighthouse as 'an observation point towards Britannia'. He later stated, inaccurately, that Brigantium could actually be seen from the south coast of Ireland. That is not true, but once Brutus and Corineus had puffed their way up to the top of the tower they may have seen the same optical illusion that many people, including us, have seen. When a low mist settles on the horizon, it forms a dark band, and on top of this, still very low and clearly far below the clouds above, the sun illuminates a white strip. It is a strip of cloud, of course, but it takes very little effort to suspend your disbelief and tell yourself that, yes, that is indeed a land, lying in the north.

The land that Ithe thought he saw was Ireland. But maybe Brutus, seeing this same illusion, thought with yearning in his heart that he was seeing the land 'far to the west, in th' ocean wide' that had been promised him by Diana.

Chapter 13

Bloodshed in Gaul

The Trojan fleet, handsomely enlarged by the ships of Corineus and his people, would have hugged the northern coast of Spain to avoid the treacherous gales of the Bay of Biscay and then turned north up the coast of Gaul, which is now France, riding the Atlantic's mighty swell until, wrote Geoffrey, 'entering the mouth of the Loire, [they] cast anchor.'

As soon as they have landed, Corineus picks out 'two hundred men' and sets out to hunt, for they must have been yearning for fresh meat. We may imagine them foraging in the dense hazel underbrush below the spreading canopy of oaks and beeches, until they find a herd of deer and succeed in killing some of them. As they return down the bank of the Loire with the dead animals slung over their shoulders, they are overtaken by a party of Gauls. Their leader Imbertus asks insolently, 'Who gave him Leave to enter the King's Forests, and kill his Game?' Corineus roars back that 'there ought to be no Occasion for Leave'. Imbertus 'shoots at him. Corineus avoids the Arrow and immediately runs up to him, and with his Bow in his Hand breaks his Head.'

They were in the north-west of what would one day become the Roman province of Aquitaine, which was occupied in the Late Iron Age by the Gaulish Pictones, whose tribal base was at Poitiers, about 120 miles south-east of the mouth of the Loire. Geoffrey does not say, but probably imagined, that the Pictones were related to the Picts of Scotland. The Picts were in fact the native people of Scotland, but in Geoffrey's time it was believed they had been invaders from Scythia, but of the same ilk, following Geoffrey's logic, as the tribesmen of Poitiers.

The local king, says Geoffrey, is Goffarius Pictus, who sets out with a large army to avenge Ibertus's death. Brutus:

sends away the Women and Children to the Ships, which he takes Care to be well guarded, and commands them to stay there, while he and the Rest that are able to bear Arms should go and meet the Army. ... At last when an Assault is made a bloody Fight ensues; in which after a great Part of the Day has been spent, Corineus is asham'd to see the Aquitans so bravely standing their Ground, and the Trojans maintaining the Fight without Victory. He takes therefore fresh Courage, and drawing off his men to the right Wing, breaks in upon the very thickest of the Enemies Ranks, where he makes such Slaughter on every Side, that at last he pierces through the Cohort, and puts them all to Flight. In this Encounter he loses his Sword, but by good Fortune meets with a Battle-Ax, with which he claves down to the Waste every one that stands in his Way. Brutus and every Body else both Friends and Enemies are amaz'd at his Courage and Strength, who brandishing about his Battle-Ax among the flying Troops, does not a little terrify them with these insulting Words.

'Whither fly ye, Cowards? whither fly ye, base Wretches? stand your Ground, that ye may encounter Corineus. What, for shame, do so many Thousands of you fly one Man? However, take this Comfort for your Flight, that you are pursu'd by one, before whom the Tyrrhenian Giants could not stand their Ground, but fell down slain in Heaps together.'

At these Words one of them, named Suhardus, who was a Consul, returns with three hundred Men to assault him: But Corineus with his Shield wards off the Blow, and lifting up his Battle-Ax gives him such a Stroke upon the Top of his Helmet, that at once he cleaves him down to the Waist.

Further deeds of extraordinary bravery follow. 'Brutus seeing him [Corineus] thus beset, out of mere Affection to him runs with a Band of Men to his Assistance.' Before long, Goffarius and the remnant of the Gaulish army have fled.

With Gaulish blood smeared over their faces and the warlike yelling of Corineus echoing in their ears, a maddened lust for further killing seems to have overtaken the Trojans. They row ever further up the Loire, negotiating its treacherous sandbanks and making frequent forays ashore: 'he sets the Cities on Fire, seizes the Riches that were hid in them, destroys the Fields, and makes dismal Slaughter among the Citizens and common People, being unwilling to leave so much as one alive of that wretched Nation.' Such attempted genocide seems distasteful to us now, but Geoffrey was writing for a predominantly warrior audience: he attributed mass slaughter like this to King Arthur too, and nobody seems to have minded. But Goffarius minds. He raises help from the other eleven kings of Gaul, and now brings his massive army bearing down on Brutus. The Trojans respond by fortifying a camp for themselves 'where the City of Tours now stands' (see plate 27).

Geoffrey's inspiration for this detail was Nennius's embryonic story of Brutus. Having been exiled from Italy for killing his father, said Nennius, Brutus had gone to Greece, but been driven thence 'because of the killing of Turnus, whom Aeneas had killed, and arrived in Gaul, where he founded the city of Tours, which is called Turnis'. In other words, the Greeks knew that Brutus's great-grandfather Aeneas had killed Turnus who, though Italian, was of Greek ancestry, and had driven him away because of this, and Brutus then named Tours after Turnus. It is a contrived and rather implausible story – why name a city after someone your ancestor had killed? – so Geoffrey invented a second Turnus who was a 'nephew' of Brutus's. This is almost impossible, for Brutus's mother died in childbirth and we do not hear of his father Silvius remarrying, but when Hildebrand Jacob wrestled with this problem in the eighteenth century he decided that Brutus had a sister called Lavinia (named after her step-great-grandmother) and that the boy Turnus was her son by a valiant warrior called Tros. Alternatively, maybe this Turnus was actually a nephew of Brutus's Greek wife Ignoge. At any rate, says Geoffrey, this young nephew Turnus fights bravely by Brutus's side in Gaul and kills 600 men, but eventually is slain: he is buried in the Trojan camp, and Brutus names it Tours in his memory. Geoffrey adds an odd comment, 'as Homer testifies', when of course Homer does no such thing, nor probably ever knew much of Gaul at all.

In Nennius's time, Carolingian Gaul was magnificently cultured and prosperous, and Tours was one of its finest old Roman cities. The spurious link between the names 'Turnus' and 'Tours' gave Nennius the opportunity of claiming it as a British foundation, and the idea clearly pleased Geoffrey as well. But it is archaeologically unlikely, for Tours dates back only to Roman times. It is built on the flat, southern bank of the Loire. A much more plausible place to imagine Brutus's camp is on the low limestone escarpment that forms the steep northern bank opposite, for here there is archaeological evidence of a settlement dating back to the Iron Age at least.

Only 12 miles upstream, where the Loire is entered by the river Amasse, is the beautiful Renaissance chateau of Amboise, and rising up behind it is the high bluff of the Plateau des Châtelliers, on which was a hill fort of the Iron Age Turones. Its remains are still there, with high banks and commanding views of the valleys and hills around (see plate 28). It is there that we may best picture Goffarius and his confederates establishing their base.

When Goffarius first approaches the Trojans' camp, his attitude is scornful. 'We shall quickly take these pitiful Fellows like Sheep, and send them about our Kingdom for Slaves.' The Trojans form their ranks outside the camp and prepare for battle. Horns blew, we may imagine, and spears rattled on shields while the Gaulish warriors (probably naked save for their warlike tattoos) yelled their savage battle cries. The Trojans rampage forwards, slaughtering up to 2,000 of the enemy and forcing the Gauls to retreat. However, Goffarius has far greater numbers on his side, and is able to regroup his warriors and mount a counter-attack so fierce as to drive the Trojans back behind their stockades.

A miserable fate now awaits the Trojans: brutal death or a return to slavery. But Corineus has a plan. In the depth of the night, he leads a party of men out of the camp and along the river into the woods. We may imagine them crouching, silent below the mossy trees, cloaked by the silvery dawn mist that often lies over the Loire and its broad valley. Then, as the sun comes up, Brutus flings aside the barricade and marches out boldly with a small cohort of men, as if to give battle. The Gauls roar in anticipation, gladdened that so few of their enemies seem to remain, and come charging forward to begin hacking down the men of Troy. Then, behind them, their ears are assailed by bellowing. The brushy edge of the woods melts into a sea of spears as the ambushers charge out. At their head is Corineus, raging like a bull, his axe spraying Gaulish blood high into the morning sky, his enemies falling helplessly before his relentless onslaught. The Gauls 'hastily quit the field; but the Trojans pursue them, and kill them in the pursuit, nor do they desist till they have gained a complete victory.'

The lust for victory is sated and Brutus, 'though in joy for this great success' wakes as if from a long, blood-soaked trance. He is 'afflicted to observe the Number of his Forces daily lessened, while that of the Enemy is still more and more.' It is time to leave behind this land of savage Gauls and 'to go in quest of the Island which the Goddess had foretold him of.'

'With the consent of his company, he repairs to the fleet, and loading it with the riches and spoils he has taken, sets sail.' They would have cast off their hawsers and allowed the Loire's relentless current to bear them back downstream, the way they had come. The smell of salt would have filled their nostrils and they would have heard gulls mewing in the blue arc of the sky above.

Chapter 14

Here Be Giants!

The consummation of the long voyage was drawing nigh. 'With a fair Wind' behind him, Geoffrey wrote, Brutus sets sail 'towards the promised Island'. To reach there, the Trojans must have negotiated the bony peninsulas of Armorica, *Ar-mór*, 'the land of the sea', which we call Brittany, and then beaten the dark green waves with their oars as they struck out boldly north. It was a perilous voyage into the unknown, yet they followed their course so unerringly that, though Geoffrey does not say so, it is difficult not to imagine the guiding hands of the gods at work.

At last they saw land ahead. Instead of brilliant white cliffs – for those do not start until 80 miles to the east – the steep rocky edge of the land that they saw would have been iron-red, and so too, ominously, was the surging tide that foamed beneath.

Totonesio littore, is where Geoffrey says they first landed, 'on the coast of Totnes', which by old usage might indicate anywhere from East Portlemouth on the southernmost tip of Devon, right up to Exeter.

William Blake painted the Trojans landing on a Devon beach, having plunged down waist-deep into the cold waves to drag the keels up onto the glistening pebbles, safe from the tug of the roaring waves (see plate 30). But most often the Trojan ships are imagined making their way into the broad estuary of the river Dart, whose river god would glory ever after in his being the first British river to receive 'my Britaine-founding Brute … with his puissant fleet',

Brutus and Corineus amongst the Neolithic remains of Les Pieres Plats, Locmariaquer, Brittany.

as the poet Michael Drayton wrote in 1622. The channel narrows between the wooded banks until suddenly it broadens out again into the glistening expanse of Galmpton Creek. Then, the banks begin to close in again, the lower branches of the overhanging oaks almost touching the grey water at high tide, and ahead lies what is now the market town of Totnes.

Later Devon tradition, recorded by L. du Garde Peach and inspired by Geoffrey's work, puts an unlikely verse in Devon dialogue into Brutus's mouth, as he finally stepped ashore:

> *Yur where I stan*[d],
> *I takes my res*[t],
> *this be my woame* [home],
> *this be Totnes!*

Totnes has a Brutus Stone (see plate 29). Some say it is the stone onto which Brutus first stepped when he came ashore, or the plinth on which the Palladium had stood in Troy itself and which Brutus had brought with him (very improbably) all the way from Italy. It is in fact a local Devonshire stone, and was probably originally a standing stone, one of several in the West Country that were used as Broadstones or *bruiters stones*, from which *bruits* or announcements were made. Its name happened to sound like 'Brutus', so this is probably one of the reasons why Geoffrey chose to associate Brutus's landing with southern Devon. The persistence of the Trojan tradition that became attached to the stone since Geoffrey's time shows the wonder with which the local people seem to have regarded his story of Brutus.

What is left of Totnes's stone is now set in the pavement between numbers 51 and 53 Fore Street: it is on the right as you walk up towards the gate, easy to miss on a first attempt despite its discrete, gold-painted label, 'Brutus Stone'. The town criers still make their announcements from it occasionally. It has helped keep the story of Brutus alive in Totnes, so when a new road bridge was built over the river Dart in 1982, they decided to call it the Brutus Bridge in his honour (see plate 31). They are the only monuments named after Brutus in the whole of Britain.

The Trojans had completed an immensely long, perilous journey to a land far beyond the safety of the Mediterranean. Great must have been their celebratory feasts, as they clustered around blazing fires at their landing place by the Dart, giving thanks to the immortal gods of Olympus.

Suddenly, joy turned to terror. All around them loomed the dark outlines of twenty-one giants wielding uprooted trees in their angry fists. Their leader was Goëmagot, who had brought his tribe storming up from Cornwall to destroy the incomers. This was not what Diana had foretold: she had told Brutus that the island had once been inhabited by giants but was now deserted. Perhaps she had lied so as not to put the Trojans off going.

Scarce had the ink dried on Geoffrey's manuscript than Henry of Huntingdon reworked this section, with the giants wading out, Cyclops-like, into the sea to try to stop the Trojans from landing at all – but that is not how Geoffrey wrote it. In his version, the giants 'make a dreadful Slaughter' until more Trojans can join the fight. Geoffrey does not say how the Trojans managed to prevail, but presumably the determining factor was technology. Against Neolithic farmers armed with sticks and stones, the giants would have been invincible. But against the sharp bronze spears of the men of Troy, they had no hope: as ever, the ancient stood no chance against modernity.

Finally, only Goëmagot himself is left, 'in Stature twelve Cubits [12 or 20 feet, depending on which type of cubit Geoffrey meant], and of such prodigious Strength, that at one Shake he pulled up an Oak, as if it had been a Hazel Wand.' Everyone is terrified except Corineus who, overjoyed,

prepares himself, and throwing aside his Arms, challenges him to wrestle with him. At the Beginning of the Rencounter, Corineus and the Giant standing Front to Front, strongly fetter each other in their Arms, and pant aloud for Breath; but Goëmagot presently grasping Corineus, with all his Might, breaks three of his Ribs, two on his right Side and one on his left. At which Corineus highly enraged, rouses up his whole Strength, and Snatching him upon his Shoulders, runs with him as fast as he is able for the Weight, to the next Shore [a distance of at least 6 miles, if the battle had actually taken place in Totnes] and there getting upon the Top of a high Rock, hurls down the savage Monster into the Sea, where falling by the Sides of craggy Rocks, he is cruelly torn to Pieces, and colours the Waves with his Blood.

The place was known ever-afterwards, writes Geoffrey, as 'Goëmagot's Leap'.

The cataclysmic death of the greatest of the giants reverberated down the centuries. As late as 1622, Drayton recalled how Goëmagot's fall

Shook Neptune [Poseidon] *with such strength as shoulder'd him withal*
That where the monstrous waves like mountains late did stand,
They leapt out of the place, and left the bared sand
To gaze upon wide heaven, so great a blow it gave.

Twenty-three miles west of Totnes is Plymouth Hawe, which many claimed was 'Langoemagot' or 'The Giant's Leap'. But really Goëmagot may have died anywhere along the rocky shore of southern Devon, where the iron ore in the rock still makes the sea foam red, as if stained by the blood of the giant vanquished by Corineus.

As the Trojans explore the island of Britain they encounter more giants, whom they drive off into 'the Caves of the Mountains'. Later, Holinshed asserted that Corineus had fought Gogmagog at Dover and Edmund Spenser, probably tongue-in-cheek, imagined a Trojan called Canutus slaying a Kentish giant called Godmer. And the myths of Arthur are full of the battles that he and his knights fought against giants, left over long after the time of his ancestor Brutus.

There are many reasons why Geoffrey and his predecessors should have imagined giants living in ancient Britain. The hefty bones of archaic human species, *Homo erectus*, *Homo heidelbergensis* and the Neanderthals, all of whom had lived in Britain during the Ice Age, along with those of their prey such as mammoths, could easily be mistaken for those of giants. Indeed, the medieval poem *Dez Grantz Geanz* says that the large bones found throughout Britain, teeth, legs and ribs and thigh bones 4 feet long, *ausi large cum un escu*, 'as big as a shield', were ample evidence of the giants whom Brutus had encountered there.

Equally, the vast, ancient standing stones erected by our Neolithic ancestors about 6,000 years ago still dominate the landscape to this day. To Dark Age minds, they were best explained as the work of giants – or even as giants themselves, turned into stone, mid-dance. But it is not as simple as that.

The presence of giants goes much deeper into mythology, to the core, perhaps, of the creation myths of the early inhabitants of post-Ice Age Britain. We do not know what those myths were, but they were likely to be similar to the earlier creation myths found all over the world – that the world had been dredged up from the bottom of the sea by a benevolent animal deity, and then shaped by other gigantic creatures. The Australian Aboriginals, for instance, have many tales of how the valleys were gouged out and the mountains were pushed up by the Rainbow Serpent's journey across the world at the start of the Dreamtime. Similarly, Siberian myths recorded by Voskoboinikov relate how Sely the Mammoth built the first dry land up out of muck dredged from the bottom of the primeval seas, and how Dyabdar the serpent then journeyed across the nascent world, shaping the landscape as he travelled. We know from their cave paintings how much the Ice Age people of France venerated mammoths, and the image of one was found recently in a cave in the Cheddar Gorge, Somerset, so the idea of a creation myth in Britain involving a giant world-building mammoth is possible.

World-shaping animals were appropriate for hunter-gatherer and nomadic societies, who shared the natural landscapes with large wild animals that they respected. But the onset of farming – the Neolithic phase of human history – led to humans starting to reshape their world for themselves and treating animals as captives, not as equals. Slowly, throughout world mythology, there is a shift away from animal deities, first to the animal-headed but otherwise very human-looking gods of the Egyptians, for example, and later to the fully humanlike gods of ancient Greece. Similarly, world shapers who were once giant animals became inexorably more human looking, until they ended up as giants. Classical Greek depictions of giants, interestingly, tend to show them with human torsos and heads, but with serpents' tails for legs – a last vestige, maybe, of the writhing body of Dyabdar.

Also, as new gods inherited the world from the original, wild, world shapers, those world shapers became demonised – so the benevolent serpent became a force for evil, and the mammoths, transformed in human imagination into giant humans, became ever more monstrous: colossal humans, who could exercise human lust and greed on a superhuman scale.

So the giants whom Brutus and Corineus encountered in Devon had been there at the start because they had shaped Britain in the first place, first as the benevolent mammoth and serpent, perhaps, later as half-animals, half-men, and finally as monstrous giants, fit only for death at the hands of the righteous Trojans.

Nobody seems to know what the original name of Geoffrey's chief giant was. Some manuscripts have Goëmagot, others say Goemagog. Later versions call him Gogmagog, a spelling inspired by the Bible, for in Deuteronomy (3.11), Og is leader of the Amorite Giants of Canaan and then 'Gog, the land of Magog' appears in Ezekiel (38.2). Japheth had a son Magog, too, said variously to be ancestor of the Scythians, the Goths and the Gauls, so it was a name aptly suited (in medieval British minds) to such barbaric, ancient denizens of Britain.

Geoffrey's 'Goëmagot' or 'Goemagog', however, might be adapted from an old British word that simply meant 'giant'. The Irish giants in the *Lebor Gabála* were called Fomorians. This name must surely be linked to the names of Cormoran, the giant who lived near St Michael's Mount in Cornwall, and Gourmailhon, a giant who lived, according to French folklorist Paul Sébillot, not far from Mont-Saint-Michelle in Brittany. Probably derived from the same root was the name of Goram, to whom Somerset legends attribute the digging out of the region's dramatic limestone gorges, and of Grim, who is said to have constructed Grim's Dyke and other southern British earthworks. Though generally said to be a byname for the Saxon god Woden, or for the Devil himself, the name of Grim surely goes back to an ancient, widely used word for an Earth-shaping giant.

Perhaps it is from this same matrix of giant names – Fomorian, Cormoran, Gourmailhon, Goram, Grim – and maybe via an intermediate name like 'Gormagor', that Geoffrey finally arrived at the name Goëmagot, which he bestowed on the giant with whom Corineus held his fateful wrestling match.

Throughout this section of Geoffrey's *History*, Corineus looms larger than life – larger, indeed, than Brutus himself. It is Corineus, not Brutus, who encounters the Gauls in the forest, and Corineus who provokes the war against Goffarius. In the subsequent battle, it is Corineus who leads the action, mobilising and directing the troops and slaying numerous foes whilst Brutus merely looks on admiringly. It is Corineus who comes up with the rouse that leads to the final victory over Goffarius. When they land near Totnes, it is Corineus who wrestles with Goëmagot and flings him headlong into the sea.

Brutus's story falls into distinct sections, like a patchwork of different tales that Geoffrey stitched together: as the English scholar J.S. Mackley observed, 'on ... occasions, he lifts lengthy passages without attributing his source.' After Brutus's voyage along the African coast, which is based on Nennius's account of the journey of the Gaels, and before his founding of London, come his adventures with Corineus in Spain, Gaul and Devonshire, which are effectively a story in themselves. They might not, originally, have been about Brutus at all. Had Geoffrey simply copied out an older story about Corineus, who came from Spain, ravished Gaul and then conquered the West Country, and simply inserted a few references to Brutus into it?

This takes us back to the idea, mentioned earlier, that Corineus's name was originally Corunus, and that he may originally have been the eponymous hero of La Coruña; not a Trojan at all, but a son of Hercules. In fact, this becomes rather self-evident from traces of this original story that Geoffrey did not bother to alter. 'In an Encounter with any Person even of Gigantick Stature, [Corineus] would immediately overthrow him, as if he engag'd with a Child,' which is just what we would expect of a son of giant-slaying Hercules. 'Take this Comfort for your Flight,' Corineus yells at the Gauls, 'that you are pursu'd by one, before whom the Tyrrhenian Giants could not stand their Ground, but fell down slain in Heaps together.' Tyrrhenia is a Greek name for Etruria, the region immediately north of Rome, and the best known giant in this region was Cacus, whom Hercules killed in Rome itself. Corineus's boast therefore associates him very firmly indeed with Hercules, making the idea that he was once Corunus, son of Hercules, very far from absurd.

When this section of Geoffrey's *History* is read as Corunus's story, it becomes ever more apparent that Geoffrey has spliced mentions of Brutus into an older text. Sentences like 'Brutus seeing him [Corineus] thus beset, out of mere Affection to him runs with a Band of Men to his Assistance', and 'Brutus and every Body else both Friends and Enemies are amaz'd at his [Corineus's] Courage and Strength' read oddly, until one realises that Geoffrey had simply inserted them into Corunus's story. Brutus's founding of Tours is spliced in because Nennius said this had happened. It stands out sharply as the only thing Brutus actually does of his own volition during the whole campaign.

At the point where Geoffrey stops following Corunus's story and returns his focus to Brutus himself, the joins show up sharply. As Geoffrey tells the story, the Trojans land in Britain and decide to settle there. They explore the 'various territories' and drive the giants away into caves. Brutus names the island after himself. Then we return to Corineus, who decides to settle in the West Country, where he enjoys wrestling giants. It is only *then* that we hear of the settlers feasting 'in the port where they at first landed', during which Goëmagot makes his appearance and Corineus wrestles and kills him. It is messy. Someone writing the story from scratch would have made them land, fight the giants in the place where they landed, and then set off to explore, colonise and name the land. But it is lucky that Geoffrey's narrative is messy, because through such messiness he reveals his sources, and allows us to glimpse back, beyond the story of Brutus, to an older, more imaginative story that would otherwise have been lost.

As shown earlier, the Crunnia myth was older than Geoffrey's *History* and it seems likely that it and the Corineus story used by Geoffrey were separate descendants of the same earlier myth. That myth might date back, like the Brutus story, to monkish musings in the Dark Ages, when there was much communication between the abbeys of Ireland, Britain and northern Spain (not least the monastery of Santa Maria de Bretoña near Ferrol, on the opposite shore of the Artabrian Gulf from La Coruña, which had been founded by Romano-Britons escaping the Anglo-Saxon takeover of England). It is even possible that the story, livened up by monkish imaginations, goes back yet further, perhaps even to pre-Roman times, when the tin trade flourished up and down the Atlantic seaboard, with West Country tin being traded from Plymouth Sound and St Michael's Mount, via Gaulish middlemen and the harbours of the Artabrian Gulf, including what is now La Coruña, whence it made its way to the Mediterranean, to form part of the bronze weapons of ancient Greece.

The version of the story in Alfonso the Wise's *Primera Crónica General* says that, when Hercules decided to found La Coruña, he named it after its first occupant, a woman called Crunna. He does not say that they had any children, but Hercules was renowned for fathering eponymous heroes and populations, so this would have been the natural conclusion of such an older Galician tale. Alfonso may have left that part of the story out simply because it did not suit his purpose: he wanted to glorify northern Spanish history through the cultural, not the biological input of Hercules. But whoever originally sang the myth of Corunus, the hero from the Artabrian Gulf who raided Gaul and settled in south-western Britain, would likely have had another agenda – to claim Hercules as an ancestor for a ruling dynasty either in the Artabrian Gulf, or in south-west Britain, or both.

A legend connecting West Country kings to the wealthier cultures of southern Europe would come as no surprise: maybe it even reflected genuine dynastic connections between the ruling Iron Age elites of Galicia and southern Devonshire. After all, Geoffrey makes Corineus's daughter Gwendolen marry Brutus's son Locrinus, and says that their son Maddan (the ancestor of the later kings) was brought up in the West Country by Corineus himself. Maybe, before Geoffrey had shoehorned Corineus's story into Brutus's, the earlier tale had been simply that Maddan was Corineus's son. We can speculate – for in the absence of an original manuscript, or a reliable reference to it, such a theory is unprovable – that a West Country Iron Age dynasty told stories about its descent from Maddan, whose father Corunus had been fathered by Hercules in Crunna in the Artabrian Gulf. Corunus had then set out by sea to ravage Gaul, and wrested the West Country from the giants. Such a story may have been recorded in Roman times and could have survived just long enough for Geoffrey to incorporate it creatively into his *History*.

The myth of Hercules, founder of La Coruña and (as we have theorised) father of Corunus had an interesting side effect too, for such a story had clearly influenced, or was influenced by, the foundation myth of Ireland, as recorded in the *Lebor Gabála*. Created about the year AD 1000, it was, like Geoffrey's *History*, a monkish compilation drawn from a variety of different sources. It relates how the Gaels of Ireland were descended from the family of Noah and how they roamed west through the Mediterranean until they reached Spain. Here, their leader Brath 'had a good son named Breoghan, by whom was built the Tower and the city – Brigantia was the city's name. From Breoghan's Tower it was that Ireland was seen' and, having sighted Ireland from the tower, the Gaels pressed on to colonise the land.

Brigantia was the Roman name for the port on the promontory called Crunna (La Coruña). Breoghan's Tower was of course the lighthouse there, known now as the Tower of Hercules, from which an optical illusion created by clouds along the horizon can be mistaken (with a willing suspension of disbelief) for Ireland. Dissecting the *Lebor Gabála*, it seems clear that the story of the earlier wanderings of the Gaels, whose leaders included a hero called Feinius Farsaid, were based upon the travels of Aeneas. In the story as it exists now, his descendants reached Spain and there was born Breoghan, whose own progeny settled in Ireland. But is this a monkish manipulation of an earlier story? Had Breoghan originally been another son of Hercules and the woman called Crunna, with a story similar to Corineus's? Had the monks in this case taken that story, kept Breoghan, but deleted his original parentage to make him a descendant of Feinius Farsaid instead?

Whether the Irish story inspired the West Country one, or vice versa, is impossible to tell. South-east Ireland, the West Country and north-west Spain were all part of the same matrix of Iron Age trade and conquest, and of later Dark Age trade and monkish communication. The best we can say is that stories were probably swapped around and adapted freely, and echoes of these survive in both Geoffrey's *History* and the *Lebor Gabála*, with Hercules as a probable starting-point for the foundation-myth of Galicia, and thus of Ireland and south-west Britain too. In both Ireland and south-west Britain, Hercules was displaced, in the Irish case by an earlier line of Gaels descended from Feinius Farsaid (Aeneas), whilst in the West Country case Geoffrey removed Hercules and turned Corunus into a thoroughgoing Trojan called Corineus.

So much we can guess from Geoffrey's *History*. But let us return now to Corineus, panting with exhilaration at having just flung Gogmagog into the sea, and to Brutus himself.

Chapter 15

New Troy in Britain

Britain, the best of Islands ... produces every thing that is for the Use of Man, with a Plenty that never fails. It abounds in all Kinds of Metals, and has Champians [fields] of large Extent, and Hills fit for the finest Tillage, the Richness of whose Soil affords variety of Fruits at their Seasons. It has also Forests well stor'd with all Kinds of wild Beasts, in the Lawns whereof Cattle find good Change of Pasture and Bees variety of Flowers for Honey. Under its lofty Mountains lie green Meadows pleasantly situated, in which the gentle Murmurs of Crystal Springs gliding along clear Channels, give those that lye on their Banks an agreeable Invitation to slumber. It is likewise well water'd with Lakes and Rivers abounding with Fish.

So wrote Geoffrey, following a similar description of Britain found in Nennius and evoking a sort of earthly paradise inspired, most likely, by the way Virgil imagined the Golden Age in Italy in his *Eclogues*. Geoffrey added later that 'the pleasant Situation of Places, with Plenty of Rivers abounding with Fish, and the engaging Prospect of Woods, make Brutus and his Company very desirous to fix their Habitation in it ... they begin to till the Ground and build Houses, so that in a little Time the Country looks like a Place that had been long inhabited.'

Everything to the west is to be Corineus's: Cornwall, asserts Geoffrey, is named after him. But the greater prize is Brutus's: 'Brutus calls the Island after his own Name Britain, and his Companions Britains: For by this Derivation of the Name he was desirous to perpetuate his Memory.'

Within a few lines of Brutus landing at Totnes, his people stop being Trojans and become Britons, and their language starts changing to what Geoffrey terms 'rough [or crooked] Greek', or British – the language later known as Welsh. What caused this transformation, he does not say: most likely, their vines had not survived the journey, so they started brewing beer from golden-seeded barley. Maybe they started tattooing their bodies with woad too. Like fruit changing colour as it ripens in August, the transmogrification of the Trojans into Britons had begun in earnest.

Samuel Palmer's *The Eastern Gate* (1879) was an illustration for Milton's *L'Allegro*, but it could be a Virgilian scene from the first mornings of Brutus in Britain, when the Trojans were hard at work cultivating the yielding earth of their newly adopted land.

Brutus 'enters upon a Design of Building a City, and in order to it, travels through the Land to find a convenient Situation.'

Like moss growing on a boulder, Brutus's journey across Britain inspired many later details. As he set out east of Totnes along the southern flank of Dartmoor (see plate 32), he would have forded the river we now call the Exe, so the early twentieth-century mythographer Lawrence Waddell imagined him naming it after the Scamander (also called Xanthus), one of the two great rivers of Troy.

Alexander Pope, in his poetic epic about Brutus, and later the pseudo-historian E.O. Gordon too, could not resist bringing him to the ancient monuments of the Marlborough Downs. Unlike Geoffrey, they both followed Holinshed by envisaging Britain being already peopled by an ancient people who welcomed the civilised southerner as their king. Gordon imagined Brutus attending the 'supreme Gorsedd' at Avebury' (see plate 34). Here, he was 'first "lifted" by the Elders to a stone sedd or seat according to a most ancient custom of the Kymry, and there crowned within the precincts of the stone circle, in the presence of a vast concourse assembled on the Earth-circle (a mile in circumference) that enclosed the Temples of the sun and moon.'

A route due north from Avebury would have brought Brutus to the infant Thames, which rises in a field south-east of Cirencester. Its banks are still narrow at Cricklade, and lined with willows, and below their overhanging branches Brutus was once imagined walking. After Geoffrey's time, once Oxford and Cambridge had become university towns, generations of scholars argued over which had been founded first. Cambridge's dons claimed their university had been founded in 375 BC by a son of Cantaber, a mythical king of Spain, who filled it with philosophers and astronomers from Athens. The medieval *Oxford Historiola* struck back with one of the 'extraneous oddments', as the antiquarian Sir Thomas Kendrick put it, 'that in the course of the Middle Ages stuck themselves like burrs upon the accommodating body of [Geoffrey's] *History*.' For it claimed that Brutus's entourage had included a group of philosophers from Athens. When they reached the Thames, Brutus encouraged them to settle there, in a place they called Greeklade, later corrupted into Cricklade. Later, these philosophers decamped and travelled 25 miles east along the Thames, to settle at Oxford. This idea was revived and adapted by the Reverend R.W. Morgan, who claimed that it was Brutus's great-grandson Membricius who transferred 'the College erected by Dares Phrygius from Cirencester to the present site of Oxford'.

Brutus had 'formed a design of building a city, and in order to it, travelled through the land to find out a convenient situation'. His foundation of 'faire Lincolne' is mentioned in the *Faerie Queene*, though Spenser probably invented this detail simply to amuse his friend Thomas Cowper, who was Lincoln's bishop. This was not the city Brutus had in mind. For eventually, 'coming to the river Thames, he walks along the shore' until the valley broadened out, and the river became a wide and unfordable expanse of grey water. Where the river Fleet flowed into the Thames and three low hills rose up, Cornhill, Tower Hill and Ludgate Hill, Brutus stopped. This was the place that he resolved, in Spenser's words, to make 'the compasse of his kingdomes seat'. And Brutus calls his city *Troiam Nouam*, 'New Troy', which Geoffrey says became corrupted into Trinovantum. It is the city we now call London.

That Brutus had founded the City of London was one of Geoffrey's most compelling inventions. It was widely believed throughout the Middle Ages, to the extent that writers sometimes called London Trinovantum as late as the Stuart period. In his poem *In Honour of the City of London*, for instance, William Dunbar (fl. 1474–1515) wrote:

> *Gladdith anon, thou lusty Troy novaunt,*
> *Citie that some tyme cleped* [called] *was New Troy;*
> *In all the erth, imperiall as thou stant,*
> *Pryncesse of townes, of pleasure and of joy,*
>
> ...
>
> *Most myghty carbuncle of vertue and valour;*
> *Strong Troy in vigour and in strenuytie* ...

The success of Geoffrey's idea stems from a partial truth, for the Iron Age people who lived in Essex, and who probably controlled the land north of the Thames before the Catuvellauni seized it in the century before Caesar, were the Trinovantes. Orosius called them *Trinobantum firmissima ciuitas*, 'the strong tribe of the Trinovantes', which the Venerable Bede misinterpreted as 'the strong city of the Trinovantes' and from this Geoffrey developed the idea of London having been the new Troy. How the Trinovantes gained their name, we simply do not know – but it is most unlikely to have had anything to do with Troy.

In 1973, Beryl Platts made a charming attempt to hijack the myth for her beloved Greenwich, which is 4 miles downstream from the City of London and once quite separate from its outward suburban sprawl. Greenwich's name is conventionally derived from the Saxon *grene wic*, 'green ford', but Platts found early references to it as Gronewic or Gronavic, and these, she argued, could be corruptions, via 'Tronavic', of Trinovantum. Her theory could only be true if Brutus had ever existed, which we know he didn't, but perhaps the original name of Greenwich had its roots in the name of the Trinovant tribe, even though they had lived on the other side of the river.

Within the myth, once Trinovantum had been founded on the northern bank of the Thames, Brutus's work as an *oikistes*, the founder of a city, was done. All that was left for him was to rule his realm from Trinovantum, watching the sons borne to him by Ignoge grow up, whilst the Britons, the descendants of the people of Troy, cultivated and expanded their fields across the green hills of Albion.

The name of Brutus's wife Ignoge is sometimes rendered Innogen. Although Geoffrey said she was Greek, he may have taken her name from the Gaelic *inghean*, 'maiden'. Shakespeare reused the name for a character in *Cymbeline*, and either he or the printer changed it to, or perhaps simply mis-spelled it as, Imogen. That is how the name Imogen came to be.

Three sons were born from the marriage of Brutus and Ignoge: Locrinus, Albanactus and Camber. Their names are eponyms for the lands that Geoffrey says they received. Albanactus's name is from Albany, the name the Scots coined for their northern realm towards the end of the Dark Ages, derived from the whole island's ancient name, Albion. Camber was named for Wales, which the Welsh called Cambria or Cymru (a name actually derived from the British *cymri*, 'compatriots'). And Locrinus received Loegria, the name the Welsh gave to England (a name probably derived from the Greek *leukos*, 'white', after its white cliffs).

From these three brother-kings, particularly Locrinus, descended the ancient mythological kings of Britain. Unlike the old Welsh pedigrees on which he based the rest of his *History*, Geoffrey provides an unbroken genealogy down for only eleven generations below Locrinus. These kings included Bladud, who founded Bath (see plate 33) and Leir, later to be immortalised by Shakespeare. After this line, Geoffrey's genealogy is broken several times when it is not stated clearly how a new king was related to his predecessors, and at times it degenerates into a mere list of names with no relationships stated at all. But the implication of Geoffrey's narrative is clear enough: one way or another, all the later British kings were descended from Brutus.

Their mythological, genealogical inheritance was impressive. Through Brutus's mother they had for their ancestors the kings of Latium, whom some said were of the blood of Hercules. Through Brutus's wife Ignoge they had Pandrasus, who was probably a descendant of Achilles. Through Brutus's descent from Aeneas's father Anchises, they had the kings of Troy and Zeus as their forebears. And Aeneas's mother was the lovely Aphrodite, the most radiant progenitor of all. It was a potent collection of imaginary ancestors, who were handed down, ultimately, to Arthur and all the British monarchs who have followed since.

Part III

The Afterlife of Brutus

Chapter 16

A Mythology for the Middle Ages

On 16 February 1152, about seventeen years after he had completed his *History*, Geoffrey of Monmouth was ordained a priest at Westminster. Eight days after that, across the Thames at Lambeth Palace, he was consecrated Bishop of St Asaph in Flintshire, in north-eastern Wales. But war in Wales between the English and Owain Gwynedd probably prevented him from ever going there. His death in 1154/5 is mentioned in the *Brut y Tywysogyon*, a Welsh copy of his own magisterial *History*.

Some say Geoffrey died at Llandaff, near Cardiff, while saying mass, but as Michael Curley showed, this last piece of information about a man who claimed to have been the mere translator of an ancient book seems likely to have arisen, ironically, from a mistranslation. In truth, we know no more about Geoffrey's demise than we do about his birth.

Backed by its royal patron Robert of Gloucester, Geoffrey's *History* gained widespread attention and popularity amongst Britain's small number of literate readers, and the many more who enjoyed listening to its tall tales of adventure and intrigue. Besides the fifty Welsh translations of his work, called *Bruts*, there are some 207 copies of the *History* surviving in Latin. The story they contained enshrined Brutus and the Trojans as the dominant theme in England and Wales's ancient history throughout the Middle Ages.

Geoffrey's *History* and its Welsh translations continued a story that started with the fall of Troy, as related in Homer's *Iliad*. But very few people in medieval Europe could understand Greek, and Homer's lengthy works were not at all well known then. Instead, therefore, readers turned to the pseudo histories of the Trojan War by Dictys and Dares whose prose style, as observed above, had probably been the model for Geoffrey's. Copies of both Dictys and Dares are often found attached to manuscripts of Geoffrey's *History*, providing an easily readable backstory for Brutus's adventures and rooting them firmly in the high deeds of the siege of Troy.

The Middle Ages was an era of credulity. If something appeared in writing and was not condemned outright by the Church, it tended to be accepted by most as canonical. Geoffrey's *History* was set to endure until the Middle

Ages themselves ground to a close. How many people understood it to be a creative combination of history, older myths and lively imagination, we do not know. Most people, busy with the more pressing concerns of daily life, seem to have accepted it credulously, and perhaps even believed themselves to be the descendants of Trojans.

'Italian-born Turk leads Albanian asylum seekers to Britain' is how a modern British newspaper might report the arrival of Brutus. But in the Middle Ages, Brutus's story was used quite differently, as Robert of Gloucester had intended, as a charter for the English kings to extend their rule right across Britain. When Edward I wanted to justify war with the Scots, he reminded them that Brutus had given England to his eldest son, Locrinus, and Scotland to his second son, Albanactus, making Scotland junior to England. Further, Geoffrey's *History* also related how Arthur had enforced this English superiority by defeating the king of Scotland and appointing a new monarch there in his stead. Such claims remained excuses for English interference in Scotland throughout the Middle Ages.

This in turn goaded the Scots kings into fabricating their own chronicles. To outdo the antiquity of Brutus, the Scots chroniclers took the parallel histories of the Pictish and Gaelic kings of Scotland, and laid them end to end – just as the Welsh and the Latin historians had done before them with their own national histories – to create an impressively long pedigree for their nation. One such early chronicle, the *Duan Albanach*, began with the Gaelic version of the Frankish Table of Nations, which made 'Albanus' (Scotland) and 'Britus' (the Britons) brothers. From this, they contrived the story that Albanus took control of 'Alba' (by which they meant either Scotland or the whole of Britain) and drove his *younger* brother Britus away across 'the Sea of Icht' (either the Firth of Forth or, more likely, the English Channel), thus making the Scots king the senior monarch in the British Isles.

The Welsh, too, played the English at their own propaganda game by using the Brutus myth to seek alliances with the Scots. Faced with English aggression, Owain Glendower (d. c. 1415), a descendant of Merfyn Frych, wrote to Robert II of Scotland, that:

> Brutus, your most noble ancestor and mine was the first crowned king who dwelt in this realm of England, which of old times was called Great Britain. ... Brutus begat three sons, to wit Albanact, Locrine and Camber. From which same Albanact you are descended in direct line. And the issue of the same Camber reigned royally down to Cadwallader, who was the

last crowned king of my people, and from whom I, your simple cousin, am descended in direct line …

Thus, the different nations within Britain used Brutus as they pleased, to support their own points of view, and thus kept him relevant to political life throughout the Middle Ages. And it was as Trojans that they all went together, with their French cousins too, on their Crusades to try to capture and keep hold of the Holy Land. As they reminded the Saracens, they were descendants of the men of Troy, returning to the region of the world from which they were sprung. And when in the process they sacked the Greek city of Constantinople in 1204, they reminded the Greeks of this too. There was no point complaining about the damage, they sneered, as they slurped vintage wines from the emperor's cellars: this is merely just revenge for what you Greeks did to our ancestors' city of Troy in the first place.

Meanwhile, back in England, Geoffrey's story proliferated. Following Henry of Huntingdon, English chronicles, from Alfred of Beverley's 1154 *Historia* to Layamon's *Brut* (c. 1200) and John Hardyng's *Chronicle* (c. 1437), based their early British history on Geoffrey. Each embellished, so allowed the stories to grow, always trying not to contradict one another.

In his survey of feudal manuals of English history, Thomas Wright printed six medieval accounts of England's history. Here, interestingly, the first two, both in French, say nothing of the island's early past but start with England's Saxon kings. But the third prefaces the story of the Saxon kings with a brief account of the island, mentioning that Britain was so called after '*un home ke aveint à nun Brutus, ke primes habita en Engleterre, après ke les geanz furent morz*' ('a man who was called Brutus, who first inhabited England after he had killed the giants'). The fourth, in Latin, starts with a rather full history of the fabulous period, founded on Geoffrey's story (which Wright omitted from his reprint). The fifth, in Latin, starts 'with a small illumination of Adam engaged with a spade digging in his garden' and comes down via Noah to Brutus and thence down to Arthur. The sixth, *Chronicles between England and Scotland sithen the commyng of Brute*, in the British Library and supposed to date from Henry VII's time, begins: 'The noble and mighty man Brute, which descended of the noble blod of Troye, with many of the same blod, arrived in this land, that tyme called Albyon, inhabited with geauntes, whom by his mighty powair slewe and overcome, and called this land Bretayne, after his awne name … .' So it is no surprise to find Geoffrey Chaucer (c. 1340–1400), in the *Complaint to his Empty Purse*, praising Henry IV as the 'conqueror of Brutes' Albion'.

Like moss and lichen gathering on the standing stones of Britain, the Trojan myth became a solid base on which many other myths and legends could become fixed. The people of medieval England, Wales, Cornwall and even Lowland Scotland used the myth as the vocabulary by which they explained their connections to their own soil. Thanks to Geoffrey's writing, they had come to see their land through Trojan eyes.

Geoffrey's story may also have stimulated a renewed interest in the Trojan myth as a whole. Jersey-born Wace's verse *Roman de Brut* (c. 1155) retold Geoffrey's *History* in verse. Then, in about 1160, about a quarter of a century after Geoffrey's *History* was written, there appeared both the *Roman d'Eneas* and Benoît de Sainte-Marie's *Roman de Troie*, romance poems retelling parts of a story that could now be seen as the prologue to the epic of Brutus. These were written in French as courtly romances to amuse the court of Henry II and his powerful wife Eleanor of Aquitaine. The *Roman d'Eneas* focuses on Aeneas's relationships with Dido and Lavinia. The *Aeneid* ends before Brutus's great-grandparents Aeneas and Lavinia meet, but in this version their relationship is explored in detail: they fall in love at once, but Lavinia is anxious to make sure she means more to Aeneas than his earlier, doomed lover Dido, whilst for Aeneas, Lavinia's love is his great inspiration for winning the war against Turnus. The story suited its time, for just as Lavinia brought Aeneas the dowry of Latium, so too had Eleanor brought Henry her great estates in France. The *Roman de Troie* focuses on a made-up love affair between Troilus, who features often in Dares's account of the Trojan War, and Briseis (Cressida), who is also being wooed by Diomedes. Both these stories filled the courtly lovers of twelfth-century England and France with memories of Troy, and enforced the blossoming conceit that their blood was nobly Trojan.

In Geoffrey's *History*, Brutus found Britain populated by giants, but where they had come from was a mystery. Sometime between 1250 and 1334 appeared the poem known as *Dez Grantz Geanz*, written in Norman French, which was also attached to some copies of Geoffrey's *History* as a prologue. Once Brutus had defeated the giants, his curiosity overcame him and, says the poet, he spared Gogmagog's life so that he could tell his story, and Brutus had this recorded for recounting at high feasts. The resulting story drew on two main sources: first, the Greek story of King Danaus of Greece, whose daughters murdered the men they had been forced to marry; and *1 Enoch* 6–7, which tells of male angels breeding with human girls, who gave birth to giants 300 cubits high, who sank into depravity and ate each other.

Thus, Gogmagog claimed that his ancestor had been a powerful king of Greece who had thirty daughters. They are given husbands, but all but one of them decides they do not want to be subject to any man except their father, so they plan to murder their new spouses. The king hears of these plans and is horrified. He banishes the twenty-nine would-be murderesses in a ship without oars or food and a terrible storm drives them to the uninhabited island that is now Britain.

The eldest daughter, Albine, leaps ashore and claims feudal rights to the island, naming it Albion after herself (Geoffrey never mentioned Britain's earlier name, but Wace did and that was probably our poet's source). Even though Albine was Greek, the poet's idea for a primal female power ruling Britain may have come from his knowledge of Britannia, who originated in the native British goddess Bride. The land is as fertile as Geoffrey had described it and the ravenous sisters gorge themselves on abundant fruits and creatures that they snare using cunning traps, and they grow enormously fat as a result. This Eden lacks men, but there are demons there called *incubi* and from their lustful couplings with the bloated sisters are born babies who grow into giants. These giants then have intercourse with their own obese mothers to produce a second generation of even more monstrous beings.

For 260 years, says the poem, these 20-foot high giants rule Albion from the hill forts that can still be seen across the land, but they are so proud and violent that none of them are willing to be subject to each other, so they fight constant wars until only twenty-four remain – they whom Brutus then defeats. Although the poet did not say so explicitly, this turns Brutus's arrival in Britain into another revenge for the Trojan War, as the giants whom the Trojans defeated were of course descendants of a king of the Greeks.

Through Geoffrey's *History*, medieval England learned not just about Brutus but also about his descendant, Arthur. By Geoffrey's time, Arthur had already absorbed the legends of many real or semi-mythical kings and heroes who had gone before him, from Bran the Blessed to Vortimer. Geoffrey's Arthur was a fairly brutal conqueror, who rampaged across Britain and Europe, slaughtering all in his path. In the late 1300s, *Sir Gawain and the Green Knight*, a poem about the exploits of knights at Camelot, opens with 'After the battle and the attack were over at Troy ...' and continues twelve lines later to tell us how 'fortunate' Brutus came 'joyfully' over the 'French sea' to found Britain 'by ample down and bay', after which his descendants became a rough-and-tumble lot who relished a good fight 'and made much mischief in troubled times.' The poem ends by reminding the reader that it was set in the time of Arthur, who ruled the land that Brutus had founded in the aftermath of the Trojan War.

It was under the pen of Sir Thomas
Malory (d. 1471) that Arthur gained
the nobler persona of Aeneas, and
Camelot came ever more to resemble the
archetypal city of Troy. But it was not a
one-way process, for by founding London
and becoming so closely associated
with the land, Brutus was gaining a
British, Arthurian depth. Eventually, the
brooding spirit of the old gods of Britain
were subsumed by Brutus, who became
the mysterious *genius loci* or 'native spirit'
of the island, and of the ancient ruins
lying beneath London's busy thoroughfares.

King Arthur defeating a giant, as imagined
in a medieval manuscript at Douai.

Through Brutus's descent from Aeneas, Virgil's *Aeneid* became part of
Britain's family history. The brightly painted coats of arms of the Middle Ages
were inspired by Virgilian precedents. The essential heraldic principal of sons
inheriting their fathers' coat of arms owed much to Virgil's mention, in book
seven of the *Aeneid*, of Hercules's Italian son Aventinus, who 'on his shield bore
his father's cognizance – the hundred snakes of the serpent-cinctured Hydra.'
When the Welsh princes and the English kings chose lions for their shields,
they were probably thinking back to the stern of Aeneas's ship, which Virgil, in
book ten of the *Aeneid*, said was carved with two lions. We know for sure that
Aeneas was depicted as a knight with a lion on his shield in a Prussian heraldic
manuscript of about 1200. When the English heralds attributed arms to Brutus,
they gave him either three crowns, for the three kingdoms of Britain (England,
Wales and Scotland) that he ruled, or else this same, Virgilian lion. Throughout
the Middle Ages heraldry reinforced the connection: the English kings bore
lions on their arms, as Britain's monarchs have continued to do to this day,
proclaiming them to be heirs of Brutus, the great-grandson of Aeneas.

The medieval kings (and the medieval myths of Arthur) owed the concept of
chivalry, too, to the Trojans. The tortuous Roman horseback games of the *Ludes
Troiae*, the 'Troy Game', which Virgil re-imagined, in book five of the *Aeneid*,
as having been initiated by Aeneas on the shore below Mount Eryx in Sicily,
became the blueprint for medieval tournaments. When we watch re-enactments
of medieval tournaments, we imagine what life would have been like in medieval
England. But within their shining helmets, the medieval knights were probably
imagining themselves as the boys of Troy, playing the Troy Game for the first

time on the beach in Sicily. We think of such knights as quintessentially Anglo-Norman: but they imagined themselves to be thoroughgoing Trojans.

When printed books were introduced to Britain by William Caxton in the late 1400s, the first title, chosen to reflect the appetites of potential readers, was his own translation of Raoul Lefevre's *Recuyell of the Historyes of Troye*, a medieval retelling of the siege and fall of Troy. Amongst the other books that Caxton typeset for his English readership was a translated *Brut* (the Welsh version of Geoffrey's story) and Sir Thomas Malory's *Morte d'Arthur*. Geoffrey's *History* itself was first printed in 1508, and even though it was in Latin it still allowed a new and expanding generation of educated readers to devour the British extension of the Trojan myth, as told by its most notable teller.

Just as Geoffrey's words were reaching more British readers than ever before, a strange new mythology was creeping in from the Continent. Joannis Annius (c. 1432–1502) of Viterbo, Italy, had the ever-inquiring mind of a true genealogist. Like the ancient Greek genealogist Hesiod before him, he saw a mass of contradictory stories about his people's origins, which he wanted to sort out. In Annius's case, there was a great mesh of material to digest concerning the extended family of Noah, into which had been woven the wanderings of the Trojans and of

Aeneas bearing a lion on his shield, from Staatsbibliothek Preussicher Kultirbesitz in Berlin (ms germ. Fol. 282 sheet LIIIr).

Brutus, depicted alongside the foundation of London in Godet's *Chronicle* (1562). He bears a lion on his shield and his flag shows the same lion quartered with three crowns.

Hercules, and a hotchpotch collection of Greek, Mesopotamian and Egyptian gods, all euhemerised or imagined to have been ancient kings. Faced with this multi-headed jumble, Annius went back to scratch and concocted a new origin myth for Europe, which he attributed, following Geoffrey's unfortunate example, to two 'lost books'. One, he claimed, had been written by Manetho in Egypt about 200 BC and the other by Berosus of Babylon, who was of even greater antiquity and authority – hence Annius's coming to be known as 'the false-Berosus'.

Annius's resulting *Antiquitatum Variarum* was an ingenious synthesis of biblical and Classical origin myths, with a bit of folklore thrown in for good measure. Noah is identical with Janus, and is the only good survivor of an otherwise evil race of giants. After the Flood, he starts repopulating the Earth from his home in Armenia. His son Nymbrotus is 'the first Saturn of Babylon', father of 'Jupiter Belus', whilst other human descendants of Noah include the likes of Osiris and Hercules.

Though primarily interested in his native Italy, Annius included some new mythology for France, creating the wise Samothes, alias Dis, a son of Noah, who rules the Celts. From Samothes descend a line of kings – Magus, Sarron, Dryius, Bardus, Longho, Bardus junior and Celtes, whose daughter sleeps with Hercules and has a son Galathes, the eponym of the Gauls. Galathes is ancestor of more kings down to Rhemus, who rules the Gauls at the time of the Trojan War, after which the Celts are ruled by Francus, son of the Trojan prince Hector. Besides providing Gaul with a list of post-Flood kings, this creative etiological system also showed how they had gained their bards and druids, from kings Bardus and Dryius.

Like so many earlier European myths, Annius's system ignored Britain. But as news of his ideas reached Britain, enquiring minds filled in the gaps. In 1489, John Bale, Bishop of Ossory, decided that Samothes and his successors must have ruled Britain as well as Gaul, and that Magus was surely founder of Noviomagus (Fishborne). The bards and druids are originally British, not French. Later, the long-lived Osiris, son of Noah's son Ham, comes to Britain to teach the inhabitants how to farm and brew. Osiris's son Neptune Heliconius becomes King of the Isles of the Sea, after which Britain is ruled by his son, the monstrous Albion Mareoticus. A terrible Iron Age ensues, during which Britain is ruled by Albion's gigantic descendants, until Brutus's arrival, five centuries later. Geoffrey had imagined Britain to have been uninhabited save for the giants themselves before Brutus came, but from now on those who embellished Brutus's story could imagine it already containing whatever peoples suited their purpose.

The giant Albion was a male manifestation of Albine, the giant anti-heroine of *Dez Grantz Geanz* and perhaps influenced by a local myth of Hercules slaying a giant called, coincidentally, Alebion, in the south of France, using a shower of rocks, as related by the geographer Pomponius Mela about AD 43. Albion went on to play an important part in British mythology, particularly in the imagination of William Blake. The rest of Annius's new mythology enjoyed considerable popularity, but only for a limited time. His stories appear interwoven into later editions of Hardyng's *Chronicle* and the popular chronicle of Raphael Holinshed (1577/86). The antiquarian Richard White of Basingstoke (1539–1611) even insisted that Annius's 'Hercules Libyus', son of Osiris, had visited Britain.

The result of all this was a grand summary of almost over a millennia and a half of British myth-making, penned by the anonymous author of *Eulogium Historiarum*, which described visits to Britain by Hercules, Odysseus, and of course Brutus:

> *Britona, hand-fast-maker shee,*
> *All clad in Laurell green,*
> *Plays on the harp what ever acts*
> *Our auncestours have seene.*
> *Shee sings how Britanny* [Britain] *from all*
> *The world devided was,*
> *When Nereus* [a Greek sea god] *with victorious Sea*
> *Through cloven rocks did passe,*
> *And why it was that Hercules,*
> *When he arrived heere*
> *Upon our coast, and tasted once*
> *The mudlesse Tamis cleere,*
> *Did Neptun's sonne hight* [called] *Albion*
> *Vanquish in bloudy fight,*
> *And with an haile-like storme of stones*
> *Kild him in field out right.*
> *And when Ulysses* [Odysseus] *hither came,*
> *What Altars sacred were* [built]
> *By him. How Bruite with Corinae*
> *His trusty friend and fere,*
> *Went foorth into the Western parts,*
> *And how that Caesar, he*
> *When he had fought and found, turn'd back*
> *With feare from Britan fierce.*

The poem was quoted in 1610 by the great British antiquarian William Camden in his great survey of British antiquity, *Britannia*, but by then something had changed. For Camden did not present this as a true account of British history: he commented merely that his readers 'may read or leave [the poem] unread at your pleasure.' The tide was turning against Brutus – but his career at the heart of British life was not over yet by any means.

Chapter 17

'One Happy Britannia Again'

amden's comment, 'which you may read or leave unread at your pleasure', indicates a step back from full credulity. It stems from the first serious onslaught on the Trojan myth, which had been made a century earlier by a leading Renaissance scholar, Polydore Vergil (c. 1470–1555).

Fuelled by the free-minded, trade-driven cities of northern Italy, the Renaissance was seen as a rebirth of Greco-Roman culture in western Europe. In such an atmosphere, Trojan Brutus ought to have flourished. But one aspect of the lost culture that seemed most desirable to the Italian merchants was the freedom to look, questioningly and critically, at everything.

By the 1400s, the Catholic Church had dominated European culture for well over a thousand years. It had accrued almost a millennium and a half's worth of written sermons, doctrines and papal orders to add to the complex teachings of the Bible itself. The sheer weight of words would have been daunting enough without the mass of contradictions they contained. Under the harsh light of independent thought ushered in by the Renaissance, its whole system seemed ever more ridiculous. Eventually, the Catholic Church was forced to reform itself, but not before protesting clerics, of whom the best known is Martin Luther (d. 1546), had broken away to form their own, Protestant denominations. And just as religious doctrine and practice was now open to question, so too were the myths that had become enshrined at the heart of European self-consciousness. Polydore Vergil held the myths of Britain steadily in his gaze, saw straight past their majesty and beauty, and concerned himself solely with one simple question: were they true?

A 'silly fiction' is how he dismissed Brutus. The Trojan hero was not mentioned in Roman histories, nor in Gildas. And how come, he asked, was Europe supposed to have been well populated by Brutus's time, yet Britain was deserted save for a handful of obviously made-up giants? 'What manner of men initially inhabited Britain, whether they were native or colonists, is quite unknown,' he wrote boldly. He concluded that the ancestors of the British had probably arrived long before the time of the Trojan War – soon after the Flood, most likely, and had remained there quietly ever since. It was a truth, he added, 'which does not diminish, weaken or obscure, the praise and glory of the Britons, but greatly increases, confirms and ennobles it.' But for all Polydore Vergil's salving of the wound, it is no surprise that his *Anglica Historia*, though finished about 1513, was not published until 1534, from the safety of Switzerland.

In the meantime, and perhaps inspired by knowledge of Polydore's work, the Scotsman John Major launched his own attack on the Brutus myth in his *Historia Maioris Britanniae* (1521). This, and Polydore's work, inspired later, bolder attacks on Brutus and the Trojan myth, but it also prompted some valiant defences. In 1544, John Bale accused Polydore of 'polutynge oure Englyshe chronycles most shamefullye with his Romishe lyes.' Dr Dee, the personal astrologer of Elizabeth I, wrote that 'if God will [allow], at an other apter time and in more apt place, marvellous agreement of the histories of Antiquity ... [then] great unlooked for light and credit will be restored to the Originalls of Brutus.' But ultimately, Brutus's defenders, unable to appeal to hard evidence, could only emulate the Church Fathers by claiming the dubious authority of precedent: such a great number of eminent chroniclers and historians had repeated the story of Brutus, they pleaded, that it must be true. Such an argument was produced as late as 1675 by Sir Winston Churchill (c. 1620–1688), ancestor of the great prime minister of the same name. We only doubt Brutus now, claimed Churchill, because he lived so long ago – but beware: in later days, people might think we are made up too:

> *Some doubt of Troy, others think Brute's a Fable,*
> *Cause that Age did, what this has not been able,*
> *Succeeding Times, if they allow our Story,*
> *Will yet as much Demur upon our Glory.*

Churchill's seventeenth-century arguments had little effect, but back in sixteenth-century England help was at hand for Brutus's myth – from genealogy.

Had Alexander the Great not believed himself to be descended from Achilles, the greatest hero of the Trojan War, and used that belief as the basis for his own quest for glory, it is perfectly possible that Homer's story may eventually have faded slowly out of Western consciousness. Instead, Alexander's heroic deeds catapulted the Trojan myth back into mainstream thought. His young cousin Pyrrhus of Epiros used the Trojan myth as a metaphor for his own war with Rome, casting himself as Achilles and the Romans as Trojans. When the Romans won, they embraced their newfound origins with enthusiasm, and thus started the new myth-making process that identified their ancestors with the survivors of Troy. Again, though, that myth may have died away, had not the family of Julius Caesar found new use for it when they claimed Aeneas as their ancestor – so that, once Caesar's family had gained the Imperial throne, the Trojan myth again found itself in the ascendant. As always, such heady times could not last, but just when the myth was nearly moribund again, first Theoderic found a new use for it in Italy, followed by the Merovingians in France and Merfyn Frych in Wales. The Normans could have dispelled the Trojan myth for good, but it happened to suit them to believe that each of the races in Britain, including themselves, had Trojan origins. Each time the Trojan myth seemed set to die away, therefore, a new ruler emerged who had a use for it.

Back in 1230, Ralph de Mortimer, the powerful Anglo–Norman feudal lord of a great swathe of the border marches between England and Wales, married Gwladus Ddu, daughter of Llewelyn the Great (d. 1240), King of Gwynedd. Llewelyn was a male-line descendant of Merfyn Frych, whose semi-fictitious pedigree ran back to Beli Mawr and Brutus. The later Mortimers were extremely proud of the Trojan ancestry they had gained through Gwladus, not least because of the connection it gave them to Arthur. They showed this off by holding Round Table tournaments and drawing up elaborate pedigrees, such as the Wigmore Manuscript, showing off their descent from Brutus, the first monarch of the whole of Britain. The potent appeal of the Mortimers' Trojan blood, both in England and Wales, began to worry the English kings. It was perhaps in reaction to their posturing that Edward I set up a Round Table of his own at Nevin, Caernarvonshire. He also proclaimed his son Prince of Wales, partly to emphasise his growing hold on Wales, but mainly to counter the rival claims of the Mortimers. Later, Ralph and Gwladus's descendant Edmund Mortimer married Philippa, daughter and heiress of Lionel, the second son of Edward III, and in 1385, Parliament declared their son Roger Mortimer the heir to the English throne. Had Roger ever become king, England would likely have seen a great outpouring of Trojan symbolism around the throne. But he didn't, so there wasn't. But Troy had not long to wait, for in 1485 Henry Tudor won the Battle of Bosworth and became Henry VII of England and Wales.

Henry's father was the Welsh nobleman Edmund Tudor, Earl of Richmond, and his mother was Margaret Beaufort, of the royal blood of Edward III. It was her blood which provided his claim to the throne but, once he had seized power, Henry played on the idea – and may have genuinely believed – that divine providence had elevated him so high because he was a Welshman of the race of Arthur and Brutus. He sometimes quartered the royal arms with the made-up arms of both Brutus and Arthur, and he called his eldest son Arthur. The boy would have become Arthur II, but he died in 1502 (so instead Henry was succeeded in 1509 by his second son, Henry VIII). In his efforts to dominate the Scots, he reminded them, in John Elder's words, that Brutus had been 'superiour and kynge' of all Britain.

Henry VII also commissioned a group of Welsh genealogists, including John Lleiaf and the bard Gittin Owen, to find him a male-line bloodline back to Brutus. They could not: Henry VII's great-grandfather Meredith (Maredudd) ap ('son of') Tudor had been a servant, without any remembered pedigree. But doubtless fearful of the consequences of returning empty-handed, the commissioners concluded that Meredith's father Tudor must have been identical with Tudor Fychan ap Gronow (d. 1367), a Welsh nobleman, descended from Merfyn Frych and thus from Brutus, 'of which Brute', they concluded, and as Lewys Dwnn reported later, 'King Henry the Seventh is lineally descended by issue male, saving one woman [Cordelia, daughter of Leir], and is son to Brute in five score degrees.'

Henry's lengthy Welsh pedigree was false. But all the same, the long pedigrees that the Lleiaf-Owen commission brought back from Wales and displayed before the Tudor court were a major stimulant to England's fascination with genealogy, an interest that has continued unabated to the present day.

Ironically, Henry already had Trojan ancestry through his mother Margaret. Besides the marriage of Gwladus Ddu to Ralph de Mortimer (who were ancestors of Henry's wife and thus of his children), other daughters of Llewelyn the Great had married into other prominent families whose lands bordered Wales, and between them they brought the blood of the Welsh princes and all their mythical forebears down into many prominent English families – Cliffords, de Bohuns, Giffords, de Audeleys, Nevilles, Fitzalans and Holands, and Henry VII's Margaret had a line going back through her father's mother's paternal grandmother Joan, who was the daughter of Margaret Wake, whose grandfather Baldwin's wife Hawise was daughter of Robert de Quincy and his wife Helena, daughter of Llewelyn.

This potently mythological blood flowed further down the royal line leading to the present Royal Family and also into the aristocratic forebears of the late Queen Mother and Princess Diana. The Duchess of Cambridge, likewise, is descended from the marriage of Sir Thomas Fairfax to Anne Gascoigne, whose mother Lady Mary Percy was great-granddaughter of Elizabeth Mortimer, the wife of the famous 'Hotspur' and sister of that same Roger Mortimer who might have been king, with his impeccable line of descent back to Brutus. From this same matrix of the intermarriages of Llewelyn's descendants come the ancestors of Lord Byron and Lewis Carroll and millions of modern Britons from Richard Dawkins to David Cameron. Some of these descendants have traced their family trees back far enough to know this, and many more have not. Bloodlines also flowed into the families of some of the early, upper-class proprietors who helped colonise the New World. Countless American families, including those of most American presidents, from George Washington to Franklin Roosevelt and the Bushes, also have descents from Llewelyn the Great, and thus from Merfyn Frych, and so from the mythical family of Brutus.

The Tudors' particular fascination with Brutus's myth may have stimulated a copycat interest in France too. Stories of the French kings' Trojan origins, which went back to Fredegar and the *Liber Historiae Francorum*, were dusted off by the French poet Pierre de Ronsard, who published the first four books of his epic *La Franciade* in 1572. In Virgilian style, Ronsard told the story of Francion (Francus), whom he identified with Hector's son Astynax. Instead of being killed at the fall of Troy, Francion/Astynax makes it safely to Buthrotum. Here he lives a life of ease, just like Aeneas in Carthage, until Zeus sends Hermes down to goad him into fulfilling his destiny by founding a new Troy in the west, and shows him a parade of his royal descendants. The story was intended to come down to the time of Ronsard's patron, Charles IX of France, but it was never finished. Ronsard's attitude to the myth is revealing: he wrote in the preface that he did not care whether the story was true, or whether the French kings were really descended from Trojans or Arabs: as a poet he was concerned only with what was possible. For Charles IX, of course, what mattered was prestige. When sixteenth-century kings postured amongst themselves, it is clear that one of the things that really mattered was having a good pedigree, real or imaginary, going back to the Trojans.

Elizabeth I's coat of arms, quartering Brutus's lions and crowns, in Norden's *Hertfordshire* (1598).

'She heard that she was lineally extract … [from] noble Britons sprung from Troians bold, and Troynouant was built of old Troyes ashes cold.' Thus did Edmund Spenser praise both queen and

London in his grand Elizabethan epic, *The Faerie Queene* (1590/1596). The poem's heroine was Britomart, an allegory of his own sovereign Elizabeth I, the last Tudor granddaughter of Henry VII. The Trojan myth came to even greater prominence during Elizabeth's reign. Not only was she descended from Brutus through both her father's parents, but also Virgil, that great poet of Aeneas's life, had written (in his fourth *Eclogue*) that, when the Golden Age returned, Justice, who had fled into the Heavens at the dawn of the Iron Age and become the constellation Virgo, would return to the Earth. This meant Justice was a virgin, so Thomas Hughes's tragedy *The Misfortunes of Arthur*, which was performed before the virgin queen at Greenwich in 1588, praised Elizabeth herself as

> *That virtuous Virgo born for Britain's bliss*
> *That peerless branch of Brute: that sweet remain*
> *Of Priam's state: that hope of springing Troy*

Within Spenser's *Faerie Queene*, just as Arthur learns of his Trojan descent, so too does Britomart discover her own bloodline back to Brutus. In describing it Spenser was able to glorify the origins of Elizabeth herself, to 'boast thy glorious descent, and fetch from heaven thy great Genealogie.'

Like Ronsard, however, Spenser the man was not so credulous as Spenser the poet, for in his *Dialogue on the State of Ireland* we learn what Spenser really thought about Britain's mythology. It is 'impossible to prove,' he stated there, 'that there was ever any such Brutus of England.' But as a source of stories, the Trojan myth was now more in vogue than ever. In 1595, Christopher Marlow wrote *The Tragedy of Dido, Queen of Carthage*, about Brutus's great-grandfather Aeneas's fated love affair. In 1598 Philip Henslowe recorded in his diary staging a performance of Henry Chettle and John Day's otherwise unknown *The Conquest of Brute with the First Founding of Bath* at his Rose Theatre, and spending £1 4s 0d to buy 'divers things' to make the giants' coats. Meanwhile, at the rival Globe Theatre, Shakespeare drew freely on Geoffrey's stories, particularly in *King Lear* (c. 1603/7) and *Cymbeline* (1611), both of which are about kings who ruled Britain in the centuries after Brutus, and which successfully evoke the island's misty, mythological past. In *Cymbeline*, the king looks back to Dunwallo Molmutius (a descendant of Brutus) as 'the first [king] of Britain which did put his brows within a golden crown' (suggesting that the earlier ones had not worn crowns, though Geoffrey himself had written merely that Dunwallo had made a new crown of his own). Brutus himself is not mentioned and a certain indifference to the Trojan myth is inferred also from Pistol's famous line

1. The giants now called Gog and Magog lead the way in the 2014 Lord Mayor's Show, a vivid legacy of Brutus of Troy's myth in modern Britain.

2. One of the gateways to South Cadbury Iron Age hill fort, Somerset, the most likely site of Arthur's Camelot, whose myth drew on the archetypal citadel of Troy.

3. Adam and Eve being expelled from Eden (depicted in the Abbey of Fontevraud, France). In the biblical world view, they were the ancestors of everyone, so Brutus and Aeneas were of course descendants of theirs and became, in turn, part of the bridge that connected the British back to the parents of humanity.

4. Joseph of Arimathea at the tomb of his great-nephew Jesus (depicted in the Abbey of Saint-Volusien, Foix, France). The myth that Joseph settled in Britain was a precursor to the myth of Brutus: both served to connect Britain to the momentous events described in the Bible.

5. The ruins of Troy, home of Aeneas, the great-grandfather of Brutus. In Hildebrand Jacob's epic poem *Brutus the Trojan*, Brutus visited ruined Troy himself during his exile, before discovering that his destiny was to found Britain.

6. Aeneas carrying his father Anchises and leading Ascanius (the grandfather of Brutus) by the hand as they escape from burning Troy. This modern representation of the iconic scene is in the Via C. Battisti, Rome.

7. Odysseus (as imaged in this fine bust in Vathý, Ithaka), whose cunning brought about the fall of Troy and precipitated everything that followed. His adventures at sea, as related in Homer's *Odyssey*, were a partial inspiration for the voyage of Brutus.

8. and 9. Homer (on the waterfront at Vathý, Ithaka) and Virgil (below his tomb in Naples, Italy). Homer's *Iliad* introduced Aeneas as one of the heroes who fought in the siege of Troy and Virgil's *Aeneid* told how Aeneas escaped from burning Troy to found a new kingdom in Italy. It was upon their foundations that Brutus's own myth was built.

10. The Papal Palace at Castel Gandolfo, near Rome, at sunset. It is said to be built over the site of the palace of Ascanius, where Brutus was born. The real, ancient city of Alba Longa extended along the ridge beyond. This is part of the crater of an extinct volcano, in which lies the Alban Lake.

11. Boys learning to row on the Alban Lake near ancient Alba Longa. Within his myth, we may imagine the young Brutus learning to master oar and sail here too – skills that would set him in excellent stead for his journey to Britain.

12. Part of the ancient sanctuary of Diana in the woods above Lake Nemi, near Alba Longa, Italy. The woodland cult of Diana was integral to the ancient kings of Alba Longa and became inextricably entwined with the later myth of Brutus.

13. One of the gateways into the now ruined city of Buthrotum (Butrint), Albania. The city was said to have been founded by Helenus, a survivor of the fall of Troy. Virgil imagined Aeneas coming here and embracing 'the portals of a Scaean gate', which resembled the original one at Troy. Consequently, this gate's excavators named it 'the Scaean Gate'. By the time Brutus came here, the Trojans of Buthrotum had been enslaved. They were amongst those whom he freed and led to Britain.

14. The oracle oak at Dodona in north-western Greece, not far from Buthrotum, where Zeus foretold the future through the rustling of wind in the leaves. Aeneas visited this place (according to Dionysus of Halicarnassus), as did Brutus (in the imagination of Alexander Pope).

15. The ancient citadel of Trikastro in Epirus, Greece, is perched upon the left-hand slope and crest of this dramatic mountain, with the deep gorge of the Acheron plunging down to the right. This is the most likely, real, location of the mythical fortress in which Pandrasus, King of the Greeks, besieged Brutus's Trojans.

16. Part of the ancient walls of Trikastro, where we may best imagine the war between the Greeks and Brutus's Trojans being waged – and perhaps being damaged by rocks hurled up from King Pandrasus's siege catapults.

17. The author exploring the ruins of Nerikos, Lefkada, Greece. When Brutus came to Leogetia, as Geoffrey of Monmouth called Lefkada, he found just such ruins perched up on the hill.

18. Brutus on Diana's island, imagined in Fabyan's *Chronicle* (1516).

19. 'The School of Homer', Ithaka, Greece, widely believed locally to be Odysseus's palace, with Mycenaean walls and steps cut deep into the rock – steps on which Hildebrand Jacob's incarnation of Brutus would have trod.

20. The great altar of Apollo facing Mount Kynthos on the Greek sacred island of Delos, which Aeneas visited to seek guidance in the *Aeneid*, and which Brutus visited for the same reason in Nahum Tate's *Brutus of Alba*. Here, Apollo bade him hasten 'To Albion, Brutus!'

21. The fountain of Arethusa in Syracuse, Sicily. Aeneas visited this famous site in the *Aeneid*, and Brutus would have done too, during his disastrous sojourn in Syracuse in Nahum Tate's *Brutus of Alba*.

22. Segesta, Sicily, a great Classical site whose foundation was attributed in Greek mythology to Aeneas. In Hildebrand Jacob's epic, Brutus overwintered here with descendants of the Trojan colonists whom Aeneas had left behind here.

23. Hercules at sea (as depicted at La Coruña by Gonzalo Viana in 1994). In Greek mythology, Hercules carved out the Straits of Gibraltar. It was through these straits in the myths from Geoffrey of Monmouth onwards that Brutus and his Trojans sailed to leave the Mediterranean. And it was at Gibraltar too, in Alexander Pope's *Brutiad*, that Brutus was visited in his dreams and urged on his way by Hercules himself.

24. A siren, depicted on the foundation arch in Orange, France. The passage of Brutus's fleet through the Straits of Gibraltar almost ended in disaster when sirens like this tried to lure him and his men away to their deaths. One later followed Brutus to Devonshire too.

25. A modern statue of the mythical King Breoghan stands proudly in front of the Tower of Hercules in La Coruña on the north-west corner of Spain. It was from here that Breoghan's descendants are said to have set sail to populate Ireland, and this was probably (within the realm of myth) the point of departure for Brutus and Corineus on their combined journey to Britain.

26. A natural indent on this rock near the Tower of Hercules in La Coruña looks like a giant's footprint, and may have inspired a story of giants living here, which in turn helped the myth of Corineus to take shape.

27. The Roman walls of Tours, France. Nennius, followed by Geoffrey of Monmouth and others, imagined Brutus fortifying his camp here during his war with the Gauls, and thus inadvertently founding the city.

28. Part of the Butte de César, on the Plateau des Châtelliers above Amboise, France, a Bronze Age round barrow in the centre of a Turonian hill fort. This is the most likely location of Goffarius's base during his war against Brutus in Gaul.

29. The Brutus Stone, Totnes. According to local legend, this is the very stone onto which Brutus first stepped when he reached Britain.

30. *The landing of Brutus in England*, imagined by William Blake. Brutus kisses the land that had been promised to him by the gods, while Corineus, his augur Gero and their followers rejoice at their arrival. *Princeton University Library*

31. The Brutus Bridge, Totnes: an ugly modern bridge named, at the suggestion of local people, after their most picturesque of local legends. *Nilfanion/Wikimedia Commons*

32. Haytor, Dartmoor, a natural rock stack of volcanic origin but of the sort that folklore often attributes to giants. In Geoffrey of Monmouth, the giants came down to attack Brutus and his people at Totnes: in C.D.'s Victorian epic, Brutus only glimpsed one up here in the wilds.

33. Bladud, one of the kings whom Geoffrey of Monmouth said were descended from Brutus, depicted in the Parade Gardens, Bath, Somerset – the city Bladud is said to have founded.

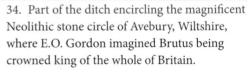

34. Part of the ditch encircling the magnificent Neolithic stone circle of Avebury, Wiltshire, where E.O. Gordon imagined Brutus being crowned king of the whole of Britain.

35. The great Neolithic mound of Silbury Hill, near Avebury, Wiltshire, was already almost a millennia and a half old by Brutus's time. This must be the 'altar of turf, in an open place' where Alexander Pope imagined Brutus assuming the kingship of Britain.

36. Inspired by their Classical educations and stories of Brutus building Troy in the Thames Valley, generations of Englishmen created their own Arcadias in England: this is Sir Francis Dashwood's eighteenth-century temple to Brutus's great-great-grandmother Aphrodite at West Wycombe, Buckinghamshire.

37. Druids celebrating the spring solstice on Tower Hill, London, with the Tower of London behind them. They follow in a tradition established by Iolo Morganwg in the eighteenth century, and into which Brutus was grafted by Reverend Richard Williams Morgan in the nineteenth century.

38. The Titan Albion, the embodiment of Brutus's island of Britain, as imagined by William Blake.

39. The Long Man of Wilmington stands 231 feet tall on Windover Hill, Sussex, and dates back for sure to the 1600s, although he could be vastly more ancient. He is akin to the now lost, colossal figures of Gogmagog and Corineus in Plymouth and on the Gogmagog Hills, Cambridgeshire, and shows how they may once have looked.

40. Looking east up Ludgate Hill towards St Paul's Cathedral, which nineteenth-century myths made into the site of Brutus's stone circle temple dedicated to Apollo.

41. The London Stone lives within this elaborate encasement, opposite London's Cannon Street Station. Nineteenth-century myth asserts that it is a relic of Brutus's foundation of London as the New Troy.

42. Guildhall, London, which is believed to stand on the site of Brutus's original palace in New Troy.

43. Gog, in London's Guildhall. Magog stands nearby. In eighteenth-century myth, they were brought here in chains to serve as porters for Brutus's palace.

44. The White Tower of the Tower of London, below which Brutus is believed to have been buried.

45. King Lud, flanked by his sons Androgeus and Tasciovanus, depicted in stone in the porch of St Dunstan-in-the-West, London. Geoffrey of Monmouth claimed that Lud was a descendant of Brutus and rebuilt Brutus's city of New Troy, renaming it London, after himself.

spoken to a Welshman in *Henry V* (c. 1599), 'base Trojan thou shalt die!' But it is possible that, earlier, Shakespeare had recognised and used the dramatic potential of Brutus. *The Lamentable Tragedy of Locrine* was published in 1595 under the initials 'W.S.' and was included in the first (1685) 'complete works' of William Shakespeare. It was only later that Alexander Pope and Dr Johnson both rejected it from their collections of Shakespeare plays on the grounds of its inferior writing, and some scholars now attribute it to Edmund Spenser. But it was signed, nonetheless, 'W.S.'.

Whoever wrote it, the play retells the career of Brutus's son Locrinus, but it starts with the last days of Brutus himself in London (Trinovantum). Having had a prophetic dream about his own death, Brutus summons his family together. He gives Wales to his son Camber, 'darling of thy mother'. Scotland is bestowed upon Albanactus, 'thy father's joy', and to his eldest son Locrinus, Brutus gives England, and the overlordship of the whole of Britain, and into his hand he places the hand of Gwendolen, the flame-haired daughter of old Corineus. Brutus dies, and the rest of the play is about the complete mess that Locrinus made of his marriage when he had an affair with Estrildis, a mistake that leads to civil war and death.

For Britain in 1595, civil war lay in the future, too. But first, came unification – or, if you believed the Brutus myth, *re*unification.

'England, Wales, and Scotland, by the first Brute severed and divided, is in our second Brute reunited, and made one happy Britannia again.' So wrote Anthony Munday.

Through the thronging streets of London, below the overhanging upper storeys of the box-framed houses, a procession slowly weaves its way, its participants clad in the bright costumes of pageantry. Here is the Lord Mayor of London in his ermine robes. There are the constables of the City in their gleaming helms. Lurching above them all are the two gilded statues of Corineus and Gogmagog, dusted off from their home in the City's Guildhall. But on this occasion, all eyes are drawn to the sight of four richly clad actors, with crowns glinting on their heads. Three younger men portray Locrinus, Albanactus and Camber, the first kings of England, Scotland and Wales respectively. And in their midst stands an older, bearded man, bearing an ancient sword: it is Brutus himself, returned to life to bestow his blessing on the new king's reign.

It is 1605. Two years earlier Elizabeth I died childless, and her English throne was inherited by her cousin James VI, King of Scots, now James I of England, whose great-grandmother Margaret was Henry VII's daughter. His own grand entry into London in 1603 took him below seven triumphal arches, loaded with Virgilian allusions. One depicted Henry VII watching James's arrival and voicing the words that Aeneas's father Anchises had uttered when he saw the shade of his future descendant Augustus in book six of the *Aeneid*: 'This is the man, this is he.' The two thrones of Britain remained technically separate, but now only one man, that diminutive, sallow-skinned Scotsman James, sat on both. The words of Merlin's prophecies, as translated in Geoffrey's *History*, rang in his ears: 'The Island shall be called by the Name of Brutus: And the Name given it by Foreigners shall be abolished.'

King James may not have believed in Brutus any more than Spenser or Shakespeare, but he was canny enough to use mythology to political advantage. So too were his subjects, including Anthony Munday, author of the 1605 Lord Mayor's pageant *The Triumphes of Re-United Britania*.

So also was the genealogist Thomas Lyte (d. 1638). By 1610, crowds of courtiers and hangers-on at Whitehall Palace stood agog before the huge pedigree he had drawn, over 6 by 8 feet in size and brightly illuminated in vivid reds, blues and gold. At its head were depicted James and his family. Up the centre of the chart rose the 'Imperial line' from the Normans. On the sides were James's other, illustrious descents – from the Saxons and their godly founder Odin, from the kings of the Scots, and from the Tudors and the Welsh kings, back to Brutus.

But the doubts and questions of the Renaissance, which had led not only to Polydore Vergil's questioning of Brutus's myth but also to the Protestant Reformation, now challenged the very principal of kingship itself. When the Civil War erupted in 1642 between James I's son Charles I and Parliament, Royalist propagandists pressed Brutus into service, arguing that he and his successors had founded and ruled the realm perfectly well without the need for democratic assemblies. But Chief Justice John Fortescue (1394–1480) had written that 'the Kingdom of Britain had its original from Brutus and the Trojans who attended him from Italy and Greece, and were a mixed Government compounded of the regal and democratic'. And the eminent judge Sir Edward Coke (1552–1634), sometime Chief Justice of the King's Bench and a leading opponent of the concept of the king's divine right to do whatever he wished, wrote, in the preface to volume six of his immensely influential *Reports* on English law, that 'the Original Laws of this land were composed of such elements as Brutus first selected from the Ancient Greek and Trojan Institutions', and by 'Ancient Greek' he had Classical democracy firmly in mind. Following this, John Sadler could argue coherently in his *The Rights of the Kingdom* (1649) that, because the kings of Troy were believed to have ruled in conjunction with councils of princes, nobles and elders (an idea taken from the Trojan pseudo-history of Dictys), so it behoved their successors in Britain to do likewise.

Charles I disagreed: he fought and lost the Civil War and was executed by Parliament in 1649. But his son Charles II was restored to the throne in 1660, and in 1665, he had his Stuart dynasty added to an old roll chronicle similar to Lyte's, which had been created originally for Henry VI in about 1450, and which included Brutus amongst the royal family's illustrious ancestors. But that seems to mark the end of Brutus being used in state-sanctioned propaganda.

Polydore Vergil's scepticism had cleared away all serious beliefs in Brutus as a genuine historical figure. When Charles II and his courtiers looked back into the past for glorious precedent and inspiration, their gaze fell not on Brutus, the founder of the decaying, rat-infested London of their youth, but upon the Romans, whose genuine achievements they sought to emulate. The king's henchman Henry Jermyn, Earl of St Albans, built his new, Roman-style Classical square in St James's and Christopher Wren laid the foundation stones of the magnificent Roman pantheon of St Paul's Cathedral, both in order to rebuild Augustus's Rome, not Priam's Troy, on British soil.

In place of Trojan Brutus, they fixed on Britannia, the Roman goddess of the isle, who had been revived in Elizabeth I's time for obvious reasons of gender, but who now came into her own. Her new image was modelled on one of Charles II's

Britannia poses triumphantly in front of Oxford University in Anthony Wood's *Antiquitates Universitatis Oxoniensis* (1674).

lovers, Frances Stuart, depicted with the flowing hair and curvaceous breasts he so admired, bearing an olive branch, or clad in armour like Athena, brandishing a trident. And so she remains, on many fifty pence pieces still in circulation, the new embodiment of the essence of Britain, in place of Brutus.

The Trojan myth lingered on longer as a political reality in Absolutist France, where it remained an essential prop for the all-pervading power of the monarchy. As late as 1714, when Nicholas Fréret made a speech denying the historical reality of Francus, the nation's equivalent of Brutus, he found himself being thrown into the Bastille.

Yet the French monarchy's love affair with Troy had an unexpected side effect, for the Trojans' escape from Greek tyranny was engrained into the fabric of the myth. When the French Revolution came, the king's opponents asserted their ancient freedoms by donning Trojan or Phrygian 'Liberty' caps, which curl forward at the tip (and which are best known in modern culture as the headgear of the smurfs). These reminders of the Trojan myth that had for so long underpinned the French monarchy were probably the last things that Louis XVI saw in 1793, when the cheering crowd watched the guillotine sever off his head.

Chapter 18

'Remember Me!'

Brutus's myth may have dropped out of Britain's official political armory, but it still had an important part to play in national life. John Milton (1608–1674) grew up with Brutus's myth firmly in his consciousness. Aged seventeen, he wrote his poem *On the Fifth of November*, celebrating the thwarting of the Gunpowder Plot, in Virgilian style and heavy with Classical references. Just as Hera expostulates against the Trojans when she unleashes war in Latium in book seven of the *Aeneid*, so too does Milton place a tirade of hatred into Satan's mouth as he looks down on James I's prosperous Britons, 'the race of Albion sprung from ancient Trojan blood', who lived in 'peace, wealth and happiness', which he hoped to upset through Guy Fawkes's plot.

Much later, in 1670, Milton retold Geoffrey's *History* in his *History of Britain*, though with mature hindsight he expressed some doubts about its veracity. He had clearly read Nennius and thus thought it likely that Brutus had been 'devised to bring us from some noble ancestor', yet he was happy to repeat the story, 'certain or uncertain ... upon the credit of those' who had told the story before, 'as the due and proper subject of story'. He even contemplated writing an epic '*Brutiad*' to rival Virgil's *Aeneid*, but instead wrote *Paradise Lost*, which, although it owes much to Virgil, is rooted firmly in the Bible and not in the myth of Troy.

Eight years after Milton's *History* came out, Nahum Tate (better known for his carol *While Shepherds Watched their Flocks*) wrote a play called *Brutus of Alba: or the Enchanted Lovers*, which was performed at the Duke's Theatre in 1678. In the preface Tate explained that he had written the play originally about Dido and Aeneas, but he then changed the characters so as not to appear arrogant in trying to improve upon Virgil. The fact that he swapped Aeneas with his great-grandson Brutus (as opposed to someone completely different) indicates that he considered Brutus to be well enough known to attract audiences in his own right. But, whilst he could not improve upon Virgil, it is revealing that he felt free to take whatever liberties he wanted with Geoffrey.

Instead of the Trojan War, Brutus refers back to an 'Albian War' in Italy, which 'our Alban State o'rethrew' (no such war, of course, ever existed, in reality or myth). 'We'll sacrifice to the obliging Storm,' says Brutus, echoing Aeneas, 'that lodg'd us on this Hospitable Coast,' but here the coast is not that of Carthage, but Sicily, where no previous incarnation of Brutus had ever been before. The Trojans, it transpires, have landed at Syracuse (a place visited briefly by Aeneas), whose queen looks on Brutus just as Dido had on Aeneas, perceiving 'Fame, worthy of your noble Ancestors – There's magick in his Language, Looks and Meen!'

Tate had to do a little rewriting to give Brutus the backstory that his audience knew and expected. To the queen, Brutus explains his exile:

> *For when Youth's Down first flowr'd upon my Cheek*
> *(Whilst practising I'th Chase the stubborn Bow)*
> *I shot at Rovers, and by fatal chance*
> *My Royal Father slew ...*

Brutus then explains how, having gone to Greece and discovered the Trojans 'by Grecian Tyranny opprest', he defeated Pandrasus and was given 'Squadrons cull'd from the Eubean Fleet' – that is, illogically, from Euboea on the east coast of Greece – in which to set sail. Just as Aeneas had married and then lost Creusa, Brutus had a wife, 'my dear Eudemia [who] sickened – dyed': he does not call her Ignoge, but presumably this was she. Instead of going to Lefkada, Brutus does what Aeneas did and visits the island of Delos in the Cyclades (see plate 20), where Apollo's oracle bade him go 'To Albion, Brutus' (where presumably the original text had said 'To Italy, Aeneas').

Aeneas went from Delos to Carthage to meet Dido, so Brutus comes to Syracuse on the south-east coast of Sicily (see plate 21) and finds the queen being courted by the king of Agragas (Agrigento), which is a city on the southern coast of Sicily, west of Syracuse. Brutus's son Locrinus, 'the fruit of my first Love, Joy of Eudemia's Life', steps into Ascanius's role. Locrinus kills Hylax, son of a leading Syracusian nobleman, but the queen refuses to punish him because she has already fallen deeply in love with Brutus. 'Impetuous passion Storms at my Heart!' she confides to the audience, whilst Brutus admits that he had thought 'no glance Cou'd thaw me, but I melt before those Eyes'.

Brutus thought he had lost his old friend Assaracus at sea, but now he unexpectedly appears in Syracuse. Brutus is delighted, but as he fears, Assaracus disapproves of his love for the queen, reminding him – in a paean of praise for Britain:

Perish a Legion nobler Lives than mine,
E're Brutus be from th'Albian Isle diverted;
Your rich Loins holds an endless Race of Kings.
Fair Albion of their Reign th'Eternal Seat,
Albion, that in the Flouds erects her Cliffs
Sits Queen o'th' Seas, whilst the aw'd Nations round
At distance wait, and in their mutual Jarrs
From this great Arbitress take Law

'Ripe Glory waits us in proud Albion's Plains,' urges Assaracus, 'And withers whilst the season we neglect.' He accuses Brutus of being 'lull'd asleep in your false Circe's charms. In vain Fames Trumpet sounds you to the Field', for 'the blood of Heroes is sold too cheaply for a Woman's smiles.'

Inevitably, Brutus's patience wears thin. 'Are these then the surmizes of my Slaves whose vile Necks from the Grecian Yoke I freed?', he explodes: 'I'll condescend to Rule this Herd no more.' But then, Brutus changes tactic, telling Assaracus he is so hurt by his friend's attitude that he may as well stab him through the heart. So Assaracus docs just that – or very nearly. Plunging a dagger into his own heart, Assaracus exclaims, 'I'll strike … that Heart of yours that's in *my* Bosome lodg'd!' Then, as he dies, Assaracus seizes Brutus's hand and whispers, 'May't prove resistless as the Thunderer's [Zeus's]. Snatch Crowns from Europe's Monarchs, grasp their Sceptres, Knit in one Empire the divided World!' Thus, Tate succeeded in glorifying Britain's monarchy whilst also knitting the plots of Virgil and Geoffrey together quite well.

Assaracus's death has the desired effect of bringing Brutus to his senses. He feels himself restored to 'my pursuit of Arms, which he conjured me with expiring Breath To re-assume', and declares, 'We'll force our way from this enchanted Coast … Give notice to the Fleet we sail tonight … I forsake the Queen tonight!'

It's not you, it's me, he tells the heartbroken queen: 'Empire cou'd ne'r have drawn me from your Feet were I the sole Adventurer I'th' War, But thousands run the fortune of my Play.' The queen's dismay turns rapidly to anger, 'Rising in rage', as her stage direction states, she yells, 'Seek, search your Fairy Kingdom through the Floods; Trust the false winds as I have trusted thee, And perish by 'em as by thee *I* perish.' Brutus can but try to turn a deaf ear: 'If like the Rocks relentless I must stand', he says: 'Make me, indulgent Gods, as Deaf as they!' The queen tries to persuade Locrinus to take her side, but he explains that he is yearning for glory: 'Th'Inhabitants [of Britain] are all of monstrous Size, Like those huge Sons of Earth that storm'd the Heav'ns, I long t'engage a Foe above my reach, And dart my Rapier at a Giants Heart.'

Once the queen realises Brutus's departure is unavoidable, anger turns to a final tenderness. Brutus imagines himself lying disconsolate by the frozen streams of Britain, pining for his lost love, but she tells him:

> *You must my Brutus promise to part hence*
> *And live remov'd from your afflicted Queen,*
> *Yet promise to Live happy too, you must*
> *'Tis all I shall enjoin you for my sake*
> *In your Eternal Absence.*

'Kind, Cruel Queen Eternally farewell,' says Brutus as he leaves. And once he has gone, she stabs herself to death.

The play's success was limited, but a decade later Tate's original script, before it was adapted into a play about Brutus, re-emerged as the libretto for Henry Purcell's opera *Dido and Aeneas* (1688). In that guise it has become one of the best-known retellings of Aeneas's story, and includes the famous aria, sung by the dying Dido:

> *When I am laid, am laid in earth, may my wrongs create*
> *No trouble, no trouble in thy breast;*
> *Remember me, remember me, but ah! forget my fate.*
> *Remember me, but ah! forget my fate.*

They could have been words from the mouth of Brutus himself.

At the end of 1688, the year of *Dido and Aeneas*'s first performance, the late Charles II's absolutist younger brother James II was overthrown by Parliament and fled away into exile to be replaced, on a more constitutional basis, by William and Mary. But he was not the only victim of the rising power of Parliament over the monarchy. The Stuarts had used the Caesars, who had overthrown the Republic and ruled Rome as autocrats, as their role models. Virgil, whose *Aeneid* had so exalted the Caesars, had ridden high in favour, so perhaps it was not surprising that now, because the ascendant Whigs looked back to the Republic for inspiration, Virgil, and all he stood for, fell out of fashion. Earlier, George Chapman (c. 1559–1634), the first translator of Homer from Greek to English, had anticipated this when he wrote that 'Homer's poems were writ from a free fury, absolute and full of soul, [but] Virgil's [were written] out of a courtly, labourious, and altogether imitatory spirit.' So in the 1700s, the Romantics held up Homer as the great, free-spirited genius, whereas Virgil's poems were 'fit to praise tyrants, and gull fools' as the anonymous *Plain Truth, or Downright Dunstable* put it in 1740. It was not until 1963 that Adam Parry put forward his 'two voices' theory, that although Virgil paid lip service to Augustus's Imperial vision, his close observation of all the misery and suffering caused by royal Aeneas's arrival in Italy shows that he had, in his heart, been a supporter of the Republic after all. But in the 1700s, the negative view of Virgil necessarily reflected upon Brutus, and was another major reason why he remained out of the political spotlight.

But Brutus was still an important link in the chain connecting Britain, emotionally, with Homer's Troy. In 1703, *The New History of the Trojan Wars and Troy's Destruction in Four Books, to which is added The Siege of Troy, a tragicomedy, as has been often acted with great applause* was published in London. This anonymous work is generally attributed to Elkanah Settle (1648–1724). The son of a Dunstable innkeeper, Settle was a king's scholar at Westminster School and started a degree at Oxford, which he did not complete. He became a commercially successful playwright in London, closely connected with the court, entertaining all classes with plays and semi-operatic works such as *The Empress of Morocco;* the *Conquest of China* and *The Virgin Prophetess, or, The Fate of Troy* (1701), about Priam's daughter Cassandra's role in the siege of Troy, which included a scene in which Helen flings herself into the burning ruins of Troy from the top of a tower. A play called *The Siege of Troy* was an adaptation of this and was performed, apparently 'with great applause', at the Bartholomew Fair in 1707 and at Southwark Fair in 1715 and 1716. If Settle was indeed the author of *The New History*, it would be no surprise, for like many of his other works, though based on scholarly material, its aims were simply to entertain his readers and make money for himself. Where he considered original material to be dull, he left it out. When he felt he could improve on the original story, he did so without embarrassment.

In many ways it was a work of genius. Settle perceived the thread running through the Greek myths to Aeneas, Brutus and modern London and penned a short work in four parts retelling the story for modern readers – not university scholars but normal courtiers, and also merchants and city tradesmen and their wives and children, both in London and elsewhere. He framed his stories as an attempt to bring out the 'true history' that had been hidden behind the clouds of fabulous myth and 'to revive antiquity out of the dust, and give those that shall peruse this elaborate work, a true knowledge of what passed in ancient times, so that they may be able readily to discourse of things that had been obliterated from the memories of most people.' Whether he really believed that a true story lay beneath the myths is uncertain: probably, he made this claim simply to make the work more exciting. In his introduction he laid stress on the connection between the Greek stories and London, promising to tell of 'how BRUTE King of the Trojans, arrived in this island of Britain; and conquered Albion and his giants, building a new Troy where London now stands; in Memory of which, the effigies of the two giants in Guildhall were set up'.

Book one retells the story of 'the most renowned and victorious' Hercules, son of Jupiter (Zeus), who is presented as a great king in Greece who only later came to be worshipped as if he were a god. Hercules is imagined more as a medieval than a Classical hero: 'in the tilts and tournaments on that occasion he bore the prize and victory, none being able to stand against him, except Jason.' Much stress is laid on Hercules's visits to Troy, which he eventually destroyed (as the genuine Greek myths relate) in revenge for King Laomedon's refusal to pay a debt. Book two picks up the story of Troy itself, and includes the aftermath of Hercules's revenge:

> The Trojans upon the departure of the Greeks, came drooping, like mournful bees about their burnt hive, and being somewhat encouraged by Priamus, now their king, they resolved to rebuild their city, more strong and large than before ... adorned with many stately palaces of the King and of his beauteous Queen Hecuba ... and of the Princess and nobles, which lifted up their gilded turrets in the air, in an aspiring manner, and peace continuing for a long time, riches increased in abundance.

Then comes the siege of Troy. Book two ends with the death of Hector and book three concerns the death of Achilles and the story of the wooden horse, ending with a free translation of Lucan's poem:

> *Sack'd Troy's yet honour'd name he goes about,*
> *To find the old walls of great Apollo out.*
> *Now the fruitless trees, old oaks with putrified*
> *And rotten roots, the Trojans ruins hide ...*

Book four concerns the aftermath, first the fates of the Trojans – Polixenia who was sacrificed on Achilles' tomb; Polydorus's murder in Thrace and Hecuba's transformation into a howling dog, all drawn from book thirteen of Ovid's

Metamorphoses, and Andromache's captivity in Greece and subsequent marriage to Helenus (which led to the founding of Buthrotum). Then come the stories that the Greeks called *nostoi*, the fates of the returning Greek kings, including a brief summary of the travels of Odysseus. Following this comes 'an account of the foundation of the Roman Empire and the arrival of Brute in Great Britain, who founded another glorious Monarchy in this island; as if it were decreed by fate, that Troy should never be totally lost, or rather, that it was not destroyed but transplanted only, to the happier European climates.'

First comes a summary of Aeneas's story, based in Virgil's *Aeneid*. There is a memorable description of Aeneas seeing Mount Etna on Sicily: 'he was much surprised to see it belch out so terribly sulphurous flames, and globes of fire; as it continues to do this very day to the terror and astonishment of the spectators; sometimes throwing out vast quantities, and streams of fire and brimstone, like flaming rivers, which imperiously beat down and destroy all before them where they pass.' Dido is glossed over in a short paragraph and quickly we have the war in Latium and Aeneas's victory over Turnus. Settle follows the genealogy given by Virgil, which is not the same as Geoffrey's, whereby Silvius was not the son of Ascanius, but his half-brother, the son of Aeneas and Lavinia. We learn that 'the Julian family who founded the empire, boasted themselves to be of the race of the gods, because it was fabled, Aeneas was the son of Venus, the daughter of Jupiter' and thus Caesar 'made his boast, declaring that a goddess was the source of his blood.' Then we hear the well-known myth that Aeneas's cousin Antenor had escaped from Troy to settle in Padua.

We then discover, with some surprise, that having reigned for seven years, Antenor died, 'leaving many sons; amongst whom Brute or Brutus, the youngest, was most active and warlike, who being dissatisfied with the part allotted him, raised war, and struggled long with various success, to make himself a sole monarch but at last, the united forces of his brothers prevailing against him, he assembled what forces he could, and seizing what ships were in the harbour, bid adieu to Italy.' This is an astonishing departure, indicating a complete disregard for all previous versions of the myth by Settle himself, and which he presumably expected his readers to share. He is known to have been extremely anti-Catholic, so perhaps he sought to distance Britain's origins from Catholic Rome.

Deviation from the original does not end there. In a couple of lines (and omitting the oracle on Lefkada, and Corineus), Brutus hears from the Gauls about 'a pleasant Island in the northern seas, which the Greeks had named the fortunate Island'. Gaining some 'auxiliary aids' from the Gauls 'he resolved to attempt it; and with a fair gale arrived on the coast of the country, now called Hampshire, where seizing on the Isle of Wight, he resided there some time to get the intelligence of the strength of the people who inhabited Britain,' and then makes landfall at Southampton.

Settle reverts to a very loose retelling of Geoffrey's myth by explaining that Britain was ruled by giants, but he incorporated the sixteenth-century ideas of John Bale (based in Annius of Viterbo) by claiming that it also had a human population, 'the relicks of the Symothes [Samothes], whom Albion and his giants had driven thither when he overcame the island'. And now great Albion, hearing of Brutus's arrival, 'raised his whole power being men of gigantick stature, and vast strength, and bearing for their arms huge clubs of knotty oak, battle-axes, whirlbats of iron, and globes full of spikes, fastened to a long pole by a chain.' The result is a massacre in which many of the Trojans are slain, and the rest retreat.

Brutus now employs cunning, waiting until nightfall and digging 'a very long and deep trench, at the bottom impeiling it with sharp stakes, and covering it with boughs and rotten hurdels, on which he caused dry leaves and earth'. The ditch helps explain why Settle had shifted Brutus's landing from Totnes to Southampton, for he probably had in mind one of the ancient ditches or dykes in the area: Grim's Dyke, a lengthy ancient earthwork on the Dorset-Hampshire border (which includes Bokerley Dyke near Woodyates), about 33 miles west of Southampton; the Devil's Ditch near Cholderton, which is about 40 miles north of Southampton, or the Devil's Ditch, which runs 6 miles west from West Stoke east to Boxgrove Common, which is about 30 miles east of Southampton.

The next day the Trojans provoke the giants into chasing them, and sure enough most of them tumble into the ditch and perish, 'and the Trojans continuing to shoot their arrows very thick, the giants were put to flight, and pursued into Cornwall, where, in another bloody fight, Albion was slain by Brute, fighting hand to hand, and his two brothers Gog and Magog, giants of huge stature, were taken prisoners.'

The captured Gog and Magog are taken 'in triumph to the place where London now stands', where Brutus builds Troy-Novant or New Troy, 'and building a Palace where Guild-Hall stands, causes the two Giants to be chained to the gate of it, as porters. In memory of which it is held that their effigies, after their death, were set up as they now appear in Guild-Hall.' Settle had invented so much that these details were probably from his imagination too: he can have had no idea in 1703 how deeply they would become embedded into London's mythology.

Brutus's descendants, Settle concludes, ruled Britain until Caesar came, and Brutus's descendant King Lud (see plate 45) rebuilt Trinovantum and renamed it Caer-Lud, or Lud's town, after himself, and 'enlarged it westward, to the stone that now is to be seen in Cannon-street' (see plate 41). And thus, rather abruptly, Settle's history, which started with Hercules in ancient Greece, ends with the London Stone.

The story was only loosely based on its sources, chiefly Homer, Virgil and Geoffrey, though Settle did not name them, and took huge liberties with what they said. But Settle's genius was to weave these together into a short and, for its time, very readable narrative, a series of tales of derring-do that thrilled readers all the more by being framed as a prehistory for London itself. Its success can best be measured by its reprints, in 1723, 1728, 1735, 1751, 1791, 1800, 1845 and 1850. It was a major factor in keeping an interest in Brutus alive far into the nineteenth century. Settle's peculiar version of Brutus's story had relatively little impact: no later writer followed the idea of his being Antenor's son or of his fighting Albion in Hampshire. But his impact on London's mythological landscape was enormous and endures to this very day.

Chapter 19

Return to Troy

'A banish'd wandering Man ... ' is how Hildebrad Jacob began his summary of the poetic themes of Brutus's story, in the introduction to *Brutus the Trojan, Founder of the British Empire: an Epic Poem* (1735): 'being inform'd by an Oracle of the Place destin'd for his Settlement [he] sets out with his Followers in Pursuit of it, finds many Adventures, and Difficulties in his Way; but, at length, overcomes those Obstacles, and establishes himself in it.'

The legacy of Nahum Tate's *Brutus of Alba* and Settle's *The New History of the Trojan Wars* was to remind those still interested in Brutus how intimately his story was bound up with that of his great-grandfather Aeneas. Though interest in Geoffrey's *History* declined and Virgil's

Hildebrand Jacob, author of *Brutus the Trojan*.

reputation was under attack, the *Aeneid* remained a staple of upper class boys' educations. For Brutus to survive, he needed to follow Tate's model and become more Aeneas-like. This, together with Milton's idea of basing an epic poem around Brutus's story, was the inspiration for Hildebrand Jacob's work.

Hildebrand Jacob (1692/3–1739) was the third son of Sir John Jacob, 3rd baronet of Bromley-by-Bow, Middlesex. Jacob's father enrolled young Hildebrand as an ensign in his regiment at the tender age of two. We know almost nothing of his army career except that he was keen, according to a letter he wrote to Lord Allington in 1710, to go to Portugal with the British Army during the War of Spanish Succession. He probably went, because his descriptions of Mediterranean and Atlantic voyages and storms at sea suggest personal experience.

Though Jacob was more than happy brandishing a sword, he was happier still when wielding a pen. After his marriage he settled at West Wratting, Cambridgeshire, and devoted himself to writing plays including *The Fatal Conspiracy*, a comedy that was performed at Drury Lane and repeated twice by command of the Princess of Wales, and essays including *How the Mind is Rais'd to the Sublime*, which was published in the same year as *Brutus the Trojan*.

Jacob's introduction to *Brutus* reveals exactly how the British viewed Brutus at the time: he was mentioned by all historians, Jacob wrote, and 'the very Disputes concerning the Truth, or Falshood of his Story, make it, perhaps, of as much Authority as that of Aeneas … for it seems to be yet no better decided, whether there ever was such a King in Italy as Aeneas, than whether Brutus ever reign'd in Britain.' Everybody, in other words, knew the story might be false, but nobody knew this for sure. Brutus made the fittest possible subject in British history for an epic poem because he was the most remote: so little was known about him, said Jacob, that all manner of poetic license was possible. But unlike Settle, Jacob was careful to spell out the difference between orthodox myth and personal imagination, summarising Brutus's story, as given by Geoffrey, and referring his readers to him for fuller details. All details not found in Geoffrey, he was careful to explain, 'are purely invented.'

Jacob's great achievement was to do what Geoffrey had omitted to do when he wrote Brutus's story almost exactly 600 years earlier – to root the story of Brutus firmly back into the world of the *Aeneid*. Though descended from Aeneas, and guided by Diana, Geoffrey's Brutus occupies a different literary world, based in pedestrian prose rather than the high-flown poetry with which Virgil had described Aeneas's adventures. That was because Geoffrey's mindset was rooted firmly in the Bible, but Jacob was a child of the Enlightenment. To him, Christianity was merely a peripheral fuzz around a radiant core populated by the magnificent heroes and high-flown language of the Classics. Suddenly, golden light bursts through the dark clouds of the medieval Christian mind and, through Jacob's imagination, we find ourselves gazing – as Virgil had once gazed – on the dazzling Mediterranean of the Age of Heroes. Here is Brutus restored to something he had never really been, but which he ought to have been all along – a Virgilian hero.

The *Aeneid* starts 'Arms I sing, and the man', so Jacob opened with:

> *I sing the Founder of the British Throne,*
> *Renowned Brutus, of the Race of Troy.*
> *Say, Muse! what Toils he bore, e're he attain'd*
> *To fix the lasting Seat of Albion's Kings.*

Everyone reading this at the time would have realised straightaway that this was a poem in the style of Virgil. Homer used Ilion as a byname for Troy, so Virgil did the same, and by doing so himself Jacob again declared his intention to write a continuation of their narrative. Similarly, because Virgil copied Homer in calling the Trojans Dardanians, Jacob was careful to do likewise. Just as Homer and Virgil often referred to characters only by their patronymics, calling Hector, for example, simply 'the son of Priam', so Jacob calls Brutus 'the Son of Silvius' (and thus the great-grandson of Aeneas). In these ways Jacob reminded his readers constantly that, in British terms, Brutus and thus the British were heirs to all the rich Trojan heritage that had gone before.

The *Aeneid* begins with a storm at sea, raised by Juno (Hera) and calmed by Jove (Zeus) at the behest of the hero's mother Venus (Aphrodite), after which Aeneas meets Dido, to whom he tells the backstory of his escape from Troy and subsequent wanderings. So, in similar vein, Jacob's epic starts with Brutus's fleet already under sail, but driven and dispersed 'Long Time by adverse Winds from Shoar to Shoar'. Diana intervenes for Brutus with Jove, protesting that 'Brutus alone … of all the race of Troy now wanders on the angry Deep, The Sport of Winds, and Waves', and is thus detained from reaching 'the happy Isle, Long by the Fates design'd him'.

Neither Juno nor Neptune (Poseidon) bears any grudge towards the Trojans anymore. But having sacrificed to almost all the gods, Brutus has neglected Aeolus, god of the winds, and it is he who is causing the storm. But Jove now commands Aeolus to calm the seas so that Brutus's fleet can land safely on the Tyrrhenian coast, where they meet Corineus, leader of those Trojans who had followed Antenor there.

It is one of Geoffrey's rare geographical slips to say that Brutus and Corineus met on the Tyrrhenian coast – which is the western coast of Italy – when he had already described Brutus sailing through the Straits of Gibraltar, on the way to Gaul. It is clear that they met on the Spanish coast, but it suited Jacob to take Geoffrey more literally, and so his meeting between the two great chieftains takes place on the Tyrrhenian coast of Italy.

They agree to join forces under Brutus's leadership for, as Corineus says, 'The Fates, our holy Prophecies declare, Have destined thee to build (but far from hence) Another Troy, an everlasting Seat.' They raise a hundred altars to Diana and Jove to seal their alliance and settle down to rest for the night: 'their watchful Fires Pierce the wide Womb of Darkness.' The following day, at Brutus's orders, they begin to repair their ships:

> *Part seek the Woods, and with repeated Blows*
> *Level the lofty Fir, or knotted Oak,*
> *While with new Noise the hollow Vale resounds,*
> *And frightened Dryads from the Haunts retire.*

Once the work is done, Corineus asks Brutus, 'favour'd of the Gods, chose[n] out From all the sons of Troy, Troy's Sons to free From Grecian Bondage', to tell his story, just as Dido had asked Aeneas to do in the *Aeneid*.

Later in the poem, we have a glimpse of Brutus's boyhood, when Diana (Artemis) tells Hermes (Mercury):

> *On Alba* [Longa's] *Hills, e'er Phoebus* [Apollo] *he provok'd,*
> *Oft with the Dawn I met him in the Chase;*
> *Oft, till the Night's Return the foaming Boar,*
> *Or nimble Hind we drove along the Plains.*

Now, Brutus tells Corineus how he brought his fate upon himself by boasting that his skills in archery were equal to Apollo's. Such brags were often the cause of misfortunes in Classical mythology, and Apollo punished Brutus's hubris by causing Brutus's arrow, though aimed at a stag, to plunge into his 'much lov'd Parent's Breast'.

Brutus recalls that he was 'Sever'd, divided, torn in blooming Youth From the lov'd branch, where flourishing I grew'. But his companion Mempricius hastens to reassure him that 'monarchs are born Less for themselves, than those they're doom'd to rule. Had Silvius thy Sire, been yet alive, Hadst thou not fled, a guiltless Parricide' then his followers would still be slaves in Greece.

We now have the backstory, as recounted by Brutus to Corineus. Exiled from Latium, he wanders far and wide through Italy, driven by the Furies (who had a particular mandate to hound those who killed their parents), until he comes to Pallenteum, which is the Palatine Hill in Rome (so not very far, actually, from where he had started). In the *Aeneid*, Evander had ruled there. Now, his elderly son Nicostron is king. Remembering the old alliance between his family and Aeneas's, Nicostron agrees to help Brutus purge away his dreadful crime of patricide by sacrificing a black ewe to the Furies. Then, he bids Brutus leave 'and be seen no longer in my Realms!'

Tearfully, Brutus takes his leave of Italy. He roams through Illyria and Thrace (i.e. the lands north-west and north-east of Greece) until his steps take him – marvellously – to Troy itself. Here, Jacob evokes the wonderful image of

Brutus poking about the ruins of his ancestral city, once the scene of fierce conflict, but now inhabited only by a handful of peasants who 'tame Flocks in Peace, and sing the Tale of Troy and Helen to their rural Pipes … Some few Tombs, Sole Testimonies of past Deeds remain'd: The Plough had equall'd all.'

Guided by the gods, Brutus comes to Greece and finds countless Trojans living in miserable slavery. His heart bleeds to see them 'Scourg'd, and insulted by their haughty Lords'. 'Fir'd by their Groans, I whispered Comfort to each wretched Man, And nobler Thoughts of Liberty inspir'd.'

The Scaean Gate, Troy, ruined now as when Brutus revisited his ancestral city in the imagination of Hildebrand Jacob (and see also plate 5).

Then, on a 'well concerted Day', the Trojans all across Greece 'bravely at once Cast off their Bonds' and escape into the woods, where they elect Brutus their leader.

They assemble their forces by the 'shady Banks' of a river. Instead of the Acheron on the west coast of Greece, as in Geoffrey's *History*, Jacob opted for the river Peneus, which tumbles down from Mount Olympus into the sea on Greece's eastern coast. He was probably thinking here of Alexander the Great, who had also assembled his great army, destined to conquer the Persian Empire, at the foot of Olympos (though the precise spot was different, for Alexander's muster was a few miles further north of the Peneus at Dion, by the river Baphyras).

The war is dealt with in a few lines: the Greeks close in with 'Their Whips, and rattling Chains', but, says Brutus, 'Our Armies Shock: Th'Assertors of fair Liberty succeed.' The Greek 'herd' disperses quickly, each formerly haughty lord now fleeing back home, collectively offering the Trojans 400 ships with arms, provisions and gold if they will go away. Pandrasus gives his daughter 'fair Ignoge' to Brutus, 'a blooming Bride, the Price of Liberty'.

Through the next one and a half books of the poem, Jacob sends the Trojans on a journey around the Mediterranean that takes in the handful of places visited by Geoffrey's Brutus, and also many of those visited by Aeneas, on his journey from Troy to Italy as related by Virgil, and even some of those reached by Odysseus, as described in Homer's *Odyssey*.

First, Brutus and his fleet pass Crete (like Aeneas, who landed there), seeing Crete's Mount Ida 'ever crown'd with Snow'. Then they sail up the west coast of 'hated Greece', passing the island of Zakynthos, as Aeneas had done, but are then struck by a storm. 'We err, uncertain, on the angry Deep' until they are swept onto the African coast not far from Carthage. They begin to build a new Troy, complete with a temple to Diana, but the locals are not well disposed to Trojans, because it was out of grief over Aeneas's departure that Queen Dido of Carthage had committed suicide. Thus, 'The Coast around Glitters with threat'ning Foes.'

The alarm at being beset by enemies, combined with her terrible ennui at leaving Greece, is too much for Ignoge, who dies. This is an abrupt departure from Geoffrey's narrative, but by killing her off Jacob makes Brutus more Virgilian: like Aeneas, he loses a woman whom he loves on the African shore, and like Aeneas, too, he is free to take another wife when he eventually reaches his goal (but Jacob's epic is unfinished, so we never find out who this new wife will be).

They raise a tomb to Ignoge on the Carthaginian shore, and depart:

> *The Rowers lash the Main: The Land behind*
> *Seems to retire in Haste, and soon our Eyes*
> *Vast, liquid Plains caerulean behold,*
> *Curl'd by the gentle Breath of Auster mild.*
> *Our Sails lightly inspir'd, an even Course*
> *All Day we held, and now the spangled Sky*
> *Smil'd on us, and each Star propitious shone,*
> *While sweet Melorus to his tuneful Lyre*
> *In many a Phrygian Strain divinely sang*
> *Old Tales of Troy, and Priam's golden Reign.*

Caerulean blue is exactly the colour of the Mediterranean under the summer sun. Auster is the deity of the south wind. Melorus is a made-up companion of Brutus's, whose name comes from the Greek for honey, *melos*. Phrigia is an Homeric name for Troy.

At dawn the Trojans sight the island of Leogecia. Geoffrey's Leogecia was definitely Lefkada, off the north-western coast of Greece, but Jacob thought it was Lampedosa or one of its tiny neighbours, between Sicily and Tunisia.

This was in Carthaginian territory and had been wasted by pirates. Forty young Trojans go ashore to hunt. They come back with mountain deer, reporting no sight of humans except for some smoke rising from an ancient temple of Diana that they had found 'in a Vale remote, amidst high Groves'.

Brutus decides to visit this temple himself, 'With Pray'r, and Off'rings ... our Fate to learn, And in what Realm to fix our Household Gods.' Jacob follows Geoffrey closely now, describing the rites that Brutus performed, his prayer to Diana and her prophetic reply. Jacob's translation of the prayer to Diana differs from others when, instead of asking bluntly where the Trojans were to live, he enquires, 'where our Household Gods may rest secure', which is the way Virgil's Aeneas would have put it. In Diana's reply, her reference to Britain being inhabited by giants is omitted. Her prophecy ends:

> *Victorious Monarchs from thy Line shall spring,*
> *And o'er the boundless Ocean spread their Sway.*

They set sail again, but Jove sends a storm that rages for four days and sweeps them back to the African coast, to Syrtes (near the Philenian Altars, which Geoffrey's Brutus had visited straight after Lefkada). Here they are attacked by a Carthaginian fleet that 'with brazen Beaks Drive on the latent Sands our lighter Ships.' The Trojans manage to sink three of the enemy vessels, and then escape under cover of night ('A safe Retreat to Conquest is allied', Brutus comments sagely).

They come next to the land of the lotus eaters, which Jacob makes an island near the African coast called Menynx (and which Ernle Bradford thought was Djerba, an island off the coast of Lybia). Odysseus's men found the lotuses there so delicious that they had wanted to remain there, thus jeopardising their mission to return to Ithaka, so Brutus is careful not to eat any himself: two Trojans succumbed, so were presumably left behind. I have eaten lotus roots and seeds myself, in Vietnam and Laos, and whilst they were very pleasant, they didn't make me want to remain there forever, but maybe Homer had had in mind a different sort of plant, such as the *cordia myxa*, as Bradford suggested, a sort of crab apple used in those parts to make a particularly intoxicating type of cider.

They nearly make it to Sicily, where Brutus wanted to make sacrifices at the tomb of his great-great-grandfather Anchises, who was buried there, but again they have trouble with the weather. Zephyr the West Wind blows them far off course again as far as Ithaka, which is off the western coast of Greece, just north of Zakynthos. It is a small island, lying long and thin along the north-eastern side of Kefalonia, with pale, limestone cliffs and low, domed mountains, which in those days were still densely covered with pines, looming above a series of marvellously deep, dark blue sounds, where ships could moor safely.

In Homer's *Odyssey*, Ithaka was the home of Odysseus and his son Telemachus, so the king there now, imagined by Jacob, was Laertes, son of Telemachus's son Arcesius (both names borrowed from the Homeric ancestry of Odysseus). Though Odysseus had been the arch-enemy of Troy, Diana opens his great-grandson's heart to the Trojans' plight, filling him with admiration for their plucky defiance of the Greek leaders on the mainland. After Brutus has told his tale, Laertes talks at length of Odysseus's deeds at Troy, and of his 'late Return ... And tedious Toils; of fair Penelope [Odysseus's wife], Her Web, her Suitors, and her kind Delays' (all as related in the *Odyssey*). He even takes Brutus on a tour of the island's Homeric sights and helps him repair the fleet:

> *Woody Zacynthos gave her solid Oaks,*
> *And Ithaca with Mountain Fir supplies*

They overwinter in Laertes's palace on Ithaka (see plate 19). Several sites lay claim to being Odysseus's palace, the most plausible being the ruins among the olive groves north of Stavros now signposted 'The School of Homer'. Here are ruins of Mycenaean walls, gateways and even dark red floors, and steps cut into the rocky hillside that may once have connected different levels of Odysseus's palace. The site commands views of the harbour bays on either side, just as Homer described it.

Their stay is marred when Brutus's nephew Turonus has a boxing match with another guest, Aretes, a descendant of the Phaecian king (from Corfu) who had helped Odysseus return home safely. The boys used armoured gloves called *caesti*, and when Turonus strikes Aretes with his, it accidentally kills him. Laertes is furious, but seeing Turonus's genuine grief he forgives him.

When spring comes, Brutus presents Laertes with the very sword that Aeneas had used to kill Turnus at the end of the *Aeneid*, and Laertes in turn gives Brutus the Trojan shield that wise Nestor had given Telemachus in the *Odyssey*, 'And Ithaca with grateful Minds we leave.' When darkness comes the wind drops:

> *And on our Masts the useless Canvas fell.*
> *All now was hush'd, and calm: our Vessels move,*
> *Born by a silent Current, nor prevail'd*

> *The Rowers Labour, or Philastron's Skill.*
> *On the smooth Tide we sail, we know not where,*
> *Nor by what secret Pow'r. At length, surpriz'd,*
> *With sweet inchanting Notes our Ears are charm'd*
> *Of warbling Birds, and straight the Dawn reveals*
> *Each vernal Beauty to our wond'ring Eyes,*
> *The flow'ry Valley, and the swelling Stream;*
> *While all the Fragrance of the new-born Year*
> *Salutes the ravish'd Sense. A pleasing Port,*
> *Secure from ev'ry Tempest that might rise,*
> *Our Navy, by this hidden force impuls'd,*
> *Unguided meets: Its verdant Banks are crown'd*
> *With fair, and blooming Nymphs …*

Like Brutus, we start in the real world and finish on an enchanted island and, like him, we are not quite sure how we got there.

Chapter 20

'To Raise the Lasting Throne of Albion'

Hildebrand Jacob had borrowed Brutus's latest adventure from the *Odyssey*, for the Trojans had reached the mythical island of Ogygia, which Bradford thought was Malta, where the sea nymph Calypso wanted to keep Odysseus captive for ever, but he escaped after seven years. She wanted to keep Brutus there for ever too, but pretended otherwise, addressing him, 'Dardanian Chief … renowned Brute, Sprung from Aeneas, and decreed by Fate To build amidst the Waves a lasting Throne.' Had she had her way, he would never have reached Britain at all.

She bids him and his men rest 'awhile' on her island and, lured by the nymphs, the men flock out of their ships. Brutus follows, 'sad, Like some fond Shepherd, who beholds from far His helpless Flock in the Invader's Hands.' He asks Calypso why she is hindering their journey. 'Blest Son of Silvius,' she replies, claiming to know Diana's will, and his fate: they may leave, she lies, whenever they choose. But this is a trick: 'Sunk in fond Delights, The Trojans sleep.' In stark contrast to the love-struck Brutus of Nahum Tate's story, who was more than happy to linger in Syracuse, Jacob's Brutus remains focused on his mission and steadfastly refuses Calypso's offers of 'Immortality and Love'. Yet his prayers to Diana seem in vain as 'The Summer wasts, and now autumnal Leaves With Fruits of vary'd Colour stain the Ground.' Diana isn't listening anymore, taunts Calypso, 'or else withdraws Her mighty Aid,' or is busy hunting, or else is 'haply, 'midst the Gods, Unmindful of the Earth, and human Fate'.

But then, one day Calypso takes Brutus on a hunt, surrounded by warlike nymphs, all across her island and on into the night. Suddenly Diana appears in the form of a dryad. 'Save a burning Fleet!' she cries. In his absence, she has caused some of the younger Trojans to start burning their ships. Brutus manages to stop the destruction by killing their leader, and the shock of fire and blood brings the others to their senses, just as Diana had planned. Into their surviving ships they hurry, and a wind bears them swiftly away.

This burning of boats comes from Virgil, who borrowed it from earlier traditions about Aeneas's voyage, which told how Trojan women, tired of a never-ending voyage, tried to force their leader to let them all stay where they had landed. Their boat-burning never succeeded and in those older stories it was Aeneas who brought them to their senses. In the *Aeneid*, a failed attempt to burn the boats led to Aeneas's departure from Sicily for Latium, and in the same way Brutus was now underway again in earnest.

It always seemed extraordinary, given how much it features in the *Aeneid*, that although Geoffrey's Brutus passed close by Sicily, he never landed there. Jacob rectifies this, bringing his hero past all the sights mentioned in the *Odyssey* and *Aeneid*, including the straits of Messina containing the whirlpool of Charybdis, and the Cyclopses threatening them from the shore below volcanic Etna. He omits Syracuse, perhaps consciously to distance his hero from Nahum Tate's romantic hero. Then come lofty Agragas; the promontory of Lilybaeum (Marsala) and, on the western coast, Drepanum below Erycina, which is Mount Eryx (Erice). On Mount Eryx is the temple to Aphrodite (now lost below the medieval castle), said to have been founded by Aeneas. Brutus finds altars to Mars there as well, something not mentioned by Virgil. 'Sacred Incense yet perfum'd the Air, And on th' expiring Embers now they pour Libations there.'

Aeneas had left behind a Trojan colony at Segesta, a few miles inland from Eryx, headed by Acestes, whose descendant Acestiades now welcomes Brutus (see plate 22). Together they pay homage to Anchises, Brutus's great-great-grandfather, whose tomb Aeneas had built down on the shore, just north of Drepanum. Aeneas had held games there to commemorate his father, so of course Brutus now held a similar festival of naval and athletic skills, in which his nephew Turonus won the main prize of 'a crested Helmet, and a Massy Shield'.

They overwinter with their Trojan cousins in Sicily. When they set sail next spring, they take with them 200 young men from the colony, one of the happiest crossovers between the *Aeneid* and Brutus's myth achieved by Jacob, for it gave the British mythological blood from Aeneas's Trojan colony of Segesta.

Scarce have they left Drepanum than a new, violent storm arises. 'Amaz'd the pale Philastron [the pilot] stood Before his useless Helm' as they are swept north-east and deposited on the Italian shore where they meet Corineus (for in this version of the story, we must remember, Corineus lived in Italy, not Spain). Here, Brutus's story of his travels ends, and 'The Leaders seek Their lofty Ships, impatient for the Morn.'

Brutus, 'on future Cares intent', cannot sleep, so Diana descends into the Underworld (where she is also known as Hecate) to seek out Somnus, god of sleep. She finds the god, 'His Head with Wreaths of drowsy flow'rs adorn'd' and he agrees to help Brutus rest: 'And in soft Sleep forget the Toils of State.' Even then, Diana's care of Brutus is not over, for when he awakes, she reminds him to sacrifice to the wind god Aeolus, to avoid further storms. That strategy, we discover, will be only partially successful.

The combined fleet embarks. Brutus's sixty ships, containing 3,000 Trojans, are now supplemented by 140 vessels containing Corineus's followers. 'Trembling beneath the Weight old Ocean foams,' as they speed south past Cape Palinurum (named after Aeneas's ill-fated helmsman, who had drowned there) and the Aeolian Isles. They pass Caralis (Sardinia), the Balearics and Orphiusa (Formentera) and then cross to the southern shore of the Mediterranean to rejoin Geoffrey's narrative by stopping at the mouth of the river 'Malvana' on the Mauretanian coast. Then they pass between the Pillars of Hercules and 'feel the warring Tide' that flows through the Straits of Gibraltar. They embark apprehensively on the Atlantic where, as Brutus's pilot Philastron reminds him, no Trojan ship has ever sailed before.

A fresh storm brews as they reach Tartessos (Cadiz) on the southern Spanish coast. Cadiz was a Phoenician colony like Carthage. It therefore made sense for King Amilcar (whom Jacob named after the father of the Carthaginian general Hannibal) to be an enemy of the Trojans, because of the way Aeneas had treated Dido. But for Jacob he was also an archetype of the shifty foreigner, so Amilcar 'feigns Signals of Peace, and opens his Port. The barring Chains remov'd, the Vessels sail Beneath the lofty Pharus [lighthouse].'

Amilcar views Brutus as 'An exil'd Stranger plough[ing] th'Atlantic Main! A wand'ring Parricide of Dardan Race.' But the king is also sensibly 'jealous of their Force, and rival Pow'r', for until now the Atlantic has been the Phoenicians' sole preserve. Amilcar therefore 'gains the Trojan Faith, now smiles, now seems to weep' as Brutus tells his story. But as soon as night falls – 'Darkness, fit for treacherous Intent' – 'the faithless Pirate his dire Council calls.' The Trojans had obviously incurred Neptune's anger, argues Amilcar, as they had been beset by storms, so 'No Tortures are too horrid for our Foe.' But Hermes assumes the guise of the king's henchman Narbal and warns that they would be foolish to fight Brutus and Corineus, whose skill in arms is famed throughout the Mediterranean. This keeps the Phoenicians debating until dawn, when their deliberations prove irrelevant:

> *And now the Morn arose,*
> *And now Salpirus, who the watchful Chief*
> *Had ever by his Side, Salpirus known,*
> *Throughout the Host, and honour'd in the Field*
> *From the high Deck, where Brutus sought Repose,*

Thrice sounds aloud his brazen Clarion,
Known Signal to depart. The Port around,
The lofty Tow'rs, and far extended Moles
As oft re-echo to the martial Voice.
Straight on the Masts the loosen'd Canvas fell,
And to their nimble Oars the Vessels move,
While daring Corineus leads the Van.
And now the Navy meets the Ocean's Wave,
High-swelling, and the Sea with Murmur hoarse
Confess'd the Tempest past …

They escape up the Iberian coast, described in some detail, surely from Jacob's personal experiences at sea. Reaching the Bay of Biscay they find themselves in the doldrums: Brutus 'mourn'd over his useless Arms' and Corineus 'rag'd, Tir'd of inglorious Ease.' But Neptune (Poseidon) sitting up on Mount Atlas hears Amilcar's daily prayers for vengeance. The god feels his 'sleeping Fury' rise at the thought that 'Seas I had shut From all Invaders, save the Ships of Tyre [i.e. the Phoenicians], Be ploughed by wand'ring Slaves in hostile Arms, By Fugitives, escap'd from Grecian Chains.' He raises a terrible storm, so that Brutus's ships find themselves:

Now on a swelling Mountain's foaming Head
Uplifted to the Clouds, now sinking low,
As in some Vale profound, th'enormous Waves,
And Wonders of the Ocean they survey,
Trembling, and pale.

Jacob had probably experienced something similar, clinging to the rails of a British man-o'-war.

Some of the Trojan ships sink, and the rest are scattered along the French coast. Brutus's ship reaches the mouth of the Loire, and the fifth book of Jacob's epic opens with him and a keen-eyed young companion, Rhesus, up on the towering cliffs nearby, try to spot other surviving ships. It is sunset and the sea before them is scattered with 'lab'ring ships, still beaten by the Storm'. Brutus orders his herald Salpirus to sound his horn right through the night, and sends men to kindle 'Far-shining Flames at equal Distance rang'd'. Brutus's careful strategy worked, and 'tow'rds th'enlighten'd Shoar the Vessels move.' Thus did Jacob, writing in the Age of Enlightenment, imagine savage northern Europe being literally *enlightened* for the first time by Trojan fire.

Before long, the old god of the Loire finds his river mouth clogged with ships. 'The destin'd Time so long foretold' has come, says he: 'A Dardan Foe in Ships of Greece arrives, To break with rude Alarms my long Repose, T'oppress with Carnage, and pollute with Blood My pure, and virgin Nymphs. What Scenes of Death, What Toils, what Strife, what Horrors they prepare!'

But of this prophecy the Trojans are unaware. They hold a council in a vale 'shadow'd round with high impending Oak' where they reflect on their long journey, tales of which 'Shall cheer our Age, and make our Infants smile.' They decide to repair their battered ships for the final leg of the voyage. Corineus, meanwhile, goes hunting for food, and of course this is where the trouble starts. For already rumours of 'A sailing Forest, and unnumber'd Foes' have spread throughout Gaul. The local king, Goffarius, sends 200 armed men led by his ambassador Imbertus to challenge the newcomers. Jacob, following Geoffrey, calls the tribe Picts and almost certainly imagined them to be cousins of the native inhabitants of Scotland – of whom the eighteenth-century English had a high-handedly low opinion.

Corineus, certainly, treats these semi-naked savages with contempt, calling Imbertus a 'wretched Slave' and telling him that the Trojans will kill and eat as many deer and boars as they please. Imbertus shoots at him and Corineus, enraged 'Like a rous'd Lion', kills him.

Meanwhile, back in the camp, Brutus watches his men repair their ships. Oppressed with concern for them all, he prays to Diana, 'O, teach me to conduct the Race I love!' In response, she 'pierc'd the ambient Cloud ... And to the Dardan Hero stood confess'd, Attir'd as she was wont, when oft they chac'd On Alba's woody Hills.' She tells him to avoid war at all costs, and remember that his destiny lies on his promised island. But now the hills are seething with Gauls, and presumably the ships are not yet ready to depart. Brutus has no choice but to lead the Trojans out to defend themselves.

Now we meet Goffarius properly, and in far more vivid detail than Geoffrey ever imagined – standing high on a hill, surrounded by his young braves:

> A Wolf enormous, by himself subdu'd,
> Grin'd on his Helmet, and the savage Spoils
> Athwart his manly Shoulders graceful hung.
> His Breast a painted Sun adorn'd: The Stars,
> The horned Crescent, and grim God of War
> Were shadow'd on his Limbs

Thus proudly tattooed like the Scottish Picts, Goffarius is 'like some fell Tiger, or Hyrcanian [leo]pard', the epitome of savage terror.

Brutus sends out his herald Pantheus with an olive branch, accompanied by some of the Trojan youths, to ask Goffarius for 'Fair Peace, and Rites hospitious'. But Goffarius cries out for revenge and his savage people concur with a murmur, 'As when loud Ocean roars, or Forests wide Bow with the Fury of some Thracian Blast.'

Inspired by Mars, the God of War, Goffarius has the Trojan youths dragged to the Pictish altars, where 'now with Oaken Boughs a Druid crown'd, Step'd forth, and sudden in their panting Hearts, Relentless, plung'd his consecrated Steel.' His vestments 'stain'd with purple Gore', the druid offers these human sacrifices to the ghost of Imbertus. The Trojans are descended from Jove (Zeus), Goffarius tells Pantheus, but he, the king of the Gauls, delights in his descent from Jove's brother Hades, 'that dread Pow'd who awes th' infernal World'.

Goffarius sends Pantheus back to Brutus, 'His Garments rent, his peaceful Laurel torn.' As he runs, Pantheus prays to Jove to 'Punish the dire, unhospitable Race' of the Gauls. Thunder booms overhead in answer to his prayer, and he hurries to Brutus's tent 'and there with Tears the horrid Scene unfolds.' So ends book five.

The Trojans will fight the Gauls and win, and will then sail away to Britain to build London. We know from what Diana says in book four that Brutus will 'consecrate to my immortal Name Such solid Tow'rs as Age shall ne'er destroy', and in a footnote below this Jacob cited his belief that 'Fanum Dianae [Diana's Temple] is one of the Names which have been given to London' (which is not quite true, but as we shall see antiquarians had speculated that a Roman temple dedicated to Diana had stood on Ludgate Hill in London, where St Paul's Cathedral now stands). Quite how Jacob planned for Brutus to have his three sons is unclear, for unlike Geoffrey's *History*, Ignoge had died in Africa. Presumably a second wife was planned for him, the daughter of a native British king whom he would marry just as Aeneas had married his second wife Lavinia, daughter of King Latinus, once the Latin War was won.

But, sadly, if Jacob ever wrote the final books of his poem, they seem never to have been published. The title page of the printed version of the first five books of his poem in Columbia University Library states that 'the latter Part is preparing for the Press'. Whether through lack of money or ill health, Jacob never published the rest. He died four years after the publication of the first five books, on 3 June 1739, at Clarges Street, Mayfair, and was buried on 5 June at St Anne's, Soho.

Perhaps Jacob had been disheartened because his poem had not caused much of a stir when it appeared. The *Oxford Dictionary of National Biography* describes it as 'forgettable', and maybe contemporary readers saw it merely as a parody of the *Aeneid* and not, as Jacob doubtless intended, as its triumphant sequel. Yet that is what it is, and the fact that Jacob never finished it seems a great tragedy. His vision of the Trojans landing at Totnes would have been worth having, as would his description of their fight with the giants. The lack of both are irrevocable losses to Brutus's story that can never be made good, but in the five books that Jacob did publish we have a very fine, very unforgettable retelling of the story indeed, uniting Geoffrey's medieval tale with the high-flown language of Virgil.

Jacob's choice of subtitle, *Founder of the British Empire*, might have a faintly absurd ring to it now that the empire has been and gone, but when Jacob was writing, genuine glories lay in the future and the élite of his generation could smell gold on the air. To their possession of Ireland and the early colonies in North American and the Caribbean, the British had already added countless trading bases along the west coast of Africa, in India and the Far East. Jacob was right, therefore, to delve into British mythology to seek inspiration and justification for what was to come. In book four, we are privy to a conversation on Olympus between Hermes and Diana. Their father Jove, they say, 'shuts from us with Adamantine Bars The sacred Records of unalter'd Fate,' yet Brutus must be the one foretold by prophecy, whose 'active Sons' would raise more altars to Hermes than anyone else, whilst Diana enlarges on her own earlier prophecy in book two that Brutus's progeny would 'o'er the boundless Ocean spread their Sway':

> *Hard tho' it seems, O Hermes, to unfold*
> *The Register of Time: Yet we have hear'd,*
> *The Progeny of Brute will reign secure,*
> *While the Earth-shaking God shall be ador'd!*
> *And know'st thou not, 'twas rumour'd here above,*
> *How to a Race from Troy in Years to come*
> *The Empire of the Ocean should descend?*
> *Decrees, we're told, in ancient Saturn's Reign,*
> *Obscurely spoke of Brute, a Dardan Line,*
> *Riches, reviving Liberty, and Arts,*
> *The Muses Seats, and new discover'd Worlds.*
> *Thus far our mighty Sire himself declar'd,*

> *And, in the Synod of assembled Gods,*
> *Pronounc'd, that Brutus was the Hero chose,*
> *To raise the lasting Throne of Albion.*

The 'Earth-shaking God' is Poseidon (Neptune) and the allusion here is to Britain's mastery of the seas. Amongst the most recent additions to the empire were Newfoundland and Arcadia in Canada, and Gibraltar, and Minorca in the Balearics, which Britain had gained through the Treaty of Utrecht in 1714. Britain had gained a firm foothold in the Mediterranean and the Union Flag was seen fluttering over the 'Vast, liquid Plains caerulean' of the Mediterranean. Perhaps it is no coincidence that James Thomson's poem *Rule Britannia*, with its line 'Rule, Britannia! rule the waves', which Thomas Arne immediately set to music, appeared a mere five years after Jacob's epic was published.

In the eyes of Hildebrand Jacob and those who read and enjoyed his retelling of the Brutus myth, the presence of British vessels in the Mediterranean was nothing new. Thanks to their descent from Brutus, the doughty mariners of the Royal Navy were simply the descendants of the Trojans, back where they belonged.

Chapter 21

Alexander Pope's *Brutiad*

T he story of Brutus had enjoyed widespread popularity for so long that it comes as some surprise to learn that, until 1718, whilst his adventures could be read in English in the pages of Hardyng, Milton, Settle and so on, nobody had ever read Geoffrey's *History* itself in anything other than Latin. Its manuscripts and printed editions (of which there were three, from 1508, 1517 and 1587) were all perfectly accessible to most educated men (whose education would routinely have included Latin), but they were not an easy read and were quite beyond all those who could read only English. But in 1718, all that changed when the Reverend Aaron Thompson (d. 1753) published a translation of Geoffrey, which he called *The British History*. It is the version from which I have quoted in this book. Going against the fashionable view of the time, Thompson adored Brutus's story and hoped passionately that there might be 'at least some Foundation of Truth discoverable in the ruins of this ancient Story of Brutus and his Successors'.

Thompson translated it all himself, but for Brutus's poetic prayer to Diana, and her reply, he enlisted the help of his friend, the angular young wit and poet Alexander Pope (1688–1744), who made a rather a good job of them. But Pope's refusal to believe in Brutus was upsetting because, full of the new ideas of the Enlightenment, the young poet treated Brutus's myth with utter disdain. Back in 1713, Pope had written in *The Guardian* about the creation of epics, take 'any old poem, history, book, romance, or legend, (for instance, Geoffry of Monmouth ...) ... Pat these pieces together, and throw all the adventures you fancy into one tale.' But you are a Catholic, Thompson reminded him, so are ready to believe in numerous stories of saints' miracles, so why not give similar credit to 'the wonders of Corineus and Gogmagog'? Pope pretended, politely, to do so, but confided to a friend that having spent a week reading Geoffrey, he would be quite 'prepared to translate, with belief, and reverence, the speech of Achilles' Horse.'

Yet over the ensuing years, Pope worked on his own translations of Homer and Virgil and found himself swept up in the magic of the Trojan myth. And so his old friend Aaron Thompson's marvelous story of Brutus, which formed a bridge between the cypress-fringed pastures of Latium and the oak-edged fields of Pope's beloved Thames Valley, wound its way into his heart.

Pope happened to belong to the circle of freedom-loving writers and politicians opposed to Sir Robert Walpole's Whig government (which, though ostensibly liberal, was still far too right wing for the circle's tastes). A member of this circle, George Lyttleton, urged Pope in 1741 to choose from 'out of the Rubbish of Monkish Annals' some theme for 'a new Edifice, that wou'd be fit to Enshrine the Greatest of our English Kings, and Last to Eternity'. Such an 'edifice' would be an epic poem, and besides telling a story it would also convey the liberal political point of view in which Lyttleton's circle believed. From such seeds germinated Pope's *Brutiad*.

I doubt Pope ever read Hildebrand Jacob's epic, but even if he had it would have made very little difference, for unlike Jacob, Pope was not in the business of marinating Brutus in the world of Virgil. But in planning the *Brutiad* as the last of his great works, Pope did look back for guidance to Milton, and followed the Miltonic plan of writing about glory, ruin and restoration. Pope's poem *Essay on Man* (1734) stood for glory; his *Dunciad* (1728/1743) represented ruin – and so in his *Brutiad*, as Professor Donald Torchiana suggests, Pope looked forward to the restoration of mankind. Brutus would be, as Pope wrote, 'as perfect as human nature will admit. A most wise legislator, an undaunted soldier, a just, moderate, beneficent prince; the example and pattern of kings, and true heroes'. Even the slight human foibles of Virgil's Aeneas would be absent from the shining character of Brutus.

Pope's Brutus was a deliberate contrast to the debauched George II, and was surely a template for what Pope and Lyttleton hoped the king's son Frederick, Prince of Wales (who was Lyttleton's employer) would become. Brutus's mission was not merely, as in Geoffrey, to find a safe home for the Trojans. Taking a leaf out of Polydore Vergil's reworking of British history, Pope imagined Britain as already inhabited, but by people living in naive savagery. Through good government, liberty, education and unsuperstitious religion, Brutus's task was to meld both races into a perfect, Enlightenment society – and thus to lay for the foundation for what Pope and his circle believed Britain could one day become in reality under Frederick (a hope that was ultimately disappointed when the prince died before his father in 1751).

By 1743 Pope wrote that his epic on 'our Brutus from Troy' was 'exactly planned'. But when it came to translating his plan into verse, he seems never to have progressed beyond the first few lines:

> *The Patient Chief, who lab'ring long, arriv'd*
> *On Britain's Shore and brought with fav'ring Gods*
> *Arts Arms and Honour to her Ancient Sons:*
> *Daughter of Memory! from elder Time*
> *Recall; and me, with Britains Glory fir'd,*
> *Me, far from meaner Care or meaner Song,*
> *Snatch to thy Holy Hill of Spotless Bay,*
> *My Countrys Poet, to record her Fame.*

Pope's prose outline of the *Brutiad* shows that he intended to take as many liberties with Geoffrey's story as Settle had done. The story opens on the Rock of Calpe (Gibraltar), where Brutus and his fleet have landed, he having used Italian gold to ransom the enslaved Trojans from all over Greece, and sought direction from the oracle at Dodona (see plate 14) in north-western Greece (as opposed to hearing Diana's prophecy on Lefkada).

The Trojans are unwilling to leave the safety of the Mediterranean. Elderly, cautious Pissander is in favour of settling on the Spanish coast and effeminate Cloanthes, who longs for an easy life, agrees. Both claim that Hercules had gone no further than these straits, and had decreed that no one should venture out into the Atlantic. But Pope's Brutus is fired with zeal and wishes to find a home for the Trojans amongst 'a people uncorrupt in their manners, worthy to be made happy'. 'Hercules was but a mortal like them,' Brutus tells his followers, 'and if their virtue was superior to his, they would have the same claim to divinity: for that the path of virtue was the only way which lay open to heaven.' He would go on alone, and leave behind 'all such dastards, as dared not accompany him'. Brutus's words fill the Trojans' hearts with desire to follow him, and at night Hercules himself appears before Brutus in a dream and urges him to venture forth beyond the ancient boundaries of Mediterranean civilisation.

Pope then imagines a scene in Highest Heaven, of the sort that Milton had adapted in *Paradise Lost* from the godly conferences on Mount Olympus dreamed up by Homer and Virgil. Light blazes forth from the celestial throne, on which sits the Christian God. Before him is prostrated the Angel of Troy, his silvery wings brushing the starry pathway, confessing 'his injustice in having overturned that kingdom, for the sins of the princes, and of the people themselves'. Now, however, the angel believes the Trojans' descendants have been suitably 'chastised and humbled [and so] it would now be agreeable to his mercy and goodness, to raise up a new state from their ruins, and form a people who might serve him better. That, in Brutus, his Providence has a fit instrument for such a gracious design.'

God raises up the Angel of Troy, so that his wings can beat strongly in his creator's brilliant radiance. Down plunges the angel through the spheres of Heaven and bursts through the dawn-blushed clouds, his wings golden brushstrokes against the deepening blue of the morning sky. His beating wings raise a steady, easterly wind that fills the Trojans' sails and speeds them out through the Pillars of Hercules, and into the surging swell of the Atlantic.

In Pope's story, the Trojan fleet heads south-west to the volcanic island of Tenerife. Exploring the lushly vegetated 'land of laziness', and finding it uninhabited, many of the Trojans long to remain there. Like Aeneas in Sicily, Brutus allows the elderly and infirm, and those of the women who chose, to settle there, giving them 'a form of pure worship, and a short and simple body of laws'. The people Brutus left behind must have become the Guanches, the native people of Tenerife who, outside Pope's imaginings, were probably of Berber origins. If so, they may have shared some of the mythology that had been spread along the northern coast of Africa in the last millennium BC by the establishment of Greek colonies, which had attributed Trojan origins to some of the coastal peoples of the region. Perhaps news of vestiges of such beliefs had helped inspire Pope in this particular flight of fantasy.

Brutus and his remaining followers sail north-east, and up the Portuguese coast. The Greeks sometimes attributed the foundation of Lisbon to Odysseus, whom the Romans called Ulysses. In Pope's version, Lisbon is called Ulyssipont, and Brutus finds it riddled with 'the wicked principles of policy and superstition' that the arch-deceiver, Odysseus, had established. Pope's great concern was with good and bad government: Odysseus's had been so dreadful that he had 'at length [been] driven away by the discontented people he had enslaved' – a dire warning, no doubt, to Walpole himself.

Now (and ignoring Brutus's adventures in Gaul) an evil spirit raises a storm that sweeps the fleet north, straight past Britain, until they see the jagged cliffs of the Norwegian coast ahead of them. Clinging to the mast, Brutus offers up a desperate prayer, and the winds die away. The glassy blue sea reflects the jagged purple mountains as they row their battered vessels into the shelter of a fjord.

They make camp as night falls and the ghostly green lights of the aurora borealis, the 'northern lights', dance and flicker overhead. The Trojans stare up aghast, whispering fearfully that this land is the dancing place of faerie spirits. Brutus, however, like an Enlightenment rationalist, realises that the lights 'may be a phenomenon of nature usual in those countries ... but that if it be any thing supernatural, they ought to interpret it in their own favour, because heaven never works miracles, but for the good.'

He is right, for, as they gaze in wonder, they spot dark shapes creeping over the heathery moors, their weapons glinting in the lurid glow of the convulsing heavens. Thus forewarned, the Trojans seize up their spears and swords, and when the Vikings fall on them they are ready. Beneath the sweeping curtains of green effulgence, the battle unfolds, short and brutal: Brutus slays the leader, and his faithful second in command, Orontes, kills the next three most important Norsemen. They take prisoners, who tell the Trojans how they sometimes visited the shores of Britain, and they hand over some slaves they had captured there. Guided by these freed Britons, Brutus's fleet sets sail west, to make landfall on the Orkney Islands.

Pope knew nothing of the sophisticated Neolithic and Bronze Age cultures that had flourished in the Orkneys, so he did not imagine Brutus staring in wonder at the great earthen mound of Maes Howe, nor walking among the great rings of tall, sharply outlined standing stones that rear up from the low-lying shore of the Ness of Brodgar. Had he known of these, Pope would surely have attributed their construction, unerringly, to Brutus himself. Instead, however, Pope thought of the Orkneys as the end of the Earth and imagined the islanders as groveling savages, living in supernatural terror of the demons they believed swirled about on the Scottish mainland, 'who forbid all access to it by thunders, earthquakes, &c.' Eudamon, an equally superstitious Trojan, thinks this confirms the Greeks' stories that the fallen Titans lay confined 'in one of the northern islands of the ocean', but the ultra-rationalist Brutus refuses to believe this.

Brutus, Orontes and some companions set out across the Pentland Firth in a six-oared boat to explore the northern coast of Scotland for themselves. As they approach the shore, a violent hurricane rises. The rowing boat pitches and drops amidst mountainous waves, until they feel a jarring crash and the timbers below them splinter on the savage rocks of John O'Groats. Half blinded by the icy salt water, everyone drowns except for Brutus and Orontes, who manage to drag themselves ashore.

A dense forest of pine trees shelters them from the worst of the storm, but a more terrible danger lies ahead. 'All at once the sun was darkened, a thick night comes over them; thundering noises, and bellowings are heard in the air, and under ground. A terrible eruption of fire breaks out from the top of a mountain, the Earth shakes beneath their feet.'

Had Brutus landed much further west, at the foot of the Black Cuillins of Skye, about 60 million years earlier, he would indeed have seen livid lava exploding out of the gaping craters of volcanos, caused by the movement of the continental plates. The geology of the region was just becoming understood in the eighteenth century and this probably underpinned Pope's idea. For it was violence of this magnitude that Pope imagined unfolding now before Brutus's eyes, accompanied by the shrieking of malignant spirits in the tortured air. Orontes screams in terror and flees like a frightened deer into the forest. But Brutus stands his ground, gazing up at the fiery frenzy and the rivers of molten lava that hiss towards him like raging bulls of molten bronze, and prays to heaven for salvation.

As the lava broils closer, Brutus's eyes are almost blinded by another, brighter light. Between him and the Hellish doom of the volcano there appears a towering figure, from whose lofty shoulders there expand two gigantic wings, like the sails of ships, blazing with a silvery radiance that makes the fiery lava seem dull. The Angel of Troy beats his mighty wings once and the lava cools, crackling like pond ice under a heavy foot: its onward flow is halted and it shatters into shards of pumice. With another beat of his mighty wings, the angel quells the volcano itself, and all is still.

God had permitted evil spirits to appear to work miracles, the Miltonic angel explains, in order to test Brutus's virtue, and to humble the pride of Orontes, 'who was too confident in his courage, and too little regardful of providence.'

When Orontes, cowering in his cave, sees Brutus looking for him, he is so ashamed that he wants to kill himself, but Brutus reprimands him gently: it was understandable that he had been terrified of the supernatural, but in future he must put more faith in God. Brutus tells Orontes what the Angel of Troy had told him: that this northern land is 'infested by men not yet disposed to receive religion, arts and good government'. Civilising them will be the work of one of Brutus's sons (Albanactus, who later became king of Scotland). Meantime, their mission lies in the south.

Back on the shore, they find the Trojan Hanno waiting with a ship to carry them back to the fleet. And with that, Pope's excursion to the northlands comes to an end, and the Trojans sail south, where Brutus's heart leaps with joy 'at the sight of the white rocks of Albion'. Instead of Totnes, Pope's Trojans land at Torbay, where William of Orange's landing in 1688 had precipitated the Glorious Revolution. Here, Brutus met with 'a kind reception', not by giants but by native Britons. The climate was free from both the 'effeminacy and softness' of the Mediterranean and the 'ferocity and savageness' of the north, so as a consequence the people, who worshipped the sun and fire but made no human sacrifices, were 'well adapted to receive the improvements in virtue'.

'At an altar of turf, in an open place' Brutus meets the druids 'offering fruits and flowers to heaven'. This must be Silbury Hill near the stone circle of Avebury, just to the west of Marlborough, Wiltshire (see plate 35). It is a Neolithic mound, built about 2400 BC. At 131 feet in height it is the tallest prehistoric monument in Europe, comparable in size to some of the smaller Egyptian pyramids. Here Brutus hears about the state of the rest of Britain: Anglesey is 'groaning under the lash of superstition, being governed by priests'; the north is 'invested by tyrants, of whom the Britons tell strange stories, representing them as giants'; an unspecified island nearby (Ireland?) is 'distracted by dismal Anarchy, the natives eating their captives, and carrying away virgins'; and yet another is 'under the domination of Tyranny ... defended by giants living in castles', including Gogmagog.

Brutus will defeat all these foes, throwing down the tyrants and exposing the trickery of the priests, who used secrets such as gunpowder to keep the people subdued by superstitious fear. Brutus will also quell discontent and rebellion amongst his own people, some of whom are keen to enslave the liberated Britons. Instead, Brutus prefers to 'polish and refine them, by introducing true religion, void of superstition and all false notions of the Deity'.

All this we know from Pope's 1743 outline for his epic *Brutiad*. The poem itself was destined never to be written and he died the following year. His failing health had forced him to lay 'aside his Epic Poem, perhaps without much loss to mankind', as Dr Johnson wrote acerbically in his *Lives of the Most Eminent English Poets* (1779–1781), for Brutus 'was of the fabulous age; the actors were a race upon whom imagination has been exhausted, and attention wearied.' But Dr Johnson could not have been more wrong.

Chapter 22

'Fair Albion's Shore'

From his earliest boyhood, William Blake (1757–1827) experienced spontaneous eidetic visions, a medical condition by which the brain convinces the eye that it has seen something that is not really there. As he sat reading by the window in his father's house in Broad Street, Soho, or walking through the fields below Dulwich Hill, Blake would see the Prophet Ezekiel sitting below a tree, or angels perched in the branches, their 'bright angelic wings bespangling every bough like stars' and the ghost of 'Milton [who] lov'd me in childhood & shew'd me his face'. Later, Blake expressed his belief that Milton's spirit had appeared 'in the Zenith as a falling star, Descending perpendicular, swift as a swallow or swift; And on my left foot falling on my tarsus, entered there.'

He read Milton's *History of Britain* and its retelling of Geoffrey's *History* swarmed through the young Blake's imagination as he walked through London's raucous streets as an apprentice engraver. This, he knew, was the city built by Brutus, the New Troy in Albion. In 1773, he engraved Joseph of Arimathea 'among The Rocks of Albion' and a few years later he painted the very moment when Brutus and his people came ashore, clad in steely blue armour and iron-red cloaks against a dun background of the British coast (see plate 30). The Trojans' arms are raised aloft in a typically Blakean gesture of praise, surrendering their mortal bodies and their rational selves to the ecstasy of spiritual wonder and awe. In their midst, the old augur Gero has thrown himself on his knees and is absorbed in a prayer of thanksgiving. In the centre of the picture is Brutus himself. He kneels as well, trembling with reverence on the margin of tide and shore, bent double to kiss the blessed sand of the living island-body of Albion.

About the time he painted this electrifying scene, the young Blake also reimagined the story of Brutus's landing, and expressed his own deeply felt sentiments about Britain's arcane origins and liberties in his poem *O sons of Trojan Brutus*. Here it is in full, and I recommend strongly reading it out loud, in as sonorous a voice as you can muster:

> *O sons of Trojan Brutus, cloth'd in war,*
> *Whose voices are the thunder of the field,*
> *Rolling dark clouds o'er France, muffling the sun*

In sickly darkness like a dim eclipse,
Threatening as the red brow of storms, as fire
Burning up nations in your wrath and fury!

Your ancestors came from the fires of Troy,
(Like lions rous'd by light'ning from their dens,
Whose eyes do glare against the stormy fires),
Heated with war, fill'd with the blood of Greeks,
With helmets hewn, and shields coverèd with gore,
In navies black, broken with wind and tide:

They landed in firm array upon the rocks
Of Albion; they kiss'd the rocky shore;
'Be thou our mother and our nurse', they said;
'Our children's mother, and thou shalt be our grave,
The sepulchre of ancient Troy, from whence
Shall rise cities, and thrones, and arms, and awful pow'rs.

Our fathers swarm from the ships. Giant voices
Are heard from the hills, the enormous sons
Of Ocean run from rocks and caves, wild men,
Naked and roaring like lions, hurling rocks,
And wielding knotty clubs, like oaks entangled
Thick as a forest, ready for the axe.

Our fathers move in firm array to battle;
The savage monsters rush like roaring fire,
Like as a forest roars with crackling flames,
When the red lightning, borne by furious storms,
Lights on some woody shore; the parchèd heavens
Rain fire into the molten raging sea.

The smoking trees are strewn upon the shore,
Spoil'd of their verdure. O how oft have they
Defy'd the storm that howlèd o'er their heads!
Our fathers, sweating, lean on their spears, and view
The mighty dead: giant bodies streaming blood.
Dread visages frowning in silent death.

Then Brutus spoke, inspir'd; our fathers sit
Attentive on the melancholy shore:
Hear ye the voice of Brutus – 'The flowing waves
Of time come rolling o'er my breast', he said;
'And my heart labours with futurity:
Our sons shall rule the empire of the sea.

Their mighty wings shall stretch from east to west.
Their nest is in the sea, but they shall roam
Like eagles for the prey; nor shall the young
Crave or be heard; for plenty shall bring forth,
Cities shall sing, and vales in rich array
Shall laugh, whose fruitful laps bend down with fullness.

Our sons shall rise from thrones in joy,
Each one buckling on his armour; Morning
Shall be prevented by their swords gleaming,
And Evening hear their song of victory:
Their towers shall be built upon the rocks,
Their daughters shall sing, surrounded with shining spears.

Liberty shall stand upon the cliffs of Albion,
Casting her blue eyes over the green ocean;
Or, tow'ring, stand upon the roaring waves,
Stretching her mighty spear o'er distant lands;
While, with her eagle wings, she covereth
Fair Albion's shore, and all her families.

These must be the finest lines inspired by the Trojan myth ever written in English. Certainly, they have not been excelled since, and I doubt they ever will, for they are based in Blake's childlike belief in the truth of Brutus's myth, and a willing acceptance – albeit with an eighteenth-century, libertarian slant – of the human emotions that the myth expressed and of the hopes and fears our Dark Age British ancestors had invested in their founding hero, and which had sustained our island so well for so long.

As Blake grew older, however, he grew more particular in his choice of mythological heroes and, having celebrated Brutus's myth as a young man, he became increasingly uncomfortable with its pagan overtones and veered away from mythology that linked Britain's past to 'the detestable Gods of Priam' and 'the covenant of Priam, the Moral Virtues of the Heathen'.

Like a Dark Age disciple of St Augustine's *City of God*, Blake turned his back on the old pact made between Britain and Troy, which he believed was embodied in the arrival of Brutus at Totnes. Yet he was so soaked in the old idea of London being the 'New Troy' that he could only displace it by replacing it with something else. So for William Blake, London stopped being Troy and started becoming a physical manifestation of the heavenly Jerusalem:

> *The fields from Islington to Marylebone,*
> *To Primrose Hill and St John's Wood,*
> *Were builded over with pillars of gold,*
> *And there Jerusalem's pillars stood.*

This verse is from his lengthy 'prophetic book' *Jerusalem*, which Blake composed, on and off, from about 1804 until he finished it off at Samuel Palmer's house in Shoreham, Kent in 1820. Blake did not present a coherent pseudo-historical explanation of how London could be Jerusalem, but instead he used poetry to circle, just as the Greek poets loved to do, around the idea. He played on Milton's retelling of Annius of Viterbo's story about Albion, the giant son of Neptune, and also on Pope's *Brutiad*, which refers to the Greek myth that the Titans, having been cast down by Zeus, were imprisoned somewhere in the western ocean and hints that at least one of them might lie groaning below the chalk of Britain itself.

Blake's Titan Albion assumed far vaster, spiritual proportions, becoming the most primal of all God's acts, 'our ancestor, in whose sleep or Chaos creation began' (see plate 38). He was 'Albion our Ancestor patriarch of the Atlantic Continent whose History Preceded that of the Hebrews'. Albion fell due to sin, but from the fallen Albion there also emerged his Emanation, the good, imaginative part of him. That 'emanation' was Jerusalem, and Jerusalem – in Blake's extraordinary imagination – was also London.

Just as the Old Testament prophets had imagined their city of Jerusalem as the stage on which God had chosen to enact his cosmic drama, so Blake imagined the same events being played out in the familiar surroundings of London. He no longer needed Joseph of Arimathea or Brutus to form bridges between the Bible and Britain, for in Blake's imagination the entire life of Christ could unfold in the streets of London and on the green hills around. From that spiritual vision sprang his shorter poem *Jerusalem*, which appears in another of his 'prophetic books', *Milton*:

> *And did those feet in ancient time*
> *Walk upon Englands mountains green:*
> *And was the holy Lamb of God,*
> *On Englands pleasant pastures seen!*

Set to music by Herbert Parry, the hymn was chosen by Prince William and Kate Middleton for their wedding in 2011 and, when Danny Boyle sought to encapsulate the very essence of Britain for the opening ceremony of London's 2012 Olympic Games, he opted for *Jerusalem* as well, and the rise of the Industrial Revolution over 'England's green and pleasant land'. But it is worth remembering that, underpinning Blake's poetic vision of London as Jerusalem, lies that much older myth, invented by Geoffrey of Monmouth, that London had been built as the new Troy, by Brutus.

Chapter 23

Angels over Dover

In 1769, twenty-five years after Alexander Pope's death, and only a couple of years before Blake penned his poem about Brutus, Pope's plan for a *Brutiad* was published by his biographer Owen Ruffhead, hoping that 'the design may serve as a model to employ some genius, if any there be, or shall hereafter arise, equal to the task'.

The challenge was taken up, at the suggestion of Bishop Warburton, by the Northumbrian-born author and moralist John 'Estimate' Brown (1715–1766). Brown drafted the first couple of books, following Pope's plan, before his attention was distracted away to other projects, including devising an educational system for Catherine the Great's Russia. What became of Brown's draft is not known.

Of all the Trojan stories, that of Dido and Aeneas was always perhaps the most popular, and helped keep the Trojan myth in the national consciousness. When the Bath playwright Prince Hoare wrote the libretto for *Dido Queen of Carthage*, which was performed in 1792 at the Haymarket Theatre, London, he included a patriotic masque at the end in which Neptune reiterates clearly the connection between Aeneas's story and the audience: 'Third from thy sire,' he tells Ascanius,

> *... shall Brutus rise,*
> *Who far beneath yon western skies,*
> *Ordain'd to empire yet unknown,*
> *On Albion's coast shall fix his throne,*
> *And crown'd with laurels, spoils, and fame,*
> *Shall change to Britain Albion's name.*

Thus far, Brutus's story had been retold by Welshmen and Englishmen. Now, in the next generation, it was the turn of a Scot, the Reverend John Ogilvie (1733–1813) of Aberdeen. Ogilvie took up Ruffhead's challenge, picking up where Pope and Brown left off and completing his own *Britannia, a National Epic Poem* in 1801, a great fusion of Geoffrey, Pope, Milton and Jacob (to whom he refers), all set within a Homeric war – not the siege of Troy, but a battle between good and evil for Britain. That is no surprise, because since 1792 Britain had been locked in bitter war against the new French Republic, and without the Royal Navy, Ogilvie's land would have been overrun by a deeply detested foreign foe. Indeed, Ogilvie dedicated his poem to the First Lord of the Admiralty, the 2nd Earl Spencer, the ancestor of Princess Diana. It begins:

> *The Chief who to Britannia's shore convey'd*
> *A train to conquest born, and sovereign rule,*
> *The first great FATHERS of her race; – his fame*
> *In arms, in wisdom; and the deeds that graced*
> *His bold Compeers, whose spears opposed the force*
> *Of barbarous hosts; – to conquer and reform,*
> *To rule and civilise, at once their aim …*

In Geoffrey, as in Virgil, it was the Olympian gods' will that Brutus should reach Britain. In Ogilvie, as in Pope, that will is God's, so Brutus's arch-enemy is an entirely Miltonic Satan. 'Prophecy,' says Satan, 'speaks of a pure religion, and a race enlighten'd free, imperial' who were destined to spread 'the light of knowledge, and of truth' in opposition 'to superstitious rites … where human victims stain our sacred altars with their blood.' Satan fears that the empire Brutus's descendants will found – the British Empire – will 'circumscribe my power; perhaps to shake, or raze mine empire, o'er the sons of Earth, so dearly bought.'

Brutus's background is explained as a backstory, starting with his killing of his father with his accidental bow shot, though Satan also sees a vision in which

> *… a hero stood*
> *Before me, of the famed Aenean line,*
> *Splendent in arms! I saw his father's blood*
> *Smoke on his sword, and knew each parent doom'd,*
> *By him, though guiltless in th'intent …*

Having collected followers from Italy, Brutus sails to Greece where the kings 'yielded' him a country called Pandrasia. Here Brutus spends 'long years … in luxurious ease', long enough for him to have his three sons and allow them to grow up, for Ogilvie had roles for them all in his story. As they 'are supposed to have been the original Progenitors of the nations which comprised Great Britain,' he explained in the introduction, each was given 'the predominant features of the national character', so Camber was 'stimulated', like his Welsh descendants, 'by the powerful motives of emulation, and by the pride of ancestry', Albanus (instead of Geoffrey's Albanactus) possessed the 'animated valour, acting in co-operation with good sense and discernment' of the Scots and Locrinus was the model of 'the dignified manners, heroic courage, and noble qualities' of an English gentleman.

Eventually, Brutus obeys God's will and sails towards Sicily (not Lefkada), where an oracle would direct him to his destined home, but Satan sends the demon Azrael to divert him, by means of a dreadful storm, to Cythera (which Ogilvie places in the Cyclades, but which is actually off the southern tip of the Peloponnese). Cythera was an imagined birthplace for Aphrodite (Venus), goddess of love and mother of Aeneas, and she had a major sanctuary there in antiquity, so it was an appropriate destination for her descendant. Brutus 'beheld the groves beloved of Venus, and the bowers sacred to pleasure, and voluptuous ease.' From the Trojans' breasts were 'cast th'oppressive weight of sadness. All the past dissolved.' The Cythereans, led by their king, Asmodeus, are 'Tutor'd to raise voluptuous thought, and wake the embers of untamed and loose desire, by smiles and dalliance' and, as Azrael had planned, the Trojans lose all interest in continuing their voyage. The Angel Uzziel persuades Brutus to continue his journey. But Brutus cannot talk his council of leaders around so, just as God sent a destroying angel to 'punish the impiety of Pharaoh', the Angel Ormul now spread misery and pestilence amongst the dissipated sons of Troy, 'chastising some by temporary punishments, and others by death':

> *no age he spared;*
> *But smote the hoary head, and pierced the heart,*
> *The blameless heart, yet innocent of ill*
> *In undistinguish'd ravage …*

The humbled Trojan leaders 'late so boastful, shrinking now from perils near in prospect … humbled now, approach'd their Monarch's sight' and they all embarked on the long-delayed voyage to Sicily, where Brutus receives Diana's prophecy. Later he recalls how

> *… at thy shrine,*
> *The rites perform'd, I lay dissolving wild*
> *In heedless extasy:– Ye know, at last*
> *The adamantine statue nodded! shook*

> *The vault, as charged with whirlwinds! All the Power*
> *Rush'd on the Prophetess, who thus inspired,*
> *Announced an ISLE, amid the western main ...*

They sacrifice two white heifers and God sends an eagle 'sailing with spreading pinions on the wind' as a sign, speeding them on to Britain. With them travel various contingents of Greeks, allowing Ogilvie to bestow blood from Athens and Sparta, and not just from Troy, upon his British readers.

Unseen to the Trojans, Britannia, the 'Guardian Power' of the island, 'this little world, by the surrounding seas as with a rampart girt', stands on the White Cliffs of Dover and beholds

> *... the Fathers of the British line;*
> *A generous people, hard, daring, free,*
> *By ills unbroke; advancing to the land*
> *That echoing, hail's the sovereigns of the main.*
> *HIGH on the foremost ship, that brush'd the wave,*
> *At hand, the Leader of th'glorious host,*
> *Known by his gesture, and th' expressive look,*
> *That, while it awes, yet pleases; took his stand*
> *On the tall prow. His limbs in shining mail*
> *Were cased. His face, and ebon-tinctured hair*
> *Stood full to sight displayd. Calm courage there*
> *And ardour rein'd by wisdom, by the voice*
> *Of cool experience ...*

As with Blake, Ogilvie's Britain, out of all the world, is special. Britannia recalled how, 'when th'Eternal call'd from night this rude orb', all the world's dry land was covered with woods and 'roughen'd with the cloud-wrapt hill' but then she saw

> *... the deep recoiling, as the cliffs*
> *Of Albion tower'd amid th' investing main,*
> *Sublimely eminent*

The Trojans are special too: this is the race, Britannia knows, 'by Heaven ordain'd ... to found a line whose fame should spread to Earth's remotest bound' and to 'free from thrall the natives'. For (as with Pope) Britain had aboriginal inhabitants, the Albians, and later we hear how once they enjoyed its 'streams, and lawns; with interchanging hills, and spreading woods embrown'd: our fathers held [these] through many an age, amid the branching oaks their empire here'. But then came the giants in their 'vessels rudely framed', descendants of the Cyclops Polyphemus, son of Neptune, who were seen 'amid the black surge plunging … its waves assailing their broad chests in vain' as they strode ashore. The Albians had lined the shore ready to repel the invaders, but when they saw the giant king, Gerontes, 'by stature raised to power' and his champion Romerus, 'the spirit died within us. From our hands the useless javelins fell.' The Albians became the giants' slaves, but one of the giants, Androgeus, grew to like them and learned their ways. Eventually he persuaded the giants to allow the Albians to retire into Wales to live in peace.

Britannia assumes the disguise of a shepherd to greet Brutus and warn him about the giants: in response he burns his ships, so his people would have no choice but to fight for victory. Brutus's son Albanus and his Athenian friend Eugenius explore the deep forest: this is the Weald, the wild woods between the North and South Downs that the Romans marched through but never fully tamed. Guided by Britannia they find the giants' fortress, 'a mighty space, fenced with a rampart, and encircling fosse, and height unequall'd'. Behind it was a river, and before it they saw a plain, untilled, for the giants lived by hunting and were too crude to farm. It was covered with 'bones and smoking gore' thrown there during the giants' banquets: 'here a carcass half devour'd, and there a head, with tusks still grinning, and extended jaws'. Ogilvie had in mind a hill fort: the nearest major one to Dover is Bigbury, on the hills immediately west of Canterbury and as a clergyman (who included several church dignitaries from Canterbury in his list of subscribers) he may have visited the city and seen the remaining banks and ditches of the hill fort in the woods. Before it to the south stretch the floodplains of the river Stour and a little tributary of the Stour runs behind, near its north-westerly defenses, so it was probably here that Ogilvie had in mind.

Satan's scheme to prevent Brutus reaching Britain has failed, so his plan now is for Azrael to stir up the giants and Albians against Brutus. We see Romerus demonstrating his fearsome strength by attacking a 'lordly bull' – one of the mighty aurochses that used to roam the Weald – which even the other giants had dared not approach: seizing it by the horns, he breaks its neck with his bare hands. The giants feast on its flesh and march to the coast, where the giant king Gerontes, pausing at the forest edge, observes the Trojan host, 'blazing shields he mark'd, and countless numbers, all employ'd, as in a city raised by magic

power, in works of general use. … the helm far–gleaming, and the mail turn'd
to the sun's broad orb; the gleam of swords waves in triumph; all announced a
foe, prepared for battle.'

Gerontes is daunted, but the 'pride and imperious courage' of Romerus leads
to battle:

> … *the woodlands give*
> *Their dire inhabitants to sight! A crew*
> *In form, in act, horrific; in attire,*
> *Shagged and rude; in stature, arms, and power,*
> *Beyond he feebler race of man, unaw'd*
> *By thunder; wielding rocks …*

Locrinus leads the Trojan counter-attack, 'flaming, as he moved', like a god
'shot from th'Olympian height':

Dover Castle, Kent, with the English Channel beyond, from an old print. The hill,
overlooking the English Channel, was Brutus's 'high eminence' from which he fought the
British giants in Ogilvie's *Britannia*.

... Arms divinely framed,
That graced Aeneas toiling in the van
Of many an host; the helm and splendent mail
Now clad his great descendant ...

Locrinus routs Gerontes, but Camber's flank is overwhelmed by Romerus, who may have won the battle had he not been surrounded by giants fleeing Locrinus, who force him to retreat with them into the trees. But now Azrael causes Androgeus to bring his Albians – Abractes from Clwyd, Caractacus from Conway with his 'steeds that on the sides of cloudy Snowdon ranged free as the liberal air', the brothers Trigontes and Segonax from 'Plynlynmmon's flower-enamell'd vales' and many more, to enforce the giant ranks. Locrinus and Romerus almost negotiate peace, but Azrael's demons cause the armies to 'rush precipitately' back into battle. Androgeus drives the Trojans before him but shows his decency by sparing the life of a young Trojan, Phraortes, at 'the intercession of his Tutor'.

Brutus now descends from his 'high eminence'. This must be Dover Castle, which is built over Roman foundations within Iron Age embankments: the idea of Trojans fighting giants there goes back at least to Holinshed in the 1570s. As Brutus marches down, Britannia 'assuming mortal form, marches before him' and battles the demon Moloch, a character borrowed direct from *Paradise Lost*. Ogilvie tells us:

... And now Britannia's Queen
Unsheath'd her sword amid the solar orb,
Drench'd deep, and streaming with its purest ray.
Th'Infernal [demon] mark'd his fate, and from its edge
Shrunk back in terror ...

Brutus 'by coolness and perseverance' prevails against Androgeus, who 'wastes his force, under the influence of passion.' Romerus kills Clitander, Prince of Mycenae, but is wounded by Locrinus, and Azrael spirits him away to safety in the woods. Now Satan himself comes up from Hell with the fiend Bethphlegon, the embodiment of Despair, just in time to prevent Androgeus from suing Brutus for peace. The armies part in the evening and we see the Trojans

Lodg'd in their tents, when now the setting sun
Play'd on the chalky cliffs, and faintly tinged
The forest' waving umbrage ...

Brutus sends Albanus and Eugenius with men to hide in the forest, ready to ambush the enemy as occasion required. The next day, just as Amazons played their part in Homer's and Virgil's wars, Gerontes' fearsome daughter Leontia takes to the field, wreaking havoc amongst the Lydians, another contingent that has sailed here with the Trojans, until Camber slays her. Gerontes defeats but fails to kill Camber and, grieving, bears his dead daughter from the field.

Britannia now summons the guardian spirits of the island, 'from groves, and caverns dark, that hear afar the torrent's roar; from grot, and haunted stream' – Dariel, Icariel, Zeruiah, Zelohim and 'Astor ... from the willow'd bank of Thamesis'. All looks set for a great Trojan victory, but God (in order,

The forces of God and Satan battle in the skies in one of Gustave Doré's illustrations for Milton's *Paradise Lost*: the scene applies equaly well to the angelic war over Kent in Ogilvie's *Britannia*.

presumably, to create dramatic tension) holds the good spirits back. Androgeus and Brutus meet in battle again and they almost come to terms, but Satan himself intervenes, wrapping the whole battlefield in darkness and casting Brutus onto the ground. Romerus is victorious over the Trojan's right wing and now Despair rushes onto the field, routing the Trojans entirely. Brutus is, truly, in despair, but God responds by allowing Britannia to unleash her celestial forces, and she in turn rouses Albanus and Eugenius's hidden army, inspiring them to assail the giants from behind. Britannia seizes Despair 'and striking Earth that opens, precipitates her to Hell.'

This is enough to save the Trojans from destruction, and they retreat safely back into their camp, Brutus being the last man to enter the safety of its walls, where he laments the loss of Locrinus. Brutus has a 'mighty heart, by hostile armies unappall'd, that bore, in perilous fight, as in the calm of peace, an equal tenour', but now, imagining Locrinus dead, he paces about his tent, imagining the giants slaughtering them all. He gives 'one burst of human passion to the lot, the changeful lot of MAN'. But then his Trojan fortitude returns. 'Yes,' he says, 'let me bear, Great Lord of Nature ... the ills that courage cannot ward. Rough is the road, and dark the passage to th'oblivious stream that bloats remembrance out. But let me face in arms the peril' with 'resolution, cool' and his bard sings of Hercules, who overcame the greatest obstacles in order to complete his labours.

But Locrinus is not dead: he has been lured into the woods, searching for his beloved Almeria, whom Azrael had also tricked into seeking safety amongst the trees earlier on. But thanks to Britannia, Almeria has found refuge with a druid, and now Locrinus finds her there.

The druid then shows Locrinus a vision of the future, akin to that which Aeneas experienced in Hades in book six of the *Aeneid*. Through Locrinus's eyes we see the Roman invasion, the breaching of Hadrian's Wall and the desolation caused by the Saxons, then the Vikings and Alfred, all lessons that Britain was 'a prey to foreign nations' while she remained in 'ignorance of maritime affairs, and want of a Navy'. We see Britain groaning under King John and papal interference, until 'the Power of Liberty descends from heaven with the MAGNA CHARTA'. Following this, Ogilvie traces the rise of Britain's commerce and naval greatness. Locrinus sees a vision of 'the splendour and magnificence of the metropolis; the Thames covered with the ships of all nations; the business, freedom, wealth, power, and commerce of Great Britain; her navy; her extensive empire in the East and West Indies; and last of all her dominions in America'. (Ogilvie notes that he would have included details of the present wars with France, but this would have made an already long chapter even longer.)

The next day, battle resumes and Locrinus returns, piercing Gerontes through the throat: 'supine he lay, and gnash'd in death his bloody mace.' Again, Brutus and Androgeus almost agree a peace treaty but Romerus intervenes and Satan 'comes forth on his native element, as the Prince of the Power of the Air' like 'the flaming meteor, that portends the fate of nations'. Ogilvie anticipates by 140 years the Battle of Britain, when the fate of Britain was again decided by battles in the clouds above Kent, for now the Angel Ithuriel swoops down, armed with the power of God and the Lord of Darkness 'is finally expelled by the thunder of Omnipotence.'

Locrinus, aided by Eugenius and some of the Albians, manage to penetrate the giants' fortress, bodily forcing up the pails of its spiked wooden walls and using them as a bridge to cross the ditch inside: their savage massacre of the giant women and children is brief and rather glossed over by Ogilvie, who focuses instead on the glory of the Trojans' triumph.

Back on the field, Romerus alone is unconquered but, covered with wounds, leans on a tree trunk for support. Locrinus faces him and the fighting stops. Romerus's 'God-like rival seem'd prepared to meet his arm,' but the giant is too badly wounded to fight. 'What nation rising through the shade,' Romerus wonders, 'O'erspreads the boundless region?' He sees a vision of the future, including Britain's warships, 'that hold the subject main enthrall'd, and speak in thunder'.

> *And now, Romerus, from the trunk that bore*
> *His weight, receding, stagger'd on the field;*
> *The vital fluid, streaming in his path,*
> *From wounds that bled afresh. His broad breast heaved*
> *With the last breath. He turn'd his languid eyes*
> *O'er his pale mates, and look'd a long farewell.*
> *They pass'd, they shut in darkness! – Down he fell,*
> *Amid the ruin of his kind, and sunk*
> *In death, without a groan: – the mighty form,*
> *No more the mansion of his noble mind,*
> *On earth low laid, to mix with kindred clay.*

So ends Ogilvie's *Britannia*, which he 'considered ... the principal literary employment of my life' and justly so, for the grand project of a full-length epic about Brutus had at last been accomplished.

Ogilvie's angels, with their arcanely Old Testament names, seem closely related to Blake's and both are derived from those in Milton's *Paradise Lost*. His Brutus is most closely related to Pope's, and to the Brutus of Blake's earlier poetry. Ogilvie certainly took as many liberties with Brutus's story as Pope had done, changing many details – no Ignoge or Corineus, no battles in Gaul, a different landing place in Britain. As far as we can tell, Brutus arrives in Britain a widower, and maybe this is intentional: for who else could he be, in Ogilvie's Miltonic vision, but the (chaste) consort of Britannia herself?

Attention, Ogilvie claimed in direct riposte to Dr Johnson, was most certainly not wearied on Brutus's story, but at 15,000 lines long, as *The Monthly Review* put it, 'few persons will be able to accomplish a progress through the whole' and I had the impression, reading the London Library's copy, that few people between then and now had struggled through it all. It would have been better if it were much shorter, but its length matches the grandeur of Ogilvie's vision. In his introduction, Ogilvie quoted Dr Edmund Bolton (1574/5–c. 1634), one of those antiquaries who had argued that Brutus was real, 'to exculpate my friend Geoffry from the charge of having invented the story ... although,' he added, 'I am not *quite* so certain of its truth.' But what really counted was the story's poetic truth, and that Brutus's story 'admits the *sublime* and the *marvelous*.'

Chapter 24

Brutus and Victoria

After Pope, Blake and Ogilvie, later writers have continued to make their own additions to Brutus's story. William Wordsworth's own reading of Milton's *History* inspired him in 1815 to write a thirty-verse poem *Artegal and Elidure*, about two of Geoffrey's mythical British kings descended from Brutus. Wordsworth started with a handful of verses about Brutus himself, who freed Britain from the giants' tyranny and 'refined' the island:

> *Whence golden harvests, cities, warlike towers,*
> *And pleasure's sumptuous bowers;*
> *Whence all the fixed delights of house and home,*
> *Friendships that will not break, and love that cannot roam.*

It was a romantic view of Britain's ancient past shared by many of Wordsworth's contemporaries – a Britain that never was, but which always ought to have been: the Britain of Brutus.

Then, in 1860, fifty-nine years after Ogilvie, it was time to retell Brutus's story again for a new, Victorian generation. The first four cantos of *Brutus the Trojan, A Poem* were published in London in 1860. Its author chose to hide behind initials, C.D.. Charles Dickens was at the height of his powers then, but so too were Charles Darwin and Charles Dodgson (better known as Lewis Carroll). Our author was probably someone of far less magnitude – not as fine a poet as Hildebrand Jacob, but a competent one capable of conjuring up some memorable images.

C.D. explained in his introduction that 'this attempt at reviving a medieval Romance, such as used to delight our forefathers, is an undertaking which may perhaps require some apology in the latter half of the Nineteenth Century, or rather some indulgence and imaginativeness on the part of the reader,' and he hoped, with typical Victorian self-deprecation, that the story 'may not prove uninteresting.' To make the poem relevant to his time, C.D. reminded his readers that 'Shakespeare's *King Lear* was drawn from these sources and the late beautiful revival of that play, amongst others, by Mr. C. Kean, is what induced the writer to search those old Chronicles, where he found the subject of the following poem, which at once impressed itself on his imagination.' Then we discover that C.D. was one of those who, like the Reverend Aaron Thompson, thought that 'the story itself ... has been generally believed to be founded on truth': this was 'the original history of the foundation of the British Empire'. This theme continues in the poem that prefaces Canto one, which asks, rhetorically, whether the reader, the 'fastidious son of modern science', would deem that everything that Geoffrey wrote 'was all a false and unsubstantial dream?'

The epic opens, perhaps not coincidentally, just after Jacob's ended, with the Trojan fleet putting out to sea from Gaul after their victory over Goffar. The 'swifter warlike gallies' lead the way and the 'heavier laden craft' follow behind, 'and flashed the sea beneath their stroke.'

> *On board, their wives, their arms, their all they bore,*
> *Advent'rous seeking o'er the salt sea-foam*
> *Upon some free and undiscovered shore*
> *A place of rest, a country, and a home.*

The Trojans are a 'fearless, frank, and handsome race ... not unaccustomed to the warlike field'. The Victorians saw humans in terms of races and this noble one was of course the precursor of the modern British: 'Full well became each open sunburnt face the Phrygian bonnet,' and C.D. admired their courage, 'who dared to try the fortune of the deep ere yet the compass or the magnet's art.'

Now we meet Brutus, 'his dark eye fixed in calm and thoughtful mood, on open space that clear before him lay; tall, but well knit his form, in prime of youth and yet of pensive melancholy mien, seldom or never was a smile, in sooth, upon his grave and classic features seen.' His leadership, as with the Victorian ruling classes, is innate: his 'mind superior makes the crowd obey.'

With Brutus is Corineus, 'blue-eyed, with curling beard, so vast his force, that fabled Hercules you might have deemed stood there in person', and nearby sits Ignoge, whom C.D. calls Iogerne. Despite the rigours of the voyage she is immaculately dressed in Greek robes, 'embroidered deep with purple and with gold', her features like a marble statue and her 'dark hair clustered on the ivory brow.' She is 'serene, but pallid, and with sadness rife, resigned to fate and to her nuptial vow.' Corineus wonders later 'if she loved that daring Chief to whom her fate was linked; or, if her heart was marble like her look' because 'some young Greek dwelt in her memory still.' Perhaps Corineus is in love with her ('love, unrequited,' warns C.D. in book three, 'withers up the heart.')

But Corineus's more pressing concern is the voyage. 'How must we steer?' he asks Brutus, 'for o'er the pathless sea no sign of land ahead as yet appears.' But Brutus is sanguine: 'still onwards hold our course; beyond these waves, doubt not, O Corinaeus, lies the land ... have confidence in me, my destiny floats on the swelling tide.' When Corineus and Iogerne remain unconvinced, spooked by the silence of the ocean, Brutus declares 'in me behold the Child of Fate! though dark and gloomy on my birth the stars arose, my course tends onwards to a brighter mark, and clouds disperse, and happier days unclose. Sprung from old Priam's race, the Trojan line of Princes lives in me.' His mother, he says, was an Etruscan princess called Lavinia, whilst his father's grandfather was 'goddess-born Aeneas' (a phrase used frequently by Virgil). But because of the prophecy that Brutus would kill his father, 'men looked askance upon me; sometimes kind, sometimes regretful looks my father gave,' so 'thrown back upon itself my infant mind learnt self-reliance, more reserved and grave.'

A thousand years after Nennius first wrote about that fatal hunting accident, C.D.'s Brutus looks back and tells us in his own words how it happened:

> *Years ran their course, – my sixteenth summer past,*
> *Approaching manhood nerved my limbs apace;*
> *I knew not all the worst, – yet vaguely cast*
> *A shadowy, black, and apprehensive trace,*
> *That half told Prophecy – as clouds obscure*
> *Before a thunderstorm, pregnant with flame,*
> *The summer sky and dim its brightness pure;*
> *I could not dream such deed, and yet it came.*
>
> *I loved the chase; upon the Alban hills*
> *To rouse the boar, or track the fleeter deer,*
> *Close at my Father's side, and far away*
> *From man's abode; how oft the pine-topped glade*
> *Rang to our horns! ...*

[Brutus's memory is faulty here: C.D. fondly imagined Italian pines, but the woods around Alba Longa are deciduous. Still, the scene is set ...]

> *In hot impetuous haste was hurled my dart,*
> *It grazed a tree and glanced aside – a cry!*
> *A fall! – the steel had pierced a Father's heart.*

On the deck of his ship, Brutus remembers the scene, 'darker than my darkest dream … I beheld him quivering on the clay; when from his side gushed forth a crimson stream'. Overcome with renewed remorse, Brutus cries: 'look down, paternal shade … pardon thy son … stern Fate decreed, and Fate must have its course.' But despite his grief, Brutus is a model of Victorian self-control: his 'deep-drawn breathing was the only sound. At length his heart, accustomed to control, more calmly beat, by the strong mind subdued.' He recounts how, exiled, he had wandered to Greece, found the Trojans enslaved and encouraged them to rise up. Like Jacob, C.D. knits Brutus's story back into the world of Aeneas, where it belongs, making Pandrasus into a son of Pyrrhus (Neoptolemus) and likening Brutus asking Pandrasus to set his people free to Priam of Troy begging Neoptolemus's father Achilles to give back the corpse of his son Hector at the end of the *Iliad*: 'with swelling heart I sued for liberty.'

As we know, Pandrasus refuses and the war begins. The Trojans fight bravely: 'what memories nerved our arm you best can know, what thoughts of ancient Ilion's [Troy's] heroes slain.' C.D. turns Brutus forcing Anacletus to betray the Greeks into a revenge for 'Sinon's fraud', for Sinon was the one who made the wooden horse, which the Greeks tricked the Trojans into taking inside their walls. Now, 'when the silver moon had sank behind the mountain crest' the Trojans crept into the Greek camp. 'The King's pavilion well I marked,' recalls Brutus, 'and led my band towards it … Over the mossy turf with noiseless tread … then sudden shouts that midnight silence broke, and rushed to arms the half-awakened foe; then many a Trojan blade with vengeful stroke laid many a son of haughty Argos low.'

Pandrasus is captured: 'Around the Monarch Trojan falchions shine, eyes flash beneath dark brows in angry mood. I would not take his life, – at my behest each swordman's point was lowered to the ground; disarmed and sad, he bent his lofty crest and yielded to his fate as Fortune frowned.' Pandrasus agrees to Brutus's demands for ships, supplies and the hand of his daughter ('strange', comments C.D., perhaps from personal experience, 'how stern parents alter in their mind when altered circumstances favour gain'). Thus, 'the Trojan Outcast won a Royal Bride.'

The poem prefacing the second canto is about the migration of birds and their unerring skills in navigation. Its cause (their ability to detect the Earth's magnetic field) was not yet understood: C.D. thought it was due to 'a mystic power' (from God, as he lets on later), and likened this to the one that guided the Trojans to Britain. The canto itself opens with the sound of axe on wood, reminiscent of the *Aeneid*, as the Greeks, 'on cloud-capped hills felled the enduring widely-branching oak' and the 'lofty pine by mountain rills sank crashing to the woodman's vigorous stroke.' The fleet is being built and meanwhile Trojans flock to the shore where 'full many a hand unwonted tries the oar' of the new-built ships.

They set sail and reach Leogecia (Lefkada). It is wooded with oak, pine and birch (a mistake, as no birches grow there). Diana's temple is reminiscent of Virgil's ivy-entangled Latium. Foxes made their lairs in the ruins, 'through the open roof the rain had sent streams on the floor', 'the wild fig tree waved its leafy head' and 'among the arbutus [strawberry tree] and cistus [rockrose] gay the aromatic myrtle shed perfume.' In the midst of this abundant growth, 'untouched Diana's Image dwelt, as if some marble majesty divine.' Brutus and his companions, Geryo, Mempricus and Helenus make their sacrifices. Brutus asks his question of Diana and settles down to sleep.

> *Scarce knew I if I slumbered, till at last*
> *Dawn through the fractured roof a silvery ray*
> *Between me and the altar gently passed,*
> *The moonlit walls seemed bright'ning into day.*
> *The radiant mist took shape before my eyes*
> *Of more than mortal beauty, strange to tell*
> *I knew the form! – yet strove in vain to rise,*
> *While clear upon my sense these accents fell*

He has seen Diana, albeit in a lucid dream, and, dreamlike, his limbs are unresponsive. Yet he hears her response and then awakes. There is 'no trace of a Supernal Being' to be seen and, like a Victorian rationalist, Brutus wonders 'if some vague delusion [had] filled mine ear'. But his wise companions are sure he had heard a 'prophetic voice'.

They follow the course described in Geoffrey, south to the African coast and then west along it, the fleet progressing like 'stately oxen ... with measured steps across the grassy vale'. Though attacked by pirates like 'bloodthirsty insect tribes', their 'Trojan valour foiled their swarthy host.' As they pass Gibraltar, Brutus comments, presciently, 'if in a future age some warlike King that towering Rock precipitous should own, what vent'rous enemy could hope to bring a force to drive him from such Titan-throne!' In the straits they see 'sea monsters round us, singular and vast'. Sailing up the Spanish coast they find Corineus, 'stout of heart as of Herculean frame'. Joining forces with him, they sail north-west to Gaul and encounter the Gauls.

The story follows Geoffrey but the description of the Gauls is inspired by Jacob, though they have become even more primitive. The archaeological ages of stone, bronze and iron had been codified in 1848, and for C.D. the Trojans were the harbingers of the Bronze Age in northern Europe. The natives, therefore, were Stone Age people, 'half clad in wolf and other shaggy hides; loose down their shoulders streamed their waving hair, axes of polished flint hung by their sides' and in their quivers were darts 'of sharpened bone and tusk of boar'. C.D.'s view was also coloured by colonialism, for his Gauls stood for any native people encountered by the civilised British: 'each Gaul among them raged, and strained his lungs, and shook his javelin tipped with sharpened bone. So ludicrous their rage, we smiling stood.' The Gaul Imbertus fires an arrow at Corineus, who simply steps aside like an Eton-educated officer, seizes Imbertus and knocks him down: 'the awe-struck horde, astonished, fled with cries of wailing sound.'

But the natives stop being amusing when they return en masse, 'with wild and savage cry'. Their advance is 'like a torrent rolled that overleaps its wonted river marge' and the Trojans 'scarce could hold our ranks unbroken by such fiery charge.' Corineus leads the counter-attack, fighting Suhardus, who has three skulls hanging from his horse's mane, 'their faded locks among its plaits entwined ... barbaric trophies bleached by sun and wind.' 'Thy head shall make the fourth!' Suhardus cries, but brave Corineus slays him and the slaughter goes on: 'lopped arms and limbs before his falchion's sweep ensanguined fell' until the barbarians 'turned, and safety sought in flight.' The Gauls buried Suhardus by the Loire, slaughtering his horse and wife to lie there with him. 'To me,' Brutus comments, anticipating the British banning Indian women from being forced to commit suicide at their husbands' funerals in 1829, 'such rites seemed cruel and abhorred.'

The Trojans travel up the Loire and overwinter in the camp that will become Tours. The Gauls muster a great army and when spring comes they attack, but (like the British Empire builders again) 'our walls were proof against such warriors rude.' Corineus leads another successful attack on them, but then the Trojans decide to leave and 'mindful of Fate, to trust the azure main and seek our long-expected Island shore.'

As Brutus finishes recounting his story, his 'eager eye descried' Britain, 'yet indistinct and dim' in a distant mist, the breakers roaring below its cliffs, but soon the haze clears and canto three begins:

Thus Iogerne beneath the rising Sun
Beheld the shores expanding to her sight,
Down to the beach the silver streamlets run,
Mingling their freshness with the surges white.

Brutus at once names the island Britain, and spies the mouth of the Dart, 'whose 'placid waters ope, as welcoming the ocean's future Lords,'

Like some secluded lake, that ne'er till now
Upon its surface boat or man had known
The Dart was cleft before the Trojan prow
Which broke with dash of oars its stillness lone.
Like living gems the kingfisher flashed by,
The melancholy heron, scared at the sight,
Rose from the shallows, and with wailing cry
Flapped his broad wings, and stretched his legs for flight.

That is just how the Dart is, along with its 'tufted oaks' with their 'gnarled and massive forms'. Ogilvie's epic was littered with references to parts of the British Empire and, copying him, C.D. likens Brutus to Christopher Columbus entering an untamed paradise. They reach an opening in the trees, whose 'broad level turf' would be suitable for 'tournaments and jousts of chivalry' such as had been held in Troy. Brutus 'sprang forth … on the grassy shore, while all the air with joyous plaudits rang.'

They camp in what will become Totnes. The following morning they all assemble 'upon a rising hill of freshest green', which is the mound where Totnes Castle stands. There was a choir of matrons and fair virgins 'led by their graceful Lady, Iogerne, with flowrets crowned and loosely flowing hair' and 'the ranks of warriors holding their hunting spears in their sinewy hands'. Brutus leads them in prayers of thanks to the 'powers divine' that had guided them:

Lit by the splendor of his [God's] *morning rays,*
That festal crowd assembled on the height,
In the simplicity of olden days.
Encircled by the hills and waving wood
Their altar of the mossy turf was reared.

Now something extraordinary happens, which neither Geoffrey nor Jacob had imagined, but of which Milton, Pope and Blake would have approved: old Helenus steps forth, 'vested in flowing robes of purest white, a wreath of oakleaves on his temples bound, with feeble steps, but eye undimmed and bright … in patriarchal green old age'. Helenus was the brother of Aeneas's wife Creusa. Virgil wrote that he had died by the time Aeneas had reached Buthrotum, but the idea that he had survived long enough to join Brutus on his voyage goes back to Holinshed at least, who states in his *Chronicles* (1577/87) that Brutus had 'made him his preest and bishop thorough out the new conquest' and repeats the idea that Cornwall had once been called the 'promontorie of Helenus', and that the 'sea haue washed awaie his sepulchre' that was once there.

   Now, in C.D.'s epic, old Helenus,

> … *told that finished were those times of woe*
> *That long had weighed down Troy's devoted line;*
> *If Gods of Greece had wrought her overthrow,*
> *And crushed her warriors with their force divine …*
> *They now might see that some still mightier powers,*
> *(Since e'en Olympian Jove to Fate must yield)*
> *Had still preserved their race in darkest hours*
> *Sublime yet vague ideas of One Supreme;*
> *His words, scarce comprehended, filled their breast*

'Thus the old Sage, in solemn train of thought, unfolded to the crowd … such doctrines as the earliest Druids taught, tho' later priestcraft wove them gloomier veil,' and 'the Trojan throng to a yet Unknown God their voices raise, with garlands decked, intoning choral song round the turf altar of primaeval days.' Ideas that the ancient British druids had been monotheistic, due perhaps to some (imagined) contact with the Holy Land, or the teachings of Pythagoras, were popular in Britain at the time, so here we have the Trojans effectively laying the foundations of the Church of England and what followed, for in the eighteenth century, John Wesley set out to reform Anglicanism (and ended up founding Wesleyan Methodism) by touring the West Country, preaching in the open air. Anticipating Wesley, Helenus decrees that the British should always worship 'under the blue vault of Heaven alone, on the broad hill-top … where the free wind pours forth its organ tone'.

   They draw lots for the land and begin to cultivate fields. Brutus and his companions start to explore: 'Elate he trod the turf, through woodland maze they wandered long' and through 'verdant meadows' where 'streamlets ran sparkling and unrestrained.' Now the woods thin out and the land rises up through holly trees to 'firm turf, amid the golden gorse' where 'some solitary thorn … clad with lichen gray, bent by the wind of Dartmoor wild' (see plate 32).

Up on Dartmoor they see a heard of aurochs, magnificent wild cattle. They must have brought horses all the way from Greece, so they pursue the cattle on horseback, like the gauchos of Columbia, says C.D., complete with lassoes. They injure the bull with a javelin and 'the forest Monarch, bellowing, turns to bay, and dares the hunters to unequal fight … his eyeballs rolling gleam with fury bright.' His horn grazes Brutus's leg. Corineus 'daringly the prostrate beast bestrode' and 'grasped the spreading horns in either hand,' while 'Brutus quickly drew his gleaming knife and plunged it in the chest.'

The huntsmen's horns, which had sounded once in the forests of Mount Ida near Troy, now ring across the tors of Dartmoor. But their celebration has an unexpected consequence, for it attracts giants, one of whom, Goemagot, comes to investigate. 'A crash was heard of interlacing boughs, as when the East wind in its fury rends their limbs asunder … Human he seemed; but all uncouth and strange, with shaggy eyebrows, and neglected beard … his rustic vesture was a thick bull's hide … .' He whirls an uprooted oak tree about his head, posturing like 'some huge Elephant on Indian plains, scorning his pigmy foes'. Corineus is ready to attack but Brutus thinks this rash, and the stand-off ends disappointingly with the giant retreating. When the Trojans go back later to search for traces of the giants, they find nothing more than bears' footprints, as if it had all been an illusion.

We had not expected the bull hunt, but maybe C.D. was thinking of the bull that Romerus slew in Ogilvie's epic. Bulls were the emblems of the Minoan kings, too: instead of fighting the mythical giants to gain control of Britain, Brutus had earned his own kingship of the isle through the slaying of the 'forest Monarch'.

Chapter 25

Brutus Reincarnated

In the final canto of C.D.'s *The Romance of Brutus the Trojan*, Brutus wanders his new realm alone, 'charmed with the beauty of its leafy gloom.' From a hilltop he sees the river Exe in the distance and follows a deer track down to Anstey's Cove near Torquay, where something spooks his dog and they hear music 'like some Aeolian harp, with plaintive call … as in a dream'. It is a mermaid, of the type reputed to haunt the West Country coast, complete with 'flowing hair' and 'coral red … lips'.

She says she is 'a daughter of ancient Proteus', the Greeks' Old Man of the Sea. She has followed the Trojan fleet all the way from Lybia, protecting it from the worst of the storms. She had fallen in love with Brutus's 'manly beauty and commanding mien' and invites him to join her in the waves: 'We will rove the ever-sounding shore,' she suggests, and enjoy 'the dreamlike music of the shell'. They will hunt sea monsters together and their sons will rule the waves around Britain. But Brutus is repulsed by a glimpse of her fishy tail and realises that she is a siren (see plate 24). 'This Isle's firm land is my allotted part,' declares Brutus, firmly.

Spurned, she turns nasty: 'Go back!' she hisses, 'and seek thy earthborn bride forlorn.' She curses him, prophesying that every few generations his descendants will suffer from childlessness, murder or exile and she proceeds to show

Brutus sees the execution of Charles I in the siren's mirror.

him his descendants in her mermaid's mirror, 'as the shades of fleeting clouds pass by, swift shall their line appear, and swiftly fade!' C.D. had in mind here the vision of the future shown by the druid to Locrinus in Ogilvie's *Britannia* but more particularly book six of the *Aeneid*, in which Anchises shows Aeneas the 'parade of heroes', the shades of all his descendants down to Augustus.

So now we see, through Brutus's eyes, the division of Britain between his sons Locrinus, Camber and Albanactus, and the subsequent history of their descendants, all based on Geoffrey, including King Leir, Dunwallo Molmutius, Lud, Cassivellaunus and Caractacus – and Boadicea, whom Geoffrey omits – and the Dark Age kings down to Arthur, who is like the last bright flare of a dying lamp, 'the noblest of thy line', and Cadwallo and Cadwallader, who was exiled by the Saxons, whereupon 'their feeble remnant mourns its empire flown.'

'Thou Prophetess of ill to me and mine!' protests Brutus. 'Must all then perish thus, in woe and grief? Is this the ending of the Trojan line?' 'Not so,' the siren replies. 'In distant woods, on misty hills … thy race still lives … by Snowdon's peaks, on Cader Idris side.' Dwelling 'upon the margin of the Western Sea', the Welsh bards 'shall sing through long dark night, by ruddy-gleaming fires, on harps of triply complicated string, the ancient glory of their Trojan sires.'

Now the mirror shows Britain's later rulers including Rhodri Mawr, Alfred, William the Conqueror and Llewelyn, then the Wars of the Roses and Henry VII in whom the 'ancient British Kings [were] revived again'. The Victorians had a particularly romantic fascination with the Stuarts, so Brutus is especially saddened by the executions of Mary Queen of Scots and Charles I, and the fate of the descendants of the exiled James II – Bonnie Prince Charlie, 'the young Ascanius of the second Troy' and his brother Cardinal Henry Stuart, who died, childless, 'on Tiber's bank' in 1807. Brutus is unimpressed by the 'garb grotesque and ordinary mien' of the Georges, but is pleased to see the British Empire being carved out 'of sultry Eastern plains', Nelson winning Trafalgar and Wellington defeating Napoleon. Finally, Brutus looks on with approval as Victoria is crowned, 'feminine and gracious … the well beloved Monarch of the Isle'.

The siren gives him a last, lingering look and vanishes into the waves and Brutus, 'deeply musing, paced the echoing strand.' C.D. may have intended to give us the rest of Brutus's life, and to build on earlier, dark hints of a love affair between Ignoge and Corineus, but he never did so. He leaves us with a Brutus suited to the Victorian age – high-minded yet practical, impeccably moral, a fearless coloniser and empire builder, with a romantic appreciation of the British countryside. His settlement of Britain seeded the British with Trojan blood, laid the foundations for the monotheistic religion that would blossom eventually into Protestantism and gave rise to a line of kings that would lead, ultimately, to Queen Victoria herself.

C.D.'s poem was a hard act to follow, but it would not be surprising if more than one twentieth-century writer had tried to pen a new epic of Brutus. Given the amount of time Brutus spent ravaging Gaul, it would have been interesting to have had an epic written by someone who had experienced the battlefields of France in the First or Second world wars. But if anyone attempted such a thing, I have not found it in print. But J.R.R. Tolkien served in the First World War and his *The Lord of the Rings* (1937–1949) certainly reflects the horrors of all-out war. His epic tale drew heavily on the *Aeneid*, and one of its heroes, Aragorn, the prince sprung from an exiled line who wanders through the northern wastes of Middle Earth, has elements of both Aeneas and Brutus about him.

I toyed with the idea of writing a new epic of Brutus a few years ago and even wrote an ending for it, and a beginning:

> *A fatal arrow, from a fated bow*
> *By my hand drawn but by the gods' will bent*
> *Laid low my high-born father Silvius*
> *In Alba Longa's woods ...*

However, as I researched this book, I found that almost every idea I had come up with, from Brutus returning to Troy to wander through its ruins, to his fighting a war against hostile tribes in Kent, had been imagined already. Such a modern epic would necessarily lack the sense of imperial destiny inherent in Pope, Jacob, Ogilvie and C.D., for that phase of our history is over now, but it could develop C.D.'s reverence for the British countryside, with Brutus roaming across his island, watching approvingly as his people cultivate the land, creating that balance of ploughlands, pasture and wild places that so many of us now long to conserve, the tamed in harmony with the wild: Demeter's cornlands alongside Pan's wild wood. When Brutus looks forward through the siren's mirror he would understand how that fatal arrow changed the world down to the twenty-first century, and witness the parade of his royal descendants continuing down to the marriage of Prince William to Kate Middleton and the births of Prince George and Princess Charlotte. But it remains unwritten.

The invented mythology of Professor Tolkien's world, meanwhile, gave rise to the gentre of fantasy fiction, out of which emerged a reincarnation of Brutus, in *Hades' Daughter* (2003), the first novel of the 'Troy Game' trilogy by

Australian novelist Sara Douglass. This is not a retelling of Brutus's story for its own sake and makes no attempt to retain the spirit of the older versions. Instead, Douglass reinvents the story as part of a broader fantasy plot of her own, and thus invests Brutus with characteristics and powers completely unknown in Geoffrey's original.

In Douglass's fantasy universe, the Greek gods are dwindling in the face of the new spiritual powers that have caused the collapse of Mycenaean civilisation. The highest supernatural power is 'the Game, a labyrinthine mystery of great power and sorcery' (an idea from the Reverend R.W. Morgan in the nineteenth century, who wrote that Troy's walls were modelled on the Cretan labyrinth). Civilisation is founded on 'the Game' and the gods had drawn on it too for their power. Brutus occupies a unique position because he is the last living descendant of any of the kings of the great cities of old. He has been trained in the civilising 'Game' and wears magical golden 'kingbands' (which are literary descendants of Tolkien's magical rings), which he has taken from the dead body of his father Silvius, who had inherited them via Ascanius from Aeneas, who had saved them from the destruction of Troy. On these kingbands the leadership of the exiled Trojans depends.

This makes Brutus the unwitting object of the desire, not of a siren, but of a siren-like goddess who wishes to rule the world. She exists presently in human form, as Genvissa, who lives in Britain, but she appears to Brutus in visions as Artemis (Diana) and lures him there, where she hopes he will 'weave with her that enchantment that would raise this land to everlasting greatness.' By the Thames she hopes to establish a new, power-generating labyrinth, which will be London.

For the first time in Douglass's writings we see Brutus through a modern, female perspective. His physical and sexual aspects, latent in earlier retellings, comes to the fore as we encounter him first – through Artemis's eyes – asleep on a beach on the Adriatic coast, 'not a handsome man, being too blunt of feature and his black eyebrows too straight, but he was well made with wide shoulders, flat belly, slim hips, and long, tightly muscled limbs.' His eyes possess 'that liquid blackness she had always craved in her lovers'. Brutus walks about naturally naked in front of his men and has his groin brushed suggestively by a henchman called Membricius, who we learn had been his lover in adolescence.

Most previous writers about Brutus had invested in him their own hopes and aspirations, but not so Douglass, so he is a darker character than ever before. His slaying of his father, we are shocked to learn, was no accident, for we find him thinking back to 'that terrible (*wonderful*) day when he had taken the kingbands from his dead father's limbs. He'd taken a great risk that day – and been exiled for it – but now that risk had been justified and rewarded.' And when Artemis tells Brutus he is destined to rebuild Troy in Britain, 'he could feel the excitement deep in his belly … he took a deep breath, tipped back his head, and opened his arms to the moonlight, as if in silent exultation.'

As in Geoffrey's narrative, the Trojans are living in Greece, the 'sorry remnants of a people … who had caused their own misfortune'. Douglass places them (correctly) in Epiros and imagines Pandrasus, their Greek captor, as the king of Mesopotama, which is the name of a village not far inland from the mouth of the Acheron. Brutus goes to Mesopotama to free them and, having made his intentions known by a messenger sent amongst the Trojan slaves, he is invited to come into the city in secret to the house of Assaracus, the Greek aristocrat who is half Trojan on his mother's side. Assaracus thinks Brutus thoroughly arrogant in his assumption that he will lead the Trojans, and indeed that he is the heir to anything but 'a rubble of smoking ash and broken dreams'. But Brutus retorts that 'while there are still men who call themselves Trojans, then there *is* a Troy to be heir to!'

The Trojans escape into the mountains and fight an abbreviated version of the battles described by Geoffrey, aided by some extraordinary, magical occurrences. Brutus's humiliation of the defeated Pandrasus is brutal and unpleasant and his rape of his new wife Ignoge (whom Douglass renames Cornelia) is worse: '*Everything* about him repulsed me,' Cornelia recalls, 'his barely clothed body, his sweat, his blunt, unattractive Trojan features, his stableyard manners, his sheer damned confidence.'

Reincarnation is a driving force in Douglass's fantasy world. She introduces the beguiling idea of Brutus being reincarnated down the ages, most prominently as that other great coloniser of Britain, William the Conqueror and later as an army major called Jack Skelton, who lives in London during the Second World War. That is a strange, smog-darkened London, in which the power-giving labyrinth created by Genvissa has survived and evolved, to become the London Underground. All this builds, successfully, on the magical aura that Brutus's myth had woven around London's older landmarks, from Guildhall and the London Stone to, ultimately, the Tower of London, where we will presently find Brutus being buried.

In Aeneas Middleton's 2010 fantasy children's novel *Tim Hartwell and The Brutus of Troy*, Tim (who comes from Tenby, Wales) encounters Brutus sitting 'on his powerful horse' by Lyn Lydaw below Mount Snowdon, his skin 'golden from the sun'. His help has been enlisted to train Tim as a hero. Battling giant beetles, Brutus whisks Tim away up the Stairwell of Travel to his magical city of Troia Nova. Here Brutus shows him the Temple of Diana and, by pulling a secret lever behind her statue, he leads Tim into a secret chamber. Here stands the goddess herself and we learn that, just as she had guided Brutus, her concern is now to aid Tim in his quest.

At Diana's direction, Brutus shows Tim a stone circle in his palace, which surrounds a milestone, later to become the London Stone. Using his magical powers Tim cracks it, as the goddess says he must, and breaks off two fragments: once he reaches the Underworld (called here the Death of Ages) these will turn into the horses that (in Homer) Zeus had given King Laomedon of Troy. Brutus gives Tim a magical rope that suspends them both in mid-air: they gaze far into outer space and, marvellously, can *see* 'the voices of many different artificial intelligence species from planets light years away'.

Their evil adversary Stratford transports Brutus and Tim forward in time to the modern Guildhall, where they find themselves in evening dress, being entertained to dinner by their enemy, who speaks to them in the manner of a Bond villain: 'What family history!' he sneers to Brutus. Back in Troia Nova, they hold funeral games for a dead comrade, which include a chasing match with Magog in what will later become Battersea Park. The city survives a vicious attack by killer spiders. We learn that the stoic ancestors of the Londoners have 'Trojan blood that holds the agony from one of the greatest wars of all mankind, the fall of Troy', and Brutus is soothed to sleep by Diana. Having helped Tim win the Shield of Aeneas from the ghost of the Emperor Claudius, Brutus guides him back to Snowdonia, where he must continue his quest down into the Death of Ages on his own.

Thus does Brutus live on in fiction, and fiction writers continue the literary game of adding ever more layers to his story, which started to be told over a millennia and a half ago and owed its own origins to Homer's songs of Troy almost 3,000 years ago, at the dawn of Western literature.

Part IV

Burying Brutus

Chapter 26

Brutus of the Kymry

From the time of Homer down to the reign of Henry VII, the Trojan myth had stood at the gateway between the golden age of the dim and distant past, and the modern age of iron and strife, shielding our ancestors from the immensity of time that lay beyond. But once Polydore Vergil had shaken Britain's belief in its Trojan past in the sixteenth century, the British found themselves increasingly bereft of roots in which they could truly believe. Adam and Eve and Noah were still there, reassuringly printed in the pages of their Bibles, but between then and the time of Arthur was a bewildering void. 'The historians tried to fill the gap with Pytheas of Marseille and Julius Caesar,' wrote scholar George Gordon, 'but fill as they might they had little success. The hole was too big, and the prehistoric wind kept coming through.'

The embryonic science of archaeology was one possible means of plugging the gap. In the 1530s, attempting to build genuine history on ephemeral foundations, the Canterbury schoolmaster John Twyne (d. 1581) reported the opinion of the Abbott of St Augustine's, Canterbury that, before the Great Flood cut Britain off from the Continent, the land was occupied by the giant Albion, son of Neptune, whose people lived in caves, hunted and gathered food and erected the great megaliths and earthworks. He was wrong, but his fascination led to a more serious study of these ancient remains that led ultimately to the modern archaeological understanding of them and of the real ancient Britons who built them.

The loss of faith in Brutus's Trojans 'laid Britain open', as Sir Thomas Kendrick wrote, 'to any invaders that an ingenious antiquary might see fit to conduct to our shores'. Twyne suggested that Britain's true civilisers were the Phoenicians, who had come looking for tin. This idea was revived by the French biblical scholar Samuel Bochart in his 1646 *Geographia Sacra*, which maintained that the Phoenicians had built Stonehenge. Phoenician Britain was a central theme of Aylett Sammes's 1676 *Britannia Antiqua Illustrata*. The idea remained popular throughout the eighteenth century and has remained floating about in pseudo-history ever since – but it is not correct.

In the time of Blake, Edward Williams (1747–1826), who assumed the 'bardic' pseudonym of Iolo Morganwg, was inspired by Geoffrey of Monmouth and Annius of Viterbo to invent a fresh origin myth of his own. An enthusiastic reviver of druidism (see plate 37), Morganwg was averse to the Trojan myth because, as his biographer Prys Morgan wrote, it 'made Welsh history subservient to a foreign myth, to the Virgilian vision of ancient Roman history.' At the start of the nineteenth century *Myvyrian Archaiology of Wales*, a journal devoted to the revival of Welsh nationalism, started publishing traditional Welsh triads (short poems containing ancient lore, originally *aides-memoire* for bards). Morganwg, who was a laudanum addict, forged a whole series of his own triads, which were published (as the third series of triads) alongside the genuine ones. Through these he erected what Rachel Bromwich has described as 'an elaborate fiction which depicted the eponymous Prydain son of Aedd as the original legislator and administrator of the Welsh nation'. Prydain was a genuinely ancient figure in Welsh tradition, but in Morganwg's second forged triad he assumed some of Brutus's roles: it was he, not Brutus, who made the 'primary Divisions of the Island of Britain', Cymmru, Lloegr and Alban, and he was one of the island's three 'Great [or Beneficial] Sovereigns'. Morganwg made Brutus wholly subservient to Prydain by turning him into a British-born character called Brwth, who was Prydain's great-grandson. Morganwg even invented a new British creation myth in his ninety-seventh triad, 'The Three Great Exploits of the Island of Britain'. This tells of 'the ship of Nevydd Nav Neivion, which carried in it a male and female of all things living, when the Lake of floods burst forth, and the horned oxen of Hu [Gadarn] the Mighty, which drew the Avanc of the Lake to land, so that the Lake burst forth no more'.

Most people realised Iolo's triads were forgeries, but some loved them so much that they wanted them to be genuine. In the mid-nineteenth century, for instance, John Williams (Ab Ithel), one of the leading proponents of Welsh nationalism and an organiser of the Eisteddfod of 1858, thought Morganwg, as Prys Morgan wrote, 'incapable of perpetrating literary deceit' and so his influence has lived on in British pseudo-history. But these details are, most certainly, inventions of Morganwg's.

Iolo Morganwg had sought to play down Brutus in order to encourage Welsh nationalistic pride, but ultimately Brutus's myth was too long-standing, too powerful, to remain subdued. In 1857, three years before C.D.'s epic appeared, it bubbled up to the surface again with gusto in *The British Kymry: or Britons of Cambria*. Its author was an imaginative Welsh clergyman, the Reverend Richard Williams Morgan (c. 1815–1889), a cousin of John Williams (Ab Ithel) and, like him, an enthusiastic reviver and promoter of Welsh culture. Two years before the appearance of Darwin's *Origin of Species* (1859), Genesis remained the main point of reference for most people's view of the ancient past, and Morgan attempted a grand synthesis of this with the works of Iolo Morganwg and Geoffrey of Monmouth, all informed by his personal belief that the Welsh were the greatest nation in the world.

Before the Great Flood, the progeny of Adam and Eve inhabit the 'White Island of the West', which is now Britain. The Flood, Morgan claimed, was remembered in two ancient sources, the Hebrew Bible (which was preeminent in world literature, as the Creator had intended) and also, and with equal authority, in Welsh literary tradition. This was because the Welsh were the senior branch of the human race, so therefore their language must be the original language of Noah. In Wales, 'the harp has never been silent – the spirit of the poet has never been quenched – the heart of the nation had never ceased to pour forth its emotions in the same tongue the Kymry of Asia first brought from the Crimea and the Caucasus.' Pre-eminent in Welsh sources were the triads, especially those 'found' (but sadly, in fact, made up) by Iolo Morganwg. Thus, the Welsh sources recall the building of the ship of Nevydd Nav Neivion and how 'Dwy Van (the Man of God, whom the Hebrews remembered as Noah) and Dwy Vach (the Woman of God, Noah's wife)' survive the great flood.

The Ark floats away from Britain and ends up, as Middle Eastern tradition asserts, on Mount Ararat in Armenia. Noah's sons' descendants populate the world – Ham's settling in Egypt and Africa, Shem's in the Semitic lands of the Middle East and Japheth's spreading across the rest of the world. In the Bible, Japheth was the youngest son but in Morgan's book, and with no obvious justification, he becomes the oldest, 'and in right of such Primogeniture the Heir of the World.' Continuing the long tradition of ascribing Europe's different races to Japheth's seven sons, Morgan provided some updates for nineteenth-century readers: the Russians, for instance, are descended from Japheth's son Mesech or Mosoch, who is, he said, an eponym for Moscow.

The eldest of Japheth's sons, Gomer (or 'Chomr', said Morgan), is ancestor of the 'Kymry, or Cimbri', the Welsh. This idea does not appear in Josephus or Isidore of Seville because the racial term Kymry, which means 'compatriots', only came into use later on in the Dark Ages, as the Romano-Britons forged a new identity for themselves in the face of the Anglo–Saxon invasion. But by 1799 Philip Yorke reported a Welsh theory that Noah's grandson Gomer had founded the Cimmerian tribe, which migrated up the Danube, into Gaul and thence to Wales, where they called themselves 'Gomeri or Cymry'. That piece of faux-etymology was surely a major inspiration for Morgan's own, ambitious scheme.

Gomer's descendants, the Kymri, flourish in the Caucasus and the Crimea, 'the Summer Land': Gumri in Armenia and the Cimmerorioi on the shores of the Black Sea recall their name. Then, about 1700 BC, a descendant called Hu Gadarn (another of Iolo Morganwg's inventions) resolves to return to his people's ancient home and begins travelling west. His followers are members of three subgroups of the Kymri – the Kymry proper, the Brythons and the Loegrwys (a name derived, in fact, from the Welsh name for England). As they travel, members of these groups are left behind, as the Locrians of Greece and Ligurians of south-east Gaul, the Brythons of Brittany, the Kelts of Gaul and the Kymry of Italy, whose name becomes corrupted from Kymry to 'Umbri'. For this reason Morgan asserted that Latin, which he said was the language of the Umbrians, is 'based on Kymric, not the Kymric on the Latin'. Old Roman family names such as Claudius, Cato, Pompeius and so on all, therefore, are ultimately of Kymric origin.

Finally, the remaining members of each tribe reach their ancestral homeland of Britain. It is still mostly waterlogged, presumably due to the Flood, so they settle on the southern chalk plateaus and in the western and northern mountains, as the three 'Pacific [Peaceful] Tribes'. The 'Elder tribe' of the Kymry, whom Morgan made into the senior descendants of Gomer, eldest son of Japheth, eldest son, he said, of Noah, hold 'the monarchic and military supremacy' and choose, of course, to settle in Wales (and they also settle in Scotland as the Picts).

The foregoing merges Morganwg's invented triads with the Bible. Now it was time to synthesise all of this with Geoffrey, a near-impossible task that Morgan tackled with aplomb, to the extent, he wrote, that Britain's Trojan inheritance 'solves the numerous and very peculiar agreements in the social and military systems of pre-historic Britain and Asia which would otherwise remain inexplicable.'

Virgil (following Dionysius of Halicarnassus) had asserted that the Trojans' founder Dardanos was born in Italy. Morgan therefore claimed that Dardanos is a descendant of the Umbri[ans], who are a branch of the Kymry. Dardanos settles in the Troad and his descendants, the Trojans, are thus the only people in Asia Minor who are not Semitic descendants of Shem. To prove this, Morgan argued that the Trojan Ganymede's original name is Gwyn the Beautiful, Erichthonius's is Eric and Venus, the daughter of 'Jove, King of Crete', is Gwen. In Laomedon's time 'the citadel and walls of Troy were rebuilt by Belin and

Nev, architects of Crete, after the model of the Cretan Labyrinth, which was also an exact representation of the Stellar Universe.' Jason and his Argonauts (including Hercules, whose original name is Hercwlf) abduct Hesione from Troy, so in the next generation Paris, in justifiable revenge, abducts Helen from Greece. After the ten–year siege of Troy, Antenor and Helenus, who 'had always been averse to the war … threw open the Scaean Gate, surmounted by a statue of the white horse of the sun' to let in the Greeks. It was not Homer who sang of this, incidentally: the *Iliad* is in fact 'a collection of the Heroic Ballads of the Bards of the *Gomeridas* or Kymry … originally composed in the Kymric or Bardic characters'. Only later is this Welsh text translated into Greek.

Aeneas, son of Anchises and Gwen (Venus), escapes and leads the survivors back to Italy, where he marries Llawen (Lavinia). His story is told by Virgil, 'a descendant of the Kymric conquerors of Italy under Brennus', one of Geoffrey's kings, who had reputedly led an army of Gauls into Italy: Virgil is, 'as his writings everywhere evidence, an initiated Bard.' Aeneas's great-grandson Brutus is duly born, accidentally kills his father and leads the Trojans enslaved in Albania to freedom.

Brutus 'resolved on emigrating with all his people to the Northern seat of the mainstock of his race – the White Island.' He receives his prophecy from Diana (whose real name was Karidwen) on Malta, which is 'called Legetta'. They join forces, surprisingly, with a colony of Cretans whom they find in Calabria and then, more conventionally, they meet Troenous (Corineus), the leader of four colonies of exiled Trojans in southern Spain. They fight their war against the Kelts of Gaul and Brutus's nephew Tyrrhi is killed at Tours. They reach Torbay and Brutus is the first to step ashore, onto the 'Stone of Brutus' in Totnes. 'The disembarkation occupied three weeks.'

Following Alexander Pope's idea of the favourable reception in Britain of Brutus, 'The three Pacific Tribes' of Britain 'received their countrymen from the East as brethren.' A 'National Convention of the whole Island' is called and Brutus is 'elected Sovereign Paramount' and 'the throne and crown of Hu Gadarn thus devolved upon him, by descent and suffrage.' Earlier, Morganwg had associated Brutus with the old eponym of Britain, Prydain, so as to undermine the Trojan myth. But now Morgan undid this work completely by using Morganwg's inventions to strengthen his own myth of Trojan Brutus and the Welsh phrase *Ynys Prydein*, 'the island of Britain', became in Morgan's book 'the island of Brutus'.

In place of the 'simple patriarchal usages' of the islanders, Brutus introduces Trojan law, including the principles of individual freedom and royal primogeniture. He names his three sons after the three tribes of the island. Morgan has no choice but to follow Geoffrey in saying that Brutus makes Loegria the superior nation, but he adds what seems to be one of his own inventions, that the Kymry in Wales retain the 'Military Leadership' under a '*Pendragon* [or] Military Dictator' in times of foreign invasion.

Though he was a Welshman, devoted to Welsh culture, Morgan lived for some time in London. The city had of course belonged to the native Britons (whose remnants survived in Wales) long before the Anglo-Saxons took it over, and Morgan sought to reclaim the prestige of London for Welsh culture. Brutus founds London and, picking up on an idea of Jacob's, Morgan argued that the alleged Roman temple to Diana, which was widely believed to have stood on Ludgate Hill, was founded by Brutus. Brutus has brought with him on his journey 'the Pedestal of the Trojan Palladium', and this he places in the 'court of the Temple of Diana', where it becomes the London Stone. The prophetic words uttered to Brutus by Diana are 'engraved in Archaic Greek on the altar of Diana in New Troy or London, and translated into Latin in the third century [AD] by Nennius' (an odd statement to make, as Nennius, who actually lived in the AD 800s, knew nothing of such verses: nor is it obvious why Brutus, a Trojan, should have written anything in Greek). Later, in his book *St Paul in Britain* (1861), Morgan argued that St Paul's Cathedral was so called because St Paul had once preached on Ludgate Hill and converted the British druids to Christianity.

The British Kymry proceeds to retell Geoffrey's history, and then actual British history. The Scythians, Saxons, Vikings and Norse become junior descendants of Noah's progeny, with 'large but soft limbs, red or flaxen hair … and flat feet' with 'a passion for indulgence in intoxicating liquors' and a religion based on 'Materialism of the grossest kind'. So as not to alienate English readers completely, Morgan allowed the Normans (who really were Norsemen) to be descendants of Welsh soldiers who had been taken abroad by Urb, a grandson of Assaracus son of Ebraucus, one of Geoffrey's kings descended from Brutus. Morgan included a fold-out table showing the 'genealogy of the Britanidae, or royal line of Britain', from Noah's grandson Gomer down, via 'Brutus, or Prydain' to Geoffrey's kings and the Welsh princes who claimed descent from them, and on via Henry VII to Queen Victoria.

By writing in his introduction that 'due weight had been allowed to all sober-minded objections of the sceptic school' Morgan indicated that he knew, in his heart, that many people would find his version of history ridiculous. Yet in fact his narrative, though cobbled together from many contradictory sources, was penned with such utter conviction that it remains a focal point for British pseudo-history to this day, and thus an important, living part of Brutus's myth.

There has been a constant interplay between fiction and the perceived reality of Britain's history throughout Brutus's story. Out of the epic poem writers, C.D. for one clearly believed that the basic story was true, and Jacob may have done too. The Reverend Aaron Thompson translated Geoffrey into English because he thought he was dealing with a true story about his people's racial origins. Similarly, their work, though ostensibly confined to the realms of English literature, helped keep Brutus's story, if not at the forefront of national consciousness, at least updated and in the minds of those who still wished to quarry it for truth about their origins. Pope and Ogilvie repositioned the Trojan story firmly back into the Christian domain and this prepared the ground for Morgan's pseudo-history, which reaffirmed the original, strong link between Brutus and Genesis. Then, only three years after Morgan's book appeared, C.D.'s new romance of Brutus turned the Trojans into instruments of divine will, seeding a druidic belief in the one God of the Old Testament in Britain. Whilst C.D. did not repeat any of Morgan's pseudo-history, its reminder of the link between Brutus and the Bible may have had an influence and helped enforce C.D.'s belief that the British really did have Trojan roots.

Because farming techniques spread east to India and west to Britain from a common point of origin in the Middle East, that whole area of the globe shares common Indo-European cultures and languages. In the nineteenth century, this similarity was explained in terms of a warrior race called the Aryans, who were imagined expanding out from Tibet to conquer both India and the West. In 1914, E.O. Gordon claimed that Brutus's myth was based in true history and that he had been a pioneer of this very Aryan civilisation in Britain. Her work owed a great debt to Morgan, because her Brutus's arrival at Totnes was greeted by the 'Pacific Tribes' of Britons, who raised him to the throne of Hu Gadarn and accompanied him on a joyful procession across southern Britain, via Stonehenge, to build Trinovantum (London) – all of which, she was convinced, had really happened.

Following this, Lawrence Waddell's *The Phoenician Origin of Britons* (1924) picked up the sixteenth-century idea of Phoenicians seeding British civilisation but asserted that these Phoenicians were Trojans. The Phoenicians were not a Semitic people at all, he claimed, but a western branch of the Aryan race and the 'ancestral pioneers of the Higher civilisation'. He wrote in chapter eight that Lord Leighton's imaginative painting of fair-skinned Britons trading with dark-complexioned Phoenician merchants 'requires an exchange of complexions,' and might benefit from 'some slight nasal readjustment in the latter [the Phoenicians] to the Aryan type'.

Aryanism remained a fashionable theory until Hitler used it as a justification for his genocide of the Jews during the Second World War. After that, most people have very sensibly shied away from it. Modern archaeology and genetics finds no support for the theory at all.

Although the Phoenicians were a major part of the trade network that ultimately linked Britain with the Mediterranean world, we know now that the Gauls acted as middlemen between the two, so it is unlikely there was much direct contact between the Phoenicians and Britain at all. But the idea has never fully gone away and as recently as 2009, Gary Biltcliffe's *The Spirit of Portland: Revelations of a Sacred Isle* claimed that the modern Portlanders have Phoenician blood. That may be true, if it came from a handful of traders, but the idea that they had any substantial input into Britain's gene pool has long since been roundly disproved. But the identification of Trojans with another Middle Eastern people, the Jews, has proved far more durable.

Chapter 27

The Man who Wasn't There

Peppered like a secret code throughout the writings of William Blake is the poetic notion that the British were identical with the people of the Holy Land. 'London covr'd the whole Earth,' he wrote in *Jerusalem*, 'England encompass'd the Nations and all the Nations of the Earth were seen in the Cities of Albion ... Levi and Judah & Issachar: Ephraim, Manasseh, Gad and Dan are seen in our hills & valleys ... Medway mingled with Kishion: Thames receiv'd the heavenly Jordan.'

Blake's ideas were a poetic elaboration of an idea that had been floating about in British consciousness since the sixteenth century – that the British were the Lost Tribes of Israel. The idea answered the same psychological need that had led earlier generations to imagine themselves as descendants of Hercules, Joseph of Arimathea or Brutus – that desire to draw up the prevalent beliefs of the Mediterranean world into the British Isles.

The Hebrews were traditionally divided into thirteen tribes, each claiming descent from the sons of Jacob (who was in turn descended from Shem, son of Noah). They were conquered by Nebuchadnezzar in 597 BC and a sizeable portion of the population was taken into exile in Babylon. In 538 BC many Jews from the southern kingdom of Judah were allowed to return to their homeland, but the ten tribes of the northern kingdom of Israel were assimilated into the Babylonian empire's population, and never reappeared.

In Jewish belief, these ten Lost Tribes remain somewhere in the east, and that when they eventually return to Jerusalem, all will be well again. When the Reformation allowed Protestants to read and hear the Old Testament in English, their imaginations were filled with tales of roaming Israelites – tales that helped in their own way to drum out the rival myths of Troy. The Protestants likened their struggles against the Catholic monarchies to the persecution the Israelites received from the Babylonians. And when the Protestant English helped the French Huguenots against their Catholic oppressors, the grateful Huguenot Counsellor Le Loyer wrote in *The Ten Lost Tribes Found* (1590), that 'the Israelites came to and founded the English Isles.'

He probably meant this entirely metaphorically, as a means of complimenting his English allies, but it was only a matter of time before serious racial theories started emerging as a result. Richard Brothers' *A Correct Account of the Invasion and Conquest of the Roman Colony Ailbane, or Britain, by the Saxons* (1822) asserted that the Saxons had originally been 'the greatest part of the ten tribes [of Israel] carried into captivity by Salmanazar [*sic*] and placed on the borders of his empire, near Georgia and Armenia'. In 1840 John Wilson's *Our Israelitish Origin* reaffirmed the Saxons' descent from Jacob and on 3 April 1894 the *Pall Mall Gazette* even claimed, absurdly, that 'Saxon' was a corruption of 'Isaac's Sons'.

This idea of wandering tribes of Israelites may have been an inspiration for Joseph Smith's *Book of Mormon* (1830), upon which is based the Church of Jesus Christ of Latter-day Saints. It tells a different story of wandering Jewish tribes but the end result, the settlement of America by 'chosen people' descended from Jacob, is the same. In Ireland, meanwhile, the descent of the Irish kings from Noah's family, as invented in the Dark Ages and enshrined in the *Lebor Gabála*, was developed into a specific, racial theory expounded in the Reverend B. Murphy's *Proof that Israelites Came from Egypt to Ireland* (1816). The *Lebor Gabála* is based around a pedigree coming down from Noah past Feinius Farsaid and Breoghan to Heremon, whose wife Tea was said, fancifully, to have been 'Pharaoh's daughter'. In 1861, F.R.A. Glover's *England, the Remnant of Judah, and the Israel of Ephraim* improved on this and on Murphy's ideas when he announced that Tea's father hadn't been Pharaoh at all: he had been Zedekiah, the last king of Judah of the House of David.

Because the British royal family was descended from the kings of Scotland, whose ancestors were of royal Irish ancestry, Queen Victoria suddenly found herself with a pedigree purporting to trace her back, via Zedekiah, to the House of David. When the British–Israel–World Federation was established in 1919, its patrons included a granddaughter of Queen Victoria and a prime minister of New Zealand. Though its membership and prestige has declined, the organisation still exists to this day, and there are many who still believe that the British royal family has sacred, Davidic blood.

Having to rely on the Irish for a descent from King David, however, was distasteful to the English and their non-Irish American descendants. So it came as a relief to some when Charles Totten (1851–1908), an American army officer, claimed in some of his many books, written mainly in the 1880s and 1890s, that Brutus's ancestor Dardanos was identical with the biblical Dara or Darda, whom the Bible makes son (Chronicles 2:6) or grandson, via Mahol (1

Kings 4:31) of Zarah, son of Judah by his second wife Tamar. Zarah had a twin, Pharez, the ancestor of Jesus. Genesis 38:3 tells how, at birth, Zarah stuck his arm out first, so the nurse tied a scarlet thread around his wrist to identify him as the elder son. This 'scarlet thread' came to symbolise the perceived bloodline that came down from Dar(d)a/Dardanos, via Brutus, to his modern British Israelite descendants. Thus, wrote Totten, if Darda son of Zarah was Dardanos founder of Troy, this would enable us to 'continue … the record of the Sacred Chronicles, and lend them greater reverence'.

Backed by such beliefs, Brutus becomes an instrument of divine destiny once again. Though Rome's empire has fallen, the empire Brutus founded in Britain can be seen to be living on through its new incarnation in the United States. And the Brutus Stone in Totnes, where Brutus first alighted onto British soil, becomes the precursor of Plymouth Rock, the stone onto which the Pilgrim Fathers first stepped when they landed in America in 1620.

It is for this reason that the American preacher Raymond A. Bradbury, visiting Totnes in 1959, could write: 'We stood upon the … bridge of the river Dart, whose placid waters once carried a mighty king of Zarah-Judah stock, namely Brutus the Trojan, to the island home for which he had been seeking … it is evident that Brutus came here under Divine leading and compulsion. He was led to the "Appointed Place for My People Israel".' To those not versed in the Brutus myth, these lines sound ridiculous, but within the context of the myth-making process, we can at least understand the complex process that led to them being written.

In 2013, a new retelling of Brutus's story, deeply informed by the ideas of Charles Totten, appeared as an e-book, *Brutus; First King of England, Prince of Troy (The Welsh Chronicles)* by Mark Hodges, an American firewood cutter and evangelist. Mostly, Hodges follows Geoffrey's story, though there are some oddities. Aeneas, rather than Ascanius, is still king of Latium when Brutus is born. After the hunting accident it is a democratic council of elders, not the king, that finds the fifteen-year-old prince guilty, anachronistically, of manslaughter and sentences him to exile 'as of tomorrow at 2 in the afternoon'.

There is a pleasant enough scene in which Brutus rests on the Italian coast, gazing out across the Tyrrhenian Sea in the moonlight and being lulled to sleep by the splashing waves, but the geography of his voyage is spoiled by his being able to see Etna and Vesuvius at the same time (which is impossible) and reaching Greece within sight of Olympus, when the mountain is on the east, not the west coast. Brutus spends five years in Greece, growing to 'just under 7 feet tall, as strong as a lion and as swift and agile as any forest deer'. He takes leadership of the Trojans there and they escape just as Geoffrey describes. When they reach Lefkada, his vision of Diana is not a manifestation of a real goddess, but a dream in which her face appears 'like an alabaster mask of a Greek actor'.

Once Brutus and his followers reach the Atlantic, his fleet is attacked by two sea monsters called 'Kronoses' or Leviathans, which, we are told earnestly, 'could pose a real danger and a hazard to seafarers.' Brutus fends the monsters off with Greek fire thrown by siege engines perched, impossibly, on the deck of his ship. After the monsters retreat, Brutus relaxes on deck and smokes a pipe, despite tobacco not having been brought to Europe from America until the seventeenth century. He is encouraged to stop fighting in Gaul by a note sent by an impatient Ignoge: 'Do we fight for fighting's sake, or do we seek a land for our children?' In the final chapter, we learn to our surprise that there are mountains in Cornwall and that Brutus died in a very precise 1081 BC (which is only three years after the conventional date for the end of the Trojan War).

To Hodges, as to many fervent Christians, science and religion remain implacable foes. He writes of Troy as 'a mighty fortress town that our men of science and history assured us didn't really exist' (this despite the fact that mainstream academia stopped doubting the existence of Troy in the nineteenth century). The text becomes interesting when Hodges moralises and attempts to synchronise the story with the beliefs of American Bible Christians. This is part of the same tradition of melding Brutus's story to meet the hopes and fears of the time that has been ongoing since his myth was invented in the Dark Ages. In many ways, Hodges does not so much intrude biblical references into the tale as reclaim the myth for a brand of modern Christianity that is itself descended from the same early Christianity out of which Brutus's story emerged. Thus, we hear that Aeneas 'wasn't known to be fond of soothsayers or those who dabbled in the occult' (in contrast to Virgil's Aeneas, who was constantly seeking auguries and guidance from the gods, and from the dead). The Trojans 'were not a weak people' because 'not many' centuries had passed since Noah's time, so 'time and mutations hadn't yet done their work in the slow stealing away of the grandeur that was once Adam. ... They were skilled in written language and manifested many of the gifts endowed on a mankind made in the likeness of their Creator' – traits that would pass down through the British and thus, by implication, to the Americans of New England. Brutus himself, ruthless in war, seems unbounded, says Hodges, by religion or a strict moral code and 'whether or not he had any knowledge of the one true god that many of the ancients spoke of, through word of mouth or inkling of conscience, there was no sign of it in his behaviour.'

Brutus's story is true, Hodges asserts, because it appears in old records, adding, 'All the modernists can give us with their Darwinian history is a lineage of endlessly reproducing biological robots. The Welsh Chronicle [the *Bruts*, those Welsh copies of Geoffrey's *History*] … gives us Arthur and Camelot. If they without guile trace themselves back to the creation of Adam and Eve in the Garden of Eden and the subsequent fall, so much the better.' But the amount of monkish guile required had, of course, been considerable.

All the beliefs described in the last few chapters, of Brutus as an Israelite, an ancient Briton, a Phoenician, an Aryan or, indeed, simply as a Trojan, are still held dearly by small minorities of people now and an appetite remains for Brutus's story to be proved true.

During the First World War, the distinguished archaeologist Sir Flinders Petrie argued that Geoffrey of Monmouth's *History* was a translation of the *Brut Tysilio*, which, he claimed, preserved genuinely ancient British traditions that might be true. In 1929, the American scholar Acton Griscom, who wished passionately to believe that his British ancestors were descendants of Noah via the Trojan dynasty, built on Petrie's ideas, arguing that Brutus's story, as given in the Welsh *Bruts*, was derived from a correct historical account of the Trojan settlement of Britain.

Inspired by such assertions, Brutus still crops up here and there in pseudo-history. Iman Jacob Wilkens's *Where Troy Once Stood* (2005) revives a nineteenth-century theory that the real Troy was located in Cambridgeshire's Gogmagog Hills, where the Cam was once called 'Scamander' (the name of one of the Homeric rivers of Troy). The 'Greeks' were Gauls and Achilles was, like Wilkens, a Dutchman. After the Trojan War, everyone packed up and sailed for Greece, taking their place names with them. The legend of Brutus 'returning' to Britain with descendants of the Trojans is taken as the final (though desperately illogical) piece of proof that this extraordinary theory must be correct.

David Hughes's *The British Chronicles* (2007), meanwhile, takes all British and Continental European mythology and attempts to deduce from it a coherent pseudo-history for Britain going back to the kings of Atlantis 'circa 45,000 BC'. His story includes Brutus as the leader of 'the Albanese (descendants of Trojans from Italy, where they became the Etruscans), the Iron Age Britons' and argues that his 'restoration' of the history of the ancient British monarchy 'is justified by the premise that all legends are based on historical fact.'

Back in the late nineteenth century, a contributor to *Somerset & Dorset Notes & Queries* suggested that Brutus's great fleet had landed on the Dorset coast at the Isle of Portland. This idea was revived by Gary Biltcliffe in 2009, who retold Brutus's story as historical fact. Totnes was too small to receive Brutus's fleet, he argued, whereas Portland had an ancient harbour 'large enough to accommodate a fleet of 300 ships'. 'In ancient times,' he explains, 'mariners, upon arrival, would celebrate their safe journey by honouring the gods or goddesses at unhewn stone altars ... there were many accounts of stones and altars existing on Portland,' and the memory of one of these exists in the name of a field near Southwell called Brutt Stone Meadow. Presumably this was actually one of the West Country *bruiters stones*, like the one in Totnes, from which *bruits* or announcements were made – but for Biltcliffe, this fortuitous survival becomes firm evidence that the Isle of Portland was the landing place of Brutus, and he proceeds to link this theory to Portland's genuinely old myths about giants – and thus to imagine Corineus and Gogmagog battling it out in their wrestling match up on the high chalk cliffs of Portland Bill.

Richard Darlow's self-published *King Bryttos and the Trojan Origins of Bronze Age Britain* (2011) seeks, meanwhile, to synthesise Brutus's story with the modern, archaeological understanding of the arrival of the Bronze Age in Britain. The fall of Mycenae was thanks to Brutus's war with Pandrasus, which weakened Greece and allowed the Dorian invasion to take place. The arrival of Brutus in Britain explains the introduction of bronze (despite the fact that bronze-working was definitely being practised here for many centuries before the fall of Troy). Chariots, roads, hill forts and so on were all introduced here, apparently, by Brutus. Archaeologists have worked out detailed theories to explain all these cultural innovations, but if only they would read Geoffrey of Monmouth, argues Darlow, they would discover the truth.

One reason why the Brutus myth continues to flourish in pseudo-history is that mainstream historians have done relatively little to explain its true, literary origins. Sir Thomas Kendrick's *British Antiquity* (1950) provides an overview of 'the matter of Britain' and includes a two-page explanation of the rise of Brutus's myth out of the Frankish Table of Nations, but that is all.

Professor Hutson's *British personal names in the Historia regum Britanniae* (1940) and John S.P. Tatlock's *The Legendary History of Britain* (1950), followed by some more recent articles by the distinguished archaeologist Stuart Piggott (1910–1996), explored Geoffrey's *History* to see how much could definitely be attributed to his borrowing from other, non-ancient sources. They identified many instances of creative borrowings, but they tended to keep silent about all the material for which they could not account. Had Geoffrey made this other material up, or was some of it derived, as I have argued in the case of Corineus's story, from older myths? Or was it all based in ancient, true historical accounts?

By not addressing the latter question head-on, they did little to put off those who were still determined to see Brutus as a genuine historical figure.

More recently, Brutus's story, with varying attempts to explain it, has featured in various academic articles and it is regularly accorded a few paragraphs in books about Britain's past such as Sir Anthony Wagner's *English Genealogy* (1983); David Miles's *The Tribes of Britain* (2005); Bryan Sykes's *Blood of the Isles* (2006) and Barry Cunliffe's *Britain Begins* (2012). Cunliffe, not untypically of the rest, attributes Brutus's story ultimately to 'the lively imagination of an unnamed British cleric'. They seem to have felt a polite need to include Britain's mythical founder in their books, yet they pass by him relatively quickly, that 'man who wasn't there' eager to move forward to more solid ground. Again, by not tackling the myth head-on, they left the way open for those who wanted to claim that his story was all true. If only it was – but the evidence makes it overwhelmingly clear that it is not: the truth of Brutus lies not in any physical reality at all, but in the enduring power of his myth alone.

From the sixteenth century onwards, the disintegration of mainstream belief in the Trojan myth generated the false leads of Britain's Phoenician, Aryan or Israelite origins. But it also stimulated the process of reconstruction from which Britain derives its modern view of the world.

What started with antiquarian interrogation of ancient stones, henges, manuscripts, languages and facial features, and alchemical probings into the properties of metals and the internal workings of plants and animals, has led to the growth of the modern sciences and the discovery of DNA.

Brutus of Troy's greatest bequest to the modern world, then, was the void he created when most people ceased to believe in him – a void that stimulated the appearance of modern science. This in turn reversed a trend: instead of being the last recipients of second-hand myths from the Mediterranean world, Britain became the powerhouse of a new world view, spearheaded by Darwinian evolution, which swept back south and east and, ultimately, encircled the globe.

Through science, we can look back and see more clearly than ever before who we really are, where we come from, and how we fit onto the greater scheme of things. Year by year we are discovering ever more of our ancestral story, back from Ice Age migrations around the world to our human evolution in Africa, our proto-hominid development in the forests of Europe and Asia and thence to all the stages of evolution that take us back to reptiles, fish and worms and ultimately to those first single-celled ancestors of ours who floated about in the warm seas of early Earth, some 3,500 million years ago, as described in my book *In Search of Our Ancient Ancestors*. Each step of the way has been mapped out by a combination of scientific disciplines, from archaeology and linguistics to anthropology, zoology, geology and genetics. Even before life began, we can trace back to the births of our own planet and of the fiery sun, and then trace the sun's own ancestry back to the Big Bang, which stands, apparently, at the start of everything.

Thanks to science, too, the more recent story of the human colonisation of Britain after the last Ice Age is better understood than ever before. Any signs of a sudden influx of Trojans is singularly lacking, but archaeology has revealed how bands of Palaeolithic hunter-gathers wandered north and were cut off by the rising Mesolithic seas; how they were joined by Neolithic farmers, then Bronze Age metal-workers from western Europe and invading Iron Age Celts; how the Romans came, and brought in Anglo-Saxon mercenaries who eventually took control of England when the empire collapsed. And how in the meantime, Irishmen from Ulster established themselves in western Scotland, creating a kingdom that would eventually fuse with the native Picts to form Scotland.

Before this was known, myths of Brutus and his Trojan and biblical ancestors were constantly being interrogated in case they might provide details of what our true history really was. But now that the sciences tell such a coherent story, we can stop interrogating myths for hidden truths about our origins. If they happen to contain some vestiges of ancient events after all, so much the better, but we don't *need* them to do so any more. Instead, we can enjoy them as literature and experience through them a certain comradeship with our ancestors who created and listened to them on the hillsides of Greece and Judea and around the hearths of Dark Age Britain. We can let their attempts to understand life, love and death fortify us, and allow their endeavours to bestow a sense of higher purpose and destiny on their lives to inspire our own.

The Trojan War was probably real enough, but the myths of Aeneas crossing the wine-dark Mediterranean to lay the foundations of the Roman Empire in Italy, and Brutus's subsequent journey to fill Britain with descendants of the Trojans, are myths. But these myths are very real in themselves. They were an essential element of our ancestors' self-consciousness, through which they rationalised their relationship with the Earth, with other races, with the gods and with time and death itself. The Trojan myths spread with urban civilisation and were an essential, edifying component of literate, city-based life.

The Trojan myths were both the products of history and also the creators of it, for they inspired the great deeds of Alexander the Great and Pyrrhus of Epiros, of Caesar and Augustus and of many leaders of nations before and after. They put fire in the hearts of the warriors who built the Dark Age kingdoms of Britain and stiffened the backbones of generations of British officers who carved out the British Empire. The tales of dauntless heroes that they contained helped instil courage in the souls of the pioneers who colonised the outback of Australia and the prairies of America.

The myths of Troy inspired three radiant millennia of poets, playwrights, historians, genealogists, sculptors and artists, from Homer and Hesiod to Euripides and Virgil, and Shakespeare, Spenser, Milton, Pope, Blake and Wordsworth and many more, and they continue to do so today.

The myth of Troy and the story of Aeneas lies at the heart of Western culture, and the tales of Aeneas's great grandson Brutus lay at the heart of Britain's identity for over a thousand years. In our ancestors' hearts and imaginations, Brutus was never just a myth: he truly lived.

Chapter 28

Ludgate Hill

Vestiges of Brutus's myth lie scattered across Britain, but nowhere are they more alive than in London, the city that Geoffrey describes him founding as Trinovantum, the 'New Troy' in the west. Four places are associated with him specifically. He is said to have founded a temple on Ludgate Hill, where St Paul's Cathedral stands; to have set the London Stone in place; to have built his palace where Guildhall now stands; and to be buried beneath the Tower of London.

In his story of Brutus's descendant Bladud (see plate 33), Geoffrey refers in passing to a temple of Apollo in London. So when John Hardyng's *Chronicle* (c. 1437) touched on St Paul's Cathedral (see plate 40), he wrote 'and Troynouaunt he [Brutus] made full specially an archflaume his see cathedrall certain, a temple therof Apolyne to obteyne' – Brutus made New Troy the archdiocese of a high priest by building a 'cathedral' to Apollo there. This enabled later writers to theorise that, in this context, 'Paul' was a later, deliberate Christianisation of the name of Apollo.

But as Brutus was guided to London by Apollo's sister Diana, would he not have built her a temple too? Fuel for such a myth was provided by the name of the Dean and Chapter of St Paul's. In his article on the subject, John Clark traced early references to a building that stood near the cathedral called variously 'Hospitium Deane' in 1407–1408 ('the Dean's Hospital'); 'domus quae fuit Diane' in 1220/22; 'Camera Diane alias Segrave' in 1452 and 'Camera Diane' in 1480. The transition from 'Dean' to 'Diane' is clear, and what was probably an accidental alteration in spelling may have prompted, and then been helped along, by speculation that this building had some ancient link to Brutus. Thus, in 1443, John Flete wrote in his history of Westminster Abbey that, when the Anglo-Saxons came, 'belief in the old abominations returned everywhere … London sacrificed to Diana and suburban Thorney [where Westminster Abbey is] made offerings to Apollo.' This was probably no more than Flete's flowery way of saying 'pagan worship returned', and of course in reality the Saxons worshipped their own gods, not the Greek ones. Flete may have been influenced by the location of the Camera Diane, near St Paul's, so concluded

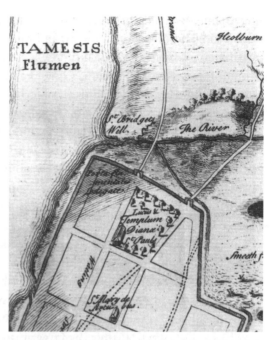

J.P. Malcolm's picture (in *Londoninium redivivum*, 1802–1807) of Dr James Woodward's bronze figurine of Diana, which was pressed into service as evidence for the existence of the Temple of Diana on Ludgate Hill.

Stukeley's map of London, showing Diana's grove on Ludgate Hill.

that if the sister was worshipped there, the brother must have been venerated in Westminster. But none of this influenced John Stow. Writing in 1592, he ignored Flete's idea and thought that there had been a Roman temple on Ludgate Hill – but that it had been dedicated to Jupiter (Zeus).

In 1610, however, William Camden reverted to Flete's idea and asserted, in his *Britannia*, that St Paul's was on the site of a Roman temple to Diana. He did not believe in Brutus, but he seems nonetheless to have been influenced, perhaps subconsciously, by the association between Diana and London created by Brutus's story. Camden argued his case on three grounds – first the name of the 'Camera Diane', and secondly the discovery, in the 1300s, of an 'incredible number of ox heads [which] were digged up' at St Paul's. Camden opined that 'the learned know, that *Tauropolia* [bull sacrifices] were celebrated in the honour of Diana [i.e. at the temple of Artemis Tauropolis on the western coast of Attika].' But mass sacrifices of cattle are known elsewhere from before, during and after the Roman period and were favoured particularly by the pagan Saxons, so Camden's ox heads can't even be taken as evidence of Diana being worshipped in Roman London, let alone in the misty centuries before. Thirdly, as a boy, Camden had seen a medieval ceremony being performed at St Paul's, whereby 'a stag's head sticking upon a speare-top ... [was] carried round about within the very Church in solemne pompe and procession, and with a great noise of Horne-blowers ... a ceremony,' he thought, 'suiting well with the Sacrifices of Diana.' But he knew perfectly well that this was simply the annual presentation of a doe and a buck by the Baud family, in return for lands that they held from the Dean and Chapter of St Paul's, and the ceremony only dated back to the 1300s.

But Camden's affirmation that a Roman temple of Diana had stood on Ludgate Hill led, twenty-four years later, to the Bishop of Norwich writing as a matter of fact that, when Christianity reached Britain, St Paul was venerated on Ludgate Hill 'while Diana [was] thrust out'. William Dugdale repeated Camden's theory respectfully. And, when digging out the foundations for the new St Paul's Cathedral after the Great Fire, Sir Christopher Wren was, as his son wrote, 'very desirous' of finding evidence of Diana's temple. Nothing was found, but Wren's hopes fuelled more speculation. In 1724 William Stukeley published a map of Roman London showing a square covering Ludgate Hill, full of trees and labelled '*Lucus* [grove] & *Templum* [temple of] *Dianae*'. When the antiquarian Dr John Woodward (1665–1728) acquired a collection, as Allen reports, of 'the tusks of boars, the horns of oxen and stags, and sacrificing vessels, with representations of deer, and even Diana herself, upon them; all of which were dug up [on Ludgate Hill]' they seemed to prove Camden right. But the sacrificing vessels were ordinary Roman samian tableware and the figurine, found somewhere between Blackfriars and the Deanery of St Paul's, simply proves that the Roman Londoners venerated Diana as one of the pantheon of Olympian deities. It scarcely proves she had a whole temple there to herself.

The idea of a temple on Ludgate Hill dedicated to Diana probably had its roots in the Brutus myth, but it took until 1735 for Hildebrand Jacob, himself a Londoner, to join the strands back together again. In a footnote to his epic poem *Brutus the Trojan* he wrote that, when Brutus reached Britain, he consecrated London to Diana, claiming that 'Fanum Dianae [Temple of Diana], is one of the Names which have been given to London'. The association between Diana's temple and Brutus was then solidified further by the inventive Welsh nationalist the Reverend R.W. Morgan in 1857, who wrote that 'in the court of the Temple of Diana [in London, Brutus] ... placed the sacred stone which had formed the pedestal of the Palladium of the mother city of Troy.' Interestingly, Morgan did not state that Brutus had *founded* the temple: he may have imagined it existing there already because, in his vision of the past, Britain had been inhabited long before Brutus arrived.

Nonetheless, the link was now strong enough for Brutus's building of a Temple to Diana on Ludgate Hill to reappear as an established fact in numerous pseudo-histories, all increasing the mysterious nature of ancient London in the minds of those who wish to believe in it. That mythical atmosphere is only increased by the second of Brutus's legacies to London – the London Stone (see plate 41).

What is left of the London Stone is set into a shop wall in Cannon Street, nearly opposite the entrance to the railway station. It used to be much bigger but centuries of wear and tear and souvenir hunters chipping bits off it have reduced it in size and now a metal grille protects it from becoming any smaller. It is made of oolite limestone, which is not local to London. It had either been brought up from Dorset or the Cotswolds or, more likely, down from the north side of the Chilterns. It has been there, and known as the London Stone, since at least 1108, when '*Eadwaker aet lundene stane*' was mentioned in a list of tenants of Canterbury Cathedral's properties in London. If it dates back as far as Roman times, it may be a Roman *milliarium*, one of a set of stones set up in Roman cities for the purpose of measuring the distances between them. Or it could have been there much longer.

In 1450, Jack Cade struck his sword on the London Stone and proclaimed himself mayor of London, a scene elaborated by Shakespeare in *Henry VI, Part Two* and used by some writers to argue that the stone had some ancient significance as a place for receiving power. Any hard evidence for this aside from the Cade story, however, is lacking. When William Camden wrote about the stone in the sixteenth century he knew of no such tradition. But it was known in medieval London as a place for settling deals and making announcements. Like Totnes's stone, it may even have been called a '*bruiters* [announcements] stone'. If so, it created a link between Brutus and a part of London that was palpably ancient, but there is no written evidence for that term being used for the London Stone. Geoffrey may have known about the West Country custom and assumed a link with the London Stone, but again, if he thought this, he did not write it (and nor did he mention the London Stone at all). This all suggests that the London Stone's entry into the Brutus myth came much later.

As awareness of ancient monuments increased, John Strype, in his 1720 edition of Stow's *Survey of London*, wondered if the stone had been 'a Monument, of Heathen Worship'. This, and Jacob's description of bloody druidical sacrifices in Gaul in his 1735 epic about Brutus, fed Blake's imagination. In *Jerusalem* (c. 1804–1820), Blake imagined the victims of the druids of ancient London who 'groan'd aloud on London Stone' and the murder of Albion 'in Stone-henge & on London Stone & in the Oak Groves of Malden, I have Slain him in my Sleep with the Knife of the Druid.' Blake's poetic association of the London Stone with Stonehenge helped in turn to fuel a wonderful, though completely unproven theory, suggested in E.O. Gordon's *Prehistoric London* (1914), that Brutus's temple on Ludgate Hill had been a stone circle, and the London Stone had been its heel stone. Some stone circles, including Stonehenge, have an outlying 'heel' stone, marking the spot from which significant sunrises or sunsets over the circle are best viewed. If the circle was for worshipping the sun god, then here was a further tenuous Brutus link, because the Greek sun god was Apollo, the brother of Diana, Brutus's divine protectoress. Maybe the name 'heel' really did recall Apollo's Mycenaean alter ego, Helios. But absolutely no archaeological evidence for a stone circle on Ludgate Hill exists, despite the unprovable argument that the old Powle's Cross, which used to stand in St Paul's churchyard, had originally been one of its sarsens.

Meanwhile, in 1798 John Carter referred to the London Stone as 'the symbol of this great City's quiet state ... "fixed to its everlasting seat"'. Following him, Thomas Pennant said in 1793 that the London Stone was 'preserved like the *Palladium* of the City'. That was no more than a metaphor, but in 1828 Edward Brayley elaborated this, commenting that the London Stone was 'like the Palladium of Troy [and] the fate and safety of the City was argued to be dependent on its preservation'.

It was only a matter of time now before the London Stone stopped being *like* the Palladium of Troy and actually *became* its pedestal. Thus, when the Reverend R.W. Morgan was trying to reclaim London for Welsh culture in 1857, he seized on the idea that the London Stone had been the pedestal of the original Palladium. Brutus had brought it with him from Italy and placed it in Diana's temple, and 'on it the British kings were sworn to observe the Usages of Britain. It is now known as "London Stone".' This presupposes that Aeneas had managed to lug it out of Troy during the city's destruction, something Virgil does not mention, and that Brutus had been able to take it with him when he was exiled from Italy – which is rather ridiculous – and that it stayed with him throughout his wanderings. Perhaps in response to such criticism, Morgan wrote to *Notes and Queries* in 1862 under his bardic name Mor Merrion, reiterating his belief that the London Stone 'was also the altar of Diana… Tradition also declares it was brought from Troy by Brutus, and laid down by his own hand as the altar-stone of the Diana Temple, the foundation stone of London and its Palladium.' So now Brutus had gone direct to Troy to unearth it and bring it on his journey. Morgan's story is probably what influenced a later story that the Brutus Stone in Totnes was, also, the Palladium Stone. It is a compelling myth that has stuck fast to both the Brutus Stone and the London Stone ever since.

Morgan wrote also in 1857 that 'the belief in old times was, that as long as it [the London Stone] remained, New Troy, or London, would continue to increase in wealth and power; with its disappearance, they would decrease and finally disappear.' He elaborated this in 1862 too, quoting what he claimed was an old proverb, 'So long as the Stone of Brutus is safe, so long will London flourish', which he claimed to have translated from an old Welsh saying, '*Tra maen Prydain, Tra lled Llyndain*'. But this actually means 'so long as the stone of *Britain* [exists], so long will London spread'. This supposedly ancient saying does not exist in any known Welsh source and John Clark argues that the proverb was probably Morgan's very creative adaptation of a genuinely old Welsh saying from the *Book of Taliesin*, '*Tra môr, tra Brython*', 'as long as there is a sea there will be Britons'. Clark points out that Morgan had not quoted this proverb in his 1857 book, most likely because he had not yet invented it.

Initially, Morgan's imaginative ideas about ancient London seem to have been ignored. When Henry Charles Coote wrote a paper on the London Stone in *Transactions of the London and Middlesex Archaeological Society* in 1881, he made no mention of Trojans. But in April 1888 an article in the popular weekly *Chambers's Journal* repeated Morgan's ideas and this seems to have pushed them at last into popular consciousness. They were an inspiration for many details in E.O. Gordon's *Prehistoric London* (1914), and in 1937, Lewis Spence's *Legendary London* cited an 'old saying' about the London Stone being the Stone of Brutus. Unaware that Morgan had made this up less than eighty years before, Spence wrote knowingly of the stone as 'the original communal fetish [stone] of London which represented the guardian spirit of the community'. Subsequent writings about the London Stone have built on this and have helped carry the myth of Brutus forward, wonderfully alive, into the twenty-first century.

Chapter 29

Tower Hill

In the Middle Ages, there used to be a giant figure of a man – or perhaps it was a life-sized figure of a giant – carved in the turf on the Hawe at Plymouth (see plate 39). By 1486, and probably thanks to Geoffrey's *History*, it was being called Goëmagot or Gogmagog. By the 1500s, it had been joined by a second figure, which, by 1630, was being called Corineus. Both figures were destroyed to make way for the Restoration fortress there.

We cannot possibly know how old the first giant was, or whom it originally represented. Maybe it had been created in the Middle Ages, having been inspired by Geoffrey's book. Or maybe it was a Roman or Iron Age depiction of Hercules, or one of the many giants who loom large in West Country myth: if so, it could have been one of Geoffrey's several reasons for locating Brutus's landing on the south coast of Devon in the first place.

In death, Corineus and Gogmagog became an inseparable pair, more like bothers than arch enemies. Emulating Plymouth, students of Cambridge University carved their images in the turf on a hillside just south-east of the city. Though the images are now long grown over and lost, their names remained, so the hills there are still called the Gogmagog Hills. The archaeologist T.C. Lethbridge (1901–1971) tried to rediscover them on the slopes below Wandlebury Hill Fort, hammering a pole repeatedly into the downland turf to find the softest patches of chalk. By 'joining the dots' Lethbridge constructed a fantastic series of images of goggle-eyed monsters, which he thought included a sun god, Gog, and his moon goddess consort, Ma-Gog. But what he had found were simply natural weaknesses in the chalk, caused by underground water: everything else stemmed purely from his imagination.

A pair of wicker and plaster statues of giants, one male and one female, lived in London in the Middle Ages and were brought out on civic occasions to be paraded through the streets from at least 1421, when they are recorded greeting Henry V on his return from France. By 1522, one had changed sex and the pair were identified as Hercules and Samson. But when they were dusted off for a parade to celebrate Queen Mary's marriage in 1554, they become 'Corineus Brittannus' and 'Gogmagog Albionus', and as Corineus and Gogmagog they appear in the 1605 records of the pageantmaster of the Lord Mayor's Show. They remained thus, Corineus and Gogmagog, until they were destroyed in the Great Fire of London.

They were remade, and in *The New History of the Trojan Wars* (1703), Elkanah Settle described Brutus capturing Gog and Magog, who were brothers of the giant Albion, and taking them 'in triumph' to London, where he chained them to the gates of his new city, 'in memory of which it is held that their effigies, after their death, were set up as they now appear in Guild-Hall.' It was this association between what were now Brutus's giants and Guildhall that seems also to have inspired Settle's idea of Brutus 'building a Palace where Guild-Hall stands' (see plates 42 and 43). Settle's fanciful notion contains a vague grain of truth, because Guildhall stands over some genuinely ancient ruins – of London's old Roman amphitheatre, though, not of a Bronze Age palace.

The giants Settle knew must have been in poor repair because in 1708 Captain Richard Saunders carved a new pair. Of these, Thomas Boreman wrote in 1741 in his *The Gigantick History of the Two Famous Giants, and other Curiosities in Guildhall, London*, one of the earliest children's books ever written, that 'Corineus and Gogmagog were two brave giants who richly valued their honour and exerted their whole strength and force in the defence of their liberty and country.' Of course, the original Corineus was the invader, but Boreman meant here that Gogmagog and the giants had been justified in opposing Brutus, who wanted to take their island from them. 'So,' he continued, 'the City of London, by placing these, their representatives in their Guildhall, emblematically declare, that they will, like mighty giants defend the honour of their country and liberties of this their City; which excels all others, as much as those huge giants exceed in stature the common bulk of mankind.'

It was Settle who first split the name of Gogmagog into Gog and Magog and as the eighteenth century progressed this name for the giant pair began to stick. Thus, 'with this, the poor soul, who had a heart big enough for Gog, the guardian genius of London, and enough to spare for Magog to boot … sat down in a corner, and had what she termed "a real good cry".' So wrote that great bard of London, Charles Dickens, in *Nicholas Nickleby* (1838/9). Their myth has also extended abroad, for further copies of them (known variously as Gog and Magog, or Corineus and Gogmagog) now stand over the Royal Arcade in Little Collins Street, Melbourne, Australia.

The London statues that had inspired Boreman were destroyed in the Blitz, and the most recent pair were carved by David Ellis in 1953. They were used in the Lord Mayors' Shows until quite recently, but now they remain inside

Guildhall, and a pair of wicker giants made by the Worshipful Company of Basketmakers come out to lead the procession. They have become London's unlikely tutelary deities – the City's guardian-gods, 'the traditional guardians of the City of London', as the official literature of the Lord Mayor's Show describes them to this very day.

Geoffrey ends Brutus's story abruptly, telling us simply that he died in Trinovantum – London – 'in the twenty-fourth Year after his Arrival'. In 1437 Hardyng related more poetically that, when the time came for him to die, Brutus 'did resign' his body to 'his goddas Dyane', she who had guided him on his journey there in the first place. And 'to increase His soule amonge the goddes everychone, After his merytes trononized [enthroned] highe in trone.' The awkward construction of these lines was determined by Hardyng's wish to rhyme 'trone' (throne) with 'everychone' (each one), so his precise meaning – if he even had one – is unknown. But the general sense is clear: that the fate of Brutus's immortal soul lay with the gods.

We learn more of Brutus's death in *The Lamentable Tragedy of Locrine*, that play of 1595 written by 'W.S.', who may or may not have been William Shakespeare. When Brutus was growing old in London, Ate, goddess of human suffering, sent him a dream. A lion strode majestically through the woods, when out from behind a thorn bush leapt 'a dreadful Archer with his bow ybent' and shot it: 'in vain he threatened teeth and paws, and sparkleth fire from forth his flaming eyes, for the sharp shaft gave him a mortal wound.'

Just as Brutus had shot his father, so now he, in the form of the British Lion, had been slain with an arrow. But who was the archer who ushered Brutus away into Heaven? Perhaps it was Diana's brother Apollo, whom the Greeks knew as the 'far-shooting' archer.

Brutus awoke, knowing he must die, wrote 'W.S.', and summoned his courtiers:

> *Most loyal Lords and faithful followers,*
> *That have with me, unworthy General,*
> *Passed the greedy gulf of Ocean*
> *Leaving the confines of fair Italy,*
> *Behold, your Brutus draweth nigh his end ...*
>
> *This heart, my Lords, this ne'er appalled heart,*
> *That was a terror to the bordering lands,*
> *A doleful scourge unto my neighbor Kings,*

Now by the weapons of unpartial death,
Is clove asunder and bereft of life,
As when the sacred oak with thunderbolts,
Sent from the fiery circuit of the heavens,
Sliding along the air's celestial vaults,
Is rent and cloven to the very roots.
In vain, therefore, I struggle with this foe;
Then welcome death, since God will have it so.

And with that, death closed the eyes of Brutus, the first king of Britain: 'Brutus, that was a glory to us all, Brutus, that was a terror to his foes.'

Fixing the burial place of Brutus was the result of almost a millennium of myth-making from Geoffrey's time onwards.

Geoffrey says Brutus was buried 'in the City he had built'. 'W.S.' describes how the ever-practical Corineus ordered the Trojans to 'sound drums and trumpets; march to Troinouant, There to provide our chieftain's funeral'. Neither says exactly where the burial took place, but Hardyng's *Chronicle* imagined 'His corps to be buryed withouten lees in the temple of Apolyne [Apollo]', which was (by inference) where St Paul's Cathedral is now, on Ludgate Hill.

But Brutus's imagined body was not destined to remain on Ludgate Hill. In 1849, Lady Charlotte Guest's English translation of the *Mabinogion* appeared in London. It included the story of the ancient British hero Bran the Blessed, whose severed head was brought back to London. It was buried below the 'White Hill' with the face turned towards France as a talisman against foreign invasion.

Nobody knows where this 'White Hill' was. However, on Tower Hill stands William the Conqueror's White Tower. The Tower is home to ravens, whose continued presence there is said to ensure England's safety: and the British for 'raven' is *bran*. This must be Bran's burial place, the Victorians decided, but soon the lines between Bran and Brutus became blurred. In 1857, our old friend the Reverend R. W. Morgan, presumably inspired by the *Mabinogion*, wrote that Brutus founded London 'on a spot known as *Bryn gwyn* or the White Mount, on the North side of the estuary of the Thames. The White Mount is now occupied by the Tower.' He then stated that, when Brutus died he 'was interred by the side of Imogene, at the White Mount.' Thus, by 1914, E.O. Gordon could write, as a matter of well-known fact, that Brutus 'was interred by the side of Imogene [Ignoge] on the Bryn Gwyn,' where the Tower of London stands (see plate 44). This is the story now repeated in many London tourist guide books. It even featured for a while in the official literature of the Tower itself.

In *Hades' Daughter* (2003), Sara Douglass reaffirmed the Victorian belief that Brutus was buried beneath the Tower of London. She imagined the corpses of Brutus and his wife being washed and taken 'to the well that sunk deep into the White Mount from the basements of the palace. There they were lowered, and placed into a chamber that had been hollowed out in the heart of the mound.'

Layer upon layer of myths, each building imaginatively on the last, had achieved something that seems almost real.

And so they set out that bright, clear morning near the end of the Bronze Age, red-haired Corineus, grey-veiled Ignoge and her three sons with noble heads hung low, to bear Brutus's body to its final resting place. Out of the palace gates they went, where the hoary old giants sat slumped and enchained, their sullen eyes bidding farewell to the great chieftain who had consigned them to their endless bondage. The procession went first west, up through the green meadow, silver with dew, to the top of Ludgate Hill. Around them swept the view – the Chilterns to the north, the North Downs to the south, and to the east the shining river broadening out into its mighty estuary. They stood within the great stone circle, where rams' horns were blown and paeans were sung to Apollo and Diana, who had guided them on their epic journey from the south so many years ago. Then they went down, past the circle's heel stone and along the track leading past the wooden huts of the craftsmen and fishermen that lined the muddy bank of the Thames.

Beyond the steep stockaded bank and ditch that marked the city's eastern limit, the ship that had borne Brutus and Ignoge all the way from Epiros still lay drawn up on the shore. Its timbers were starting to rot but nobody could bear to break it up. They continued along the riverside, startling the herons and other marsh birds up from amongst the reeds until they came to the low hillock they called the White Mount. They recited the pedigree of Brutus, son of Silvius, son of Ascanius, son of Aeneas, son of Anchises and Aphrodite, and sang a paean to her, the slender-ankled goddess of love. Then, they lowered Brutus's body into the receptive, fertile earth of his island of Albion, which he had named Britain after himself. And so they buried Brutus of Troy, builder of cities, the founder of Britain.

> *Do not weep for me, Britannia:*
> *It is I, Brutus,*
> *Who sleeps below your dreaming hills.*

Select Timeline

BC

c. 9,500	Start of the present, uninterrupted human habitation of Britain after the Ice Age
c. 1194–1184	Trojan War
c. 1135	Very approximate birth year for the mythical Brutus
c. 1103	Arrival of Brutus in Britain, within the myth
c. 1079	Death of Brutus, within the myth
c. 780	Hesiod's *Theogony* composed in Boetia
c. 700s	Homer's *Iliad* composed, perhaps in Chios
753	Traditional date for founding of Rome
c. 320	Pytheas visits Britain
55 and 54	Caesar's two failed invasions of Britain
19	Death of Virgil, having almost finished the *Aeneid*.
c. 7	Death of Dionysius of Halicarnassus

AD

33/34	Crucifixion of Jesus
43	Claudius conquers Britain
410	Roman legions abandon Britain
413–430	St Augustine writes *City of God*
455	Vortigern's son Vortimer defeats the Jutes
461	Death of St Patrick, who converted Ireland
518	Arthur's victory at Mount Badon against the Saxons
539	Death of Arthur
c. 520	Frankish Table of Nations compiled in Byzantium
640	Death of St Cuanu
820s	Nennius's compilation of the *Historia Brittonum*, under Merfyn Frych
c. 1135	Geoffrey of Monmouth's *History of the Kings of Britain*
1485	Accession of Henry VII
1534	Polydore Vergil's *Anglica Historia* refutes the Brutus myth
1590/96	Edmund Spenser's *Faerie Queene*
1670	John Milton's *History of Britain*
1703	*The New History of the Trojan Wars* first published (last edition 1850), probably by Elkanah Settle.
1718	First English translation of Geoffrey's *History*
1735	Hildebrand Jacob's *Brutus the Trojan*
1741–4	Alexander Pope working on *The Brutiad*
1757	Birth of William Blake
1801	John Ogilvie's *Britannia*

1822	Richard Brothers asserts Israelite origin for the Saxons.
1857	Rev. Richard Williams Morgan's *The British Kymry* reasserts Brutus as a real historical figure.
1860	C.D.'s, *Brutus the Trojan*
1914	E.O. Gordon claims Brutus was an Aryan.
2003	Sarah Douglass's *Hades' Daughter* turns Brutus into a fantasy hero
2004	*Troy* movie released in cinemas
2013	Mark Hodges's *Brutus; First King of England, Prince of Troy*
2015	Publication of this, the first biography of Brutus

Brutus's Family Tree

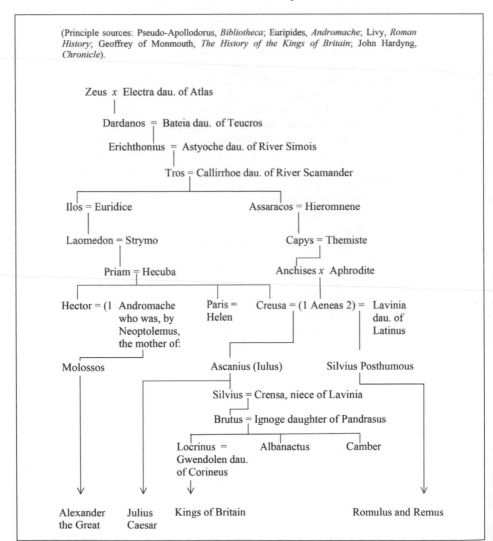

(Principle sources: Pseudo-Apollodorus, *Bibliotheca*; Euripides, *Andromache*; Livy, *Roman History*; Geoffrey of Monmouth, *The History of the Kings of Britain*; John Hardyng, *Chronicle*).

Zeus *x* Electra dau. of Atlas

Dardanos = Bateia dau. of Teucros

Erichthonius = Astyoche dau. of River Simois

Tros = Callirrhoe dau. of River Scamander

Ilos = Euridice   Assaracos = Hieromnene

Laomedon = Strymo   Capys = Themiste

Priam = Hecuba   Anchises *x* Aphrodite

Hector = (1 Andromache   Paris =   Creusa = (1 Aeneas 2) = Lavinia
who was, by   Helen   dau. of
Neoptolemus,   Latinus
the mother of:

Molossos   Ascanius (Iulus)   Silvius Posthumous

Silvius = Crensa, niece of Lavinia

Brutus = Ignoge daughter of Pandrasus

Locrinus =   Albanactus   Camber
Gwendolen dau.
of Corineus

Alexander   Julius   Kings of Britain   Romulus and Remus
the Great   Caesar

Acknowledgements

I am indebted to the many people who have encouraged and helped me in my journeys, both intellectual and physical, not least Anxo Abelaira (Galician Society of Celtic History); Mark Bonthrone; Dean Bubier; Céline (tourist office of Tours); John Clark; Professor James E. Crimmins; Nick Crowe; Jill Drysdale (Totnes); James Essinger; John Galani; Eleanor Ghey (British Museum); Craig Goldman; Professor Fransisco Javier González García (Associate Professor of History at Santiago de Compostella University, for helping clarify many points concerning the name and myths of La Coruña); Dr Harry Gouvas (director of the Museum of Arts and Sciences in Preveza, without whose help I would never have found Trikastro); Alistair Hogarth; Cliff Jones; Raimond Kola (director of Butrint); Alan Langmaid (Totnes); David Lee; Matt Lewin; George Logothetis; Trevor McCallum; John D. McLaughlin; Jeff Saward (Labyrinthos); Andrew Shapland (British Museum); Gabriel Swift and Julie Mellby (Princeton); Natalie Taylor (Flat Holm); John Townsend; Ann Walsh (Reef TV); Professor Calvert Watkins (Harvard); David Williams … and my sincere apologies for the many omissions I know there must be in this lists. I am enormously grateful too to Linne Matthews, my commissioning editor, and to Jonathan Wright and all his colleagues at Pen & Sword for making this publication possible.

Above all, my thanks go to Scott Crowley, for accompanying me on my journeys, for allowing me to subvert holidays into research trips, and for driving us many thousands of miles around Britain, Europe and Turkey following the trails of the elusive Trojans. He negotiated the hair-pin bends of the Epirote Mountains with aplomb, wove through the chaos of Istanbul without demure and made so much possible that without him would not have been. Ευχαριστώ!

Bibliography and References

Ackroyd, Peter, *Blake*,Vintage, 1999.

Adolph, Anthony, *In Search of Our Ancient Ancestors: from the Big Bang to Modern Britain, in Science and Myth*, Pen & Sword, 2015.

Adolph, Anthony, *Tracing Your Aristocratic Ancestors*, Pen & Sword, 2013.

Allen, Thomas, *The History and Antiquities of London*, 1827, Woodward quote 1, 23.

Al-Razi, *Muluk Al-Andalus*. Manuscript 'Mo' includes this detail. This is admittedly a 'Spanish version of a Portuguese translation dated around 1300', so it is possible that the Galician connection was included here because of Alfonso's story and was not in Al-Razi's original text. However, as Professor Francisco Javier Gonzalez Garcia of the the University of Santiago de Compstella wrote to me, the phrase 'the city now called La Coruña' may 'indicate that there was a reference to this site in the original Arabic text and that all that was done (in the Portuguese or Spanish translations) was to update the place name' because, in the 900s, the site was called Crunnia. So, despite the uncertainty, the evidence at least admits the possibility that the myth linking Hercules to the founding of La Coruña is an ancient one, and that is as much as we can expect.

Ashdown-Hill, John, *The Third Plantagenet*, 2014.

Ashe, Geoffrey, *Camelot and the vision of Albion*, Book Club, 1975.

Asher, R.E., *National Myths in Renaissance France*, Edinburgh University Press, 1993.

Augustine, *Sermon* 105.10.

Bale, John, *Chronicle of Lord Cobham*, 1544, ch. 8.

Bale, John, *Illustrium majoris Britanniae scriptorum, hoc est, Angliae, Cambriae, ac Scotiae Summarium* ... ('*A Summary of the Famous Writers of Great Britain, that is, of England, Wales and Scotland*') (1548/9).

Barber, Richard, *Legends of Arthur*, The Boydell Press, 2001.

Bartrum, Peter, *Early Welsh Genealogical Texts*, University of Wales Press, 1966: for Arthur's ancestors see particularly pp. 93–4.

Beard, Mary, North, John and Price, Simon, *Religions of Rome*, vol. 2, sourcebook, C.U.P., 1998.

Bede – *Bede's Ecclesiastical History of England*, ed. by Sellar, A.M., 1907, ch. 2.

Biltcliffe, Gary, *The Spirit of Portland: Revelations of a Sacred Isle*, Roving Press, 2009, pp. 116, 121–2.

Blake, William, *Jerusalem*, London Stone, plate 27, lines 30–4; druids, plate 94, lines 23–5.

Blake, William, on 'angelic wings' is quoted in G.E. Bentley (ed), *Blake Records* (1969), 508; on seeing Milton's face is quoted in Geoffrey Keenes (ed.), *The Letters of William Blake*, 20; on Milton's spirit entering him is from Edrman (q.v.), p. 110; his poem *O sons of Trojan Brutus* is at the start of Blake's poem-play *Edward III* , which is included in his 'Poetical Sketches' (1769–1778); 'detestable gods' is from Erdman (q.v.), p. 122; 'covenant of Priam', *Jerusalem*, p. 98, l. 46; Jerusalem's pillars, 'To the Jews' in *Jerusalem*; Albion as ancestor, *A Vision of the Last Judgement*, 191; Albion as patriarch as quoted in Erdman, 554 and 558; London covering the Earth, *Jerusalem*, p. 79, lines 22–35.

Bonedd yr Arwyr, see Bartum pp. 93–4, 30 b & 33. These pedigrees only show four generations between Kerint to Brutus so they are probably earlier attempts than the later, longer version I have quoted in the text.

Bord, Janet, *Footprints in Stone*, Heart of Albion, 2004.

Boreman, Thomas, *Gigantick History*, 1741.

Bradbury, Reginald A., 'Brutus the Trojan', in *The Kingdom Voice*.

Bradford, Ernle, *Ulysses Found*, Sutton, 1963.

Brayley, Edward Wedlake, *Londiniana: or, Reminiscences of the British Metropolis*, 1828, 1, 17.

Broch, Herman, *The Death of Virgil* (1945/1995), trans. by Jean Starr Untermeyer, p. 264.

Bromwich, Rachel, 'The Character of the Early Welsh Historical Tradition', in Chadwick et al, *Studies in Early British History*, C.U.P., 1954, pp. 83–136, on the authenticity of the *Bruts*.

Bromwich, Rachel, 'Trioedd Ynys Prydein: The *Myvyrian* 'Third Series' – I', Transactions of the Honourable Society of Cymmrodorion (1968), her comments on Iolo Morganwg's forgeries and fictions on p. 332.

Byrne, Francis J., *Irish Kings and High-Kings*, Four Courts Press, 1973.

C.D., *Brutus the Trojan. A Poem*. Cantos I, II, III, & IV, Hamilton, Adams and Co, 1860.

Caesar, *Conquest of Gaul*, quote from i. 33, 2: some books say that this phrase was used as early as 122 BC, but I have never found any evidence for this.

Calasso, Roberto, *The Marriage of Cadmus and Harmony*, Vintage, 1994.

Camden, William, *Britannia, or, a Chorographicall Description of the most flourishing Kingdomes, England, Scotland, and Ireland*, George Bishop and John Norton, 1610, St Paul's, p. 426; 'may leave or leave unread' from chapter on Oxfordshire.

Carter, John, *An Architect*, 1798, p. 765.

Ceka, Neriton, *Buthrotum, its history and monuments*, Migjeni, n.d.

Ceram, C.W., *Gods, Graves & Scholars: the story of archaeology*, Book Club Associates, 1971.

Chatwin, Bruce, *The Songlines*, Picador, 1987.

Churchill, Sir Winston, *Divi Britannici* , 1675.

Clark, John. 'The Temple of Diana' in *Interpreting Roman London*, Oxbow Monograph 58, 1996, pp. 5, 6.

Claudian, *Against Rufinus*, 1.51–2.

Condi, Dhimiter, *Butrint: History, Monuments and Museum* (Argjiro, n.d.).

Cooper, Helen, *Sir Gawain and The Green Knight* (Oxford World's Classics, 2008).

Cope, Julian, *The Modern Antiquarian* (Thorsons, 1998).

Cornell, T.J., *The Beginnings of Rome* (Routledge, 1995).

Creighton, John, *Coins and Power in Late Iron Age Britain* (C.U.P., 2000), pp. 140, 143.

Cunliffe, Barry, *Britain Begins*, O.U.P., 2012, p. 7.

Cunliffe, Barry, *Iron Age Communities in Britain*, Routledge, 4th ed., 2005. Cunliffe, Barry, *The Extraordinary Voyage of Pytheas the Greek: the man who discovered Britain*, Allen Lane The Penguin Press, 2001.

Curley, Michael J., *Geoffrey of Monmouth*, Twayne's English Authors Series, 1994, esp. p. 133.

Darvell, Timothy, *Prehistoric Britain*, B.T. Batsford Ltd, 1997.

Dee, John, 1577, B.L., Cotton MS. Vitellius. c. vii. f 206v.

Dez Grantz Geanz (see Mackley, below).

Dickens, Charles, *The Life and Adventures of Nicholas Nickleby*, 1838/9.

Diodorus Siculus, *Bibliotheca Historica*, on the origin of the Gauls, 4.19.2 and 5.24.1; on the name of Britain, 5.1.4.

Dionysius of Halicarnassus, *The Roman Antiquities of Dionysius of Halicarnassus*, translated by Earnest Cary, 1937, repr. 1968.

Ditmas, E.M.R., 'Geoffrey of Monmouth and the Breton families in Cornwall', *Welsh Historical Review*, vi, 1972–3, 451–61.

Douglass, Sarah, *Hades' Daughter*, Book One of The Troy Game, Tor Fantasy, 2003, pp. 19, 28, 42, 501, 56, 60, 73, 631.

Drayton, Michael, *Polyolbion*, 1622.

Duan Albanach, quoted in William Skene, *Chronicles of the Picts, Chronicles of the Scots, and other early memorials of Scottish History*, 1867, p. 57.

Elder, John, 'To the moost Noble, Victorius and Redoubted Prynce, Henry the Eight …', 1534, BL, Royal MS 18 A, fol. 38, published in *Bannatyne Miscellany*, vol. 1, 1827.

Erdman, David V. (ed.), *The Complete Poetry and Prose of William Blake*, Bantam Doubleday Dell, 1988.

Eusebius, *Demonstratio Evangelica*, book 3.

Floriano Cumbreño, A.C., *Diplomática española del periodo astur. Estudio de las fuentes documentales del reino de Asturias (718–910)*, Oviedo, 1949–1951, vol. 1, p. 155. This shows that the place name Crunnia existed in the region, and *presumably* was the place later called La Coruña.

Fortescue, Chief Justice John, *Commendation of the Laws of England*, posthumously pub. 1543.

Fox, Robin Lane, *Travelling Heroes: Greeks and their myths in the epic age of Homer*, Penguin, 2009.

Frankish Table of Nations, Vatican Library, Rome, Vat. lat. 5001, a copy made about AD 1300, as quoted by Goffart (q.v.), pp. 133–165.

Frazer, Sir James, *The Golden Bough*, 1890, repr. Wordsworth Reference, 1993.

Funari, Salvatore, *Myths, Legends and Customs in Greek and Roman Sicily*, Kompass Media Centre, 2001.

Geoffrey of Monmouth quotes are from Rev. Aaron Thompson's translation, *The British History, Translated into English from the Latin of Jeffrey of Monmouth*, 1718: this switches randomly between past and present tense, so for consistency I have altered all quotes into the present tense. Lewis Thorpe's 1966 translation, and the 2007 translation by Michael D. Reeve and Neil Wright, are also excellent.

Geoffrey of Monmouth, *The Prophecies of Merlin*, quotes from 7, 206 and 212.

Gerald of Wales, Description of Wales (quote from 1, ch. 3).

Gildas, *De Excidio Britanniae* ('*The Ruin of Britain*'), 1, 25.

Glendower, Owen, quote from A.G. Bradley, *Owen Glyndwr and the last struggle for Welsh Independence*, 1901, p. 160.

Goffart, Walter, *Rome's Fall and After*, The Hambledon Press, 1989, pp. 133–165.

González García, Fransisco Javier, 'The Legendary Traditions about the Tower of Hercules', *Folklore*, 125, 3, December 2014, pp. 306–321.

Gordon, E.O., *Prehistoric London: its mounds and circles*, 1914, heel stone quote p. 13, Tower of London p.107.

Gordon, George, 'The Trojans in Britain', *The Discipline of Letters*, Clarendon Press, 1946, p. 37.

Green, Miranda, *Dictionary of Celtic Myth and Legend*, Thames and Hudson, 1997.

Griscom, Acton and Jones, R.E., *The Historia Regum Britanniae of Geoffrey of Monmouth with contributions to the study of its place in early British history*, New York, 1929.

Gunten, Ruth von, *Segesta*, La Medusa Editrice, 2006.

Hardie, Philip, *The Last Trojan Hero: A cultural history of Virgil's Aeneid*, I.B. Tauris, 2014.

Hardyng, John, *Chronicle*, name of 'Crensa' ch. x; archflaumes ch. 14; on death and burial of Brutus ch. 16.

Harleian ms 3859, version A, pedigree I, in John Morris, *Arthurian Sources*, vol. 5, 'Genealogies and Texts', Phillimore, 1995, p. 42.

Henslowe's diary, quoted in Wiggins, Martin and Richardson, Catherine, *British Drama (1533–1642): A Catalogue*, O.U.P., 2014.

Hodges, Mark, *Brutus; First King of England, Prince of Troy (The Welsh Chronicles)*, Mark Hodges, 2013.

Holinshed, Raphaell, et al, *The First and Second Volumes of Chronicles* (1586), repub. as *Holinshed's Chronicles*, AMS Press Inc, 1965). Helenus: 'Hist. Descr. of the Iland of Britaine', ch. 9, 10; Annius: 'Hist. Eng.' bk 1; Brutus, 'Hist. Eng.' bk 2 ch. 1–4.

Hughes, David, *The British Chronicles*, Heritage Books, 2007, vol. 1, ix and xiii and vol. 2, p. 389.

Hunt, Leigh, quote from *The Indicator*, no. ix, 8 December 1819.

Hutson, Professor A.E., *British personal names in the Historia regum Britanniae*, California University Press, volume 5 of their 'publications in England', 1940.

Hysi, Ylber, *Discover Butrint: its history, archaeology, and religious cults*, Gent-Grafik, 2008.

Ingledew, Francis, 'The Book of Troy and the Genealogical Construction of History: the case of Geoffrey of Monmouth's 'Historia Regum Britanniae', *Speculum*, 69, 3, 1994, pp. 665–704.

Isidore of Seville, *Etymologia*, ix.2.102.

Jacob, Hildebrand, *Brutus the Trojan, Founder of the British Empire, an epic poem*, 1735. Using 'Ilion', I, 15; III, 51, etc; 'Dardanians', I, 10; III, 53, etc; 'the Son of Silvius' IV, 85.

Jacob, Hildebrand, letter to Lord Allington, West Wratting, Bodleian Library, Oxford, Rawlinson MS 861, quoted in Kenneth Jacob, *Pedigree of the Descendants of William Jacob of Horseheath, who died in 1508*.

James, Simon, *The Atlantic Celts*, British Museum Press, 1999.

Jarman, A.O.H., *Geoffrey of Monmouth / Sieffre o Fynwy*, University of Wales Press, 1966.

John Clark, 'London Stone: Stone of Brutus or Fetish Stone – Making the Myth', *Folklore*, 121, 1, April 2010, quotes from pp 45, 48.

Jordanes, *De origine actibusque Getarum (The Origin and Deeds of the Getae)*, translated by Charles C. Mierow, iv, ix (58).

Kallimachus, *Oxyrhynchus Papyrus* 31.

Kendrick, [Sir] T.D., *British Antiquity*, Methuen & Co. Ltd, 1950, 'burrs' p. 15, 'ingenious antiquary' p. 132.

Knight, David J., *King Lucius of Britain*, Tempus, 2008.

Laing, Lloyd, *Celtic Britain*, Granada, 1981.

Laurén, Giles, *The Other Trojan War: Dictys & Dares*, Sophron, 2012.

Lebor Gabála, First Redaction (R1), in the *Book of Leinster*, as translated by R.A. Stewart Macalister for the Irish Texts Society (1938–1956), quote about Brigantia from redaction 1, 25.

Lethbridge, T.C. *Gogmagog, the Buried Gods*, Routledge and Kegan Paul, 1957.

Levi, Peter, *Virgil, a life*, Tauris Parke Paperbacks, 2012.

Levis, Howard C., *Bladud of Bath*, 1919, repr. West Country Editions, 1973.

Lewis, Rev. Lionel Smithett, *St Joseph of Arimathea at Glastonbury*, James Clarke and Co., 1992.

Life of St Erkonwald, see Morse, R., (ed), *St Erkenwald*, D.S. Brewer, 1975, describing St Augustine converting England's pagan shrines to Christian use.

Livy, *Roman History*, 1, 1–3.

López Alsina, F., '?Pro utilitate regni mei: las ciudades y la orla costera del Miño al Deva en el reinado de Alfonso IX de León?', in *Alfonso IX y su época*, A Coruña, 2008, p. 202–203, in which he shows that the placename La Coruña was documented before 1140.

Lucan[us], Marcus Annaeus (AD 39–AD 65), *Pharsalia*.

Mabinogion translated by Jeffrey Gantz, Penguin Classics, 1976.

Mackley, J.S., *The Origin of the Giants: the first settlers of Albion*, Isengrin, 2014. This translates *Dez Grantz Geanz* (B.L., Cotton Cleopatra D.ix ff. 67ra–68vc).

MacLagan, Robert Craig, *Scottish Myths*, MacLachlan and Stewart, 1882.

Maund, Kari, *The Welsh Kings: the Medieval Rulers of Wales*, Tempus, 2000.

Mayor, Adrienne, *The First Fossil Hunters*, Princeton U.P., 2000.

McLaughlin, John D. 'The Milesian Legends', published on clanmaclochlainn.com.

Meirop, Marc van de, *A History of the Ancient Near East*, Blackwell Publishing, 2004.

Middleton, Aeneas, *Tim Hartwell and The Brutus of Troy*, Royal Middleton Publishing, 2010.

Milton, John, *History of Britain*, 1670.

Monarchy of Britain, the (lost poem), see B.F. Roberts, 'Geoffrey of Monmouth and the Welsh Historical Tradition', *Nottingham Medieval Studies* 20 (1976) (29–40) p. 31.

Monthly Review, The, January 1802, p. 364.

Morgan, Prys, *Iolo Morganwg*, 1975, quotes from pp. 67, 71.

Morgan, Rev. Richard Williams, *The British Kymry: or Britons of Cambria, outlines of their history and institutions, from the earliest to the present times*, 1857.

Morris, John, *The Age of Arthur*, Phillimore, 3 vols., 1973–77.

Nennius, *Historia Brittorum* (*History of the Britons*) J.A. Giles's translation (1848) and also the version printed by John Morris in vol. 8 of his *Arthurian Sources* (1980). Dating Nennius is problematic. One version has a prologue dated 858: the earliest text of it (known as version H, in Harleian Ms 3859, copied about 1100) seems, from internal evidence, to date from 828/9, but even this copy contains various obvious additions or 'glosses', some incorporating changes suggested by the writer's master, Beulan. A preface not found in the earliest versions, but perhaps copied from an older source that does not survive, attributes the work to Nennius, 'pupil of the holy Elvodug'. St Elvodug died as Bishop of Bangor in 809, so perhaps the earliest version of the *Historia Brittonum* was that old: his pupil's work cannot have been before 796, for an event of that year is mentioned. William Skene was keen to date the original slightly earlier, to about 770, and suggested that the original writer was not Nennius but a historian called Gildas, though not the famous one. But the more recent assessment of John Morris seems safer: he thought the original *Historia Brittonum* could be dated pretty safely to about 809–829 – and that it was by Nennius.

Newman, Paul, *Lost Gods of Albion*, 1987: new ed. The History Press, 2009, p. 106.

Norwich, Bishop of, quoted by W. Longman, *A History of the three cathedrals dedicated to St Paul in London*, 1873, p. 59.

O'Rahilly, Thomas F., *Early Irish History and Mythology*, Dublin Institute for Advanced Studies, 1946.

Ogilvie, Rev. John, *Britannia*, p. 932 and argument to book 17.

Olalla, P., and Priego, A., *Mythological Atlas of Greece*, Road Editions, 2001.

Orosius, *Seven Books of History against the Pagans*. Brigantia and seeing it from Ireland, 1.2; on rejecting Aeneas, 1.18; Trinovantes 6.9.

Owen, Gittin, quote from 'Gittin Owen and Sir John Leiaf's books' in Lewys Dwnn, *Heraldic Visitations of Wales*, ed. Sir Samuel Rush Meyrick, 1846, 1, xv.

Parfait, Tudor, *The Lost Tribes of Israel: the history of a myth*, Weidenfield & Nicolson, 2002.

Peach, L. du Garde, *Unknown Devon*, John Lane The Bodley Head Limited, 1927.

Pennant, Thomas, *Some Account of London*, 3rd ed, 1793, p. 4.

Petrie, Sir Flinders, 'Neglected British History', *Proceedings of the British Academy*, viii. 1–28.

Piggott, Stuart, 'The Sources of Geoffrey of Monmouth, 1. The "Pre-Roman" King List', *Antiquity*, 15, 59, Sept. 1941.

Platts, Beryl, *A History of Greenwich*, David and Charles, 1973.

Pope, Alexander, *The Guardian* (78, Wednesday, 20 June 1713); on Achilles' horse, Pope to Blount, 17 September 1717 (in Joseph Warton, ed., *The Works of Alexander Pope, Esq*, 8, 1803); on monkish annals, *The Correspondence of Alexander Pope*, iv, 348–49; on character of Brutus, Pope's character notes for the Brutiad, Ruffhead; on his epic being 'exactly planned', Pope to Spence, Ruffhead, pp. 188–9.

Price, Rev. W. Willis, *East Portlemouth and its patron saint Winwalloe* (n.d.).

Pryor, Francis, *Britain BC*, Harper Collins Publishers, 2003.

Red Book of Hergest, translated in *Trioedd Ynys Prydein*. ed. Rachel Bromwich, University of Wales Press, 1961, originally from the collection of Robert Vaughan of Hengwrt (1592–1666) and accepted by Bromwich *et al* as genuinely old.

Respondek, Lothar, *The Mystery of Silbury Hill*, Cromwell Press, 2005.

Rydberg, Viktor, *Teutonic Mythology*, 1887.

Ruffhead, Owen, *The Life of Alexander Pope*, 1769, p. 410. The original plan for Pope's epic about Brutus is B.L. Egerton Manuscript no. 1950.

Ryan, William and Pitman, Walter, *Noah's Flood*, Simon & Schuster, 1998.

Sebillot, M., *Traditions de la Haute Bretagne*, 1882.

Servius, *Commentary on the Aeneid of Virgil*, x.167.

Seters, John van, *Prologue to History: the Yahwist as historian in Genesis*, Westminster/John Knox Press, 1992, esp. pp. 60 and 123.

Settle, Elkana, *The New History of the Trojan Wars and Troy's Destruction in Four Books, to which is added The Siege of Troy, a tragi-comedy, as has been often acted with great applause* (1703: some later editions printed by Sarah Bates). The work was anonymous but the author was almost certainly Settle.

Shakespeare, William, *Cymbeline*, 3.1.59–61.

Skene, W.F., *Chronicles of the Picts, Chronicles of the Scots, and Other Early Memorials of Scottish History*, H.M. General Register House, 1867.

Skene, W.F., *The Four Ancient Books of Wales*, Edmonston & Douglas, 1868.

Snell, Daniel C., *Life in the ancient Near East*, Yale U.P., 1997.

Spence, Lewis, *Legendary London*, 1937, pp. 170–1.

Spenser, Edmund, *Dialogue on the State of Ireland*, 1598.

Spenser, Edmund, *Faerie Queene*, Prince Arthur 2, ix, 55–x, 69; Canutus 2.10.9; Brutus founding London 3.9.46; Elizabeth's ancestry 3.9.33 and 38.

Squire, Charles, *The Mythology of Ancient Britain and Ireland*, Archibald Constable & Co. Ltd, 1906.

Strabo, *Geography*, Pretania, 1.4.2; Acheron 6.1.5; Artabrians 3.3.5: Opiscella 3.4.3.

Tacitus, *Germania*. The origins of Tacitus's pedigree can be traced to Pliny, who mentions the Ingaevones, Herminones and Istaevones in his *Historia Naturalis* (c. AD 77), but without linking them up in a genealogy. So widespread is Indo-European culture that the best parallel to this system exists in Vedic India, where the *Puranas* record the descent of the *brahmins* (priests) and *ksatrias* (warriors) back to a sun-born flood survivor called

Manu Viavasvata, who in the most developed tales had ten children, but in the earliest had only three, Naghaga, Narasyanta and Iksvaku, whose names seem to correspond with Tacitus's Ingaevones, Herminones and Istaevones.

Tate, Nahum, *Brutus of Alba: or the Enchanted Lovers*, 1678.

Tatlock, J.S.P., *The Legendary History of Britain: Geoffrey of Monmouth's Historia Regum Britanniae and Its Early Vernacular Versions*, University of California Press, 1950.

Timagenes, *History of the Gauls*, as quoted in Ammianus Marcellinus, *Roman History*, 15.9.

Torchiana, Donald T., 'Brutus, Pope's Last Hero', *The Journal of English and Germanic Philology*, 61, 4, Oct. 1962, pp. 853–867.

Totten, Charles, *The Philosophy of History, or, The Scattering of the Holy People*, 1891.

Twyne, John, *De Rebus Albionicus Britannicis* as quoted in Sir Thomas Kendrick, *British Antiquity*, Methuen & Co., 1950, p. 106.

Tzakos, Christos I., *Ithaca and Homer (The Truth)*, Athens, 2005, trans. Geffrey Cox.

Vergil, Polydore, *Anglica Historia*, 1534, 1555.

Virgil, *Aeneid – Virgil, The Aeneid*, translated by John Jackson, 1908, repr. Wordsworth Classics, 1995.

Virgil, *Eclogues – Virgil, The Eclogues and The Georgics*, translated by C. Day Lewis, Oxford University Press 1963, 2009, quote from *Ecl*. iv, ll. 4–7.

Vogiatzis, G., *Lefkada*, Toubi's, 2007.

Voskoboinikov, M.G., *About Evenk cosmogonic legends. Languages and folklore of Northern people*, Novosibirsk, 1981, reporting Moronenok, a member of the Evenk tribe living near Lake Baikal, speaking to M. I. Osharov in 1923.

W.S., *The Lamentable Tragedy of Locrine*, 1594, quotes from prologue and act 1 sc. 1.

Waddell, L. A., *The Phoenician Origin of the Britons, Scots and Anglo Saxons Discovered by Phoenician and Sumerian Inscriptions in Britain by Pre Roman Briton Coins & A Mass of New History*, 1924. Phoenicians were Trojans, ch. 7, Lord Leighton, ch. 8.

Wagner, Sir Anthony, *English Genealogy*, O.U.P., 1960.

West, M.L., Hesiod: *Theogony & Works and Days*, O.U.P., 1988.

West, Martin, *The Hesiodic Catalogue of Women*, Clarendon Press, 1985.

William Stukeley, *Itinerarium curiosum*, 1724, 112, pl. 57.

Williamson David, *Brewer's British Royalty*, Cassell, 1996.

Wren, Christopher junior, *Parentalia*, 1750, pp. 266, 296.

Yorke, Philip, *The Royal Tribes of Wales*, 1799, pp. 45–6. Yorke cited 'Owen's History' as his source.

Index